Advance Praise for *Battledoors: The Golden Slate*

"Brian Wilkinson blazes new trails in both science fiction and the supernatural with his latest book, *Battledoors: The Golden Slate*. Daring to go beyond the conventional boundaries of storytelling, Wilkinson manages to craft a brilliant tale about adventure, youth, and hope."
— Mike Marts, Editor-in-Chief, *AfterShock Comics*

"Brian Wilkinson is a tremendous talent with excellent writing skills."
— Brian Michael Bendis, Writer, *Marvel Comics*

"A fast-paced fun book with a rollicking adventure that draws the reader right in... an amazing read that was incredibly fun and entertaining, with a gripping story and vivid setting. Recommended!"
—Roger Hyttinen, author of the Ghost Oracle series

"Wilkinson is a wizard with words."
— Taylor Sloan, *Dragon's Lair* Book Blog

D0104773

COPYRIGHT INFORMATION

BATTLEDOORS: THE GOLDEN SLATE

Book I

Brian Wilkinson

BlueMoon
PUBLISHERS

For Owen,
My son, my best friend, my pride and joy.
This is the first of many gifts for you.

I love you to the moon and back.

TABLE OF CONTENTS

PROLOGUE   7

ACT I: A FORK IN THE ROAD   14
CHAPTER 1   15
CHAPTER 2   30
CHAPTER 3   42
CHAPTER 4   55
CHAPTER 5   62
CHAPTER 6   82
CHAPTER 7   91
CHAPTER 8   103

ACT II: RUNNING TO GROUND   117
CHAPTER 9   118
CHAPTER 10   127
CHAPTER 11   139
CHAPTER 12   150
CHAPTER 13   163
CHAPTER 14   173
CHAPTER 15   179
CHAPTER 16   190
CHAPTER 17   203
CHAPTER 18   212
CHAPTER 19   221

ACT III: DOWN THE RABBIT HOLE   234

CHAPTER 20   235

CHAPTER 21   250

A SNEAK PEEK AT *BATTLEDOORS: THE BLACK SPYRE*   261

AUTHOR'S NOTE   265

ABOUT BRIAN WILKINSON   267

BOOK CLUB GUIDE   268

WRITE FOR US   270

THANK YOU FOR READING *BATTLEDOORS: THE GOLDEN SLATE*   271

PROLOGUE

The wind rushed in through the open doorway, causing their ears to pop and their eyes to water. As the two harried travellers plunged through, they didn't notice that there was at least a two-foot clearance below them, and they toppled over one another into the new space. Wherever they were, the air pressure had changed enough to cause them momentary discomfort. The air was thicker and more humid here as well. The dampness wasn't much of an issue, since sweat was already pouring off them in droves.

Disentangling himself from his sprawled-out young friend, Edgar Culshaw began to scramble on his hands and knees over to the still-open doorway. Reaching out, his fingers struggled to find purchase, and panic began to take over. At last he covered the last few inches to get a firm grip so he could swing the door closed. A split second before it slammed shut and offered them a moment's respite, a grey hand shot through the shallow opening to block it. There was a mingled howl of pain and frustration on the other side as the door caught and pinched the too-smooth fingers. The door began to open once more, until Edgar threw all of his weight against it.

He looked desperately to his young companion, who was still busy searching the ground for his glasses on his hands and knees. "Help me, you fool!" Edgar screamed.

"Where are my glasses?" asked his panicked friend.

"Forget them and help me!" The door surged forward once again, nearly knocking Edgar off his feet. The young boy gave a frustrated growl and leapt to his friend's aid. Once they had their combined weight against the door, it stopped groaning as feverishly against the assault from the other side. The grey fingers were still in the doorway, and they could hear angry growls and barking beyond. *Groundlings, no doubt*, thought Edgar. *Worse and worse.*

"Grab his fingers!" screamed Edgar.

"YOU grab them!" the boy screamed back.

Neither of them wanted to touch them. They were smooth and without wrinkles, cold and damp, like a defrosting piece of meat. Both had experience being at the end of those hands in the past, and it sent chills down their spines to think of it.

"Just do it!" yelled Edgar.

"No!"

"We'll DIE if you don't!"

"Then we'll die! I'm not doing it."

"For the love of…" Edgar reached over and with his eyes closed began to pry the fingers off. He resisted the urge to squeal as his hand slipped over the frictionless and freezing grey digits. It took all of his willpower to finish the job, but Edgar managed to clear them away and finally get the door shut. They breathed a little easier once they heard the satisfying click as the door shut into place. Once closed, this particular kind of door wouldn't open up to reveal the same space, but that didn't mean there weren't other doors nearby that couldn't be used instead. The man to whom the grey fingers belonged wouldn't be far behind. The chase had gone on for days without signs of letting up.

"Yuck! Gah!" Edgar held his hand out like it had been dipped in sewage, and he searched for something to rub his hands clean. He finally grabbed the young boy's shirt to do it.

"Stop that!" protested the boy. "I'm going to have to burn this shirt, and it's the last one I've got!"

"If you don't like it, next time YOU grab his hand! This way at least we both get to suffer somewhat. Share the load, so to speak," Edgar said. He took a moment to appraise his condition in a puddle near the doorway. It was a poor reflection, but it was the best he could do.

I look terrible, he thought. Where once he had been clean, polished, and well-kept, the reflection showed a man who looked half-starved, as though he'd been living on the streets. It wasn't too far from the truth.

He was a little over twenty-five years old and would have been called handsome had he bothered to cut his hair and wash his clothes. He lived the life of a scholar, so he claimed to those who bothered to ask. To him, that meant that such trivial things like hygiene were beneath him. He had given in to societal pressure only to the point that he agree to wear a suit in the first place. It was a fine, calf-length frock coat that had been all the rage a few years earlier. It matched nicely with his woollen breaches. The one area out of place on his person, and one he would not bend on, no matter how much his mother pleaded with him, were the thick, black goggles he wore on his forehead when they weren't covering his deep blue eyes. *One must keep some element of mystery about one's person,* he figured. The goggles painted him as some sort of adventurer. A man of mystery.

A man who invites trouble, more like, he thought, given his present situation.

His young companion, on the other hand, was less of a fashion icon and more like the spewed-out contents of an old rummage sale. The boy had to settle for one of Edgar's old blazers, a cap, and torn shorts. The shoes were too small for him, and his big toe was sticking out of the left one. He was lucky to have that much, though Edgar kept promising to do better by the lad. The boy was a servant in his father's house, and what little education he had was from Edgar, though Edgar's mother hadn't seen the point in it. She allowed Edgar keep the boy much the way one would keep a dog. To her, it was 1895 and they were too modern to worry about educating the help. She also wanted Edgar to settle down and marry, but he couldn't be bothered with it. Marriage was for peasants.

Once he was finished cleaning his hands against the boy's shirt (and ignoring the squirms and protests), Edgar took a minute to get a look at his surroundings. The door, now closed, was as plain and ordinary as any other. If he were to open it now, it wouldn't even lead to the same place. That's how it worked here, after all. The rules were different each time someone was in the World, but one truth remained: you never knew what was behind any given door, and you opened them at your own risk.

"What *is* this place?" breathed the boy as he took in their new surroundings. He stood with his head tilted back to take in the place as his jaw dropped open in wonder. They were in a giant glass-domed greenhouse with thousands of trees, plants, flowers, and bushes covering practically every square inch. The rounded edges of the room were made of stone, metal, and marble, with a few statues covered in ivy. Some were misshapen gargoyles, while others looked like gods or goddesses at rest. It was a beautiful place, but also quietly ominous.

"My God," said Edgar as his gaze went up and up. The boy was distracted by the architecture and plant life, but what had Edgar's attention were the hundreds of doors built into the walls and up into the curved glass ceiling. Toward the bottom they were dark brown oak and blended in with the surrounding walls or rocks. As they got higher, they became light wood and then stone. Higher still, they were frosted glass. At the top, where the sun was shining through, there were clear, though indistinct shapes shimmering and rippling in the dome. In small script on each of them lay hints and clues as to what lay beyond.

Gorgeous, thought Edgar. *Not just that, though. Dangerous, too.* He shuddered as he imagined the potential chaos a room like this could cause. The layout, however, revealed its purpose clearly enough. "It's a hub."

"What's a hub?" asked the boy.

"Like a train station. A central meeting point that every path eventually crosses," Edgar muttered absently. As he worked his way down the line, he read the inscriptions: "Avalon," "Ruin," "The Smith," "The New World," "The Block," "Chance," "The Albion," "Yellowcake," "The Mechanical Man." None of the names, places, or possible creatures meant anything to him and wouldn't unless he decided to go through one of them. Doors like this were always a risk, and rarely was there a reward. You rolled the dice and took your chances. Survival was optional.

Time was running out, however, and soon he'd have to make a choice.

"You hear that?" asked the boy, pulling Edgar's attention back to the situation at hand. There was a faint *boom* in the distance. "There it is again!"

Boom.

"Could be anything," Edgar said, though fear clutched at his belly.

Boom. Louder this time.

"I think we need to get going," said the boy, suddenly afraid. "It's him. He's here already!"

Boom.

"Can't be. It's too fast. He's never that fast," said Edgar dismissively, though he didn't sound as sure as he would have liked.

Boom, boom, boom.

The sounds were faster and more insistent.

"Edgar?" The boy began to cry, and Edgar almost admonished him. Looking at him, though, Edgar was reminded that this was only a child, after all. If he could do better, he would. It wasn't fair that he was trapped here, Edgar knew. The boy was in the wrong place at the wrong time, and if he hadn't adored Edgar so much, he wouldn't have been caught up in the whole mess. Not for the first time, Edgar knew that he had to get this boy free of the nightmare, no matter the cost.

BOOM!

The sound was deafening and scared up a flock of strange-looking birds in the distance. They shrieked as they flew up toward the apex of the dome and away to safety. Behind that noise came harsh snapping and snarling, and the pair knew their time was up.

"Right, then, time to go," said Edgar wearily. He fumbled at his waist to bring up the golden object that hung there freely. The parchment was smooth and clear as the words twisted themselves into shape and the choice was put before him. He had to blink several times to make sure he was reading what he thought he was reading.

Finally, he thought. *A choice that isn't a choice.*

Relief seeped into his body, and the tension flowed out. The path was obvious, and he was content. He made his choice, and the slate thrummed its acknowledgement.

"What did it say?" whimpered the boy. Edgar couldn't fault the boy for being afraid but was incredibly proud to see that he had fought back the tears, and a look of grim determination was now asserting itself.

He'll be a great man, thought Edgar. *Far greater than I ever was or could be.* Ahead of them, deep into the jungle, the howling and barking continued to get louder. It wouldn't be long before they were upon them.

"It's the end," he said. "The conclusion. The next door is the last door."

Relief spread over the boy's face. "Really? Oh, don't lie to me, Edgar. Is it true?"

"It's true," he replied quietly. Behind him, an ancient oak door hummed, and the outline of the doorframe glowed white until it gently burned through the vines that had grown over it. Calmly, he walked over to the door and put his hand on the doorknob before looking down at the boy.

"This is it," he said. "Before I open it you must make me a promise. This story is over. Its tale is told. You must never read it again."

"Of course not," said the boy, eager to get through. "Why would I ever want to come back? I've never been so scared in my life."

"And yet you are the bravest person I've ever known," said Edgar.

"Why are you talking like this? Let's go! Why aren't we going yet?"

"Promise me," repeated Edgar.

"Open the door! Let's go!" yelled the boy.

"*Promise* me," Edgar insisted.

"Fine, I promise. I don't understand! Let's go!" Edgar opened the door, and the boy quickly passed through. As he passed, Edgar saw the boy's smile touch his lips, and a twinkle at the corner of his eye. That little smile was something Edgar loved about the boy. He hoped it would get him the love of his life one day.

The moment was brief, however, because when the boy noticed Edgar wasn't with him, he stopped and turned. "What are you doing?" he yelled as he began to see what was in his friend's mind. Behind Edgar, the woods began to shake and shudder. Like a blooming flower, the shrubbery and trees began to part as one, but rather than reveal the beauty within, an oozy blackness seeped out and corrupted that idyllic place. Dozens of small black shapes began to pour out of bushes and swell over the greenery. Trees bent and snapped, plants and flowers were trampled. Under that wave of darkness, glorious day seemed to turn to hellish night. In moments, all that beautiful green life would be as cold and ruined as black death.

At the forefront of that terrible wave was a monstrous grey shape. He was the thing that even the darkness feared, for it crashed at his feet and swam about his person, but it never touched him. Edgar knew who and what he was.

It was death given form. The thing clenched and unclenched those smooth grey fingers. It rose up and fixed its dead stare on Edgar, who shuddered involuntarily. The mouth parted, and bone-white teeth appeared like daggers in the dark.

"Ahhh, there you are," said the man coolly.

Ignoring the threat, Edgar turned to face his friend again. He even managed to smile, in spite of the boy's terrified expression. "'And he lived happily ever after,'" Edgar intoned. "I am honoured, evermore, to be your friend." With that, he unclipped the golden slate and tossed it into his friend's confused hands.

The full realization at what Edgar planned came too late. Once the truth was clear, the boy dropped the slate and screamed in denial at his friend's actions. He began to run for the door to pull his friend through and away from the approaching horde that was surging forward inexorably, like a wave from a tsunami. The last thing he saw of his friend was a small, sad smile and a wink before that particular door was shut forever.

Alone on the cool cobblestone ground in the alley, weeping against the door, the boy didn't hear the small chime from the golden object nor notice as its golden glow dimmed and faded away. All that it read, in ancient black ink, were the words:

This Battle Has Concluded.

ACT I

A FORK IN THE ROAD

CHAPTER 1

"Cause and effect. Action and reaction. The notion of consequences. All of these revolve around the idea that there is no choice, no action we can take in life that doesn't produce a result. Mind you, it isn't always the result we intended or even wanted. Thoughts?"

Ms. Gerow put down the text and surveyed the class. The hope was to see bright, excited, interested faces, but instead half of them weren't even looking at her. A few had their heads down on their desks, three were texting each other, and maybe one or two were looking her way, but that seemed more coincidental than purposeful. It wasn't her fault that Shakespeare was dull and impossible to understand. It was full of "thee" and "thou," "wouldst," and "couldst." If that weren't bad enough, Shakespeare was also famous for making up words when none existed that fit what he wanted to say. How could anyone have had a conversation with that guy? It was cold comfort to the students in Ms. Gerow's fourth period English class at Morton Academy to know that audiences four hundred years ago were often as clueless as to what was going on as readers today. Despite all the evidence that Shakespeare might best be left in the past, Ms. Gerow contended that *Romeo and Juliet* was a romantic masterpiece and swooned every time Romeo opened his mouth.

"Anyone at all? There are no right or wrong answers in English as long as you can provide evidence to support your opinions!" she said with enthusiasm. Considering it was early June and there were only a few days left of class before the glorious summer break, it was impressive that she could muster any energy to keep trying. The best students could do was try to avoid eye contact, since that seemed to be teacher-speak for "pick me." Owen Thomas accidentally made eye contact.

"Yes! Owen, please share your thoughts."

Owen groaned inwardly. He was fairly new to the school; he and his father had just moved recently to the downtown Toronto neighbourhood. They were living a comfortable life in Guelph until his mother had died in a work accident, and they'd come to the big city for a "fresh start." It had been anything but. Between the traffic, the hordes of people, and the kids in his new school that were essentially total strangers to him, Owen felt exhausted. Lonely, too.

At sixteen, Owen was just now starting to come into his height. While he was still a bit shorter than most of the boys in his class, his love of gym class meant Owen was in pretty decent shape overall. The only thing that wasn't reasonably polished was the mop of brown with a hint of red hair on his head and a faded t-shirt that professed his love of *Transformers*. Being fashionable or popular wasn't something he was interested in, anyway. Owen spent most of his days trying to blend in to the point of being invisible. He still wasn't ready yet to join the rest of the human race. Too much time was instead spent thinking of all the time he wasn't going to be able to spend with his mother.

He sighed and did his best to answer the teacher's question. "Well, I think Romeo was doomed no matter what."

"Interesting," cooed Ms. Gerow. "Elaborate. What do you mean?"

Owen sighed again. "Romeo went and married Juliet, which I think is just stupid. After all, he's only twelve, and she's only twelve. How can they know what love is? It's just ridiculous." He paused and coughed when he saw Ms. Gerow's face darken. Taking Romeo's name in vain was apparently not a good idea. "Anyway, when he meets up with Juliet's cousin, Tybalt, the next day he sees that Tybalt wants to fight him. Romeo has a choice to fight or to run away. He can't just ignore the problem, or he'll get stabbed. The other option is to fight the guy and risk his relationship. He's got to make a decision.

"So he makes a choice, and there are consequences. He picks door number one: walk away. Only because his marriage to Juliet is this big secret that no one else knows about except Friar Laurence. Instead, Romeo's buddy Mercutio steps up to the plate to defend his honour. Mercutio doesn't understand that Romeo is refusing to fight because Tybalt is now his cousin through his marriage to Juliet, and he doesn't want to hurt him. Romeo tries to stop Mercutio from doing this and messes everything up. Tybalt stabs Mercutio, who then dies cursing Romeo. What makes me mad is that Romeo didn't ask Mercutio to fight his battle, so Mercutio kind of has it coming. No one asked him to fight. That was his call. Seriously, he needs to get over it. Anyway, what gets Romeo banished and sets off the whole play on a downward spiral is that Romeo gets angry, grabs a sword, and kills Tybalt for what he did to Mercutio. He made a choice. There was the cause. Murder, death, and banishment were the effect. I'm not sure door number two would have been any better. Probably a similar result.

"Damned if you do, damned if you don't," Owen said. "Pardon the language."

You'd have thought Ms. Gerow had just witnessed the invention of the wheel, she was smiling so much. Owen kind of hated that about teachers. It's not that they didn't mean well, but they got so excited over you knowing an answer that you felt a bit like a dog expecting a treat. Owen also hated this kind of reaction because it provoked an equally negative response from some of his classmates. He could hear a couple of grumbled insults and felt unseen eyes staring daggers into his back. It felt like most of them would rather be stupid together than smart individually. Action and reaction. Cause and effect. Choice and consequence. Only a lot more tribal and a hell of a lot more frustrating.

"Yes! Yes, yes, yes!" Ms. Gerow exclaimed with a small smattering of her own applause filling the room. *Please stop*, Owen thought. "Excellent example, Owen! Anyone else have an example?" She cast the net out into the ocean again, hoping to reel another one in, but the kids were mentally flopping about and gasping for breath.

As she looked about, Owen felt a sharp jab in his lower back. No need to look. It was always the same.

"Good work, Owey-boy!" hissed James Vanier from the seat behind him. The sarcasm and malice dripped off his tongue each time he spoke. He wasn't much bigger than Owen, but the black-haired kid was a thug through and through. Slim build, designer clothes, and if they tested his score in cruelty, it would be through the roof. "Maybe I oughta stab you like Mercury got stabbed."

"Mercutio," Owen hissed. "Mercury was a winged god." He wanted to add the word "moron" to that sentence but knew that would only make things worse. *Just let me go back to being invisible*, he thought.

No such luck.

"What's that, ape-face?" James snapped back. The jab came again. A quick glance showed it was a ruler with one end sharpened. Nice. Who wouldn't want to make an educational tool into a deadly weapon? This kid had sociopath written all over him.

"His name is Mercutio, *moron*," Owen replied, this time failing to apply the filter. *Uh-oh*. At once, Owen regretted the insult. Not that James didn't deserve it, but this meant another friendly beating on his way home from school. *In for a penny, in for a pound*, Owen thought. "Try listening and learning. Even Walmart values the ability to understand basic language skills, and you'll need all the help you can get. *Can* you say 'Welcome to Walmart'?"

Another jab, this one much harder than the last. Owen fought back a small cry and was sure James had drawn blood. Before another blow could land, Owen heard a small cough and looked to his right to see Lucas Walton, James's friend and bodyguard, give a quick nod in the other direction. As one, James and Owen looked to see Emily Lloyd, a girl in their class (and quite possibly an angel on Earth, thought Owen, given her beauty), raising an eyebrow at James.

"Stop it," she said in a harsh whisper. Her eyes were blazing and her jaw was tight.

Even James hesitated when she spoke. With silky brown hair flowing down past her shoulders and a beauty mark on her cheek, she looked like a statue come to life. She was wearing an amazing plaid mini skirt with a nice, breezy blouse top. Somehow, she was the only one in class not sweating. The very idea was a ridiculous notion. Emily Lloyd did not sweat. She glowed. The best thing about her in Owen's mind was that she didn't seem to know how gorgeous she was. She treated everyone the same and never behaved like a princess. No one would have blamed her if she wanted the royal treatment, and they all would have given it to her. Owen knew he was putting this girl on a ridiculously high pedestal that no normal human could reach, but that was also kind of the point. It allowed him to daydream without popping the bubble, and since he was living in his head so much these days, it was a nice shift in emotion from the constant grief over his mother. Emily, the *real* Emily, would be just as flawed and insecure as any other teenager he met, including himself. He hoped to have the opportunity to get to know the real her at some point, warts and all.

"S-s-shut up, Lloyd," James muttered. It was half-hearted at best, and you could hear the stutter. You could tell that he was rattled that she'd even spoken to him, much less admonished him. "Look at your books or something."

"Yeah, whatever," she said. "'Look at your books or something?' Dude, that's lame. Maybe you were right, Owen." (*OH MY GOD, SHE SAID MY NAME*, Owen screamed inside his own head). "Though I think Walmart might be too good for him. As far as I know, they have a policy against hiring morons."

On Owen's right, Lucas groaned and awkwardly shifted in his too-small desk. At just over six feet and tipping the scales at about 230 pounds, he was a giant in the grade eleven class. Either he'd been held back a lot, or his parents fed him other small children at night to fatten him up. From the way he was shifting in the confining seat, it seemed as though he was getting ready to get up and deal with whatever mess James had gotten them into this time. He knew that even cherubic Emily Lloyd might have pushed James too far. Lucas looked at his friend and saw veins starting to pop on James's forehead and his face go a shade of deathly grey. Before James could explode and Lucas could extricate himself from his desk, Ms. Gerow unwittingly came to the rescue.

"Oh, James!" she said happily. "You look worked up about this!" James just stared at her stupidly, as though he'd come out of a coma. Unbelievably, the teacher thought he was upset about the stupid play.

"I do?" he asked.

"It's okay, I am too!" she said.

"You are?"

"Sure, you shouldn't be punished if you were provoked."

"That's… right," he said with a grin as he looked at Owen triumphantly. "Thank you."

"For what?" Ms. Gerow looked puzzled. At this comment, James realized that she wasn't backing him up, and she hadn't heard their conversation just now. She was still talking about that stupid play and that stupid emo bastard, Romeo. James hated that play and hated Romeo even more. The guy loves one girl one day and cries about how he'll never love anyone else. The next day he meets Juliet and says the same thing. All that guy does is whine. James had often voiced the opinion in class that someone should just stab him and get it over with. It was one of the few things Owen silently agreed with him on.

"For understanding, Ms. Gerow," James said, covering up his earlier confusion rather smoothly. "You're always so understanding." At that, Emily rolled her eyes and shifted back to face the front. No one could suck up like James. Somehow, the true nutcases always seemed to slip by the notice of teachers.

"Thanks, James! You just made my day. Okay! Time for one or two last thoughts? Anyone?" At this, Ms. Gerow locked eyes with poor Bea Wells, who looked up to glance hopefully at the clock and found the doe-eyed teacher instead. Bea was a nice enough girl, though a bit blunt and prone to speaking without thinking. For most kids, that would be social suicide, but Bea happened to be best friends with Emily. That afforded her a certain level of protection. It was hard to keep quiet when you saw her, given that Bea liked to wear uber-hip shirts, shoes, pants, and glasses that were too big for her face, not to mention she had braces that looked like they'd been forged in the dark ages, but the kids here, for the most part, were really respectful and embraced differences. It was pretty cool, actually. "Bea, how about you? Do you think Romeo should be banished from the city for killing Tybalt? James seems to think he should be let off the hook because he was pushed into the situation."

Bea, who was prone to panic attacks, looked like she was going to throw up. Ms. Gerow just stared at her and waited patiently while Bea turned various shades of green. She swallowed down what Owen hoped was a ball of saliva as Ms. Gerow just continued to stare. Man, that was irritating. Teachers thought they could wait, and knowledge would just spew out of you. The only thing that was going to spew out of Bea with any kind of depth and abstract meaning was her lunch.

"I think Romeo and Tybalt should just be friends," Bea offered as beads of sweat started to form on her forehead.

This was too much for Eddie Robitaille in the back corner. He was sitting by the door and already had his bag packed. "*Brilliant*," he said sarcastically. "Romeo will pull his sword out of Tybalt's gut and they'll go get some ice cream. Maybe sing a song or two." He let out a frustrated sigh when he saw Bea's confused look. "They can't be friends, Bea, because *one of them killed the other.* Can we go now?"

Ms. Gerow pursed her lips disappointedly and looked at the clock. "Very well. Make sure you study for the quiz tomorrow." She had to raise her voice at the end as every dead body in that room suddenly shot to life and made for the door. You'd have thought there was a prize for the quickest person to leave waiting on the other side.

Owen got up and was bringing up the courage to speak to Emily when he was shoved sideways into a desk and then continued down to the floor. Bea honked out a brief spurt of laughter. When he got the nerve to look up he saw pity in Emily Lloyd's eyes. She turned and gave Lucas a look of disgust as James grinned triumphantly at what his thug friend had just done. Lucas, at least, blushed slightly in embarrassment. Though whether he regretted pushing Owen or regretted the fact that Emily saw him do it was a mystery. Owen suspected the latter.

"What happened?" asked Ms. Gerow. James and Lucas wore no expression on their faces as they stared at Owen. *Cause and effect,* thought Owen. *Action and reaction. If I speak the truth, a beating is sure to follow.*

"Nothing," muttered Owen through gritted teeth. "I tripped."

"Yeah," agreed James. "He's awfully clumsy. You should be more careful, Owen!"

Ms. Gerow giggled lightly and said to be careful in the future. By the time he got to his feet, Emily and Bea were just passing through the doorway. Lucas and James were not far behind.

God, teachers are so clueless, thought Owen. All the time things happened right under their noses, and they either never knew about it or pretended it didn't happen. Kids texted each other, insulted each other, cheated, and even stabbed each other, and the teacher just hummed a little tune to themselves and blathered on about stuff that didn't even matter. *It's a wonder any of us survive the high school experience*, Owen thought bleakly.

"At least it's only another couple of weeks until summer," said Owen.

"What's that?" asked Ms. Gerow.

"Nothing. Just talking to myself."

"Ah! Like Prince Hamlet!" exclaimed Ms. Gerow.

Owen fought rolling his eyes as he left the room.

IT WAS a long, hot walk home for Owen. Luckily, it was also event-free because James and Lucas were pulled into the principal's office at the end of the day. Apparently they had found a book of matches, a trashcan filled with paper, and had not denied themselves the opportunity to see what would happen next. Though why anyone would want to start a fire on a day as hot as this, Owen didn't know. He was just glad he didn't have to watch over his shoulder.

His school, Morton Academy, was located amongst a sea of old University of Toronto buildings not terribly far from Yonge and Bloor. It was an old building, prone to creaking floorboards, musty smells, and a 1970s vibe. Like most buildings near the core of the city, it had "flair," as his father put it. Owen didn't care about flair. He missed his home in Guelph and his friends there. He'd give up "flair" for home in a heartbeat.

About the only good thing his school had to offer was how close it was to Yonge Street. So far, this was Owen's favourite part about the city. It was one of the longest streets in the world, at 1896 kilometres (this was about the only fact he could remember from Ms. Kanerva's geography classes), but it was also the coolest street in Toronto. From here, he could go south to Yonge and Dundas Square. This area was a smaller version of Times Square in New York, but totally cool because of the video billboards and the shopping at the Eaton Centre. You never knew what might be going on as bands and events happened here all the time. It was months off, but Owen was already begging his father to let him go there for the ball drop on New Year's Eve.

Owen also liked Yonge Street because it had used bookstores, comic book shops like the Silver Snail, video game stores, cool places to eat, and culture galore. Sometimes he took back streets and alleys just to avoid the temptation to spend what little money he might have. All of the lights and displays helped him clear his mind at the end of the day. Distractions were always welcome. Distractions kept him from thinking. They kept him from being lonely. They kept him from remembering.

His walk home regularly took him up Yonge to Bloor Street, then west through Yorkville. Now THIS was rich-ville. Celebrities prowled through here all the time, partly thanks to the swanky shops and film festivals. You never knew who might see. Brad Pitt, Will Smith, Chris Pratt, Jennifer Lawrence, Keith Richards, Bono, anyone, really. Beyond here, he passed the Royal Ontario Museum, otherwise called the ROM, and the bulk of the University of Toronto campus. Then came the crossing of Spadina into the neighbourhood called the Annex, which was where he called home. The Annex was a kind of hippie community in Toronto. Artists, writers, musicians, and academics all flowed into the area. The place always seemed to stay young thanks to the constant influx of students from the university. The whole place seemed focused on sushi, which Owen hated. He preferred the businesses on Yonge Street that were a bit more commercial and people went about their day. There, he felt he could be a little more anonymous and fade into the crowd. Here, everyone was looking to join hands and sing.

Owen and his father lived in a small apartment on Walmer Road. It wasn't much of a building to look at, greyish blue, with white balconies that either overlooked garbage bins on one side or the large Metro grocery store on the other. The building itself sat directly on top of the subway line, and though he'd long since gotten used to it, every now and then he was still woken in the night by the low sounds of rumbling underneath. Guelph had been a quiet place with stars in the night sky. Now, Owen had the lights of the big city pouring in through his windows and the slow changing colours of the CN Tower in the distance.

There are no stars to wish on here, Owen thought sadly as he looked into the blank night sky. The light pollution from the city washed out the stars. He wanted to look at them and to try to count them. It had been his favourite game with his mother. The two of them would sit in their backyard and stare up at the constellations. He could name them all: the Big Dipper, the Little Dipper, Orion's belt… and his mother would listen and laugh and talk about the stories that inspired their names.

"Orion was a hunter," she told him one cool May evening. "He was a gigantic, fierce warrior who many men feared."

Owen loved her stories and curled deeper under her arm. "Was he brave?"

"Oh yes, he was brave," she agreed. "Maybe a bit foolish, too."

"Why? What did he do?"

"There's one story that says he fought with a huge scorpion. The battle was long and ferocious, and in the end, Orion killed it."

"Good for him! I hate scorpions," Owen said with a shudder. Any kind of bug freaked him out, to tell the truth. He wouldn't scream and run, but he would step quickly in the other direction. Orion had just become one of his heroes for killing something that might give him nightmares.

"Not so fast," his mother said. "It wasn't as simple as that. The battle wasn't easy, and Orion was wounded. It was a bit of a cosmic balancing act. Orion, the brave, was supposed to represent all the good things in the world. The scorpion, full of venom, was the bad. You can't have good without evil, you know. How else would we know what was good or not? So, according to the stories, while Orion may have killed the scorpion in the end, the scorpion's venom also killed Orion. One can't exist without the other. They needed each other to balance themselves out."

Owen scrunched up his face at that. Being killed by a bug was not something he wanted to contemplate, certainly not for a mythical figure who had ten seconds ago become a hero to him.

His mother chuckled as she saw the look on his face. "Don't like that, do you? Well, little one, as luck would have it there are two versions of the story. If you don't like that choice of how it ends, let me offer you another. Instead of the battle to the death with the scorpion, another story tells about how he chased after the Pleiades, seven beautiful women. Whether it was for true love or the thrill of the chase, I'm not too sure."

"What happened to them?"

"They tried a few things. They first turned into doves to fly away. That wasn't much use, because Orion was so big. So they begged the god, Zeus, to protect them. Zeus agreed to help and changed them all into stars, out of his reach.

"He was sad for some time until he saw the goddess Diana and chased after her from a very far distance. Diana's brother, Apollo, wasn't a fan of Orion, and he made a bet with his sister, who was good with a bow and arrow, that she couldn't hit a black speck off in the distance. Diana took the bet, fired the arrow, and killed Orion."

Owen was appalled. "That's not a better story! A GIRL kills him? At least in the other one he got to fight a big scorpion!"

"Hush, little one. The story isn't quite done," his mother said. "When Diana saw what she had done, she felt bad for Orion and changed him into a star like the Pleiades and placed him in the heavens with them. There, she said, he could continue his chase forever. Look up, Owen. You can see the three strong lights that make up his big belt. He's there, right now, chasing the women he loves every night. As the Earth circles around the sun and day becomes night which becomes day once again, he always chases them."

"Why doesn't he give up? Isn't it sad that he can't be with them?"

His mother hugged him close. "It's a little sad, I suppose. But at least he knows that they're there. It's just in his nature to follow them. They inspire him every night, and he reaches out to be with them. It's kind of like me and you. Whether I'm there with you or not, I'm always in your heart. You can't see me or touch me, but you feel me and you know that I love you."

"I love you, too, Mom. You're right. That's the better story. That's the one I'd pick."

"Me too, little one. Me too."

A star had streaked by at that moment. Just a flash, but they both saw it. His mother gave a contented sigh. "Make a wish, sweetheart." He made a wish for a hundred more nights like that one. Every shooting star since then had been the same. None of them ever came true, but it didn't stop him from wishing.

THE DOOR to the apartment banged open clumsily and snapped Owen out of his reverie. He'd been sitting in the large, comfy chair by the window for what seemed like hours. The apartment was dark, save for the flickering light of the television in the next room.

"A little help here!" his father called.

Owen hopped up and rushed to help his father, who was struggling with no less than ten grocery bags at once. Owen helped lift them onto the counter and peeled off the plastic loops from where they bit into his father's arms. Once free of them, Owen's father let out a long sigh and rubbed the red, raw indents on his arms.

"Wouldn't be so bad if it weren't for the milk!" he said, panting.

"Dad, you should have come get me first. You don't have to carry this on your own," Owen said.

"Nonsense!" said his father. "I can carry bags across the street! I'm all muscle. I'm more than muscle. I can destroy Superman with a wink, I'm so powerful."

This always made Owen smile. Superman, his father was not. At 155 pounds and 5'8", with a receding hairline, goofy glasses, and a huge grin, his father was more like Spider-Man's Aunt May. Still, his dad was a superhero in Owen's eyes. When his mother died, his dad had been there every step of the way. Not once did Owen feel forgotten. If anything, it had brought them closer together.

"Now, what would you like for dinner? It's eat-out night," said his father. Eat-out night didn't necessarily mean they were going to a restaurant; it just meant that no cooking was allowed. They'd go out, pick something up, order-in... just no cooking allowed. It was kind of funny that his father had just gone to all this effort to buy food and then refused to cook any of it.

"Taco night?" Owen ventured.

"Tacos *again?*" his father asked in mock exasperation. Even though he did his best to sound frustrated, Owen knew it was all for show. His father loved tacos just as much he did, though it did wreak havoc on their digestive systems and their bathroom a few hours later. It was a running contest to see which one of them could create the worst death cloud of foulness. Much as he tried, Owen's dad won every time. It was like walking into a mist.

"I think I can take you this time," Owen said with a grin.

"You're on, but just to warn you, I'm going with extra jalapeño tonight."

And so it went on. Taco night was just part of the routine that they had going. It was part of "making things normal again," as Owen's dad put it. Normal, Owen had argued in the past, would have been staying back in Guelph at their house, but that hadn't happened. His dad had been offered a promotion at work in a new office being built in Toronto, and the opportunity was too good to pass up. Though his dad never said it out loud, Owen thought part of the reason for the move was because his dad just couldn't stay in their old home any more. The grief the memories stirred up was too much. Owen once came home early from a friend's house and caught his father crying in the bathroom. His father denied it, saying he pulled a nose hair, of all things, and that made his eyes water. As best he could, his dad didn't cry, and he tried not to be sad. Owen loved his father for it but sometimes wished the two of them could just cry together for a while and get it out of their systems.

So, like clockwork, they came back to the apartment, shared meals, watched Netflix, television, or seasons of *Lost*, *The Walking Dead*, or *Battlestar*

Galactica to devour while they talked about everything except her. They talked about school, work, the noise from the subway, about tacos, about breaking wind, and about trying to choke each other out of the bathroom. For his part, Owen tried not to bring up how much he missed Guelph or the troubles at school with jerks like James and Lucas. He avoided talking about Emily and the insane crush he had on her. Even though he knew his father would be excited and interested in Owen's love life, it seemed somehow unfair for Owen to talk about new love when his father had lost his. For his father's part, he tried to make up for all the changes by just being there. It helped, even if it wasn't quite enough.

Later that night, during a commercial break for *Modern Family*, Owen's father emerged choking and gasping from the bathroom. "You did it," he whispered. "You finally did it. The son has surpassed the father." With that he fell to his hands and knees and then onto the floor, making a fake death rattle.

Owen had to laugh out loud. "You're such a dorkster," he said. "Dorkster" was part of the language his mother had given them. Swearing and insults just hadn't been in her, so the closest she came was this reworking of the word "dork." At worst, it meant someone was being incredibly silly. It was one of his favourite words in the world.

"Water!" moaned his father, who pretended to be feebly grasping for his son.

"Get your own!"

"A gas mask!"

"Now you're just being ridiculous."

"I'm finished!"

"Stop!"

"It smells of death and old people in there!"

"Whatever. I know my own flavour. That stuff is gold."

With that, the two of them broke into hysterics. *Laughing is good*, thought Owen. *Laughing is not remembering she's not here.* Owen's mother never cared for their contests, muttering "dorksters" as she walked away with a small grin.

The mood didn't last too long, as gradually the two of them just sat there looking at each other with small, sad smiles. "Am I doing okay?"

Owen's father asked. "As a dad, I mean. I'm trying. I've never been a father to a sixteen-year-old before, so I'm checking in."

"Yeah, Dad," Owen told him. "You're the best."

He meant it with all his heart.

THE NEXT morning they were back into the old routine. "Cereal?" his dad asked.

"Cereal," Owen replied. They would chat about what was coming up in the day, what they needed to do, and talked about what they might have for dinner. Again they talked freely about everything except her.

It was on the tip of his tongue to tell his dad about the confrontation he had the day before with James and Lucas, but the words died away. He'd just worry. He was too cool of a dad to call the school and rant about bullies harming his son. That sort of stuff just made things worse most of the time. But he would offer to drive him, pick him up, and maybe even try to teach him how to fight. He did, once before, after a kid in the fifth grade had been stealing Owen's lunch. It hadn't seemed odd at the time as his father was a giant to him then, but seeing this thin, short man show him how to throw a punch now seemed a bit silly. Instead of fighting that fifth-grade terror, Owen had offered him half a sandwich one day. It turned out that the kid never got a lunch from his parents because they had both been laid off and money was tight. When Owen told his mother and father about this, they beamed with pride. "You're a better man than I am, son," his father said. Each day, his parents packed him an extra sandwich and piece of fruit.

Once breakfast was done and the routine was observed, the two got into the elevator and headed down into the world. Owen got out first in the lobby to make the trek to school while his father continued down to the garage and to their car. Without fail, his father fired off two quick honks of the horn as he passed Owen at the corner and continued on to work. It might have been routine, but as far as routine went, it was pretty nice.

CHAPTER 2

N ice ended four and a half blocks away.

"There he is!" came a shout from behind. Instantly, Owen's spine tingled and his feet and hands went numb. He knew that voice and knew that if he stopped to look, it would just give James Vanier an easier time of catching up to him and making his life hell. Instead, Owen quickened his pace ever so slightly.

No good. James noticed and took it as his cue to begin the bullying from afar.

"Think THAT'S going to help?" he called. "You think shuffling your stupid ass up the street like you're going to piss your pants is a defence? Slow down, buddy. Take your beating like a man."

Owen refused to answer. Instead, he kept his focus and didn't stop walking. Why answer? Answering would only make it worse. His only hope was that if he kept walking and stuck close to the morning crowd of commuters, maybe he'd blend in and James would lose his nerve.

No such luck.

A hand reached out to grab his backpack, pulling Owen back and to the right into an alley. As he spun around, fists clenched so hard the nails were biting into the palm of his hands, he saw that James wasn't alone. Lucas, tall, burly, and mute as ever stood beside him, arms folded across his chest, his gaze drifting over the crowd to see if anyone was making a fuss. No one shouted out a protest — hell, no one even looked their way, and Lucas relaxed slightly. James, meanwhile, prowled like a cat back and forth in front of him, blocking any hope of escape. The nails bit deeper into Owen's flesh. Soon there would be blood, but would it be his own or his attackers'? Odds were it was going to be his own. Desperate, Owen called out to a stranger on the street.

"Hey, Mom!" he shouted. He hoped the obvious bluff would confuse the two long enough for him to make a break for it. He waved at the perplexed stranger and walked toward her. The woman didn't play along in the slightest. She barely cocked an eyebrow. The ruse only gave Owen time to make it past James before Lucas's two beefy hands shoved him into a group of garbage cans. Last night's table scraps from the adjoining restaurant scattered all over the place. A couple of rats scurried out from the dark corners of the alley.

The woman paid attention to this for an instant and looked as if she was debating whether to say something and come to Owen's defence. *Please do*, he begged in his mind. James and Lucas fell into hysterics, however, and James told the woman that they were really old friends and that Owen was just goofing around. Rather than look to Owen to confirm this, the woman walked off with obvious relief. Whether she believed James or not was irrelevant. She was off the hook. Much as he wanted to rage against the woman, Owen couldn't really blame her. Even if she wanted to, what could she do to help? *That will never be me*, Owen thought. *I won't ever walk away when I know something isn't right.*

Once the woman was out of sight, James picked up a rotting tomato and tossed it into Owen's lap. "'Mom'?" he asked. "You called for your *mommy*? I almost believed it, too." He started to snicker at this and picked up another tomato. This time, when he threw it he missed him, but the splatter against the wall still glanced off onto Owen's back.

"Hey, Lucas!" snapped James, tossing a glance at his partner. "How'd you know he was lying?"

At this, Lucas grunted. "Mom's dead," he said bluntly. You could barely hear him as he spoke. It was so low and rumbling, you'd think a semi truck had just driven past. It was the most Owen had ever heard him speak. Usually he just made low, guttural sounds like a caveman.

James's eyes widened in delight. "That right, Owey-boy? Your mommy DEAD? How did she die? She look at your face? She kill herself rather than live with a piece of crap like you? That's what I would have done. I'd look at you and end it all right there and then." With this, he delivered a vicious kick at Owen's leg. Then another. And another.

Owen felt a rage building inside of him he'd never felt before. *Tease me,* he thought. *Push me around. Say what you want. Do what you want. But don't ever, EVER, bring my mother into it.* His fist was still balled so tight, he thought he would break his own fingers. Blood trickled through them already from scraping them on the ground as he broke his fall. Before he could react, however, rescue arrived.

"What the *hell?*" came an outraged voice from the mouth of the alley. "What are you two doing? Leave him alone!" James and Lucas instinctively took a step back. The first rule of being a good bully is not to get caught and to deny it outright, even if everyone can plainly see that you're guilty.

Owen cautiously peered around them to see who his saviour was. There stood Emily Lloyd, hands on her hips in the kind of pose that even Wonder Woman would have envied, mouth pursed in anger and the fiercest glare in her eyes. Just off to her right stood Bea, arms folded, attention focused on a street sign, a wall, the pavement, anything but what was going on. Apparently she knew when to develop a quick, temporary case of blindness. Emily, however, wasn't going to do the same.

In that moment, Owen was more in love than ever. He was also dying of shame and embarrassment. He wasn't weak; he could fight back, but the last thing he wanted to do was make an enemy. It went against his plan for invisibility. Besides, something about these two, James in particular, suggested that they weren't all bluster. When he looked in their eyes he saw the kind of danger they warn about on nature channels. They had predator blood in them. James, in particular, looked like he could kill if he were pushed far enough. Owen didn't want to find out.

Once James and Lucas saw that it was only Emily, they laughed, and James delivered a fresh kick to Owen. "That is ENOUGH!" she yelled.

"Walk away, Emily," James said in bored tones over his shoulder.

"Fine, but he walks with us," Emily replied curtly. Her tone offered no hint of bargaining.

James's reply was less than eloquent. He began throwing random pieces of garbage at the girls. Emily moved out of the way as a rotting cabbage exploded by her feet. Half-eaten pieces of chicken were thrown next. Bea, still not looking directly at anyone, managed to dodge a chunk of watermelon. Lucas didn't throw anything, nor did he stop his friend. Instead, he stood his ground in between the two groups as garbage and insults flew by his head in equal measure.

"He's busy," James yelled back. "Giving me that Walmart training we talked about yesterday. Right, Owey-boy?"

Nothing is better for giving a kid a bout of courage like a beautiful girl standing nearby who is being assaulted by garbage. It was a chance to be noble. A chance to be chivalrous. A chance to come to a lady's defence (forgetting that she had just come to his moments before) and to protect her honour! Owen had seen many of his friends sum up guts they didn't have moments before to do some brave things. Some asked out girls way out of their league, while others performed gymnastics or acted like idiots in a bizarre attempt to get some positive female attention. Owen's own particular brand of courage was his wit. Emily was standing up for him and he wanted to — no *needed* to — show that he could hold his own.

"Right, James," he said agreeably. Loudly, even. Too loudly? Owen then looked to Emily and — he never would have thought he'd have the guts before — winked at her. "It isn't going very well. So far, he can't spell 'Walmart' and is frustrated because I told him he isn't allowed to eat out of the garbage cans. Lucas, meanwhile, is practicing for his job as a lightpost. As you can see, though, no light, but he is doing an excellent job of imitating an inanimate object."

As James whirled around to face him, Owen did something that surprised everyone, himself most of all. He found all of his frustration, anger, and courage and channelled it into one mighty blow that landed right on James Vanier's face, his left eye in particular, knocking the kid backward and causing him to topple onto all the garbage he'd just been tossing. Lucas, not knowing how to react, let his jaw drop and glanced quickly from Owen to his friend on the ground.

Bea snickered at this, finally allowing herself to look at what was happening. "Holy crap!" she said. "Owen found some *balls*!" Somehow, the tables had turned in short order. Owen may have been the one on the ground a moment ago, but now as he stood there shaking and dusting himself off, the two thugs were slightly diminished and less threatening. Emily relaxed a little, smiling at the corner of her mouth.

Snap!

The quick, slight sound may as well have been deafening in the little alley. James had said nothing, nor had Lucas, but actions were louder than words. His face purpling in anger and his whole body shaking, James revealed a few inches of sharp, gleaming steal in his hands. He had just pulled out a switchblade.

Even Lucas looked surprised. His eyes widened slightly, and he took a tentative step back. He said nothing, did nothing else, but if someone as big and frightening as Lucas Walton moved backward, that told you it was serious.

"You. Are. *Dead*," James hissed. "*No one* touches me. *No one* touches my face. *No one* does that and gets to live." His voice was so calm and measured, he was practically whispering. The menace and hate dripping out of his mouth was chilling. Lucas cautiously stepped in front of his friend, hands up in a gesture of surrender, trying to block his friend or calm him down. It only lasted a moment or two before James literally stared Lucas out of the way, but it was enough time for Owen to scramble up the alley to where the two girls were waiting. They didn't need to be told to run — they just did.

The second he got past Lucas's bulk, James took off after them, and Lucas reluctantly followed. Before they could get to the mouth of the alley, a garbage truck rolled in front of them, blocking the path. Muttering a curse and screaming bloody vengeance at the driver, James and Lucas lost precious seconds trying to find a way around.

Owen, Emily, and Bea, meanwhile, had never run so fast in their lives. They zigzagged through the throng of commuters, muttering a quick apology whenever one of them clipped someone. They didn't stop long enough to hear if their apologies were accepted, however, not with James somewhere behind. Though they couldn't hear or see him, not one of them had a doubt that he'd be following right behind, and the last thing they wanted to happen was for him to catch up. That look in his eyes had more than just scared them: they were terrified.

Once they were around the corner and down Yonge Street, Owen started to look for a place for them to duck inside. Most of the stores, other than the few eateries, were closed this early in the morning. They passed storefront after storefront, but each was locked, cold, and dark inside. Owen hoped that wasn't a sign for what might happen to them if they didn't find a place to hide. Finally, he spotted a large wooden, weather-worn sign rocking back and forth in the slight breeze that read "Tabula Obscura." The window front was full of books, and he could see movement inside. Best of all, the sign read "open." Behind him he could hear muffled angry shouts from people complaining about some unseen inconvenience rapidly approaching. Owen had one guess as to what might be trying to push through the crowd.

"In here!" he said, reaching out to grab Emily's hand. It sent a momentary thrill through him when her hand squeezed his, but it seemed to be out of relief rather than anything romantic.

"Done and DONE," said Bea, breathlessly pushing past them both. She really wasn't in the best shape.

The three of them rushed into the store so quickly that they tripped over themselves as they wedged through the door. The light chime of the bell at the top of the door welcomed them as Owen pushed the door shut and ducked down behind the book display. Beads of sweat dripped into his eyes, causing them to sting. His heart thundered madly in his chest.

"And what do you think *you're* doing?" came a gruff, unfriendly voice.

"Shhhhh!" hissed Bea.

"I beg your pardon?"

"Can't you just be *quiet?*" asked Bea. She turned around in a huff and blinked in surprise as she remembered she was in a store. A man in his late thirties stood before them, hands on his hips, and one eyebrow cocked back like the hammer on a gun. His faded nametag read "Carl," and if he wasn't happy before, being told to shut up inside his own store certainly didn't put him on a plane to Pleasantville. Bea stammered a bit when she saw the look on his face and perhaps — too little, too late — added an "Uh, sir?"

She flashed her sweet smile at him, which was slightly creepy, given her braces. She looked more like she wanted to eat him than charm him. Owen was trying to summon the courage to go back outside when Emily once again came to the rescue. "We're sorry, sir," she said sweetly. Hell, it was almost hypnotic. "We're a bit late for school, and I just wanted to look inside your store for a minute. She's mad at me for slowing her down." She smiled again and tilted her head. Her hair flowed gently with the movement, almost in slow motion, like the after-picture in a shampoo commercial. Owen stared dumbly.

A few more muffled complaints were heard outside, and Owen knew that Carl's decision would either save them or get them killed. A few seconds passed before his hair-trigger eyebrow eased back down his face. "Fine," he muttered. "But leave your bags at the counter. No bags allowed!"

The three of them let out a collective sigh. Just before they unslung their backpacks, Owen caught a glimpse of James and Lucas as they lumbered past, looking around wildly and craning to look over and past the crowd. They never slowed down and were quickly out of view. Owen dropped his bag on the front counter by the register. "Not there!" shouted Carl. "I need to cash out customers. How can I do that if your stupid bag is in the way?" A quick glance around the store showed that there was no one else there to be inconvenienced.

"Sorry, sir," apologized Owen. He moved his bag off to the side, essentially putting it in the front window. Anyone passing by would probably think the thing was for sale.

As Emily and Bea did likewise, Owen slowly appraised his surroundings. The place was incredible. From floor to ceiling, there were books. Hundreds of them. No, more likely *thousands*, Owen guessed. All of them looked incredibly old, except for one rickety metal stand filled with moldy paperbacks, many of them trashy romances. In the centre of the room were two large circular pillars, also lined with books. Beyond them was a dirt-covered glass door, partly open, that Owen could see led into a dimly lit back area, also filled with books, but the view was blocked by a lightly billowing curtain. He felt drawn to the back room and wanted to explore it, likely just because it wasn't something meant for most to see. Owen loved little mysteries like that. He saw it as a touch of magic leaving an impression on the real world for mere mortals to experience.

Off to the left of the forbidden room was a large wooden staircase that had an incredibly ornate banister carved into the shape of some sort of animal. It looked a bit like a dog crossed with an alligator to Owen. Black and somewhat sinister. Not something you'd want to run into if you expected to survive. On the wall there was a faded picture of a hand pointing up those ancient stairs with the promise of "more books" on the second floor. It was all old, *wonderfully* old in truth, and strangely beautiful, in Owen's opinion. Others might call it a mess. Or a hoarder's nest.

Beyond the entrance, Owen could see that it would actually be a bit difficult to navigate the space given all of the texts. Nevertheless, he reverently began to move forward into the space, letting his fingers slowly trace the gold lettering of the titles on some of the spines. Emily, likewise, was staring in wonder at the place. Bea, however, was all business as she faced Carl down. "So," she said earnestly. "What do you sell here?"

It was a stupid question, no doubt about it, but what made it an *amazingly* stupid question was that she was utterly sincere. Carl just stared at her, flummoxed, but before he could do the eyebrow thing again, a soft chuckle came from the office doorway behind him. An ancient man slowly crept out of the office, putting extra weight on the cane in his right hand as he stepped. His hair had all gone white and matched the bushy, patched grey beard. He had the most wrinkles Owen had ever seen and produced even more when he smiled. It was the smile that would later be what Owen remembered most clearly. Despite his age and despite his wrinkles, when the Bookkeeper smiled all age seemed to wash away, and the twinkle in his blue eyes lifted their spirits. If he could have, Owen would have immediately adopted the man as a grandfather.

"Why, we sell magic here, my dear," said the Bookkeeper with a sly smile.

There was no sarcasm in his answer and no mockery; only sincerity.

"Just about to throw them out," growled Carl. "No respect! Bunch of stupid kids. Probably want to steal from us."

"Carl, enough," said the Bookkeeper patiently. He spoke quietly but firmly as Carl ground his teeth, not liking being told to back down. It had the air of a conversation had many times before.

"You know what they're like!" Carl protested feebly.

"*Enough.* I will attend to our customers. Why don't you go over the inventory for me?" asked the Bookkeeper kindly.

Carl lingered, not liking this idea. He leaned in and whispered in a hushed and gentle voice. "But sir, you know you shouldn't even be out of bed. I can handle this." The concern in his voice surprised Owen a bit. Given how rude Carl had been moments before, it was touching to see his concern for the Bookkeeper, and Owen made a quick mental adjustment of his first impression.

"I'm not dead yet," chuckled the Bookkeeper. "Your concern and your friendship mean the world to me, Carl. Still, it is my store and my duty to help the next generation. Particularly if they want to read! Imagine such a thing with young people! No cellphones, no iPads, no devices or video games systems, but rather books! Wonderful! If I need you, I'll call, my friend."

It was obvious Carl wasn't going to change the old man's mind. Reluctantly, with one final scowl directed at the trio, he went into the office and closed the door. "Now then," said the Bookkeeper, "where were we?"

"You were telling us you sold magic," said Bea. "I don't see any wands, robes, or owls, though. I know my Harry Potter and my Tolkien. If you did, you might have more people in your store. Probably not, though. It's really old. You don't have anything magical." You had to give it to her: Bea could be blunt. Most people might be kind, patient, or attentive. Not Bea. She cut through whatever she thought was nonsense like a hot knife through butter.

It didn't faze the Bookkeeper, however. He just chuckled and let loose one of his twinkling smiles. "Indeed, I do," he said. "We sell magic of all sorts here. We sell dreams, memories, life, death, and even immortality of a sort. We have stories about faraway lands, about dreams fulfilled, about hopes dashed, and about the incredible potential of the human spirit. In these books lies the answer to Douglas Adams and his secret meaning of life, the universe, and everything! These books are the result of writers who became more than mere storytellers, but creators of worlds and lords over the beings they have conjured. All books have a sort of magic to them, do they not? I'm sure you've felt it."

"Kind of," Emily said, playing along. "Like when an author describes something and I can see it in my mind. It becomes more and more real the deeper you get into the story." Owen knew exactly what she meant. He'd felt that way often when his mother told him stories. His heart gave a slight pang of grief at the memory. His eyes darted away so he could distract himself. Once again, his gaze fell on the curtain and the hidden room.

"Yes, quite," said the Bookkeeper enthusiastically. "And if you're truly under the spell, you can also hear, smell, taste, and touch the world you're visiting. A good book transports you away. It lets you take part in the journey of its characters and lets you feel what they feel. There are even those precious tomes that feel as though they are recorded truth rather than clever fiction. Sometimes we would even rather dwell in the worlds within the books than the one we live in."

"Like *Twilight*!" gushed Bea. It was the only book she'd ever read. Owen got about twenty pages into it to see what all the fuss was about. It seemed a bit too romantic for him, so he dropped it, but he could see why it would be so appealing for others. Not wanting to offend either girl, he held back his overall thoughts just in case they didn't fall on the same side of the fence.

The Bookkeeper laughed out loud. "Yes, even like *Twilight*, I suppose. Still, I must admit that however tempting it is to 'live' a story, I have found that real life is always much more interesting and often stranger than fiction itself."

"Not *my* life," grumbled Bea. She had always been a bit disappointed with her life. Braces, the glasses, the mismatched clothes. She wasn't completely clueless and knew that whatever popularity she had was a reflection of the attention given to Emily, but she took it anyway. She'd trade her life for someone tough like Tris from *Divergent* or badass like Katniss from *Hunger Games* or anyone from anywhere that inspired her. She thought it would be cool to have super abilities and her fictional boyfriend would be someone sweet like Neville Longbottom from the *Harry Potter* books. He was like her: brave, cute, and under-appreciated.

"I think you'll find that even your life has mystery, romance, and a hint of adventure," The Bookkeeper said. "After all, you found your way here, did you not?" All three shifted uneasily at that comment, not wanting to think about what lay in wait for them if they stepped outside too soon. Though they hadn't seen or heard James and Lucas in the past few minutes, they couldn't be too far.

"In this shop, all dreams are possible. Whether it is in the shared dreams that authors have given us or in the challenges and adventures of the characters themselves, there is more than enough magic for a hundred lifetimes. So please, look around and see what catches your eye. If you feel drawn to something, pick it up and see if it fits. Try it on, so to speak. Don't resist the pull, or you might miss out on something extraordinary." Owen could have sworn the last comment was meant specifically for him as the old man locked eyes with him for a lingering, knowing moment, but he didn't know what the Bookkeeper could have possibly been referring to. After a moment, the Bookkeeper nodded sagely and took their silence for understanding. "I am here should you wish to ask any questions."

"Thank you very much, sir," Emily said politely. With a nod toward Owen, she and Bea moved off into the section labelled "Romance" while he drifted toward the science fiction section. Most of the books he glimpsed were old editions of classics from Jules Verne. He looked in vain for more slightly modern fare like *Ender's Game* by Orson Scott Card, *Hominids* by Robert J. Sawyer, or *Hyperion* by Dan Simmons. Instead, he found old green and brown books with yellowing paper. None called to him, so he left them all untouched.

As he wandered up and down the aisle, he found himself edging closer and closer to the back room, almost unconsciously. Each time he paused, he strained his neck to try to get a peek into the dim back room. The only sign as to what might be back there had partly fallen down and was resting on yet another shelf of books lining the doorway. It read "Heritage Collection," which probably just meant older than the old books in the main area (if that was even possible), but Owen's curiosity was piqued. There was no sign saying it was off limits, so if he were to go back there and Carl or the Bookkeeper was angry, he had a clear excuse.

But still he hesitated.

His eyes were fixed on the room, even as his hands casually picked up and put down books on the shelf as he worked up the courage to step back there. A quick look showed the Bookkeeper gazing out the front window while the soft giggles of the two girls floated over the book stacks from somewhere else in the store. He took a deep breath and slipped past the rippling curtain into the back room and the mysteries it contained.

CHAPTER 3

James Vanier had never been so angry in his whole life. He was still holding the knife and still intending to put it to good use, but the red haze of anger he had been in had subsided enough to give him the common sense to hide it in his shirt sleeve. He paced up and down the street, looking for that piece of crap Owen and the two girls who couldn't keep out of it.

One way or another, he'd make sure they got what they deserved.

With each step, he fantasized about catching up to them and delivering the first strike. He imagined them begging for forgiveness and offering him money. Emily would say anything to calm him down. Maybe she'd even offer to be his girlfriend, and be with him forever. She'd even want him to get rid of Owen. She'd beg him to do it. Hell, the only reason she even stuck up for him was because she felt sorry for him. Emily was really on his side all along. For her, he'd start with that little jerk's eyes.

He fought down laughter at the thought of the sound it would make.

Part of him knew this was wrong and attempted to reject it. But the fantasy just wouldn't quit. The knife would ultimately finish this story for him.

Behind him, Lucas panted along, not wanting to lose track of his friend. Lucas was loyal like that; he'd never let James wander into something alone. He knew that James meant to do harm — serious harm — but hoped he could prevent it from coming to that. As far as Lucas was concerned, James could kick and keep on kicking whomever he wanted so long as it ended there. When James pulled the knife, he could see that Lucas had honestly not known what to do. Being on James's side was all well and good, but he was fairly certain that Lucas was not interested in going to jail, which was exactly what would happen if James got his way. On the other hand, he could tell that Lucas was aware that getting in the way might mean going to the afterlife a lot sooner than he'd like, perhaps by "accident," and that Owen kid, at least, wasn't worth it. Either way, the choices weren't too appealing.

"No, no, no, no, NO!" yelled James. He pulled up short before the end of the block, causing Lucas to crash into him. The knife fell out of James's hand and skittered to a stop by the curb. Lucas quickly scrambled down to pick it up and retracted the blade. He stuffed it in his pockets and looked around wildly at the adults passing by to make sure none had seen it. No one stopped, slowed down, or screamed, so they were in luck. James wasn't really worried about the people, since owning a knife wasn't illegal or anything, but Lucas probably figured that the more of a show he put on about being concerned someone saw them would give him more of an excuse not to just hand it back over to James.

Not an option, as far as James was concerned. "Give it to me!" he hissed.

Lucas just shook his head and nodded toward all the people around. The look said "not a good idea," and James got the message and let it go. Though he'd never admit it out loud, James was kind of happy to be relieved of the blade. Now that it was out of his grip and the adrenaline had worn off a bit, he began to shake and realize how close he'd come to murder. It wasn't the first time, either. When he was younger, his little brother, Marcel, broke one of his toys by accident. Marcel was only three and curious. He hadn't meant any harm, and he certainly didn't understand what the problem was. To James, though, this was a personal attack. He raged at this mother and father about what his brother had done while they patiently tried to explain to him that it hadn't been done on purpose. James knew better. His parents clearly liked the little boy better than him. He was cuter, softer, and still liked to cuddle. They always took his side and told James he needed to be a better big brother and look out for Marcel.

He looked out for him, all right.

One day the boy was at the top of a small flight of stairs and hesitantly about to take the first step down them. James helped him down the rest of the way. As the boy lay crying at the bottom, cradling a broken arm, James was right there being brave and stroking the boy's hair when his parents came around the corner. "It was an accident," James claimed. "He fell down the stairs." The truth had been a much darker thing, and as hard as he tried to deny it to himself, James knew that he had meant for his brother to die. This realization freaked him out, but what scared him even more was that he wasn't as freaked out as he should have been. His overall calmness seemed abnormal. He thought his parents would sense the monster in their elder son and send him away. As he held his sobbing brother, he wanted to take it all back and vowed never to let something like that happen again.

Now that Lucas had the blade, by accident, he was off the hook. In his mind he was holding his brother and trying to soothe him. Since then, he and his brother still had their share of arguments, and more than once James had to make Marcel pay for being the better-loved, but at least there were no more repeats of the stair incident. Now that Lucas had his knife and James regained some of his control, there would be no new incident to regret today, or so he hoped. Owen and the girls still had to pay, that wasn't even a question, but not the ultimate price. As long as he kept his mouth shut, Owen would probably live through it. James looked to Lucas and thought about where his prey could have gone.

"Look, they can't have come this far," James said. "We would have seen them. Owey-boy, maybe, but not Emily and sure as hell not Pig-face. Piggy wheezes if she has to stand up." While the crowds were still there, they had begun to thin out enough that you could look up and down the stretch of Yonge Street and make out most of the faces. "That means they ducked into a store somewhere. Let's go back."

Lucas looked at his watch and tapped at the face. Time to go was the implication. James slapped Lucas's wrist out of the way. "I don't care what time it is. Screw school. No way am I going to go to class and have those idiots show up with grins on their faces because they got away. You want them talking? Bragging about how they beat us? At the very least, I need to give Owey-boy a fat lip to help shut his smart mouth."

It was no use arguing, Lucas knew. The talk now was of hitting, not stabbing, and Lucas relaxed somewhat. For the big kid, James knew, that was better. Hitting was fine. Punching was fine. Lucas could get behind that easily. James just hoped to find Owen all alone, however. He didn't want Emily to see him like that, and neither did Lucas; James knew he too harboured a secret crush on the girl. Most of the guys at Morton did, so that was hardly shocking. He was big and mute, and she was beautiful and had the sweetest voice. James knew Lucas didn't want any harsh words directed at him to come out of her, not that it would help his chances either way.

The two of them started back down the street, pausing at each store long enough to get a good look at who was inside.

THE SECOND Owen passed into the darkened room, it was as if he'd entered a completely different world. He wasn't aware of how much noise from the street filtered into the store until it was suddenly and totally absent. Above him, a light fluttering could be heard in the exposed rafters from some unseen bird whose sleep he had just disturbed. Faint streaks of light came in from on high and illuminated books, tables, and lamps, all of them wholly similar and unremarkable in the labyrinthine store. With dust and cobwebs pouring out of the corners of the room, some might call the space spooky. To Owen, it was peaceful. He could imagine himself staying in this room for hours, doing nothing and being perfectly content.

It was clear that no one had been in this room for quite some time, and Owen was worried that he wasn't supposed to be back there. There was no sign suggesting that he shouldn't be, however, and the door *was* open. If they didn't want him back there, he rationalized, they wouldn't have made it so easy to get into. As he browsed, he mentally prepared a list of excuses should either the Bookkeeper or Carl find him and take offense to his bold wandering.

As with the room before, there were no books that stood out to him, yet Owen couldn't help but shake the feeling that there was something back here waiting to be found. He pulled books off the shelf at random to get the heft of them and to read their titles, but time after time he was disappointed with them and returned them. How did the old poem go? *Water, water, every where/nor any drop to drink?* Samuel Coleridge had been talking about sailors on the open ocean dying of thirst and being surrounded by salt water. It must have been unbelievably frustrating to be around that much water and to know that drinking it only meant you'd die faster. For Owen, being around this sea of books was a similar frustration. If he just wanted a book, all he had to do was reach out and grab one, but it wasn't likely to satisfy him. If he just held out a few more minutes, the right book, the fresh water, so to speak, could be found and he might end his thirst.

That's how Owen felt: thirsty. He was parched and needed to solve the ache in his mind and heart. Back here, in this room, was the key. He could feel it. He closed his eyes and took a deep breath. He counted to five and felt certain that when he opened his eyes the first thing he saw would be what he was after. "One," he began. "Two… three… four… five." With the last number, he poured every thought, hope, and prayer he could muster into it and opened his eyes to see…

Nothing. Not a single thing. His disappointment bordered on grief.

"Whatcha *DOIN*?" asked Bea in a fake deep voice. She didn't ask loudly, but it scared the crap out of Owen, who yelled and lost his footing. He knocked over a pile of books trying to steady himself, which then knocked over another pile of books. The domino effect stopped after five stacked towers of books went crashing against the far wall. Several of the books got tangled in the cords of the window shade and pulled it from where it hung in the frame. What was a moment ago a few thin beams of light was now a full shaft that nearly blinded Owen, who had gotten used to the gloom.

Bea snorted twice as she laughed. "You are such a dork!" she wheezed. Emily, standing beside her, stifled a laugh as she carefully climbed over the fallen books to get to Owen. His face beet-red, he accepted her outstretched hand, and together they worked to get him back onto his feet.

"Thanks," he mumbled.

"You're welcome," she said with a smile. "Y'know, you're kind of cute when you're falling over. That seems to happen to you a lot, haven't you noticed?"

Cute? Me? Oh god, thought Owen, *don't screw this up.*

"Yeah, but only when you're around. I guess you have that kind of effect on me," replied Owen. It was the smoothest line he had ever used, and either it was going to backfire or she'd go for it. He'd never put anything on the line like that before. Before she could even answer, he wanted to take it back just in case she was offended. His lips opened to speak, but he closed them again to see how it would play out.

"So you're saying I knock you off your feet?" she said while laughing. It sounded like sunshine. "Dude, that's really corny."

Mid-blush, something shimmered behind Emily that distracted Owen before he could speak. "Owen?" asked Emily, a bit surprised that the flirting had already come to an end. She waved her hand in front of his face. "Hellooo? Earth to Owen."

"Sorry," he said, and he meant it, but his attention was still fixed on the object that had caught his attention. "There's something…" He gently pushed past her (she smelled wonderful as well, he had time to notice) and stepped over to the glass cabinet that was now bathed in the sunlight from the window. The panes of glass were all covered in dirt, but there was a faint golden glow from something inside. He tried to pull open the door, but the ornate lock kept it firmly in place. As he wiped a bit of dirt off for a clearer look inside, the golden glow seemed to thrum and pulse, as though it knew him and was calling for him to come closer.

"Ah, you've found it!" came the Bookkeeper's voice from the doorway. Bea, still enjoying the awkward display between Emily and Owen, hadn't noticed him coming in and let out a squawk.

Karma, thought Owen as he grinned at Bea. *What goes around, comes around.*

"My apologies, my dear. I did not mean to frighten you, as I'm sure you did not mean to try to deafen me."

"S'okay," said Bea, blushing. "Sorry!"

"Not at all, not at all," soothed the Bookkeeper, chuckling once again. "No one has bothered with the Heritage Collection room in ages! I see it hasn't held up very well, and Carl hasn't been as diligent in his dusting as he assures me."

Emily quickly began to try to tidy up the place by restacking books. This caused a bout of laughter from the old man. "Scattered or stacked, I don't think there's much difference, do you?" he asked. Emily carefully put down the books she was holding and apologized again, but the old man waved his hand to get her to stop and winked so she'd know it wasn't a big deal. Owen, meanwhile, was still standing transfixed in front of the book in the display case. "As for you, lad, you seem to have found my most prized possession. It is a book of unparalleled magical ability."

"What is it?" breathed Owen. He hadn't been able to look away save for a glance or two at the older man. Through the dirty glass he swore he could see movement, but it must have just been a trick of the light.

"Not something to be trifled with, at the very least," said the Bookkeeper. With surprising grace, he waded through the destruction of his back room to join Owen. "It's a very special kind of book," he continued. "Unique even among those made in a similar style. It has been in my possession for a very long time. How long, I think I shall keep to myself, as telling you my age would just depress me."

He unlocked the cupboard with a small silver key and laid his hand on the latch. He turned to look at Owen and peered at the boy over the top of his glasses. "No one has looked at or read this book since I put it in here. In fact, there are few who exist who can truly and properly read it. If I am *old* (and let us agree that I am and be done with it) then it is *ancient*. Remember what I told you of the magic in books?" Owen nodded politely. "Good, then I don't have to repeat myself. If all of the other books in this store have magic in the words that live on in the imagination, this one captures you and makes the story as real as life itself. It holds your attention until the story is done and will profoundly impact the way you view your existence and the world around you. In short, it will change your life.

"Have I sold it enough? I ought to write dust jacket summaries." The Bookkeeper chuckled at his own remarks and looked to Bea and Emily for support. Emily stood stock-still and Bea raised an eyebrow.

"Who would make a jacket out of dust?" Bea asked dully.

"Never mind, never mind," said the Bookkeeper, waving her off. He turned his attention back to Owen with excitement in his eyes. "Shall we take a look?"

Owen nodded eagerly.

The old man open swung the door, and the reflected gold light intensified to a new level. Once all the way open, it seemed to dim slightly. It was almost as though it had woken up and stretched and had now returned to sleep.

"It is called a *Battledoor*," said the Bookkeeper.

It wasn't anything like any book, or door for that matter, that Owen had ever seen before. For one thing, it wasn't bound like a book. There was no clear title page, and it was thin and solid. It had a short wooden handle and a face with lightly folded pieces of paper. The outside rim was coiled gold with the occasional leaf or design done with great care by a woodcarver over what must have been months of work. It was a masterpiece of craftsmanship spoiled only by the relatively normal, though clearly aged, paper in the middle. At a casual glance, he might even have mistaken it for a hand-held mirror without the glass. Maybe even something his grandmother may have had once upon a time. It was old and beautiful and represented something lost, though what specifically Owen couldn't have put his finger on. Other than being obvious about how you would hold the thing, Owen had no idea how to read it, much less how it could be the greatest story he would read in his life. He figured he could read every word on the Battledoor in under a minute and be done with it. It had to be some kind of joke.

Yet he could not deny he had been drawn to the thing. Owen pursed his lips and tried to hold back his growing disappointment. The Bookkeeper seemed to really think he had something special here, and rather than hurt the old man's feelings, Owen decided to go along with it.

"It's nice, sir," Owen said politely, swallowing loudly. The Bookkeeper eyed him appraisingly, clearly looking for more of a reaction. "Uh, it's *very nice?*"

"How do you read it?" Emily asked. She and Bea had come closer to get a better look at it. "All the papers are folded over. It's not like a normal book."

"Indeed, it is not," sighed the Bookkeeper as he turned away from Owen. For a moment he looked a little bit sad and disappointed, but Owen waved the thought away. *Why should he be sad or disappointed? What was I supposed to do?* thought Owen. *Maybe he's tired? Carl did say the man hadn't been feeling well.*

"The closest I can describe it is that it is very similar to an early form of the 'Choose Your Own Adventure' books that were popular in the 1980s," began the Bookkeeper. "Children would read the stories and be given an option. Whatever they chose, the book would take them in different directions to one conclusion or another. It might lead to a new branching path of the story, a pleasant conclusion, or an untimely end. Quite a lot like real life, actually, when you think about all the decisions one makes over the course of our short time on Earth. Most of those stories were quite quick, and many of the endings led to death or tragedy and were, if I say so myself, less than satisfying.

"The mechanics are similar here. You begin reading and a choice is given. Make one, turn the page, and deal with the consequences. What is remarkable about this Battledoor, unlike many of its cousin and brother books, is that once you make the decision, you're forced to follow the flow of the story. You can't go back and change your mind to see what lies down the other path, as much as you might wish it. And, you must finish the story. Yes, that much is unavoidable."

The tone and wistfulness the Bookkeeper used hinted at a deeper story, but Owen could tell that it wasn't the time or place to ask, nor would he likely get an answer that he would understand if he did.

"If it's one of a kind, what are all of those?" asked Bea. She was pointing at a stack of similarly shaped objects on the shelf below. On top of the stack were a few thin strips of leather with silver buckles.

"Good eye, my dear," the Bookkeeper said encouragingly. Bea blinked at the praise. "These are hornbooks, cousin to the Battledoor. A hornbook is just what it sounds like: a book made partly of wood and the horn of an animal. The parchment the writing is on is made of vellum." He paused at this point as though he was about to say something else. Instead, he cleared his throat and continued. "Vellum is animal skin that has been cleaned and stretched over a frame and is used as paper. In a few cases, human skin has actually been used to create vellum."

"Gross!" Bea said and made a yacking sound. Emily didn't look very impressed either.

The Bookkeeper wasn't fazed. "Yes, 'gross,' but to its credit, vellum is much more useful and durable than paper. Something written on vellum two hundred years ago would still be perfectly readable today and will be perfectly readable long after anything you might print off from your home computer tomorrow."

He held up the hornbook for them to get a better look. "A hole is left at the bottom of the handle of the hornbook so you can put it on a belt. This was quite common when they were popular. That way you wouldn't lose them. Here, try them on!" He passed belts out to Owen, Emily, and Bea, who all slipped the belts on. Despite their obvious age, the leather was soft and supple and fit nicely around their waists. On each side were a set of rings that you could hook objects on. Owen imagined the most likely use in the past would have been for keys. The belts had a bit of a steampunk-style quality to them. They fit perfectly but hung loosely at the same time.

"Very nice," said the Bookkeeper as he looked appraisingly at them. "Children would wear these belts when the hornbooks were popular, which was between the fifteenth and eighteenth centuries. Most hornbooks were limited in their use, though. Some had the alphabet on them, while others held passages from various scriptures. When they needed them, the children could use them to jog their memories or give them skills when the need arose." He grabbed at least three hornbooks off the shelf. He passed them over to Bea and showed her how to clip them onto her belt.

"Not very fashionable, are they?" she asked. She twisted and turned like a runway model showing off the latest designs. The hornbooks made a light knocking sound as they bounced off one another. "Look! I'm a wind chime!"

"Ha! Perhaps they weren't going to turn heads, but knowledge never goes out of style, young lady," said the Bookkeeper. "Remember that and you will do just fine."

He turned his attention to Emily. "For you, my dear, something tells me that you need something more than a simple reminder. I sense that you are wise beyond your years and will take the right paths, as long as you're able to make an informed decision. This, I think, would make those travels easier for you."

He pulled down another hornbook, this one slightly larger than the rest. It was a rusty blue and covered in dust. The Bookkeeper took a deep breath and blew it clean before presenting it to her. "*This* is the *Index*."

"An index?" asked Emily. "For what?" As far as she knew, indexes were in the back of textbooks or encyclopaedias to make it faster for you to find what you were looking for in the book. Rather than read through the whole thing, you flipped to the index searching for a random term like "pineapples" or something and saw that "pineapples" were mentioned on pages 42, 44, and 89. The Bookkeeper was right in that an index would shorten her path to knowledge, but it was kind of useless without a book or story to serve as a reference point.

"Not just 'an' index, but 'The' Index," he replied. "Capital 'T' and capital 'I.' It is a companion piece for the Battledoor. Where one goes, the other should be as well."

Owen blushed at this thought, because he knew what was coming next. The Bookkeeper had just paired him and Emily up as though he'd read the deepest desires of Owen's heart and was bringing him to life. Suddenly Owen wasn't just playing along but eager to turn the page. It was a literary matchmaking service.

"Go ahead, lad, and take the book," said the Bookkeeper, who gently gestured toward the golden object. As Owen hesitantly reached for it, the old man gave a final warning. "Just remember that once you start, you must see it through to the end."

Swallowing loudly, Owen picked it up. It was silky smooth and cool to the touch. At first nothing happened, but then again, what had he honestly expected? Fireworks? Music? He felt foolish holding the thing. It was like he was a little kid again and expecting to see Santa Claus or the Easter Bunny.

Just as he was about to thank the man and return the book, a faint pulse formed inside Owen's hand where he gripped the wooden board. He wanted to let go of it, but it felt almost as though the Battledoor was a part of his own arm, and even if he wanted to drop it, he couldn't. As he admired it, the Bookkeeper grabbed a long piece of thick, corded string hanging from Owen's belt and clipped it to the Battledoor. In a hushed, reverent whisper, he said, "It's yours, now," and took a step back. "It's been a long time."

Owen waved it back and forth, almost like a tool that has long since missed a firm hand. It felt like the right thing to do. "It's so light!" he said.

"Yes, but be careful *where* you swing it, lad. It's meant to be enlighten a person, not bash them," chuckled the Bookkeeper. "Though if you look it up, many associate a battledore (that's with an 're' at the end rather than an 'or') with an early kind of racquet used in a game similar to badminton or table tennis. Where they got that notion is beyond me." He laughed again at his own joke, but no one else joined in, though they smiled at the old man's ability to amuse himself.

"I'll be careful with it," promised Owen. He stopped waving the book around and brought it down to finally read it. His hands reverently paused over the delicate pages, and he allowed his fingertips to brush them.

"What does it say?" Emily asked curiously.

Two pieces of paper were folded neatly together, and an inscription neatly flowed over them both. Both because Emily asked and because he felt compelled to say the words anyway, Owen read the front of it out loud. As the old man had said, the ink was crisp and the words were clear.

THE BATTLEDOOR

Not all doors are meant to be opened, and no decision should be lightly made.

Once you make your choice, know that there is a price that must be paid.

If you are ready, open the first door and step through.

With that act, the story before you shall begin anew.

Follow the path or choose to fight;

Use all of your wits and all of your might.

The end is what you make of it once the story is told,

So until then, find your courage and don't fear to be bold.

Something had changed, Owen knew. Exactly what, he couldn't say. Like the Earth had shifted beneath his feet or colours were suddenly gone, but no one noticed. No one but him, that was.

Shaking slightly and chiding himself for being so silly, Owen folded open the two sides of the paper back and out of the way. Underneath, written in large letters that spanned the whole page, was a simple command and two options that Owen read out loud:

A NEW STORY BEGINS...

CHOOSE YOUR PATH:

'The Front Door' or 'The Alley'

"I'd pick the alley myself," said a cool voice from the doorway. There stood James Vanier and Lucas Walton, clutching one of the backpacks Owen, Emily, and Bea had stupidly left in plain view in the shop window.

"Fewer witnesses that way."

CHAPTER 4

O wen, Emily, and Bea stared open-mouthed at James and Lucas. They had been lost in the Bookkeeper's fascinating world of books and had forgotten why they were in the store in the first place. Now that James and Lucas were here, the place felt dirtier and molested, its beauty now tarnished.

For his part, Owen felt anger and embarrassment rising in him in equal parts. The Bookkeeper deserved none of this trouble, and they had brought it to his front door. That shame led to anger at James Vanier and his stupid threats and bullying. Owen had put up with it in the past because it had been an inconvenience at most, as it interfered with his brooding and loner behaviour, not because he was weak. Now it was more than just an inconvenience — it was an injustice that threatened everyone in this room. His grip tightened on the Battledoor. He barely noticed as it thrummed in reaction.

The Bookkeeper was not unaware of the tension in the room. "Friends of yours?" he asked Bea innocently.

"Uh, no," said Bea as she rolled her eyes. "This moron has been chasing us and trying to scare us. He's kind of a joke without a good punchline."

"And for that, you can pay as well, Pig-face," said James, who was still staring intently at Owen.

"Enough," Owen said, his eyes fixed tightly on James. "I've put up with your insults, your pushes, your pokes, and your crap long enough. I'm sorry you're a sad, sorry excuse for a human being, but you need to let that go and grow up. Turn around, walk out of here, and just leave us alone. We'll do the same thing, and that'll be the end of it. This is ridiculous."

"It's too late for that," said James as he and Lucas began to advance. Lucas looked less certain than his friend.

"There's no need for any of this!" sputtered the Bookkeeper as he stepped in front of James and Lucas, hands outstretched and motioning for them to calm down. Lucas reached out and shoved the man to the side, sending him sprawling through a stack of books and onto the floor. It wasn't much of a push, but you didn't need to put much force into it to move a man that ancient.

"No!" screamed Emily. "What is wrong with you? He's just an old man!" Lucas hesitated and blushed but made no apologies or attempt to help the old man. Emily made a move to go to him, but in the crowded space that meant pushing past the two boys in front of her. She knew that the direct approach meant getting thrown into books herself, and she couldn't chance hurting the Bookkeeper more than he already had been. He was weakly struggling on the floor.

Emily's indecision was ended for her. "CARL!" shouted Bea. "Come look! We're stealing things!"

On cue, Carl rushed into the room to see what the commotion was all about, eyebrow cocked and ready to fire insults and abuse like a shotgun blast. When he saw the old man in a heap, he let loose a torrent of foul language aimed at no one in particular. "What is going on in here! What have you done! You're a bunch of thugs, thieves, and low-life delinquents!" Spittle flew from his mouth as he started to foam like a mad dog. His eyes were wide and crazy as he stood protectively over the downed man.

"Turn around and leave us alo…" began James coldly. He was interrupted by a book upside the head. Carl was indiscriminately picking up books and tossing them. James took another hit in the arm, while Lucas ducked a particularly heavy-looking dictionary.

"Get OUT!" screamed Carl. "I'm going to call the police! You're lucky I don't have my baseball bat handy!"

The Bookkeeper reached an unsteady hand up and touched Carl's arm. He was gasping and looked to be in terrible pain. Carl shrugged the arm off at first before realizing who it was. He looked down as the old man began to clutch at his chest, right by his heart.

Carl fell to his knees then and cradled the man's head. "What's wrong? What is it? No, you can't do this to me!" He continued to plead, and tears started coming to his eyes. He looked accusingly at the group and focused his vision on James. "*You*. Come here and help me with him." His eyes shifted to Lucas. "Go to the front desk and call for an ambulance. NOW."

Lucas was briefly immobile due to indecision. Seeing as this was partially his fault, he seemed to judge calling an ambulance to be a good move at this point. He gave James a shrug and received a snarl in response. As Lucas rushed off, James bent down and ineffectually tried to help.

Owen looked down into the old man's eyes. Whatever else happened, he would not leave the man. He wasn't there when his mother had died and couldn't console her or tell her that everything was going to be okay. This old man might not be blood, but what had happened to him was in part because Owen had chosen this store to duck into. He vowed to be brave and face the consequences, come what may. *Cause and effect*, he thought. *Choice and consequence. I'll deal with it.*

"Get some water," Carl barked at James.

"Yes, of course, cool," said James. "Cool" was not really the appropriate word, but he looked relieved to have an excuse to be out of Carl's reach. James sat up and was comically turning his head left and right wildly for a source of water. Momentarily distracted, James did not see the Bookkeeper open his eyes, look at Owen, and wink.

Owen was so taken aback that he nearly laughed out loud. The old man was faking it! He wanted to hug him and spare Carl his misery, but he knew this was a golden opportunity to get out of here, preferably before the police showed up.

A sharp intake of breath behind him let him know that he wasn't the only one now in on the deception. Emily put her hand on his shoulder and drew him back slightly.

"I can't see any water!" said James in rising panic.

Carl's exasperation was palpable. "Then get up and go look for some, you idiot!" he yelled. "There's a small kitchenette in the office. Hurry up!" James scrambled to his feet and fled from the back room.

Other than the window he spotted when he first came in, the only other exit Owen had been aware of was the front door. That wouldn't work with both James and Lucas lumbering around. Knowing there was no other choice, he grabbed Emily's hand and was about to make a break for it when suddenly she pulled him the other way. "Back here," she hissed.

He turned to see Bea standing by a dark brown door. *That wasn't here before*, he thought. He was almost sure of it. But then it *had* been dark when he entered the space. The grain and design of the door almost made it look like another bookshelf.

"What are you doing back there?" barked Carl. "No use trying to hide. The cops'll find you. They aren't blind." Bea shifted slightly to face Carl, and when he saw the door, the confusion on his face was obvious.

"What the?" he said. "There ain't supposed to be no—"

"Go," said the old man, cutting him off.

Carl goggled at the sudden clarity and vitality coming from the Bookkeeper. "*Go*," the old man repeated insistently. "The story has started. and adventure is waiting beyond the next doorway."

"You were faking?" said Carl. A vein was throbbing on his forehead.

"Hush, now, Carl. I'm fine."

"What are you talking about?" asked Owen, breaking into the exchange. "What about you? They'll be back in a minute."

"It chose you. I have tried many times to read it, but it stayed cold and quiet. If I could have gone back, I would have. It glowed for you. It opened for you. Now you but have to open the door and step through."

"Come with us," Owen suggested. "We'll call the police outside. It's not safe here with them."

"Oh, we're quite a bit safer here than out there, I expect," said the Bookkeeper with a knowing smile. "But here is where I belong. I've accepted it. My role was to wait for a reader and a new protagonist to pick up where I left off. That person is you, my boy."

"This isn't a story!" Owen said. "This isn't some stupid adventure. This is real life, and you need to MOVE!"

"There is magic in the world, my boy, even if you can't see it."

Emily reached out and gently touched Owen's hand. "Owen," she said. "Look."

Reluctantly, he turned to look at her and saw she was facing the door itself. Carved above the handle were the words "The Alley" in the exact same font and shade he had seen in the Battledoor. It was impossible. He fumbled at his hip and brought up the paddle to look once more at the worn parchment, only it wasn't the smooth vellum it had been minutes before; now it was as sleek and smooth as glass. The Battledoor itself was shifting and changing shape. It had two strong handles on each side to grip and looked more like a computer tablet than a centuries-old adventure book. The ornate trim still laced around the edges, giving it an added layer of sophistication. The design of the edges bled out in the corners onto the screen itself. It was both futuristic and classical all at once. Steampunk in gleaming gold, with a glowing silver-white screen. It resonated with power.

"The book chooses the reader and changes itself to adapt to their needs, perspectives, and wants," said the Bookkeeper, who was also transfixed by the object. "Now all the reader must do is make the choice to go on the journey."

"This is crazy," said Carl in a daze. "You kept going on about magic books and new worlds, but I just thought the sixties had been unkind to you." The old man smiled and patted Carl's hand.

Owen looked at the Battledoor again. The two choices were still there. *What the heck*, he thought as he tapped "The Alley." The other option disappeared, while his selection grew in size and occupied the centre of the screen. It flickered twice, and the screen stopped glowing. Ahead, the strange door frame glowed slightly and shuddered. A small click and a brief whoosh of wind could be heard through the keyhole. Tentatively, as though he were afraid it would burn at his touch, Owen grabbed the handle and turned the knob.

Bea was less patient. "Great. It's a magic door. Big whoop. Now open it. Let's go!" She pulled Emily through the door and into the alley beyond. Owen stepped through with one last glance behind him.

"Good luck," said the Bookkeeper as he winked one last time. "See it through to the end!"

"HEY!" yelled James Vanier, who had reappeared in the room, sloshing a glass of water. "What the hell?"

"Go!" yelled the Bookkeeper. Owen didn't need to be told twice. He tried to pull the door shut, but as he began, several more volumes fell into the doorway, making for an effective stopper. He pulled once, twice, three times, trying to close it before giving up and chasing after the girls.

"Lucas!" yelled James. "Get in here!" Sure enough, the giant lumbered back into the room while still holding a phone to his ear. James smacked the phone away and began pushing his friend to the open door, pausing only long enough to deliver a sharp kick to Carl. Lucas pointed to the old man still lying on the floor, a questioning look on his face. "Forget him," said James. "Owen and the girls are getting away. You called the ambulance?"

Lucas nodded.

"Good enough," James said. "Let's go. They don't know our names. Didn't see any cameras, either. Forget them. Hurry up!"

"Leave them be," warned the Bookkeeper. "That doorway is not meant for you! You must not go through it! You don't belong there! Not *you*."

James turned his attention back to the old man. "Well, we're not going back to the front door so you can get us arrested. If you're smart, you'll say it was a false alarm. If I see a cop after this and he so much as touches me or looks at me sideways, I'll be back to burn this place to the ground. It doesn't look like it'd take much to make it go up in flames, either." He reached out and plucked a book off the shelf before opening it and smelling the musty odour it gave off. "Just like I thought. Fire hazard." He tossed it into the old man's lap. With a last shove, he pushed Lucas through the door.

"No!" yelled the Bookkeeper from behind them. "There are consequences!"

James ignored him as he knelt down to remove the books keeping the door from closing. Once the last thing blocking it was removed, he looked smugly back at the pair.

"Remember what I said: 'fire hazard.'" He pulled out a lighter and flicked the flame for emphasis. Then he laughed and snapped it closed. One problem at a time.

Then he shut the door behind him.

Once closed, the room seemed almost as dark and dreary as ever. Try as he might, Carl could not see a door any more, just more shelves and books. The Bookkeeper sighed and nodded agreement with Carl's assessment, though it didn't make him feel any better.

"Not to worry, Carl. Their story is just beginning," he said. He hoped he sounded more convincing than he felt.

CHAPTER 5

Walking up and down Yonge Street, Owen had darted in and out of more than a few of his fair share of alleys. They were great for cutting down travel time if you could stand the smell of garbage, stale water, small, scurrying wildlife, and perhaps the odd homeless person or two.

This was unlike any alley he'd ever seen before.

It was Toronto, and not Toronto, all at the same time. The buildings still bordered the alley, but they seemed impossibly high, almost without end. The brickwork and architecture was familiar, but vines, plant life, and other greenery clung to it as though nothing had lived here in a thousand years, leaving Mother Nature free to reclaim what was rightfully hers. The alley smell was still there, but sweeter somehow, and there were signs that people had been through recently. Owen saw the odd bits of garbage and faint wheel tracks from where tires had passed through the little collected pools of water.

He stumbled along more than ran because he was so distracted by the oddity of the place. Ahead of him, Bea and Emily were making slightly better progress as they went along hand-in-hand. He did his best to focus on them so that he could catch up, though he caught flutters of movements in the bushes at the side that got his attention from time to time. He shook his head to clear it. Obviously he was still in Toronto. The Bookkeeper's talk about magic and books had just gotten to him.

Or was that just a lie to calm himself down? The place just didn't look right. The alley was longer and far narrower than he was used to and had curves and bends. They weren't far from the door they had come through, though Owen doubted he could find it again easily. The plants covered almost every square inch of wall space and flowered out into the main path. Owen felt like a lost lamb being herded down the space, since there were no other doors he could see to try to take, and the breaks between buildings were few and far between. He had been tempted to go down the first new alley until he had seen a huge black shape shuffling down it toward him. It looked like a man with a huge load of laundry on his shoulders, only this load of clothing was half the height again of a normal man. It was only a glance, but Owen could swear that he saw eyes blink at him from the top of the pile.

Nerves. That's what it must be. Just nerves.

By the time he finally caught up to the girls, he was covered in sweat. The day had become hot and humid, even for Toronto, though Owen was no longer certain this was Toronto.

Bea was struggling with her cellphone and smacking the already cracked screen. "Can't get a signal," she muttered. "Thing won't even *work*. Why would that happen? Where are we?" she asked. She was panting and wheezing from the unaccustomed exertion of rushing down the alley. "It's like Chinatown without the Chinese people, Chinese food, or decorations."

"I don't think it's Chinatown, Bea," said Emily, who was rolling her eyes. She checked her phone as well, but it was similarly dead. As was Owen's. Wherever they were, it was a blind spot for technology.

Owen looked at Emily thoughtfully, ignoring Bea entirely. It was impossible, but he needed to hear it from someone else. "You don't think…" he asked as he raised the Battledoor in a half-hearted gesture. Magic was nuts, wasn't it? Owen wanted Emily to laugh at the idea, but instead she bit her lip and nodded.

"This isn't Toronto," she said. Owen's heart dropped a little.

"Of course it is," insisted Bea. "Just south of Yonge and Bloor. We're in some messed-up alley beside the main road."

A cable on the road coiled up into the bushes off to their right. Emily shuddered, not wanting to see the rest of it. "It's not," she insisted. "It's like Toronto, but… not."

"Like a funhouse mirror," Owen offered. So she had noticed the similarities, too. It was almost as though someone had taken a picture of an alley in the city and Photoshopped in plants while skewing the perspective.

"Exactly. It's kind of… Not-Toronto."

"Whatever. You guys are nuts. Fine, though, I'll indulge you. Let's get out of the 'funhouse,'" said Bea. She clearly expected them to come clean and tell her they were messing with her. When that didn't happen and she saw how serious Emily and Owen were, she finally started to look a bit freaked out.

"How?" asked Owen. There weren't many options. Going back meant either finding James and Lucas or running into the walking Laundry Pile. He knew two of the three weren't friendly and wasn't interested in seeing about the third. When he mentioned the creature to Emily and Bea, they looked doubtful but didn't press him for more details. Things were weird enough without trying to make them weirder.

"Can I freak out now?" Emily asked, only half serious, as a nervous chuckle came out of her.

"If *you* freak out, I'm going to start screaming," Bea said.

"Okay, okay," Owen said. "Let's all agree to freak out on the inside for a few seconds. Once we're done that, we need to figure out how to get out of here."

Emily and Bea nodded at him and stood silently for a moment or two. Once they all more or less got themselves under control, Emily broke the spell.

Emily pointed to the Battledoor. "What does it say?"

Owen lifted it from his waist and looked at the screen, the brilliant gold sides sparkling in the shafts of daylight that reached the alley floor. The screen was flat white and looked as though it had never been used. "Nothing," he said. "It's blank."

"That's not it," said Bea. "It was a paddle-thing. That's a blinged-out tablet. Kind of cool, but not the thingy."

"That's it," Emily confirmed. "When James and Lucas were rushing about and you were trying to talk to the owner, Owen, I saw it change. It kind of melted, then smoothed out."

"Why didn't you say anything?" asked Bea. "I mean, HELLO! You might warn us that some gold-thingy is melting on Owen and changing into an iPad or something! That's the kind of thing you tell your friends!"

Emily shrugged. "I thought the guy was dying! It didn't seem appropriate!"

"You didn't, huh?" said Bea, bordering on hysteria. "Does it now seem like something worth mentioning? Now that Toronto has gone green and laundry is coming to kill us?"

"To be fair, I don't think it was coming to kill us," said Owen.

"You be quiet!" snapped Bea as she whirled on Owen and brandished her pointer finger at him. "This is your fault! Why did you have to get beat up, huh? Why couldn't you run faster?"

Owen felt his temper rising. "Hey, no one *asked* you for your help."

"Yeah, well no one asked you to be a wimp!" she shot back.

"*I'm* a wimp? You can barely breathe right now! I stood up to those guys twice when he started in on you!"

"Then you let an old man fake a heart attack so you could run away!"

"You ran out the door first!"

"Coward!"

"You're a coward!"

"No, I'm not!"

"Yes, you are!"

"Am not!"

"Are too!"

"I could take them BOTH down!" she yelled. The two of them were standing face to face like matched boxers on a prizefight poster. Emily began to snicker, then laughed outright.

Neither Owen or Bea looked impressed. This made Emily laugh harder. Finally, the absurdity of what they were saying got through to Owen, and he smiled despite himself. Bea started to laugh as well. Gradually, the laughter settled down and the silence crept back into the alley.

Finally, Emily broke the silence. "Standing here isn't going to help," she said. "Let's keep moving. It's gotta lead somewhere."

Not having a better idea, Owen and Bea fell in line.

BLINDED BY determination to catch up to his targets, James failed to notice how the world had changed. Lucas finally had to grab him to get his attention and was almost slapped in the face for the effort. James was so angry, he was ready to lash out at both friend and foe.

Lucas had felt it was worth the risk. He had seen a low, dark shape dart through the undergrowth at the side and tried to point it out to James. Avoiding the careless blow from his friend, Lucas still got hurt as he stumbled back over a thick vine lying across the floor and went sprawling onto the wet pavement.

At first, James didn't stop. Then, shaking his head in frustration, he finally halted and spun around angrily. Lucas was still lying chest-down on the ground and was just starting to push himself up. To his credit, Lucas hadn't cried out when he'd fallen, though he'd obviously hurt himself. There was blood on the palm of his hand. Lucas stared at it dumbly and looked about for a place to rub it off. He reached out for a large leaf but drew his hand back when something low, black, and many-legged skittered away from the base of it. He opted instead to wipe his hand on his pants.

"Idiot," James said through gritted teeth. He was as kind to his victims as he was to his friends, though at least friends had nothing to fear as long as they stayed on his good side. Lucas weighed twice as much as James and could do more damage with one fist than the other could do with his whole body. Still, the incident with the knife was too fresh in Lucas's mind to decide to pick any kind of fight.

Unsteadily, Lucas pushed himself to his knees and slowly got back on his feet. He shambled over to a nearby stump and sat himself down to rest. This seemed to infuriate James, who wanted to keep moving, but Lucas said nothing, and James didn't leave.

Instead, James finally took notice of the odd sights and smells that had tripped up his lumbering companion. Lucas tried to point out the strange things he saw, but James wanted to dismiss them as just another oddity in a bustling city.

But the differences were just too many. It was unlike any place Lucas had ever been and yet, in a strange way, it felt like he had been here before. It was an impossible case of déjà vu. He wanted to say something, but the words were caught in his throat. Instead, he gaped about, trying to figure out where they were. Perhaps it was just a private garden or something. On the heel of that came the Bookkeeper's words to James: "*You don't belong there.*"

It sent chills down his spine, though why he couldn't say, but he couldn't let it get to him. Probably worried about his stupid plants or something. He looked at James and was about to set off again, but he could tell that the fear and uncertainty on his face had struck a chord.

"It's just that old idiot's garden or something," James said, his eye twitching with stress, though he didn't sound as certain as he forced himself to look.

Lucas was doubtful.

"Let me make it even more simple, since you seem to have taken stupid pills today," said James. "If we stand around here, we're going to get caught. If we get caught, we could get arrested. We know that old guy was probably faking, but that doesn't mean he won't get the cops to believe it. The sooner we get out of here, the better. And if we catch Owey-boy and those two girls as well, so much the better. At this point, I don't really care."

Defeated, Lucas reluctantly nodded but still made no attempt to move. He was just so *tired*. Exasperated, James turned around and started off at a light jog down the alley again. "Whatever, man," he called back over his shoulder. "Get caught. Don't care."

Lucas shifted uneasily as James ran ahead. He knew it was impossible, but the plants looked as though they were moving and encroaching on the alley. He heard leaves rustle in a way that wind alone could not recreate. The large boy knew something was deeply wrong with this place, even if James seemed to be in denial about it. Ahead, James disappeared from view around a curve in the alley.

He looked at his palm to see the gouge that had caused the bloody mess all over his pants and grimaced as he picked a pebble or two out of his raw flesh. Ahead of him, one of the black shapes from the undergrowth made a clicking sound. Leaves and stalks bent, and a rustle rippled up and along the edge of the growth. It was too fast. It was too *creepy*.

A low buzz began to sound from the plants, and all at once the movement stopped. Long seconds passed, and Lucas was sure that whatever had caused it had decided to move along. He was about to go back to picking at his palm when a black shape fluttered up past the leaves into view.

That's when Lucas knew for sure that the world had gone crazy.

This, thing, whatever it was, was unlike anything he'd ever seen before. Attached to a bulbous head with many multifaceted eyes, the creature had three black wings, translucent blue eyes, and a long, whip-like tail. Rather than short, stubby legs, it had two on the front that were long and spindly and two shorter, slightly muscled legs on the back. It was a cross between a cat and a fly, and Lucas knew that if he were to reach out to grab it, the thing would fit comfortably in the palm of his hand.

The cat-fly floated up slowly and seemed to sniff the air. It didn't hover smoothly but bobbed up and down clumsily, displaying none of the stealth or speed it suggested it had in the undergrowth. Lucas had an uncomfortable image of how slowly a cat can move when stalking its prey and then explode in a blur of movement for the final distance and the promise of a fresh kill.

As though it was reading his mind, when the cat-fly crossed half the distance to him from the far wall, the wings suddenly sped up, and Lucas was sure it was about to attack him. Instead, the creature thudded to the ground and skittered over to where he had fallen and began to lap up the blood from his palm that was on the pavement. In seconds it had finished and its frenzy passed. When it began to sniff the air again, Lucas quickly looked down to his raw palm and the caked blood. The creature sniffed again and slowly moved its grotesque head until it stared straight at him and started to beat its wings. As it slowly rose from the ground, Lucas stuffed his hand into his pocket and quickly shuffled off after James.

Something was wrong with this place, Lucas knew. It felt like the world was broken and glued back together wrong. He ran to catch up with his friend, but not before he quickly felt in his pockets to make sure the knife was still there.

OWEN, EMILY, and Bea began to slow down after a while. It had been ages since the Pile of Laundry Man and his side street, though the path since then had grown all the more linear and dull. The growth was more or less constant, and the buildings still loomed large on each side. There were no more doors to be seen. Windows were plentiful, but all of them were too high and out of reach. They had even tried to boost Bea up to one of them at one of the rare spots along the wall where plants (and the noises in the undergrowth) weren't growing, but her fingers could never reach anything they could grab, and even if they could, Owen doubted she had the upper body strength to pull herself up by her fingertips. Owen knew he couldn't do it at any rate. In the end, all they could do was continue forward.

After what felt like hours, they finally came to a fork in the road. To their right, the path curved around a building and looked much the same as everything that had come before it. To the left was a similar path, but in the distance they could see moving shapes and a large open space signifying that the buildings they were passing between weren't endless after all.

They took a moment to weigh their options and figure out their next move. Bea was for the alley and avoiding the moving shapes. So far nothing had bothered her here, so when it became clear that the alley was still going on and on and perhaps they weren't still in the city, she was all for staying safe. Owen looked down the side street and suggested that they tough it out. They needed help — he knew that much — and playing it safe wasn't going to get them far. Besides, he figured they could probably outrun another Laundry Pile if they saw one.

That made Emily the tiebreaker.

You could see that she was torn between her best friend and her belief that Owen was probably right. The hesitation seemed to scare Bea, who started to plead with her friend to just keep going down the alley. Reluctantly, and with an apologetic look to Owen, she agreed. He merely nodded and gestured for them to go on.

They didn't get far, however. After two or three more bends, the alley refused to let them go on. Though the walls kept going and the path was clearly there, the plants had fully encroached on the space. Trees had grown up and split the pavement, while vines dangled through their branches and up along the walls. The plants, including odd-smelling purple flowers, were waist-height in some places. From within the jungle, a faint droning could be heard in the distance.

If they were going to go that way, they'd have to cut their way through. Owen didn't know much about where they were now, but pushing ahead into the unknown was probably a bad idea. Ahead, the plants on the ground rustled ominously.

"Let's take a break," he suggested, if only to spare them having to turn around and face the side street. It was the only way they could go, he knew, but he thought giving Bea a few moments to warm to the idea and suck up her courage probably couldn't hurt.

They sat in silence for the most part. Bea quietly rocked back and forth while Emily picked at the few stones on the ground. Owen watched as she rolled one beneath her fingers before picking it up and tossing it to the side. Yesterday, heck, even a few hours ago, he would have given anything to be able to spend this much time with Emily Lloyd. It would have broken his rule of staying invisible at his new school, but the heart wants what the heart wants. He wanted to reach out and comfort her, to draw her close to him and have her rest her head on his shoulder and breathe in the sweetness of her shampoo. How he felt right now it was more likely that Emily would be the one doing the comforting. She was the strongest one of the three of them. He had no doubt of that.

Owen sighed and had to hope there would be a later time when he could make this dream of being with Emily a reality. Hitting on a girl while trapped in some sort of book seemed insane and was probably bad manners or something. Though he knew it was probably futile, he grabbed the Battledoor again to see if new options had presented themselves.

Nothing.

As he held it, he wondered again about how it had morphed into this cool, broken ebook. As he tugged on it, he saw that it wasn't just string that held it to his waist, but a thick golden cord that seemed to snap back into place like a retractable yo-yo. His eyes followed the string up to his waist, and he saw that it wasn't just the Battledoor that had changed. The belt around his waist no longer felt old and worn, but instead was strong and thick, though still flexible. An ornate symbol depicting an open book with trees, rays of light, and other small indistinguishable shapes coming out of it appeared where a belt buckle ought to have been. It was only decoration and not a proper buckle, because as Owen looked, he couldn't see any way to fasten, loosen, or tighten the belt. Without even trying, he was reasonably sure he couldn't take the belt off even if he wanted to. That might make showering an issue later on. If showers were still a thing he was going to get to experience in the future.

He mentioned this to Emily and Bea, who felt down to their own waists to discover the same thing. Where Owen's belt was a deep golden, Emily's shone silver and Bea's was a slightly greened copper colour. They each had designs etched into their belts as well. Emily had a circular maze-like design, while Bea's looked like a hammer and anvil.

"I like yours better," complained Bea as she evaluated the design on Emily's belt. "It's much cooler. I have tools. I'm wearing a tool belt."

"That's it!" said Owen excitedly.

"What's it? Are you calling me a tool?" asked Bea suspiciously. She was always on the lookout for an insult.

"No, no, no," hurried Owen. He grabbed for the Battledoor and brought it up to look at once again, but the screen was still blank. "What's this thing do? It's a book, right? Gives you choices and really pulls you in to the narrative."

"What narrative?" Bea asked.

Owen didn't answer, just gestured wildly about them. Bea looked for something in particular, but a light dawned in Emily's eye. She snatched at the hornbook she remembered was hanging on her belt. It was a slightly dark shade of blue, rectangular, with lines of pulsing white stretching across the edges. Where Owen's slate was ornate and detailed, Emily's was streamlined, sleek, and futuristic. The face of the book had become a silver-white touch screen. She flipped the blue slate over in her hands several times and tapped at the screen, though nothing happened.

"I don't get it," Bea said. "What are you guys doing?" She was looking to her own hornbooks, but seemed disappointed. They were simple bone-white hoops, but upon closer inspection each had different etchings into the fine surfaces. Bea tossed envious glances over to Emily's slate more than once.

Emily was now shaking the hornbook and tersely telling it to turn on with various commands and gestures. No result.

"Think about it," Owen said, pulling her attention back to him. "My Battledoor is a book of some sort, and we're in it or something. That's what the old man hinted at, anyway. Now that we're here, in book-land, it changed. It doesn't look like it did back home. You guys were given different things to wear, though, so maybe they can help us out."

"We *are* home," Bea insisted. She looked to Emily for confirmation but was crestfallen when she was ignored.

Emily finally gave up with the slate and let it fall back to her waist. "Nothing," she said. "It's useless. Or I'm useless."

"*You're* not," Bea said pointedly.

Emily looked ready to argue with Bea, but Owen refused to give up on his train of thought. "What kind of book did you get?" he asked her.

"He said it was an index," she said. "I don't see how that can help us. Doesn't matter, anyway. It won't turn on."

Owen frowned. They had to be missing something. "I can't get anything from the Battledoor, either." He turned his attention to Bea, who was turning over her oversized rings and listening to them clink as they bumped into each other. She looking at them from all angles and letting the small amount of sunlight reflect off them and onto the walls. Her hornbooks were instructional aids, so the old man had said, but from the look on Bea's face the instructional aids needed an instruction book.

She bashed them together, to no avail, though she did like the sound. Finally, she just let them drop to her waist, where they made sounds like wind chimes. Bea did a slight turn and produced a jingling sound. "Cute, aren't they?"

Emily walked over to her and lifted one of them up. The rings didn't come free from the belt, though Emily could see where a fine but strong thread connected them. Unlike the Battledoor or Emily's index, it looked like a sharp tug could pull it loose, but there wasn't really a point in trying that now.

"There's writing on it," Emily said as she examined the things. "It's like a child scratched it in." She squinted hard but couldn't make it out. Unlike the Battledoor and the Index, there was no screen, just the empty hoop that you could fit your hand through. Emily did just that, though tentatively, as though she was afraid her hand might get cut off. Once again, however, nothing happened. She wiggled her fingers for effect.

"Three for three," muttered Owen. He was so sure that one of them, at least, would have a clue as to what to do next. Now all they had were three cool belts with broken accessories.

Emily sensed his disappointment. "Hey," she said, walking over to him. "At least now we know to keep an eye out. Since it's hard to look at our own waists all the time, we should keep checking each other out." Bea sniggered at this comment while Owen's face flushed red. He hoped that she hadn't noticed him watching her roll pebbles earlier.

"It's a good idea," agreed Owen. "Now all we need to do is figure out where we are. I'd really like to know that."

"I'd like to know where we are as well," agreed Bea. "But I'd rather know how to leave it than go sight-seeing."

"Since that's not in the cards, I think we know what we have to do next," Emily said. Owen was relieved she said it, because Bea did not look at all happy. To her credit, she nodded sullenly and did not complain.

The three picked themselves off the ground and dusted off the dirt before heading back to the side street and the open space beyond.

In the distance, small flames spouted into the air, followed by muffled shouts and howls. As they strained to see farther down the side street, Owen also could smell a foul odour, not unlike a vacuum cleaner that gets stuck and burns rubber. *And onions. Rubber and onions.* The one made him gag and the other made his mouth water, though he'd never been a fan of the other. He didn't realize he was so hungry.

The three of them lingered at the mouth of the side street for longer than Owen would have liked. They were fine at the moment, but judging by the growl in his stomach, they'd need food soon and a place to rest. Down the side street they might find both, or they may find a world of trouble.

There wasn't really an option, so Owen steeled himself and took the first step. Before he could take his second, he was tackled to the ground and banged the side of his head off the pavement. The white flash from the shock to his brain made it difficult for his eyes to focus on the person who attacked him, but his ears worked just fine. James Vanier was on top of him, laughing.

"Hey, Owey-boy! Found you!" He lightly smacked Owen's face. Already dazed and his head throbbing, Owen barely felt it. James delivered a second to be sure.

Emily wasted no time. She grabbed James around the shoulders and tried to pull him free. He didn't even look her way when he grabbed her wrist and pushed her off. James smacked Owen a third time, harder still.

"Now that I found you, maybe you can tell me WHERE THE HELL I AM?" James yelled. "One second I'm in the dirtiest store I've ever seen, and the next I'm on a jungle safari tour! What's up with that?" Another slap.

Owen attempted to mumble an answer, but his mouth felt like it was filled with cotton.

"What's that?" James asked, lowering his ear to Owen's mouth. "No smart answer, dipshit?"

"Stop it!" yelled Bea. "He can't help you. We don't know where we are."

"*Someone* knows," James said, shooting Bea a look that made her go impossibly pale. "Gotta make sure it isn't him. Due diligence and all that."

Emily was back once again, unsuccessfully trying to pull James off. "Get off him, you idiot!" she screamed. "Like it or not, we're in this together! It's a book!"

James goggled at her, trying to figure out if he was mad about being insulted or if she was trying to make him feel stupid. He paused to look at her, though he made no effort to get off of Owen.

The momentary reprieve gave Owen a chance to shake off some of the cobwebs, though his head was still throbbing. He propped himself up on one elbow so he could try to shake off the other boy. It would all be for nothing if Lucas was right there about to slam him back down, but mercifully the large boy was nowhere in sight.

Thank goodness for small miracles, Owen thought bitterly. He tried to push up more, but James shifted his weight to put more pressure on Owen's chest to force him back down. "Get off me," he said.

James ignored him. "Make sense or I crack a rib," he said to Emily as he repositioned himself so that his knee was pressing down on the side of Owen's chest. Emily took another swing at him. James grabbed her wrist and bent it painfully. She cried out and after a moment stopped resisting. Satisfied by his own power trip, James let go of her wrist, and she began to rub it gently immediately.

"It's a book," she repeated, gesturing toward the Battledoor now partly pinned underneath Owen. "The man back at the store said books have magic in them, and the Battledoor has the most of all. We thought he was just old and lonely."

"I just thought he was crazy," opined Bea.

"A little bit of that too," said Emily. "It offered a choice to Owen: 'The Front Door' or 'The Alley.' It was just a stupid book, and we were about to leave when you showed up. Owen touched the option for the alley, the screen went dead, and we went through a door that said the same thing."

"Oh, that makes perfect sense. Thank you for explaining it so clearly," James said sarcastically. "You guys are so full of crap." Despite his words, there was no conviction behind them. As much as he didn't want to believe them, part of him clearly did, or Owen thought he'd be protesting a lot more. "I mean, come on, a *book*? I don't even like to read."

"Me neither," mumbled Bea.

"That's because you can't," James snapped. "I didn't pick any book, Lloyd."

"No, but you're kind of reading over the shoulder. You followed us through the door," Emily said.

"I *did* try to close it behind me..." Owen grunted from underneath James.

"...But there were books in the way," James finished. "Lucas and I followed you after we figured out the old man was faking a heart attack. I *think* he was faking it, anyway." James shuddered as though he was trying to rid himself of some unpleasant memory. From the way he shifted his gaze from each person, it was clear that he didn't know what to do next. Owen knew that James thought hurting him was fun and all, but it wasn't going to get him anywhere. Plenty of time for his crap once they got out of this mess. If James thought more about it all and decided it was Owen's fault... he let that train of thought fade away. Going down that path wasn't going to lead anywhere pleasant.

"If Lucas came with you, where is he?" asked Emily.

"Don't know, don't care," James said with a shrug. "Back there, somewhere. He tripped and I left him."

"You left him?" Emily asked incredulously. "How could you just leave your friend like that?"

"Because he's weak!" James shouted suddenly, the red haze threatening to bubble to the surface. "Because he wanted to sit and rest and whine and moan and point at bushes. He's probably still there and crying for his mommy the way you three are!" James's anger was threatening to boil over. It would only take a small nudge now. Still sitting on him, Owen felt his hands clench tighter into the boy's shirt.

"And now you tell me I'm in a book, and I'm supposed to just believe that crap? You're all just trying to make me look stupid!" James raged.

Then, quietly, all the more terrifying because of how quiet he said it, James added, "I'll kill you," in a hushed whisper.

He raised his fist to strike Owen, but the blow never landed. A huge brown shape crashed into the boy, knocking him back several feet and into the wall. As James slumped down to the ground, the brown mass continued to jump all around him and let loose barks that sounded uncomfortably close to thunder. If it was a dog, it was the biggest any of them had ever seen. Foam and slobber dripped out of his mouth, and two large fangs poked out and up from its lower jaw. It used both paws to bat at James, and its sharp claws tore at his clothes.

James Vanier began to scream.

Owen scrambled up and back to avoid accidentally getting raked by those same claws, while Bea and Emily huddled in the entrance to the side street.

"Help me!" screamed James. "Help!"

Two ham-fisted hands closed around the dog's back and tried to pull him off. Lucas Walton had finally appeared, huffing and sweating, and was now struggling to free his friend. The massive dog turned its attention to Lucas every so often to nip at the hands, making it difficult to get a good grip.

James continued to scream, and Lucas continued to struggle. Owen looked from the two boys to the two girls. To run now meant another reprieve, but they were dead tired on their feet as it was. They wouldn't get far. More importantly, Owen couldn't live with himself if he could prevent harm from coming to another human being, even if it was James Vanier. After what had happened to his mother and living through the impact that it had on himself and his father, Owen knew that he couldn't just stand by.

Wordlessly, he got up and launched himself onto the dog. His body weight was enough to shift the dog away, though Lucas nearly lost his grip. Together, he and the giant pulled the dog back enough for James to scramble away and get to his feet. James's shirtsleeve was torn and ragged, and his arm was covered in several light scratches. Thin trickles of blood seeped through a few. Owen thought James must have horseshoes stuffed where the sun doesn't shine to have gotten away with so little physical damage.

"What is that freaking thing?" James yelled. As he backed up, he stumbled over a crumbling brick and picked it up as a makeshift weapon. Lucas and Owen, meanwhile, lost control of the dog as it wrestled free and bounded toward James again. Rather than throw the brick, James dropped it and tried to run but stopped short as he came up against the wall. The dog snarled and leapt forward, paws out, and opened its mouth in the direction of James's throat.

A sharp whistle pulled the dog up short.

"Emery, oi!" came a deep, gruff voice that sounded like wet gravel rubbing together. "'E's friendly, mayhaps."

Emery, the dog-by-way-of-hippo, landed two paws on each side of James, pinning him to the wall. The mouth came closer, but instead of teeth, a giant, wet, slimy tongue came out instead and licked the entirety of James's face at once.

All attention had been on the boys and the dog, so no one had seen the Laundry Pile approach. In full light, the thing was still huge, at least ten feet tall, with bulging shoulders and a squat, small head with big eyes in between its shoulders. If the thing had a neck, it was swallowed by muscles. The bulges under the dirty, loose-hanging fabric looked like linen in the dark, but in the light it was corded muscle. The arms were similarly large and the chest wide and expansive. The legs, on the other hand, were short and stout, though neither looked like they should be strong enough to support the man.

Bea shrieked and hid behind Emily. Emery answered the thing with a bark and a howl.

"Tha's enough, all of ye!" shouted the Laundry Pile as he plugged his tiny ears with his sausage-sized fingers. "No more bleatin', all right? Gods, yer noisy." He ambled over and gave the huge dog a tug on its collar to pull him away from the wall. "My apologies, lad, if he hurt ye. Ye were shoutin' and fightin', and he don't take kindly to that sort of behaviour."

"Just get it away from me!" yelled James pitifully. He pushed the dog back as the Laundry Pile guided it away. Emery looked wounded that his new friend was now rejecting him.

"I told him 'friendly,' and he were friendly," growled the Laundry Pile. "Ye push him again and we'll see how he reacts to other commands." James was slightly cowed by this, and Owen could not resist cracking a smile. Wisely, he kept James from seeing it.

"Thanks for your help, sir," Owen said. Manners were important, even if he was freaked out. Also, he didn't want to see an angry Emery.

"Sir, he calls me, eh?" said the Laundry Pile to Emery. The Pile raised either an eyebrow or a muscle to show his interest, but it was hard to tell the difference. It was *really* hard not to stare. The dog looked up at him and wagged his long tail, the end of it extra bushy like a duster. "How d'ye like that? Well, at least ye pass fer polite, which is good enough for me. That one there," he said, nodding in James's direction, "could take a lesson or two from ye."

"He's a slow learner," Owen said. James flushed red at this, but the Laundry Pile let out a huge belly laugh.

"Name's Mangus," he said, offering a huge hand out to Owen. The handshake was a bit awkward, as Mangus's hand swallowed easily the whole of Owen's hand. Not just the hand, but part of the forearm as well. Mangus didn't seem to care and shook Owen's whole arm up and down.

"Owen Thomas," Owen replied. He introduced his friends next, saving Lucas and James for last. Mangus shook each one's arm, though James's was the only one he did so grudgingly.

"If you don't mind me asking, where are we?" Bea asked.

"Don't know, huh?" said Mangus with a chuckle. "New around here? Not been no one new in years. You hit your head? Maybe confused?"

"No, we're definitely new," said Owen. "We have no idea where 'here' is, though we'd like to leave it. No offense."

"How can ye not know?" asked Mangus. "'Ere is where we are, where we are is here. Same as it always was."

Emily tried to explain. "We came through a door," she began. She stopped suddenly because Mangus had to turn his whole body to face her. He eyed her cautiously.

"No ye didn't," he said cautiously. "Ye couldn't have. He told us it was done with."

"Who did, sir?" asked Owen.

"Prove it," said Magnus, suddenly suspicious of them.

"How?" asked Owen. "The door we came from is way back there." He gestured down toward the alley. Mangus licked his lips and cleared his throat. The friendliness seemed to have gone out of him, and he shifted uncomfortably.

"Do ye have it?" he asked.

"Have what, sir?" Owen replied.

"Don't play coy. Th' book."

Owen hesitated.

"Well, do ye have it? If ye came from... elsewhere... I'd have me proof."

Owen reached behind his back and began to swing the Battledoor forward. Magnus held out his arms and gestured for him to stop.

"No, don't show me! I changed me mind! I don't want to know. I don't want to see it, and I don't remember seeing you." He began to gather his things and called out to Emery.

"What's wrong?" asked Emily. "What are you afraid of?" Two small chimes could be heard at the end of each question, but they were faint and hard to pinpoint.

"Yer a Protie," said Mangus as he stared at Owen. "Can't be, s'impossible. But there ye are. He said it was done, damn him."

Bea sniggered. "He called you a perogie, Owen!"

Mangus growled and stared down Bea, who let out a squeak and ducked back behind Emily. "He's a *Protie!*" he repeated forcefully. "There ain't supposed to be no more of 'em, neither."

Emily cautiously put a hand on Mangus's arm to try to calm him. "Sorry, sir, no offense was meant. Can you explain what you mean?"

Mangus sighed in frustration. "A Protie is short for 'protagonist'," he explained. "The main character. The person the story bends around and the World changes for. I saw some shiftin' in the walls earlier but thought it might have been the drink. I'm partial to drinks, ye know. Do you have any?" He looked back to Owen. When no drink was offered, he scowled and continued. "But there ain't supposed to be no more. Supposed to be gone. The story lives on and goes on, but nothing new happens. Left to live and grow on its own. 'Happily ever after' 'n all that."

"Sounds like an episode of *Seinfeld*," James muttered.

Owen was fascinated. "Why aren't there supposed to be any more?"

Mangus ignored him and started down the alley back the way the teens had appeared. He whistled for Emery to follow, which the dog obediently did.

"Wait!" Owen called. "Sir! What am I supposed to do?"

Mangus kept on walking. "Don't know," he called back. "But I don't want to be around when t'other one finds out that damn thing is back in the World. That's 'World' with a capital dubya, fer reference. Just startin', ye see. Ye just got here. Time to get gone, which is what I aim to do."

"Can you at least tell us what's down this street?" Bea called to him.

"Market," Mangus said. "Thugs. Thieves. Store owners. Lawyers. Be careful or they'll rob ye blind. If ye get there, that is." He eyed the door once more. "If it lets ye get there in one piece. Ye think yer there, but yer not. Hrm." He continued on that way for some time more, all the while muttering to himself. Just before he passed around the corner, he paused and Owen felt hope rise in his chest. *Maybe he's going to come back and help.*

"Don't eat the great fruit," Mangus said after some consideration. He nodded in satisfaction. "Gives ye terrible gas." Then he and Emery continued on.

CHAPTER 6

"This is bullshit," James said bitterly after a short while of more walking.

They were at an impasse. A thick wall of plants and vines had grown over the alley, making any further progress difficult. There were faint smells and sounds on the wind that suggested they weren't too far from the market that Mangus had told them about. However close it was, it was going to be difficult to get there.

The group had been mostly silent as they walked down the alley, each one processing what they had seen and heard since they got here. The plants were getting thicker on all sides, and the unseen creatures continued to rustle from somewhere in the underbrush. From what they could tell, the sun was still shining brightly high above, but the combined might of the tall buildings and the encroaching plant life cast a gloom over the procession.

"What is?" Bea asked.

"This," James said, gesturing all around them. "All of this. The alley, the plants, your stupid face, Piggy, that giant freak, and this little prick, Owey, who thinks he can pull one over on me."

Owen sighed. "Right, man. *Totally* on me. I'm the psychopath who torments other people for the fun of it. I'm the demented loser who pulls a knife on people when he doesn't get his way. *I'm the reason people go out of their way to avoid you.*"

A low growl emanated from within James throat. "Shut up," he said quietly. Too quietly. A quick glance at Lucas's face, and Owen saw the big kid cringing and shaking his head. A warning.

But Owen had had enough. "Why do you do us all a favour, and *you* shut up. Dickhead."

Lucas threw his hands up and started to walk away.

James exploded forward with his hands outstretched and reaching for Owen's neck. Surprised, Owen took a step back and was lucky that the movement was enough that James's fingertips only brushed the skin as they raked down his chest. Not able to stop, James continued forward and smashed right into Owen, and the two of them went down to the ground.

James was on top of Owen and trying to sit up so that he could begin his assault. Owen had a hold of at least one of his arms and landed a feeble blow to James's side with his free hand.

"Stop it!" Emily yelled out. "Lucas, do something!"

Lucas still hadn't turned back around. He just shrugged.

James, meanwhile, had gotten his arm free and managed a glancing blow against the side of Owen's head. Lights exploded in the corner of Owen's vision, but he continued to try to grab James's arms to stop them from landing another blow.

Instead, James got control of both of his arms and forced them to the ground. Owen tried to bring up a knee into James's groin as a last-ditch effort, but James lifted himself up out of the way before placing a knee of his own into the centre of Owen's chest.

Then he began to allow his weight to go down and begin crushing Owen's sternum. Owen began to gasp for breath.

As he thrashed about, Owen managed to brace his foot against a large chunk of concrete, and he pushed against it, allowing his hip to shift James's weight off of him. Unbalanced now, Owen was able to shove James away toward the bushes and a small outcropping of rocks. The bushes fluttered as he landed.

"You're dead," James said. There was no anger. No rage. He spoke as if it were a simple fact in a textbook. He picked up a large rock to get the heft of it and got ready to throw it. If the thing connected with Owen's head, it would split it like a tomato.

"No!" screamed Emily. Bea looked on, horrified, with her hands up to her mouth.

Before James could follow through, one of the vines from the mass of plants whipped out and wrapped around his hand and wrists. Now it was James who screamed.

"Get it off!" he yelled out pathetically. He pulled at his arm to get it untangled but screamed even more. The tendrils all had small, thin hooks and his pulling left light scratches that soon started to bleed.

Lucas leapt forward to help his friend, but before he could reach him, several of the cat-flies he had seen earlier flew out of the bushes and crashed into him. Bea and Emily were similarly assaulted by its friends. The things were slow and stupid, though, so it was easy enough to keep them at arm's length. They didn't appear to be dangerous as long as you didn't let your guard down. If they got too close, the fangs looked as though they could do serious damage.

James began to scream in earnest at this point. More tendrils and vines had emerged and grabbed his other arm. He lunged forward, pulling despite the bleeding it was causing him and then was suddenly and viciously pulled back off his feet.

Owen, still on the ground, looked from Lucas, Emily, and Bea, who were for now fighting off the cat-flies with relative ease, to James, whose whole upper body had now disappeared into the undergrowth.

Cursing, Owen got to his feet and ran toward James. Just before his feet disappeared into the bushes, Owen grabbed them and began to pull. He got James about halfway out when new vines began to loop around James, and the tug-of-war match once again bent in favour of the plants.

Desperate, Owen picked up the very same rock that James had about to murder him with and began to smash it down on the vines. At first nothing happened, but after several more blows the vines began to split, and a thick fluid began to pour out of them.

Owen alternated between smashing the vines that had a hold of James and pulling the boy back, inch by inch. James's head finally cleared the brush, and he blinked in surprise to see that it was Owen who was saving him. His expression unreadable, Owen flinched when James, now with one arm free thanks to Owen's smashing, grabbed a rock and was getting the heft of it. With one long look at Owen, James snarled and brought down the rock as hard as he could on the last vine holding him. Thin trickles of blood rolled down his arm and onto the rock, making the surface wet and slippery. The vine let go, and James dropped the rock. Before the vine fully disappeared, it grabbed the rock as as a consolation prize.

Bea, Emily, and Lucas were still working away on the cat-flies, but nothing seemed to faze the things for long.

"We need to do something!" Emily shouted back at Owen.

Owen felt at his pockets for something, anything, that would help. His hand hit the Battledoor, and he brought it up to see if it had any suggestions.

It did.

It was not comforting.

CHOOSE YOUR BATTLE:
'Strange Brew' or 'Straight Through'

Well, that can't be good, Owen thought. The keyword was "battle." He shouldn't have been too surprised, however, since the stupid slate was called a Battledoor. Still.

He relayed the two options to the group.

"Pick one!" Emily yelled.

Owen's hands hesitated over the slate. The alley now had a door off to the right marked "Strange Brew," but the other door wasn't obvious.

"It's through there," James said, pointing to the plants that had just tried to eat him. "I can't see very far, but there's a gate."

"The market is just beyond it," Owen said.

"I'm not going through there," James said, and he held up his bloody arms to show his argument why. "I'll take Door #1."

Owen bit his lip and after a moment nodded. He tapped "Strange Brew." An unknown level of danger was better than a proven one. He had barely gotten to James in time. He didn't want to see what was at the end of those vines.

"This way!" he shouted. He ran over to the door and pulled it open. Once again there was a brief hiss and rush of air that practically sucked him through to the other side. James came behind, followed by Bea, Emily, and finally Lucas, who battered away one last cat-fly before he pulled the door shut as he went through.

OWEN COUGHED and sputtered and spat as the liquid stung his eyes. All around him his companions were doing the same. Wherever the door had taken them, this new place was dark, fragrant, and very, very wet. They were all up to their chests in a liquid vat filled with what very much smelled and tasted like hot beer.

James was moaning somewhere in the dark. The alcohol, no doubt, stung all the fresh scratches and cuts badly. *Serves you right*, thought Owen.

"Everyone okay?" he called out.

One by one they answered.

"I'm okay," Emily answered.

"Me too," Bea confirmed.

James moaned an "okay" and Lucas grunted.

"I'm very well," came another voice in a slight Italian accent. "Very considerate of you!"

It was dead silent after that.

"Okay, you guys heard that too, right?" James said.

"Hello?" Owen asked. The darkness was receding somewhat as his eyes got used to the dark. A light, dim and red, became more apparent, and he was able to see the others as they all came closer together. "Who's there?"

A small man with a bald head and a thick mustache popped out of the brew in front of them. Owen wouldn't have been surprised if he had said "It's-a me, Mario!" from the way he looked. "I am!" said the man. "You're just in time!"

"For what?" asked Bea. "Because if it's about going somewhere else to pee, I'm afraid you're too late."

"Oh, for Pete's sake…" yelled James. "Tell me you did *not*…"

"Can you help me?" asked the little man. "I was out for a walk, and I seem to have fallen in. I can't quite reach the walkway up there, and I've been stuck for some time!"

Owen looked up to see a metal path above them. He reached up, but it was too far away. He jumped as best he could, but it still was a bit too far. The water was pulling him down too much to really make a go of it.

In front of him, the little head bobbed on the surface. Owen assumed the man was short, but the visual effect made him look like he'd been decapitated.

"Sure, we can help you," Owen said.

"Good!" said the little man. "Why?"

"Because we can. And because we're all stuck."

Owen looked around for a ladder or another way out of the brew. James kept trying to reach the walkway, or at least it looked like that was what he was doing the way he kept his arms straight up in the air to avoid the stinging alcohol.

The fumes were starting to bug Owen as well.

Seeing no easy solution, Owen's eye paused on Lucas's intimidating size. The walkway was too high even for him, but if Lucas could lift someone up, they might be able to reach it.

"Lucas," Owen called out. "Give me a hand?"

The big kid nodded and heavily dragged himself through the liquid over to where Owen and the bald man were.

"Oooh, he's a big one, isn't he?" the man asked.

"Yes, sir," Owen agreed. "If it's okay with you, Lucas will lift you up so you can grab the metal railing."

Without waiting for an answer, Lucas practically threw the man up into the air. Now more than high enough, the man scrambled onto the walkway, looking quite pleased with himself.

"Great!" Owen called up. "Good job, sir!"

"No, my name isn't 'sir,'" said the man. "You may call me 'Sensei.'"

Okay, then. "Sure," Owen said. "Is there something up there that can help us?"

"Maybe," Sensei said. "I'm just out for a walk. I'll see if I come across something."

And with that he wandered away.

"Well, that was pointless," James said bitterly. "Whatever. Hey, dummy, lift me up."

Lucas obeyed. Soon enough, James was up on the walkway.

"Why do you let him talk to you like that?" Owen asked Lucas quietly.

Lucas shrugged. "You did good," he said. Seeing the confusion on Owen's arms, he clarified. "The plants. You're okay now. Just don't push him."

Owen considered this. As he did, Lucas turned and lifted Emily up next. Surprisingly, James reached down to help her up. Next came Bea. Finally, it was Owen's turn. As he helped him to his feet, helping being something Owen never would have thought James Vanier was capable of doing, a look of understanding seemed to pass between them.

Together, they turned and laid down on the latticework to reach down for Lucas. The weight was nearly too much for them, even working together, but they struggled and pulled until all of them were up on the walkway.

"Now where we do we go?" Emily asked. There was a faint chime in the air.

Before they could locate the sound, the dim lights suddenly went bright, and a loud claxon sounded in the air.

"CONTAMINATION DETECTED. CONTAMINATION DE-TECTED. DISTILLERY DISTRICT SECTION 2099. CONTAM-INATION DETECTED."

They all looked at each other in shock and surprise.

"That's probably not for us, right?" Bea asked.

A door slammed open ahead of them, and a man's eyeball appeared in it and looked all around before fixating on the group. "FILTH!" he thundered. "YOU'VE RUINED MY LATEST BATCH! GUARDS!"

"RUN!" Emily shouted. Bea needed no further encouragement, nor did James and Lucas. Owen hesitated, thinking of the Battledoor. If this was the battle, there might not be anything to outrun.

As he considered his options, the eyeball retreated, and several men in high hats and clothespins on their noses ran in. They were all holding wooden spoons and waving them about. Owen turned to run after his friends.

The metal walkways were a twisting maze suspended high over what looked like dozens of different vats. Each one had a different colour, a different smell, and in a few cases they had different-looking textures. There was even one where purple and green swirled around. *And now I know where Joker was created*, Owen thought. *Now all we need is Batman to save us.*

The guards were falling farther and farther behind and James let out a whoop of excitement. That whoop faded when ahead of them two large double doors split open and the biggest man they'd ever seen in their life pushed his way through holding a large firehouse.

"CONTAMINATION!" he thundered. One eye was larger than the other, with the pupil fully dilated. He had on a red and black lumberjack shirt that clashed with the large tuft of yellow chin hair on his face. He lifted up the huge hose and pointed it right at the group.

"Look out!" Emily yelled. She, Bea, James, and Lucas all dodged to the right, but Owen wasn't quite fast enough. He caught part of the blast of steaming liquid dead centre, and it propelled him back right into the guards and then back beyond them. The liquid pushed so hard that Owen dropped over the ledge. He would have fallen to his death, but the rope his Battledoor was attached to snagged on a loose nail, and he swung limply under the walkway.

"THAT'S ONE!" yelled the giant. "INTO THE DRINK WITH HIS STINK!"

Above him, Owen heard footsteps approach him and then continue on. He expected to be caught, but when no one looked for him, he assumed they all thought he must be dead. He couldn't see anyone, but he heard the giant move on, and one by one the guards and their rattling wooden spoons all faded away.

Once he was sure he was alone, he began to swing back and forth as gently as possible so that he could reach up and save himself. The rope looked strong, but he didn't want to test its strength or take a chance that he could cut himself free. He pumped his legs and little by little built up enough momentum that he was able to reach out and grab the walkway. He pulled himself up and unhooked the rope from the nail.

The room was empty and silent. He was alone.

Things were not going well for him so far. *Not much of a protagonist, am I?* thought Owen glumly. All he had done in this grand story was get beat up, chased, and harassed. Now he was soaking wet and smelled like a combination of sour beer and wet cat. He had also lost his friends.

Well, two friends and two... well, he didn't know what James and Lucas were. Not friends, that was for sure, but they weren't exactly enemies, either. Owen didn't like them, but he couldn't bring himself to hate them. Ever since his mother died, words like "hate" and concepts like death had taken on a new level of meaning. They were a lot more permanent and a lot more absolute. Owen treasured life to a degree he didn't know was possible now. Every moment meant more. Anything good in the world needed to be nurtured. He had seen that good in Lucas. He hoped it existed in James.

He sighed. It wouldn't matter how much good either of them had unless he found them first. He hoped they got away.

"ATTENTION!" boomed the loudspeakers. "THE INTRUDERS HAVE BEEN CAUGHT. CONTAMINATION IS CONTAINED. DISPOSE OF BATCH 2099."

The alarm stopped, the lights shut off, and Owen was left in the darkness. His friends were captured. That wasn't good.

"EXCITING NEWS! NEW INGREDIENTS HAVE BEEN FOUND. PREPARE TO BREW BATCHES 2308, 2309, 2310, and 2311."

That was worse.

CHAPTER 7

As his eyes got used to the darkness, Owen thought over his options and decided there weren't any good ones available.

He could leave and get help, but so far there wasn't any help to be found in this strange place. He could charge in and try to rescue his friends, wherever they might be. He could sit still in the dark and freak out some more. No matter what he did, his friends might suffer as a result. Cause and effect. Action and reaction.

Time to make a choice.

He pulled himself to his feet and walked back to where he last saw his friends. He wasn't going to abandon them, no matter what. He hadn't been able to do anything for his mother. She was there one moment and then just gone. He had wished a thousand times in his mind and in his dreams that he could have warned her. That he could have stopped her. That he could have saved her. In those moments, she got to live. He would come home from school having daydreamed the whole time, and he'd even half-believe himself until he opened the door and found that she was gone.

But his friends weren't gone. Not yet. Not if he could help it.

He looked to the Battledoor and shook it. The thing was stubborn and blank. Not even a dim glow to help him through the darkness. "Whatever," he said to himself. "Fine. I'll be the Protagonist. I'll play the game. I'll see the story through to the end. You could help me out a little, though."

Nothing.

That was fine. He would do what he had to do.

He got to the path his friends had taken before he had been blasted by the hose. He ran down the length of it, only stopping every now and then to listen for any clues, since he couldn't see very far in the dark. On his fourth stop he heard a low rumble of voices. He increased his pace.

When he finally came across Emily and the others, he nearly gave himself away. He burst into a room and pulled himself up short on the catwalk before he got too close to the edge and revealed himself to the group waiting below.

There were at least a hundred guards, who were all now wearing chef's hats and aprons. They tapped their spoons together in what seemed like applause. Ahead of them was the giant man who was squatting down on his haunches. His friends were all chained up and suspended over four different coloured vats of steaming liquid.

The giant man smiled and held up his hands to get them to stop applauding.

"THANK YOU," he thundered. It looked like he hadn't been shouting earlier. Apparently, this was just the way he talked. "WE ARE GATHERED HERE TO MOURN AND TO CELEBRATE. WE MOURN THE LOSS OF BATCH 2099."

There were a few cries of "contamination" and "filth" and "dirty" from the chefs. The giant nodded sombrely.

"BUT WE HAVE CAUSE TO CELEBRATE! I, YOUR HUMBLE BREWMASTER, HAVE FOUND FOUR NEW INGREDIENTS!" He gestured to the four chained-up people struggling over the vats. Bea was screaming in terror. Emily and James were as silent as Lucas, who hadn't stopped struggling since Owen arrived.

"A NEW FLAVOUR FOR EACH SEASON! WE WILL BE THE TOAST OF THE WORLD!"

"You'll be toast once I get out of this," James said.

"SILENCE, UGLY ONE," the Brewmaster said. "YOUR BATCH WILL BE THE WINTER OF OUR DISCONTENT TO MATCH YOUR UNPLEASANTNESS."

"I hope you choke," James spat. Then, as if inspired, he started spitting into the liquid below him. The chefs all laughed and jeered.

"GOOD! ADDED SEASONING!" The Brewmaster looked to the others to size them up. "THE SQUAT ONE SHALL BE SPRING, FOR SHE LOOKS LIKE SHE NEEDS TO DO SOME SPROUTING YET. THE LARGE ONE SHALL BE SUMMER AS HE IS FULL OF HEAT AND ANGER. THE PRETTY ONE IS FALL. AS IT HAS BEEN SAID, NO SPRING NOR SUMMER BEAUTY HATH SUCH GRACE AS I HAVE SEEN IN ONE AUTUMNAL FACE."

"John Donne," Emily said knowingly.

"QUITE," said the Brewmaster. "YOU SHALL BE A FINE VINTAGE."

"Wait, am I the squat one?" Bea asked, suddenly offended.

"BEGIN."

The chefs all cheered, and the chains began to squeak as the four were slowly lowered toward the vats. Owen needed a plan. He looked to the Battledoor again, hoping to see something written there that would give him a clue of what to do.

Nothing.

"Fine," Owen said. Either the door wouldn't or couldn't help him. Maybe it was Owen himself who just hadn't figured out how to use it yet. Ahead, Lucas, Bea, and Emily all struggled to free themselves while James looked strangely calm about the whole thing. It was like he was expecting it and was relieved that the end was now here.

"But it's not the end," Owen said to himself. "I'm the Protagonist. The story revolves around me. And I say this isn't the end."

He took a deep breath and stood up on the walkway above the distracted crowd.

"Stop!" he yelled. No one heard him.

This was unexpected. He started jumping up and down, but still there was no reaction. He yelled as loud as he could, but he could barely even see himself. There he was, in plain view, standing above two vats of liquid while his friends were about to be boiled alive, and he couldn't be the hero he had just psyched himself up to be.

That's when James saw him. He mouthed something at him, but obviously Owen couldn't hear him. James repeated himself and gestured as best he could with his arms tied up at his waist. He seemed to be moving his hand up and down and then wiggling his fingers. Owen didn't have the faintest clue what that meant.

And then he got it.

It was a bad idea. It was also a purely James thing to think of doing.

But he didn't have a better idea.

So Owen stood over one of the giant vats, positioned the Battledoor to allow some modicum of privacy and decency, pulled down his zipper, and let the good times roll. Improbably, across the way, James started laughing.

The Brewmaster arched an eyebrow at this unexpected behaviour before his nose started to twitch. As soon as he recognized the scent, he snapped his head around to zero in on the source.

"NO! CONTAMINATION! JUST... WHY WOULD YOU DO THAT?"

All at once, the room went dead, silent save for the sound of the trickle coming from Owen into the vat. "Umm," Owen said. It was not his best speech.

"FILTH!"

"Actually, urine is like 95 percent water and sterile, so you can drink it," James put in helpfully.

"Gross!" Bea yelled. "Put it away!"

Now aware that he had his hands full, though thankfully hidden by the Battledoor, Owen dutifully complied. "You will stop this right now and release them!"

"WHAT?" said the shocked Brewmaster. "WHY?"

"Because," Owen said, fumbling for a reason. "I am the Protagonist!"

That brought more than a few gasps from the audience. No one was taking him seriously, however. The reaction was more that Owen's declaration was tasteless than something real.

"YOU ARE UNCLEAN. YOU HAVE NOTHING TO SWAY ME."

"I have this!" Owen shouted, and he brought up the Battledoor. He *really* hoped that it would take this moment to do something truly impressive. Totally dramatic. The kind of stuff that books are made of. Explosions, maybe! Fireworks! A really bold font!

Nothing. Nada. Zip.

"*Fu*—!" he began, but before he could finish, he saw that all of the chefs were now on their knees before him. The Brewmaster looked confused and annoyed.

"HMM," grumbled the Brewmaster. "I'LL ALLOW IT."

"Good," Owen said. He searched around and saw a staircase off to the left that led down to the floor of the factor. He walked down it as quickly as he could while making sure to hold the slate up clearly for all to see. "Now let them go."

"NO."

"What? You just said…"

"THAT'S NOT HOW IT WORKS."

"Yes, it is! I said so!"

"YOU AREN'T VERY GOOD AT THIS. YOUR GOLDEN SLATE ALLOWS YOU TO CHALLENGE ME AS PER THE RULES OF THE WORLD. I, HOWEVER, WILL SET THE CONTEST. SHOULD YOU WIN, YOU GET TO LIVE."

"What about them?" Owen asked, pointing at his friends.

"THEY LOOK FLAVOURFUL."

"No, I mean, they get to go free as well. All of us."

The Brewmaster considered it. "NO."

"What if we make a deal?" Owen asked. "A bet?"

"I'M WAITING."

"If I win, we all go free. You don't stop us."

"YOU WON'T WIN."

"Then it's no big deal for you to bet me on this. Since you're so sure, that is. Still, just to pain the full picture... if you win," Owen said, pressing on, "you get to add me as well. Maybe as a limited time promotion. Potable Protagonist. Like Crystal Pepsi."

"I DON'T KNOW WHAT THAT IS. IT SOUNDS DISGUSTING."

"Okay, well, you've got me there. But it was popular! People all over the place want it again! So, there's that. And... and... you can have the Battledoor."

Another gasp from the chefs let Owen know that this was a big deal. A few of them even dared to look up at was going on. Owen had crossed over from brave to something that bordered on sacrilegious in offering up the Battledoor. Even the Brewmaster looked taken aback.

"VERY WELL," the Brewmaster said. "LET US BEGIN."

A short time later, Owen found himself sitting opposite the Brewmaster at a massive counter. His friends had been cut down (temporarily, the chefs insisted, and they would be chained right back up once Owen lost so they could be liquefied), and they stood by him, nervous and shaking. After they'd been brought down, the chefs hosed all of them, Owen included, in freezing cold water to get all of the alcohol off them. The force of the blast was so strong that Owen figured it was going to peel off a layer of his skin.

Now they stood and prepared for battle. Emily had one hand on his shoulder, and she squeezed it for support. It didn't bring him much joy.

On the other side sat the Brewmaster, sporting a huge grin. The contest, he announced, would be a drinking game. Each person was to get a special glass of Batch 1104 in what was described as the giant's barrel. They were to match drink for drink until one passed out.

In the hands of the Brewmaster, the giant's barrel looked like a child's sippy cup. In front of Owen, he could have comfortably taken a bath in it.

"Well, you're screwed, Owey-boy," James said unhelpfully.

"Stop it," Emily snapped. "Be supportive."

"Okay. I'm certain you're going to die. Good for you!"

"I don't want to be a drink," Bea whimpered.

The Brewmaster lifted his thimble and swallowed it in one gulp. "YOUR TURN," he said casually.

Well, crap, Owen thought.

"GO ON, THEN."

Owen had to stand up and lean over the edge of the barrel to look inside. It was a dark liquid with a few white, swirling shapes in it. He could have sworn they were letters, numbers, and other characters.

"A BREW FIT FOR A WRITER," the Brewmaster said. "THEY SAY ALL THE BEST WRITERS ARE DRINKERS. LET'S TEST YOUR METTLE AGAINST THEM, SHALL WE?"

Owen was far from a prude, but he was not a drinker. He was sixteen. There had been a few parties back in Guelph at his buddies' houses. Brody had a number of good ones. They always seemed to get out of control, however, and when people started bringing beer or other stuff over, it didn't make things better. Other than the odd beer or two, Owen had abstained from lack of interest. His tolerance for the stuff was likely somewhere just above a hamster's. This was not going to end well.

He had been provided a smaller cup with which to scoop his portion out of the barrel. He filled it and brought it to his lips. He downed half of it and wanted to retch. It was beyond awful.

"Suck it up, Owey-boy," James said. "I don't have plans to die today. Bad enough Bea here is toast, but I want to get home to watch Netflix."

Bea went pale. Emily glowered at James. "You can do it."

Owen hesitated.

"DO YOU CONCEDE ALREADY?" the Brewmaster asked.

"Um, no," Owen said, his mind racing. "But can I go to the bathroom?"

"YOU AREN'T DONE DRINKING."

"You didn't say there weren't any pee breaks when you announced the rules."

The Brewmaster considered this and looked over at his soured batch. "BUT YOU HAVE ALREADY URINATED."

"I wasn't finished."

The Brewmaster looked annoyed, but he allowed it. Owen was led away by some chefs, who directed him to a door down the hall on the right. No one followed him, but the promise from the Brewmaster that he only had a couple of minutes before his friends were doomed quickened his pace.

In the bathroom, Owen paced back and forth, trying to figure out how to get them out of this mess. It wasn't going to end well. He couldn't drink any more from the small cup, let alone the whole barrel. There was no way he could win.

"Can you help me, please?" came a familiar Italian accent from one of the stalls.

Owen knew that voice. "Sensei?" he asked incredulously.

"Yes," Sensei said. "I need your help."

"You and me both! This giant guy called the Brewmaster has us captured, and I need to save my friends and get out of here. We're stuck!"

"Can you give me some paper?"

"Uh, sure?" Owen said while checking his pockets. "Do you need to write something down?"

"No."

"Oh," Owen said. "*Oh*." He went into the next stall, tore off a sheet, and passed it down to the hand below.

Sensei emerged a moment later. "That is the second time you have saved me. Thank you!"

"You're welcome. Maybe this time you could help me?"

Sensei nodded and went to the sink, but either he didn't understand or wasn't really paying attention. The man was all calm, but there wasn't much going on upstairs. He washed his hands. Then he dried them. He turned to look at Owen as if to say something. Then he left.

"Seriously?" Owen said to the now-empty room.

Having stalled as long as he could and coming up with no reasonable ideas, Owen made his way back to the contest table. Emily and Bea looked at him with hope in their eyes, and it was all he could do not to break down and cry.

"READY?" asked the Brewmaster.

Owen steeled himself and looked up into the giant's eyes. Well, as best he could anyway, with one of them being so much bigger and wilder than the other. He picked up the cup, slammed it back, and drank the contents in one shot. He even managed not to gag.

The Brewmaster laughed. "VERY WELL. CONTINUE."

Owen's confidence dipped. One cup, fifty or sixty to go, until he matched the giant on just *one* drink. Still, he stood up and filled the cup again.

James was not impressed. "I'm just going to be over here making up my will while we wait, okay?"

"Not helping, dude," Bea said.

"Shut up, Pig-face," James said. "Or I make sure you die first."

"Enough," Emily said firmly. "Cut your crap and watch your mouth. Stop calling her that and show some respect!"

Owen brought the cup up to his lips and prepared to drink. "Hello?" came a voice. "Excuse me?"

Everyone, the Brewmaster and Owen included, turned to look incredulously as Sensei wandered into the room.

"WHAT IS THIS?" thundered the Brewmaster. "TREACHERY?"

"I seem to be lost," Sensei said. "Can you help me?"

"Uh, Sensei," Owen said. "I would love to help you. I'm kind of occupied right now. Maybe if I can *get away* for a moment I'll help." He hoped the hint was subtle enough. If there were a distraction or anything that the man could offer, now would be the time to do it.

"I can wait!" Sensei said helpfully.

"WHAT IS THIS?" repeated the Brewmaster. "IS THIS ANOTHER ONE OF YOUR ILK?"

"No, thank you, no milk for me," Sensei said as he sat down beside Owen. "You're the one who helped me, aren't you? Nice to see you! Well, kind of see you. My eyes aren't what they used to be."

"That's too bad. Maybe if we *get out of here* I can get you glasses."

"No thanks! My eyes are good enough for reading, and that's enough for me."

Emily dug in her pocket and pulled out a pen and a scrap of paper. She began to scribble on it furiously. Owen did his best to keep the attention on himself.

"Sorry, Sensei. I'm kind of *caught* here, and I can't *get away* to *save my own life!*"

Watching all of this with one huge eyebrow arched, the Brewmaster seemed uncertain what to make of it all. "WHERE DID THIS MAN COME FROM?" he asked his chefs. They all looked to each other and shrugged.

Emily passed the note to Owen, who passed it on to Sensei. He took the note and opened it up before looking at it for a good ten seconds. "Huh," he said.

"Yes?" Owen asked hopefully.

"Turns out I can't read!" Sensei said happily.

"Oh my god," Bea moaned.

"That's too bad," Owen said as he tilted his head toward the Brewmaster. "We could use some help."

"Yes, me too! I'm a bit lost."

"YOU SAID THAT. YOU WILL NOT BE LOST ONCE I THROW YOU INTO ONE OF MY VATS AND BOIL THE FLESH FROM YOUR BONES."

"That's not very nice," Sensei said.

"He's *not* very nice," Owen whispered.

"What?"

"*Help us,*" Owen hissed.

"WHAT?"

"I really can't hear you."

Frustration boiled over the edge. He just couldn't take it anymore. "He's holding us captive, and you have to help us escape!" Owen shouted.

The Brewmaster roared and leapt to his feet, smashing his head into the ceiling. "TRICKERY! DECEPTION!" He then slapped at the table and sent the giant's barrel splashing down all over Sensei.

All at once, the little bald man was a blur of action. He hopped up on his feet, jumped onto the Brewmaster's hand, and ran up the length of his arm before leaping and punching the giant into the larger of his two eyeballs. The giant screamed and fell backward, howling in pain. He landed on many of his chefs who couldn't get out of the way in time.

"That was rude," Sensei said. He looked toward the others, who were staring at him in shock. "The power comes from the waist. You punch, pivot, and thrust. That's how you do a good takedown, you understand?"

They nodded.

"Do you know the way out?" he asked.

"No, but let's find out together!" Emily said. She ran forward and grabbed the old man's hand and then pulled him along behind her. The Brewmaster and his crew were struggling to get to their feet, which was a particular challenge for the giant in the confined area. Owen and the rest didn't need an invitation. They took off running right behind her. They didn't make it more than fifty feet or so before the rattling of the wooden spoons started to sound behind them.

"Just so you know, I hate rudeness," Sensei said over his shoulder to Owen. "You were both polite and helpful. It's good to pay the debt. It's good karma."

They made several more turns at random to try to throw off their pursuers. All at once, they came to a door with a window that showed daylight on the other side.

"Ah, perfect, thank you!" Sensei said.

"Wait," Emily said. "Where does that lead?" A faint chime sounded once again from somewhere. In the time that she looked around for the sound, Sensei had already disappeared through the door.

"SEAL THE DOORS!" shouted the Brewmaster somewhere behind them.

"Quick! Go!" Bea yelled. She was almost into the doorway when Lucas grabbed her from behind and pulled her back. Another split-second and the metal grate that snapped down into place would have sliced her in half.

"Damn!" James said in admiration. "We nearly had sliced ham for lunch!"

"We need a way out!" Emily said to Owen. "Check the Battledoor!"

Owen lifted up the Battledoor. It was once again lit up.

CHOOSE YOUR PATH:
'Short Cut' or 'Long Road'

The choice was obvious. Maybe now that the battle was done, the road home was just around the corner. Delaying made no sense. Owen confidently tapped "Short Cut," and a new door appeared on top of the metal grate, blocking the way that Sensei had just gone.

"Go, go, go!" Emily shouted.

Bea wasted no time. She grabbed the handle and twisted it. She leapt through without looking and quickly tried to back up as the ground beneath her feet crumbled away and began the long descent down the cliff and onto the jagged rocks below. She landed hard on her stomach and desperately scrambled with her arms to hold on to something to halt her descent.

She grabbed the edge of the doorframe just as the rest of the outcropping fell apart beneath her. Her fingers began to slip.

CHAPTER 8

Just as Bea was about to fall, a hand grabbed her wrist and held her firmly in place.

"Not so fast," James grunted. "I may need you as a human shield later on."

"Holy crap!" Emily yelled unhelpfully.

Owen looked to the Battledoor, which was flashing a warning red. The message on the screen was flickering in and out as if unsettled.

THE END

Between heralding the end of their lives was the occasional reversion to the previous choice. The screen presented option one (death) and then option two (the other path), and he had to time it perfectly or else the selection would be final.

"Pull her through!" Owen yelled.

With a final heave, James lifted Bea up, and Lucas slammed the door shut behind her. Bea was hyperventilating from the panic of nearly having died.

Behind them, the Brewmaster exploded into view. One of his precious vats spilled over, and the liquid began to descend on them like a wave. Above them, somewhere in the dark corners, a small creature stirred to watch what was happening with interest.

"Owen!" Emily yelled.

Option one.

Have to time it just right.

Option two.

He nearly tapped it when it snapped back.

Option one.

The wave was maybe ten seconds away.

He took a breath, closed his eyes, and opened them again with renewed focus.

Option two barely appeared before he tapped down, hard. The door instantly changed, and Lucas wasted no time opening it. Before them was the alley they had been in earlier, and they all ran through. Owen got the door closed just before the wave hit it. The liquid slapped against it, and as the door faded from existence in the alley, all that was left was the wet outline of where their door had just been.

They were back in alley now and on the other side of the plants. Their side trip had only advanced them a short distance. The quiet and peace of the alley was back, and the market was up ahead. The relief was surreal and confusing.

"Time to get moving," Owen said with what he hoped was confidence.

An uneasy truce had formed in the group since Owen had risked everything to help James back in the alley and again with the near-disaster at the distillery. There was no easy banter and no signs of friendship between the two parties, but with nowhere else to go and everything riding on Owen's shoulders, the accepted attitude seemed to be "don't want some, don't start some."

It made Owen uncomfortable to have James and Lucas with them, but he couldn't deny that a group of five was more intimidating than a group of three. It seemed to offer Bea some comfort at least to have more familiar faces around. She hadn't whined or complained as they set off to see the market Mangus spoke of. It was probably the shock of nearly having been boiled alive.

Before long, all the indistinct shapes they had seen earlier began to take form as the hustle and bustle of a market. More Laundry Pile men could be seen (it was hard not to notice their hulking shapes), more recognizable and similar-sized people to themselves, as well as smaller, Hobbit-like people meandering about below their waists. Animals of all shapes and smiles prowled about freely or were kept in cages waiting to be sold or perhaps even cooked. None of them spoke as each new sight stole their voices from them.

As they headed toward the market, the walls slowly pushed back, which was a welcome relief from the narrow alleyway. The plants began to thin out as well and stayed back from the market, as though they feared they'd end up as fodder for some of the more foul-smelling concoctions. The smell of standing water and decay was gradually replaced by whiffs of flowers and food from the market. Each of them was salivating and licking their lips in anticipation. Without talking about it, the pace quickened slightly. Owen checked his pants pocket and found a handful of coins and a crumpled five-dollar bill. Hopefully this place accepted Canadian currency. The prospect of starving or dying of thirst with money in his pocket seemed ridiculous.

The market began sparsely enough, almost as though the place were giving them a chance to get used to the strangeness of it all. They passed a few outlying vendors, clothing mostly, as men and women neatly arranged their wares on tables. There were necklaces, rings, dresses, coats, and other odd items that Owen couldn't identify. One was a box with glass wings and another was what looked to be a clock with four hands instead of the normal two.

Owen quickly learned that it was a mistake to allow himself to become too interested in the wares. More than one vendor called out to him and chased after him to try to get him to buy. They would shout out numbers, and when Owen didn't respond they'd shout out lower numbers. One or two reached out to grab him and hold him. He gracefully declined, and most let him be. James, on the other hand, told a few where they could go in colourful language. Even then they weren't deterred until Lucas started to glare at them. Eventually they gave up trying with him.

The girls were fair game, however. They seemed delighted with just about everything, and the vendors were happy to show them. When neither

Emily nor Bea looked to be ready or willing to buy, more than a few waggled eyebrows at Owen, and knowing nods suggested the vendors were trying to get him to pay up for them. Tempting, but no.

The most interesting thing Owen saw was a selection of hornbooks. They looked much like the ones the Bookkeeper had in his shop, complete with the hand-held mirror shape with holes on the end. He wanted to take a closer look, but the group showed no sign of slowing down. Explaining he felt like shopping wasn't something he thought would go over well. Besides, with Lucas and James here and so quiet (not unusual for Lucas but for James would be like talking to a pitcher in the middle of a no-hitter), he didn't want to break the mood.

A comfort was that after the strangeness of Mangus and Emery, they were a bit more prepared to deal with the strange sights of the people around them. Most of them looked like they were wearing dark, wet rags, though bits of silver lining and fine belts showed it to be more of a fashion trend than an indication of poverty. Several other Laundry Piles (he would have to find out the correct name soon to avoid causing offense) moved about slowly, as did short — very short — stout men with large moustaches and bald heads. There were plenty of shapes and sizes in between. Some looked like anyone you might pass on a busy city street, while others looked like they were out of a science fiction movie. Owen saw one man with tattoos that ran up his arm to his neck in a pattern that zigged and zagged like a maze. Owen followed the ink trail as it shot up past his cheek but was taken aback when he noticed the man's entire eye was stained black, even the pupil, where it ended in a blade-like design.

Once they reached the mouth of the side street, they paused all at the same time. Ahead of them and off to the distance was the biggest shopping area any of them had ever seen or heard of in their entire lives. The entire market rested on the slope of a downward-facing hill and had a buzz to it like an anthill. Buildings still made a border of the market, but they were farther off and no more oppressive than they would be downtown. Here, in fact, they looked rather inviting and showed a mix of stone, brick, metal, and glass. It was a modern day cityscape with an eighteenth century-quality flea market running between them. It was an oxymoron of style, but the clash of cultures seemed to work. Colours from clothing, carpets, flags, and fabrics fluttered about while the incredible noise of the voices and movements of the people blended together into the kind of white noise Owen had only ever heard before at a stadium full of people. Here and there they could see short plumes of smoke rising from one shack or another, which hopefully meant food. The smell of it was intoxicating and nearly blotted out every other sense they had.

"Got any ideas, Owey-boy?" asked James. His eyes darted from one strange person to the next, and he winced any time one of them got too close or locked eyes.

Owen looked at the group and saw the same fatigue and hunger in their faces that he felt must have been showing on his own. The need to get out of this World (capital "dubya") and get back to their own was a priority, but they could hardly do that if they collapsed before they got there. He picked up the Golden Slate at his waist to see if there were any options being presented. It was dark and cool to the touch. He guessed they needed to stay the course for a little while longer yet. Despite being the so-called master of this thing, Owen felt more like its prisoner. He sighed. "Battledoor's got nothing. It's empty, and so are our stomachs," he said. "I guess we should see if we can get some food."

Emily and Lucas nodded their agreement while James gazed past them at the city. Only Bea wrinkled her nose at the idea of eating food cooked by and prepared something she might accidentally step on in a city park, but she kept quiet.

When a person is hungry and tired, practically anything will do. Desperation overrules taste every time. Owen could remember being so wiped out one day during a trip to a theme park with his father that he fell asleep with his head resting against a low brick wall. It had hurt when he woke up, but before he fell asleep he could have cared less. Needs are like that, he supposed. They can make anyone do something stupid or dangerous just to get over that hump, consequences be damned. He'd read news reports about people who had been stuck out at sea and tried drinking salt water. It only made things worse, and rarely did those people survive. Salt dehydrates you. The more you drink, the thirstier you got. The only thing worse was dying of hypothermia. You get so cold that your body eventually tells you that it's boiling hot, and you get out of your clothes and die even faster. Brutal. The flip side to all the negative was another report of a man charged with theft, only to find out he was stealing food to his feed kids back home. No other choice, or so he felt. Consequences be damned.

Owen hoped it wouldn't come to theft or desperation. The consequences back home for theft could involve a rap on the knuckles and a call to your parents, which at the moment Owen wouldn't mind at all, but here the rules were undoubtedly different. For better or worse, he wasn't interested in finding out.

There were many stalls selling food, but most were rejected instantly. As hungry as they were, seeing live scorpions impaled on skewers, assorted other insects, charred meat that looked like the least desirable part of an animal, or fish and eel that looked deadly to the touch dissuaded them. Several stalls were selling caged cat-flies like the one Lucas had seen in the alley, though for what purpose, no one stopped to ask. Finally, rising out of the rubble of the shacks and stalls around them was a tavern called The Pauper's Tavern. It wasn't much to look at, but since Emily pointed out that "pauper" meant "poor man," they figured it was worth a shot.

One after another, they filtered in through the doorway. The place wasn't much to look at, but there was a free table and stools for them to sit on. Ignoring the crunch of garbage under their feet and pushing past the customers, several of whom seemed to be heavily under the influence of the drink, they sat down and relaxed.

"My feet are dead," complained Bea. "I need a massage."

"Yeah, well, I wouldn't ask anyone in here for help," said Owen. Several men and a Laundry Pile laughed loudly from a booth in the corner. One of them slapped a serving girl on her behind as she went by. She turned around and slapped the man right back. He was stunned for a minute before he roared laughter in approval.

The girl made her way over to the table and cast a wary look at the group. Owen hoped that all the sweat and grime they had accumulated since coming through the door made them look less out of place. "What'll ye be wantin'?" she asked tersely.

"Water," Owen said, wanting to please her. James was bad enough. He didn't want to get slapped by a waitress. "Five of them." Hopefully, they were free.

"Water," she said doubtfully. "Ye don't want the latest from the Brewmaster?" Considering his friends had nearly been turned into new flavours, he shuddered to think of what the current batch was made from. It must have been popular, though, because from her tone, Owen didn't think anyone had ever ordered water from her before. Given the drunken festivities in the tavern, he supposed he could understand her confusion.

"Yeah. And some food, please."

"Ye want ta be specific?" she asked.

"Whatever *you* think is good," James said smoothly. He had leaned forward and was giving her this goofy grin. The swagger and supposed "charm" was meant to win her over, but she was older and had heard it all before and from more convincing sources. James, apparently, wasn't worried about getting slapped. Owen thought he might even enjoy it.

The girl sighed and rolled her eyes. "Food, fine. Ye can have the platter special. I'll be right back with yer *waters*," she said with a hint of derision. As she moved off, James revved his arm back to slap her in the backside, but Emily grabbed him before he could follow through.

"Do NOT," she hissed through clench teeth.

James grinned and lowered his arm. "You got it."

Emily ignored him and turned her attention back to Owen. She looked just as mad at him as she had been at James a minute ago. "Are you crazy?" she said. "How are we going to pay for this?"

Owen was flustered at the sudden attack and then a bit annoyed. This was a point to raise *before* ordering, not after. "Why didn't you stop me, then?" he asked.

"I thought you had some sort of plan!"

"I do. We eat, then we try to pay."

"With what? A man out there wrote 2,000 down on a glass jar he tried to sell me!"

"I have a five-dollar bill," Owen said sheepishly.

"How do you figure that's enough to pay? Even back home that wouldn't buy much more than a drink! You don't know if they'll even take it!" Emily said.

"Maybe it's exotic or something," Bea offered. Lucas grunted something that might have been a laugh. "You know? Ooooh, blue! Shiny paper! See-through as well!"

The serving girl interrupted before he could reply. "Here you go," she said as she plunked down the glasses. Some of the liquid sloshed over the sides. "The finest water we have to offer." The sarcasm was evident, but at least it didn't seem as though she had overheard their conversation. She moved off before anyone could say anything. Owen just shrugged at Emily.

Before they got back into their argument, each of them had downed their water at a gulp. Owen didn't think he'd ever had something so brilliant before. It wasn't the best water; that wasn't what made it so amazing. It was that his throat was sore and cracked, and the water felt as though it restored everything. It was glorious. The relief was temporary, however, as the thirst came back almost immediately. They were all severely dehydrated.

James grandly motioned to the serving girl to bring five more. "Lady of the Water! More of your finest!" She looked annoyed, but James threw her a wink anyway. Owen thought the girl actually blushed slightly as she turned away. However unlikely, she actually seemed to like him. *That makes one of us*, Owen thought.

"Don't worry about cash, Em," said James as he continued to look at the serving girl. "Dine and dash. It's the only way to pay." Emily looked horrified. A dine and dash was where you ate and then ran out before the bill was paid. Owen had seen it in the movies once or twice but had never thought to do it. The very idea disgusted him. If you wanted something, you paid for it. Either you did, or someone else got saddled with the cost. Free was a good price, but not at someone else's expense.

"We'll pay," insisted Owen. He didn't know how, but he'd certainly make the attempt. When the woman brought them their platter a short while later, talk of pay slipped away and the hunger took over. The food looked much better than what they had seen in the market. Roast potatoes, sliced fruit (one of which was oversized and slightly oozing, and he heeded Mangus's warning to avoid it just in case it was the "great fruit" he had talked about), and a few choice cuts of meat. It didn't quite taste like beef or pork, but none of them asked, because none of them really wanted to know. It was delicious.

They ate quickly, and after a time, as Owen's belly began to fill, he started to feel anxious about the bill coming due. He saw Emily pocket a small amount of bread and thought that was a smart move. He wanted to do the same, but every piece he picked up found its way into his mouth. In no time at all, the plate was clean and they had drained a third cup of water. When the waitress came back with a slate in hand, Owen dreaded whatever was about to come next.

"The damage," she said. "Who's it go to?"

"Him," said James as he pointed at Owen. No hesitation. The jerk even let loud a belch, which he then blew in Bea's direction. "Meat mist," he named it.

Bea gagged a little at the smell. "Gross!" she said. Lucas cracked a rare smile at the edge of his mouth.

The serving girl passed Owen the slate, and other than a jumble of numbers, he couldn't out make any of it. Calmly and as though it was a perfectly acceptable thing to do, he reached into his pocket and deposited his money onto the slate. There was a crumpled five-dollar bill, a dollar twenty-five in quarters, two dimes, a nickel, and a subway token. *That's worth at least three bucks,* he thought inanely, though he didn't figure that would impress the girl much.

Once he was done, he looked up at her and smiled awkwardly. She stared at him and didn't say anything for what felt like a full minute. "And what's this?" she asked.

"Money?" asked Owen hopefully. She started shaking her head. "No?" he asked. He did his best to feign confusion. Emily was looking into her lap. James just kept on grinning.

"Harris!" she shouted over her shoulder, her eyes not leaving the assortment on her slate. There was a clattering of pots in the kitchen, but no one came out. "HARRIS!" she yelled again, this time so loud that the entire room fell silent.

Well, crap, thought Owen. Actually, he thought of a word much fouler and worried that its namesake would make an appearance in his pants if he didn't think of something quickly.

"WHAT?" came the thunderous reply. From the boom of it, Owen expected a Laundry Pile or worse to come crashing through the kitchen door, but when it swung open it was a short man, no more than three feet tall, who came through. Owen nearly laughed, but the men around the door quickly scattered away from the little man as though he were radioactive.

"They's tryin' to rob us," the serving girl said simply.

"What? No!" Owen shouted back. What they had done was close to theft, that much was true, but it was an honest theft. *God, there's an oxymoron for you*, thought Owen. Harris began to move toward them and flung a whole table out of the way. The thing was easily three times as big and heavy as he was, but Harris chucked it as though it was made of cardboard.

"We gave her money!" Owen insisted. Again, technically true. "This subway token is worth at least three bucks!"

Harris leapt onto the table, scattering half-filled drinks to the floor. Bea gave a shriek as her water splashed all over her lap. The little man reached out and grabbed the front of Owen's shirt and lifted him off the floor. "What's bucks? You either pay in proper currency or with your teeth."

"There, there!" Owen yelled, pointing to the change on the floor.

Harris did not look impressed. "Cheap coloured paper and scrap metal? Do I look stupid to you, boy?"

He actually looked like many things to Owen, all of them strange, but it wouldn't be smart to say so. "No, sir?" he said.

Harris shook him up and down a little. James guffawed at this until the serving girl smacked him up the side of his head. "That's a light tap from my girl," Harris said. "You don't want one from me. Keep your mouth shut."

James nodded and for once kept his mouth shut. He was enjoying this. Bastard. Harris turned his attention back to Owen. "What else you got for payment?"

"Nothing," said Owen. "That's all the stuff I have in my pockets."

"Is that so?" asked Harris. The little man then turned Owen totally upside down and began to shake him in an attempt to loosen something of value. No more coins fell out, but the Battledoor slipped from his waist to dangle directly in front of the man's face. "*No,*" he breathed, his eyes widening in shock.

A murmur arose from the tavern at the sight of the book, and several men bolted for the exit. The serving girl let loose a slight yelp, as though she'd been pinched again, though no one around the table had moved.

"It can't be," Harris said, his eyes swaying back and forth in time with the slate.

"It isn't," said Emily in a rush to cover up what it was. "It's a fake. We bought it in the market. He thought it would look cool."

It was a good attempt, but Harris saw through the lie. "And why would he need to be cooled down?" He reached out and stroked the surface of the screen and scoffed. "It's not even warm." Owen's face was turning purple from being held upside down, but Harris stared into his eyes anyway. "This," he said slowly, "is adequate payment."

"Not. For. Sale," Owen choked out. The blood was pounding in his head.

"Sell it to me!" yelled a voice in the back. "I'll pay for yer food and give ye lodgings!" Harris's head whipped around to try to find the source of the voice. Others chimed in from all over the room, bidding over top of one another. Most offered money, though some promised a place to live, unlimited food, clothing, animals, and one even offered him a wife. The bids came quickly, too quickly, and a fight broke out between two men who made the same offer at once.

"Calm yerselves!" yelled Harris as he surveyed the oncoming disaster, but it made no difference. The bids were still coming, the arguing was fiercer, and soon blows were exchanged and drinking glasses started flying through the air.

One fight dissolved into a shoving match between a couple of men with overgrown beards. Lucas, Bea, and James got out of their seats and out of the way as more men scrambled over one another to get to Owen, Harris, and the Battledoor. It was almost comical until one of the men pulled out a long blade and stabbed the companion he'd been having dinner with only moments ago right in the stomach. The man groaned and sagged to the floor as he desperately tried to keep his insides from spilling out. More blades appeared, and soon blood stained the floor, along with scraps of leftover food.

Harris's eyes were wild as he saw the chaos in his bar, though he still had a firm grip on Owen. As he opened his mouth to try to shout them down once more, one of the brawlers crashed into the side of the table he was standing on and sent him, along with Owen and James, sprawling. Harris lost his grip on Owen as they tumbled down to the floor. Owen tucked his body just enough so that he didn't split his head open when he landed.

He was pulled to his feet so fiercely, he thought Harris had him once again, but he was relieved to see that it was Lucas. Bea and James were already running out the door as Lucas and Emily helped drag Owen along. Thankfully, the confusion in the bar covered their escape, but they weren't more than a few feet down the street before the first batch of fighters stepped out of the door, looking for them.

"Let go!" shouted Owen at Lucas, who obeyed without hesitation. Owen almost stumbled and fell, surprised that the boy had responded so quickly, even though he'd asked him to do it. Now free of the burden, both

Lucas and Owen ran quickly alongside Emily until they caught up to Bea and James.

The end of the market lane ended in a T intersection, and James looked wildly left and right. "Which way?" he called out. Around him and Bea, shop owners were already moving in and pushing their wares.

"It doesn't matter!" Owen yelled back. *Just make a decision*, he thought. "Go left!"

Behind them, the bar had nearly emptied, and at least twenty men were shoving their way down the street. Shop owners were tossed back into their stalls, with one flimsy shack crashing down entirely. Blades gleamed in the light as they approached.

As they were running, Owen noticed the crowd thinning out slightly. *Not thinning*, he realized. *Getting out of the way.* The lack of a crowd helped them to run faster but gave the same advantage to their pursuers.

On and on they ran. They turned left, right, left again, but at each step the mob was close behind them. What was worse, a few clueless shoppers decided to join in the chase without even knowing what was going on. They smelled opportunity, even if it was nameless.

Though they had a bit more energy, thanks to the meal, it was all for nothing. The last turn they had made wound up being their last. The market lane was long with no breaks, and soon they were at a stone brick wall, about fifteen feet high. They had put a bit of distance between them and their pursuers, but in another thirty seconds they'd be dead.

"What do we do now?" shouted Emily. James and Bea were at the wall, scrabbling at it to find purchase and somehow climb. Owen was panicked as well and twisted left and right, looking for an escape, when he was reminded of the Battledoor as it slapped against his thigh.

The screen was no longer blank, and two choices once again presented themselves, though instead of the fairly benign "path" option as before, the word "battle" ominously repeated itself.

CHOOSE YOUR BATTLE:
'The Fairies' or 'The Furies'

Frustrated, Owen didn't know what to do. Neither option was especially clear or inviting, and the prospect of fighting was downright terrifying after what had happened with the Brewmaster. He looked up and saw that the wall was no longer flat, but two doors were now carved into the face. The one on the left read "Fairies" on the door handle, while "Furies" was carved into the right.

Emily rushed over and glanced over his shoulder at the slate. "Your call," she said. "But make one."

The mob was nearly upon them. Ten seconds at the most. He needed to make a choice. Fairies were cute and harmless, like Tinkerbell from *Peter Pan*. Furies were angry Greek monsters, and the name didn't sound especially inviting. *Tinkerbell or angry monsters? Better safe than sorry*, Owen thought as he tapped the option on the left. Within seconds, both options faded and the slate went dead once more. "Left door!" he shouted. "Left door!"

Bea fumbled at the handle until it finally turned. With Lucas's help, they flung the door open and were almost sucked inside. Wherever the door led, the air pressure was slightly different. Bea was through, first followed by Lucas. As James went through he hooted in excitement. "Dine and dash, bitches!" he yelled at the mob.

Now it was just Owen and Emily. He kept one eye on her and one back toward the mob. Harris was at the head of it, his little legs moving almost in a blur. It'd be funny if Owen didn't know he was planning to kill him and rob his dead body. Owen looked back to Emily in time to see her leap through. Now that she was safe, Owen dropped the Battledoor down to his waist and ran to the door. As he slipped through the entrance, he grabbed hold of the door to close it behind him. Harris shrieked in anger, but the door finally closed with a satisfying shudder, and the noise of the market and street was instantly cut off.

ACT II
RUNNING TO GROUND

CHAPTER 9

Cold, smooth hands gripped the black tar-coloured railing while dead eyes stared out across the city. From this impossibly high vantage point, he could see just about everything. The ebb and flow of the market, the rooftops of the tall buildings, the greenery of the forested areas, and the lights of the hub, all of them glittering at the edges of his vision. Far off, he could see the flickering fire lights dancing off the jail far from the rest of civilization. Though it was still daytime, night somehow always clung to that part of the World. For that reason, and a few others, it was one of his favourite places to pay a visit. The screams and pleading were soothing.

What he saw, he owned. It was a world he controlled and a world that feared him. It was all his, save one place. Away in the distance was the castle that even he was forbidden to visit, try as he might. The place glittered, whether the sun was shining on it or not. It was a beacon of hope, of eternal promise, and nearly the definition of heaven on Earth. Being who he was, he couldn't go there. It was the day to his night. Not even the Groundlings could pass the threshold. That would change soon, he expected.

It would change, or he would see the thing crumble and fall.

His time was near, that was for certain, because the book was back in the World. More than the subtle clues such as the rippling in parts of the city or the discontent his many eyes and ears reported to him — he felt it. The air itself seemed charged with it, like a heat haze settling over the city. Gradually, the World bent and shaped itself to the Protagonist. The person who was seeing the great works with new eyes. You could have a dozen people read a book but all of them would experience it differently. Like a film. Like poetry. Like music. Like death.

The changes were there. Buildings were affected, then the market, now the rest of the city. It was all the same and yet much different. Most wouldn't notice the changes since, after all, they were just a minor part of the stories this and many other places told. And there were many places you could go and see if you had vision. And he had travelled, hadn't he? Always wandering.

Wandering, but not without an eye for detail. When you were high above it, all the differences in things that ought to be familiar screamed out for your attention all the more to make sure you noticed. Electric lights and moving signs appeared where stone and fire braziers had previously pockmarked the view. Glass and metal stood in for mud and brick.

The World had bent again, finally, after all these years, and now he only needed to make sure it bent to his will. And it would. It was inevitable.

Several Groundlings slunk carefully out of the building to join him on that high balcony. Half of them had wings, but at this height they did not want to test their endurance. To be at the top of the Black Spyre had always been forbidden unless the master invited them. Once called, to refuse most likely meant death. When you were summoned to the tall, necrotic black flesh structure, you knew it was bad. The doors opened to let loose Hell. No one with any sense walked into the Spyre willingly.

All around him, scores of creatures called Groundlings skittered and mewled. The name wasn't wholly accurate, as only some were bound by the rules of gravity, and en masse they could merge together into a dark wave where even the bravest soul was apt to drown. Their skin was pitch black, and as they moved around one another, it was like trying to track the movements of shadows upon shadows. The man knew of the shadows, of all the dark places, and was at home in them. For most, it was madness. For him, it was a comfort.

One Groundling, slightly larger than its cousins, eased its way out of the throng and fluttered up on bat-like wings before settling on his Master's shoulder. Its back legs were powerful and sharp, which more than made up for the small hands on the wings. The legs were for shredding, ripping, and tearing. The front claws of the thing were for delicately holding whatever came loose as his hungry mouth fed. The thing was an indiscriminate killer, and while its claws bit into the Master's shoulder, the Master let out no cry of pain. The creature was a vicious, blunt instrument that was both deadly and efficient. No wonder the Master had named the thing Hatchet.

At the Master's feet crouched a small black and brown dog-thing, and it was the rare exception to the brood in that a bit of colour seeped into it, though it was no less deadly if provoked. The short, black fur was shiny and new, save for a ripple of spiky protrusions following the length of his spine. The tail curved upward and was barbed at the tip. His ears were quite large and floppy and his eyes deep and kind-looking. It was the rare, overconfident visitor who might put out a hand to pet the dog, thinking it was friendly, until his mouth opened wide and tore the fingers off. The worst part of this dog-thing, named Basil, was his unrelenting bark. It had the power to drive people crazy with how loud and insistent it could become.

There were scores more, both alike and unlike the two beside their Master, both here and in the other places. All low, all black, all capable of terrible acts. The commoners were terrified of them and swore that they had crawled to the surface from some horrible abyss. Some muttered that they came from the Margins, but that was mostly ignored as superstition. The Groundlings clung to the surface of the World like an infection that could not be gotten rid of.

No wonder the Master liked them so much.

Which came first, no one was certain, as both entered the lives of the people of the World at around the same time. Either it was the Master or the minion. Chicken or egg, ultimately the debate was pointless. Neither were welcome, and both made themselves at home anyway. No matter where you were in the city, if you looked up you could see the Black Spyre blotting out the skyline as it sat there, watching.

And waiting, thought the Master. "Basil," he said in a husky voice. *How long has it been since I've spoken?* he wondered. The dog sat back on his haunches and looked expectantly at the Master. "Fetch the looking glass."

At this Hatchet let out a slight screech and swooped down to claw at Basil's backside. "Go!" the bat creature howled. "Fetch, stupid mutt!" He continued to harass the dog until Basil tentatively snapped back at him. Hatchet laughed and flew back to the Master. The bat-creature was special amongst the Groundlings because he'd developed speech. Some could muster a word or two, but Hatchet's talent made him invaluable to the Master.

"Leave the beast be," said the Master. From his tone, you could tell this was something he'd often said before, but the lack of conviction showed that he didn't really care. They were Groundlings, one and all, to him. So long as Hatchet was useful, he was allowed his perks, though even the bat knew not to press his luck too much. If the Master spoke, he obeyed.

"As you say, Master, so shall it be done."

"Until you get bored again, anyway."

Hatchet chuckled lightly. "Sometimes I do forget myself," he said.

A long silence fell on the room, broken only by the occasional shuffling or snarling of the creatures as they waited patiently. Basil finally reappeared, the silver looking glass between his teeth. Hatchet swooped down and buffeted the beast about the ears with his wings until Basil started barking. All of the Groundlings flinched at the sound, though it did not slow the bat-creature. "Move faster next time!" Hatchet shrieked.

Without hesitation, the Master smacked Hatchet across the room and sent it crashing into the wall. "You were told," he said emotionlessly. He reached down and lifted the looking glass from the floor in front of the dog. Basil craned his head up, hoping for some recognition, but none came.

Hatchet clawed up the wall but made no move to fly over to the Master's side. "So I was, oh mighty Master. I beg your forgiveness."

The Master ignored him and stretched out his looking glass. As his eye passed over the city, he noted the subtle changes along with the large. Animals were slightly different, as were the men. Not so much as you'd notice day to day, more like a passing fashion trend. *It bends but doesn't break*, thought the Master. *It's still early.*

"Bring him here," he said after a time.

The Groundlings were instantly in a frenzy of action. They shrieked and clambered over one another back into the building. If not for the double-wide door opening, they would have crushed one another. Seconds later, hundreds began to flow back outside, like a tide of blackness or the ocean at night. One would strike to the surface above its cousins, only to be swallowed again by the encroaching tide. It was no wonder they were so feared. It was said that to be swallowed by the Groundling tide was to be buried alive. The truth wasn't nearly so peaceful. One did indeed suffocate once in the mouth of the swell as the victim was eviscerated slowly to the point where they choked on their own blood.

This time the beasts were more restrained. The swell slowly parted around the head and shoulders of a huge, mountainous shape. The Master would have called the thing repulsive to begin with, but the claws and teeth of the Groundlings had done it no favours. His eye was swollen, gashes lined his face, and several of his teeth were missing. Mangus had experienced better days.

The Laundry Pile, as Owen had called his kind, hadn't gone as far or as fast as he had hoped once he saw the Golden Slate was back in the World. Still, he had not expected his kind neighbour woman to give him up to the Groundlings when he told her why he and Emery were leaving. He had brought the damned woman groceries, after all! He shovelled her snow! Cut her lawn and fixed her fence! There was no loyalty left.

His bag packed and resting on his huge shoulders, Mangus was minutes from going down the alley and out toward the outlands and the savages beyond when they came upon him. Any crack in the ground, in a brick, or from the darkest part of a shadow was child's play to a Groundling. They oozed, squeezed, clawed, and tore through an obstacle. From all sides they appeared, and Mangus could do little more than hope for a quick death. He roared and tossed his belongings, pitiful though they were, but the black tide swallowed and shredded it all. He'd shake ten free only to have twenty take its place. The best he was able to do was keep them from his dog, or so he'd hoped. Emery was still in the hovel they called home, not twenty feet away. He could hear the dog howling and barking to get out so he could come to his master's aid. The dog was the only thing trying to help him. All his neighbours (his friends, so he thought) seemed to be away from home all of a sudden.

He fought hard, but in the end he had been swallowed. He feared for the moment when the claws would come and when the blood would flow, but it happened in drips and drops, more accidental than anything. *They're playing with me*, he thought. *Like a child plays with his food before eating it.* After hours of blackness and expecting death at any moment, light had come back into the world, and it was more terrible than the void. He assumed it was the Margins. He screamed until he could scream no longer. Finally, after an eternity, he was expunged from the shadows.

From the shadows and into the presence of death itself. He was face to face with Vellum, the man the Groundlings called Master.

He averted his eyes as much as he could, but the terrible face was hypnotic and kept pulling his attention back to it. Mangus knew that one of the things men, women, and beast alike feared was the darkness. You didn't know what was in it, and you would pray for light to come and show your fears to be baseless. Though the great big man wasn't afraid of much; after all, most would be crazy to try to fight him, he did fear the dark. He'd have nightmares where his home was in blackness and terrible things lurked in the darkness. It would all be okay if he could turn on a light, but every light he came to would not work, and the panic would grow. Each light dead, until one would come on but would be so weak that it made it worse, because now he could only see himself, and that made him much more vulnerable. He hated that weakness in himself, and before coming face to face with the master of the Groundlings, he would have said it was the worst fear he had ever known.

Now he wished for the dark again so he could be out of the light. Safe. Afraid. Anonymous.

He nearly wept when Vellum caressed his face.

"You are grotesque, aren't you?" said the man. His voice was barely above a whisper, though Mangus flinched at it anyway. It was a bit absurd to be called ugly considering the company they found themselves in at the moment, but Mangus wisely nodded agreement to the statement.

"Speak," said the Master.

Mangus said nothing. He was silent until Basil sank his teeth into his calf. Then his speech was nothing but a mangled howl.

"Eloquent," The Master mused. "Now use your words."

"What do ye want?" asked Mangus.

"What I always want. Your love. Your devotion. You are one of my subjects, are you not?"

He had never been elected, crowned, or celebrated, though none had challenged Vellum as he rose in power, and none even thought about it after he claimed the Black Spyre for his home. There had been talk, but once enough people disappeared, so did any thoughts of uprising. Mangus nodded.

"So speak."

Mangus knew it was no use feigning ignorance. The World had changed, and from where he sat Vellum could see it as well as feel it. To deny it would mean death. "A boy," he said. "An' the Slate. 'e had it."

"A boy," muttered Vellum. "Indeed. And the book, too. You are certain?"

"Yes," gasped Mangus as one of the Groundlings' tails tightened around his throat, its spikes digging deeper and deeper. "It glowed gold. I knew what it were right away."

"Why did you not speak of this to anyone? Why did I have to hear it from Deirdre Lorimer? You knew she was one of mine, did you not? Looks harmless, but she has a taste for cruelty. In truth, the crone has never been of much use, though I'm told she's now enjoying her new home and her new pet dog. Emery, was it?"

Magnus flinched at that. "Was on me way to do jus' that."

"In the wrong direction. Deirdre mentioned the Outlands."

"She misunderstood, tha's all."

"Did she," he said. It was not a question. "Alone?"

"Pardon?"

"The boy. Was he alone?"

"There were two others there. Boys," he added. He told the truth, but not all of it. Mangus wished the boy and his friends no harm, particularly the girls. They had seemed nice enough. Hopefully Vellum and his Groundlings would be on the lookout for a group of three, not of five. It was a small resistance, but it was something.

"Where were they going? Must you make me ask every question?" The Master's eyes glowed dangerously, and Mangus knew he must tread carefully.

"The market," he said. "They were goin' down the Alley, didn't know where else to go. I guess they didn't want to push through the growth (there's weird stuff in those plants, as ye know). I said t'go to the market. Tha's all, I swear it."

At this, the Master swept his long deep brown cloak over his shoulder and looked back out on the city once more. Mangus felt the Groundlings begin to shift over his body and resisted groaning as a new gash appeared on his chest. Mangus wracked his brain desperately, trying to think of some other detail, no matter how minor, to try and appease the man.

"He was a Protie!" he shouted. "Pretty sure!"

At this, Vellum glanced over his shoulder. "What did you say?" he asked, ice dripping off every word.

"A... a... Protie," said Mangus. "Ye know... a Protagonist."

"I know what that is," said Vellum. "I'm not an idiot. Do you take me for one?"

"Wha? No! O'course not!"

"You must think so, if you're trying to educate me like I'm a child."

"No! Just tryin' to be clear!"

"And now you think I'm slow."

"Yer twistin' my words! He's a new Protie, tha's all I'm saying. Makes sense, him havin' the Slate. Though I don't think he knows how ta use it. But he's the one in charge."

Knots twisted in Vellum's stomach. For years he had ruled this city. For years, it shaped itself to his vision and followed his path. *He* was the

Protagonist, not some boy. To hear another named to his position would not do.

"You are mistaken, oaf," said Vellum. "I'm the only one in charge here."

Too late, Mangus realized his mistake. He regretted it the full minute it took him to fall before he hit the ground.

CHAPTER 10

Relief flooded over Owen as the door shut. He turned to smile at his companions and to make sure that everyone was okay. It was at that moment that James shoved him and grabbed at the Battledoor.

"You dick!" yelled James. "I'm tired of you, and I'm tired of your stupid-ass gold slate *crap.*" He grabbed and tugged at the book, but the gold thread connecting it to Owen's belt held firm and seemed to grow tighter. "Give the damn thing to me! I want out of here!"

Owen began to wrestle with James at this point, not allowing the boy to get a firm grip or pull any harder. "Get away from me!" he shouted. "Let *go!*"

"You let go!" James huffed. There was desperation in his voice, Owen noted, a kind of panic. The bully wasn't used to being pushed around, chased down streets, or being in the middle of a bar fight. He hit Owen, a wild punch that did no more damage than to annoy. Owen similarly fought back, putting a chokehold on James until the two of them fell to the ground, still grappling for control of the Battledoor.

Lucas made a move to join in the fray, but Emily put her hand on his arm, which was all it took to halt him in his tracks. James was his friend, but Emily was the object of his dreams, so Lucas was torn. Even if he wanted to, he couldn't do anything that might hurt her, physically or otherwise. He sighed and backed away.

Bea, on the other hand, got right into the thick of it. She ran up behind James and leapt onto his back. He let out a whooshing sound as the wind was unexpectedly knocked out of his chest. James managed to roll her over his shoulder, but the move exposed him to a right hook to the jaw from

Owen. He briefly saw stars as he fell back and Owen separated himself from him. The two of them lay on the ground, breathing heavily, neither of them making a move to start up again.

"Finished?" asked Emily tersely. She had her hands on her hips and a disgusted look on her face. Owen's heart felt a pang of hurt that she was unhappy with him, but it was fighting with his anger. He couldn't remember being so angry before and was a bit in awe of himself. Where all of those feelings had come from, he had no idea. He nodded and looked away, embarrassed.

James, too, nodded sullenly, but he made one last move and reached out to snatch at the Battledoor on Owen's waist. Still tethered to the boy, James was at least able to read the screen. The two choices were still there, though "The Fairies" was highlighted in red. He tapped at the screen to try to get a result, but nothing happened. The Battledoor itself thrummed in his hands, and the gold colour seemed to darken. *It's reflecting off his hands,* thought Owen dismissively. James's hands were caked in dirt and red raw from the fighting, scratches, or some leftover food from the tavern.

After a few seconds of trying, James got angry at the lack of result and flung the door back at Owen, who barely had enough time to stop it from hitting him right in the nose. "I'm done with this place," said James as he dusted his hands off. "I'm done with it, and I'm done with you idiots. Get us out of here, Owey-boy. Do it now. Or I'll end you and cut the thing from your corpse."

Though it wasn't a request, Owen could hear the pleading in his voice, buried down deep. *He's scared out his mind,* thought Owen. "I will," he said. He meant it, too.

"And who the hell *picks* 'fairies'?" James added as he backed off. Unexpectedly, he started to laugh. "That's just random, kid."

Owen was about to get angry again and point out that "fairies" sounded a lot less dangerous than "furies" when Emily started to laugh too. Beaten, Owen joined in, though the joke was lost on Bea and Lucas, who looked at each other dumbly.

As Owen explained the options that were given to him by the Battledoor, Bea and Lucas seemed to agree that he'd made the right choice, though Bea correctly stated that any choice was better than being run down and killed by a drunken mob. Rather than put them more on edge, Owen decided to gloss over the fact that the Battledoor was talking about a battle to fight. He didn't want to think about what a battle might entail. *Not that it really matters now,* thought Owen. *The choice was made, and now we have to face the consequences. Cause and effect.*

"First order of business," Owen said in what he hoped was a confident-sounding voice. "Take a look at where we are. This is... wow."

The new area they were in was a beautiful grotto with long, curved walls and a high, glass dome ceiling. Trees popped up all over the place with a few stone paths that spread throughout the space. Where they went was uncertain, since they couldn't see more than twenty or so feet in front of them due to the denseness of the jungle. The way ahead was obscured, while behind him was the door they came from, and hundreds more spread out on both sides both horizontally and going up vertically far above them. The entire wall and ceiling all the way up to the peak of the dome was covered in a pattern of doors. Some were stone, some wood, some metal, others glass and marble. It was beautiful and terrifying all at once. "Where are we?"

Wherever they were, going forward they weren't going to lack options. Rather than be comforting, this thought was almost crippling. When it came to making a decision between two things, people could pick one or the other and be reasonably content. It happened all the time. If you couldn't make up your mind, a simple flip of a coin did it for you. You had a fifty-fifty chance. Having hundreds of options, on the other hand, was awful. How could you hope to make a choice and be happy, knowing that there were hundreds of other ways things could have worked out? Owen thought high school was a lot like all of these doors. His dad wanted him to take every subject out there: English, math, science, art, music, whatever. "Take it all," his dad said. "It gives you more options for the future."

Easy for him to say. Sometimes having too many choices was overwhelming.

"Thoughts? Any idea what this place is meant to be?" asked Owen.

"Maybe it's the glass greenhouse from Hell," offered James unhelpfully.

"Huh," Lucas grunted as he looked around. He seemed to have an idea where they were, but before Owen could ask, Bea butted in.

"Are you sure that matters right now?" asked Bea. "Where we are? What about the fairies?"

"You don't see them?" James teased. "They're all over the place." Everyone ignored him.

"I think we also need to control the Battledoor, if we can," offered Emily.

"Control it?" asked Owen. "How?"

She shrugged. "Make it explain things," she suggested. "Like 'what are we supposed to do?'"

There was a faint musical note in the air, like a wind chime. It added to the surreal effect of the place.

Owen nodded. "Like an instruction book or something."

"Yeah," Bea said. "Ask it how to leave. So we can get out of here. Or maybe take us to some place like a donut shop or something so we can call someone."

"A donut shop, Piggy? Don't you think you've had enough to eat?" James asked. He looked to Lucas for support, but the big man grimaced and shook his head. James got the hint and fell silent.

"If only we knew where 'here' was," said Emily. Once again, the sound of a faint chime could be heard. A quick look around showed nothing that would have given off the sound

"Can you just tap to close the book?" asked Bea. "My mom has that on one of her eReader thing-ys."

Owen tried. "Good idea, but no joy."

They talked more and discussed options. Should they stay and wait for someone to come by? Maybe they should explore. Why not climb a tree to get a look around? Round and round the discussion went, but no clear solution presented itself. The one suggestion that didn't really come up was trying the doors. For Owen's part, he worried that it might become a bit of an *Alice in Wonderland* scenario, and he wasn't interested in climbing down deeper into the rabbit's hole. The farther they went, the more doors they went through, the harder it might be to get back. The flip side of that equation was that a door was what got them here in the first place and would almost certainly be the thing that would lead them back.

After a while, the discussion faded and a silence hung over the group. Though they were all thinking it, Owen was the first to say it: "Let's try the doors."

Not waiting for an answer, he walked up to the door they had come through and tried pulling at it, but the thing wouldn't budge, no matter what he did. This one, at least for the moment, was closed to him. Part of him hoped it would open back up to the market, since by then the mob would hopefully have dispersed. Now that it wasn't an option, he felt strangely relieved and free to try the others. He walked off to the right and read off the nameplates above the door handles.

"'Hunger,'" he read.

"No, thanks," said James.

"'Worms.'"

"Eww! No!" squealed Bea.

"'Nothing.'"

No one immediately objected, so he turned the handle of the heavy oak and stone door and was surprised at how smoothly it moved. He swung the door open and saw... nothing.

"What is it?" asked Emily.

"Nothing," he said. "It's like a large broom closet, but made of stone or concrete."

"Anything in it?" asked James hopefully.

Owen stuck his head in to be sure. There was room for all of them to fit in there, but that was it. There wasn't a broom, a mop, even a cobweb. It was utterly pointless.

"To be fair," Emily said. "The room *is* as advertised."

As a group, they continued on like that for a while. They would read off the nameplate and decide as a group if it was worth checking out. They avoided anything that sounded gross, terrifying, or problematic (such as "trolls," "flames," and "telemarketers") and tried the few that sounded less likely to cause trouble. "Clouds" was full of clouds, but since they could see no indication of a floor, they didn't want to risk hopping through and finding themselves a thousand feet above the ground. "Grasslands" opened into endless fields of green. It was beautiful but vast. Lucas and James played a game of "paper, rock, scissors" to decide which one of them would stick their head through to see what was on the other side of the door. James lost and was quite gracious about it. He stuck his head through and looked around the side but told them it was more of the same. He actually hopped through at this point (Emily let out a small sound of fright) and walked a few feet before looking around the door. He said he saw nothing but the door itself. From the back of it, he could only see the frame, and from the front he could see through to where the rest of them were. He guessed that if it were closed, the door might still be there, but it might disappear as well. They decided that while they could see a great distance, there was nothing to see and that might be the end of them. Besides, they couldn't risk having the door disappear and stranding them there should they want to come back.

They moved on. "Winter" was a stark landscape that matched "Grasslands" in its vastness but chilled them all when they held the door open. "Light" was blinding to look at, and they shut the door quickly. Other doors were just strange. One lead to a sea of Lego blocks, others had things in them like a bottle collection, old couch covers, and blank cassette tapes. "Monkeys with Typewriters" was pretty trippy, Owen had to admit. Hundreds of them, several smoking, sat writing page after page, then taking it out and throwing it away. One flicked a cigarette at them when they opened the door, while another flung its dung their way.

The next was a word none of them had heard before: "Paramnesia." They opened it to see it led to some place where it was night, with only a poorly lit corridor in a building, possibly a hospital. Faint, blue-hued forms wandered distantly down the corridor, looking at them in wonder. One of the forms was quite squat and looked as though it had on huge glasses. When it saw them, it started to penguin-walk towards them excitedly. "Close it!" squeaked Bea, and no one objected.

The next was labelled "Dust," and the world inside revealed nothing but statues of people. Or at least they looked like statues until a desert wind kicked up a gust from nowhere and one of the statues blew away in the gentle breeze. The face of that statue had been frozen in a scream, a heavy shoulder bag roughly thrown around its shoulders, and it had been made to look as though it was reaching out to some unseen person or thing.

Another was called 'The 7th Parallel.' It was a futuristic world with flying cars and a huge city in the distance that seemed to reach into the clouds. A car streaked by them at that instant, a woman with an 'o' of surprise in her mouth as she pointed at them. Moments later, sirens erupted all around them and they closed the door hastily.

More doors, more oddities. One led to an office clerk sitting disinterestedly at his desk. He looked at them, seemed not at all surprised, and said, "My turn again?" The nameplate read "Harold." He looked like a Harold. Bored, glasses, burned out. They closed the door. Another led to a cave, one to a waterfall, one to a city, one to a factory. On and on.

All in all, fascinating as it was at times, the experiment was quite disheartening. While all the doors led to one thing or another, none of them was a clear way home or even hinted at a way for them to further the story. Unlike the Battledoor, which had so far led them to new and interesting places, these doors were random words, thoughts, or ideas with no focus or point. *It's almost like stumbling through someone's subconscious*, Owen thought. *Stream of consciousness thinking. Like Ms. Gerow was talking about. The idea that someone writes or thinks whatever pops into their heads without planning.* Like grocery shopping without a list or a plan. Just pushing the cart up the aisle and scooping things off the shelves without looking at them.

"This is getting us nowhere," Owen declared after shutting the door on "Poetry." The other side had been nothing but a collection of slips of papers with random words written on them. Ms. Gerow would have leapt in instantly and done a backstroke through it. "The Battledoor said 'fairies,' so I think we should just find them. I think that's what we're supposed to do."

Emily bit her lip. "Do you think that's a good idea? The book did say 'choose your battle.' We picked 'The Alley' before and nearly got trampled to death."

"I don't know what else we can do," said Owen. "The old man told us that Battledoors were like the 'choose your own adventure' books that I used to read as a kid. Not every path took you to something horrible."

"It's not like it's taken us on vacation so far," Bea said.

"Every path has had you freaks on it, so it's all been horrible," James said.

"Like you're any better," Bea said. James glowered but let it go.

"I read them too," said Emily. "And you're right, because you could finish the book and get a happy ending. But most of the choices took you to a dead end or even had your character get killed off. I got frustrated reading those things because it felt like no matter how I wanted to continue the story the main character would die, lose, or something else awful would happen. They were totally random."

Owen knew she was right, but they were out of choices unless they wanted to try their luck with the doors. Instinctively, he felt that would be the end of them. They were incomplete ideas, these doors, not true paths, or at least not the paths they were meant to take. These doors were the dead ends of the "choose your own adventure" books in terms of finishing their own story and getting out of the World.

He looked to the others for suggestions, but Bea had none and James muttered something about Owen being their "glorious leader" and kicked a stone. Emily was deep in thought. Lucas wasn't even looking at him. He was still gazing up at the dome and along the walls, though what he was seeing was a mystery. Owen couldn't see a thing through the thick tree canopies they had been under since they arrived.

"What do you see?" he asked Lucas.

Lucas ignored him and walked over to the nearest tree with low-hanging branches. Wordlessly, he jumped up to grab the lowest branch and hauled himself up. For such a big person, he was surprisingly graceful as he pulled himself up hand over hand and disappeared into the thick canopy. He wasn't gone more than a minute before he quickly came down and leapt to the ground, dusting off his hands and clothes. He had a huge grin on his face.

"What is it?" asked Owen. "Do you know where we are?"

He grinned and nodded.

"Okay, dummy," said James. "Don't keep us in suspense. Spill it."

"Yonge and Dundas Square," he said gruffly. "Pretty."

ONE BY one they climbed the tree to see for themselves and could not deny the big boy was correct. Without a doubt, they were looking at the Times Square of Toronto, though twisted ever so slightly. The outline of the area matched, and from their new vantage point they could finally see across the space and even up its walls. The screens, the signs, the billboards, the scramble pedestrian crosswalk, all of it, all there. It was bigger, though. Quite a bit. The actual square was walkable, but this place was pulled and stretched at least ten times bigger. The layout, though, was right. Close enough, anyway.

To Owen, it was a huge relief. If the world of the Battledoor was so much like Toronto, that meant that the cityscape, twisted and bent though it might be, was still largely the city they knew. The sight was hope, and until that moment he hadn't known how much he needed it.

The square wasn't entirely comforting, however. It was brutally overgrown, as though humans had abandoned it. The size was intimidating. After all, they had been walking up the row of doors for the past two hours and didn't seem to be even halfway. From up high, it didn't look quite so big, but on the ground it was another. It was like the rules were different for your eyes and for your feet, Owen mused. Even calling it Yonge and Dundas Square now would be a misnomer, considering this place was all curved into a bowl shape. While the buildings were still there, none of the familiar stores or shops survived the transition. The essence of the buildings was there, but only in appearance. Every square inch of them was covered in doors like the ones they had been trying. The lights and screens were wrong, too. Instead of commercials or ads, they were static images that seemed to pulse and undulate. They moved, they flowed, they rippled, but they didn't change. They were all mostly a golden white light, though there were some reds and blues in the mix. It was beautiful, but it wasn't home.

The best part of being up so high was that Owen could see there were breaks in the trees and a few patches of open space. In one of them, near the centre of the room, was a building with a very faded sign on top.

"What does it say?" asked Emily.

In fright, Owen nearly lost his grip and tumbled from the tree. He hadn't heard her climb up. "Sorry," said Emily apologetically. "Did I scare you?"

"No, no," he lied with what he thought was a convincing voice. "Just lost my grip. No, you aren't scary. I'm not scared. Not." He took a breath. "Hi, how are you?"

I sound like an idiot, he thought. *She's going to think I have brain damage.*

She smiled at him. "I'm fine, sailor. Now that we're both fine, can you tell me what you can see?"

He nodded and hesitantly looked away from her. *It's her eyes. I could drown in those eyes.* He shook off the cobwebs and focused back on the task at hand. "I can't quite make it out," he said. "The writing is all faded." He squinted and thought he could make out an "I," "f," and a "t."

"'Information Booth,'" finished Emily, who was full of excitement. "Owen! If this is Yonge and Dundas, there's an information booth in the middle! Remember? You can also get discounted tickets for shows there."

Owen hadn't been to any theatre shows in the city. That was something his mother loved, and she had planned to bring him once he was older and "developed an appreciation for it." He never went with her, but sometimes she and his father had driven into the city to go see them on their big date nights. The memory made him sad, but he pushed it down.

"Looks like we have somewhere to go now," he said, grinning.

Emily grinned right back at him, and for an instant Owen was lost. He was in this strange place, at the top of a tree, with the girl of his dreams and in a perfect moment. He was summoning up the courage to tell her that he liked her but the moment was broken when she started to scramble back down to the others. "Come on!" she called back to him. "We have to tell the guys!"

By the time Owen got down, the mood had passed and Emily was filling Bea, Lucas, and James in on what they saw and suggesting they head out at once.

"Pass," said James with a dismissive wave.

"What?" asked Emily incredulously. "It says 'information'! We can go and find out where we are!" Once again, the faint chime sounded, though only Emily heard it. She flicked her hair at the sound, as though trying to get rid of an annoying fly.

"And *I* said 'pass'," repeated James. "I'm not going in there." He motioned at the jungle and stone paths that led away from the wall. "You know it's not going to be as simple as walking up and asking someone for directions. Crazy stuff will happen. I'm not interested. I'll wait here."

Emily looked furious and was about to start shouting, but Bea broke in first. "Me too," she said. When Emily glared at her, she rushed to apologize. "I'm sorry, Em, but I'm kind of freaked out. I don't want to go."

"We're *all* freaked out," Emily said, staring daggers at her friend. "But we can't just sit here!"

"I can," said James, who promptly sat down. "You go check it out. We'll wait." He tossed a wink at Bea, who looked ashamed of herself. She had chosen to stay with someone who insulted her constantly rather than go with her best friend.

"I'll go too," Owen said.

James laughed at this. "Sure you will, Owey-boy. You go on your little date with your new little girlfriend and bring back a brochure or something. Don't forget to bring us back a snack or something. Maybe a t-shirt that says 'I went to a messed up version of Toronto and all I got was this lousy t-shirt.'"

"At least he's not a coward," Emily spat out at him. James flushed an angry red but said nothing. "Come on, Owen. Let's go."

The two of them started down the stone path and looked back to see Lucas shuffling along behind them. "What, you too?" asked James as he looked at his friend. The big boy merely nodded, and James waved him off. "Yeah, whatever," he said. "Who needs you?"

Emily reached out and took Lucas's hand. "Thank you," she said while giving his hand a slight squeeze. His ears and cheeks pinked slightly, and he gave a slight nod. She dropped his hand and looked back to James and Bea. "We'll be back soon. Wait here."

Bea had tears in her eyes. "I'm *sorry*, Em!"

Emily only nodded. "I know. Don't worry about it. Be back soon."

"We'll see," James said ominously.

CHAPTER 11

The three explorers stuck to the stone path as closely as possible. Owen and Emily were up front as Lucas silently plodded along behind. Owen wasn't happy about the big lug tagging along as he was desperate for some alone time with Emily, but it was a bit more reassuring to have the extra muscle. Owen noticed that Lucas could be protective of Emily, and that was fine by him; that much they had in common.

Emily had insisted they stick to the worn stone path as much as possible, even though it seemed to wind up and down paths throughout the forested area. The argument was sound: if anything came crashing out at them, they could run faster and easier than trying to hop over branches and stir other things in the jungle that might best be left alone. Lucas merely nodded, and that seemed to settle any sort of debate.

Owen suggested they create some sort of means to follow their path back to their friends. Something like the trail of string Ariadne gave the Greek hero Theseus, so he could find his way out of the labyrinth once he killed the half-man/half-bull beast called the Minotaur. Owen always did love that story. Dark caves, adventure around every corner, and an unseen and terrible danger! Now that he was in a story just like it, the whole thing was far less exciting. Reading about it was better than living it in this case. They emptied their pockets, looking for something they could use, but came up short of anything practical. Owen had nothing at all since he'd given everything he had, unsuccessfully, to Harris. Emily had her shoulder bag with her, but all that was in there were a few books and a can of hair spray. Lucas had a crumpled subway transfer pass.

Getting home was important. He realized that even if they managed to get home, he wouldn't be able to take the subway back to his apartment and his father. Ah, his father. He must be freaking out by now. They had been gone more than long enough for his dad to be worried. His mind would go to dark places, Owen knew. First his wife, now his son was missing. Being in the World wasn't really Owen's fault, but he couldn't shake the guilt anyway. He had to get back. His father was all he had left.

Emily sneezed beside him and blushed. Owen smiled a little. Maybe, if things went well, he'd have more than his father in the future. Just then, Lucas passed Emily a tissue, and she took it gratefully. The big guy was quite pleased with the whole thing. *Then again*, Owen thought, *I might need to step up my game.*

"Ideas?" Owen asked. Emily was all for pressing on and forgetting about leaving a trail, but Lucas had that thoughtful look in his eyes again. Paying attention to that look the first time revealed their location and gave them something to work toward, so Owen wasn't ever going to discount him again. "What are you thinking?" he asked.

Lucas walked over to the side of the path and rummaged around for a moment. His hand closed on a broken old branch, and he pulled and pulled at it until it came free from the tangle of undergrowth. It wasn't a huge branch, maybe three feet long, but when carefully laid on the ground, it was the first marker in their makeshift trail of breadcrumbs.

"That'll do," said Owen. "We'll put a new one down every fifty feet or so or just before we lose sight of the previous one. Good idea."

Lucas blinked hard at the compliment. Possibly it was the first one he'd ever gotten. In that moment, Owen realized that perhaps he was just as guilty as many other people in making judgements too quickly. Lucas was smarter than he looked, was kind to Emily, and might have a soul. James, on the other hand, was debatable.

"That's just going to slow us down," complained Emily. "We can be there in half the time if you aren't pulling out branches for a tree fort."

"It's safer this way," Owen said. "I just want you to be safe." He blushed at this comment, and she seemed to slightly as well. Lucas's face betrayed no emotion, but he didn't blink for a while. It had been his idea, after all, and for the same reasons, but the girl did not blush for him.

"Thanks," Emily said. "All the same, I don't need protecting. I'm not a delicate flower that either of you need to shield from a gust of wind. As I recall, Owen, I've saved your hide once or twice in the past couple of days."

"Yeah, from him!" Owen said pointing at Lucas, which led to a small snicker from the kid. "Shut up!" Owen said.

"And *you*," Emily said to Lucas, causing him to shut up. "You're not so tall that I can't crush you if you step out of line." Now it was Owen's turn to laugh as Lucas blushed and looked flustered.

Before they moved on, Owen caught a slight grin from Emily, along with a tiny wink. Man, this girl was *cool*. And certainly not to be underestimated!

Emily was right about one thing: it did take forever for them to make any progress. Owen and Lucas would take turns pulling up branches and then have to rush off after Emily, who would only wait a few seconds before starting off again. Every so often, to make sure they didn't lose their way, one of them had to climb a tree to get a bead on their target. Only once or twice did they have to backtrack to a fork in the road when it was decided they were drifting off course. Wisely, neither Lucas nor Owen pointed out how easy their stick trail would make the return trip go smoothly.

Though it was slow going, they pushed ahead and finally came out of the thick paths of trees to a clearing, and they could see the Information Booth up ahead. The thing was mostly dark glass, and they were dismayed to see that the sign and area around it looked weather-worn and beaten, neither of which suggested that it was still in use. Looks could be deceiving at their current distance, and they hadn't come all this way to give up before getting a closer look.

Emily started off at once, and Owen rushed to keep up with her. Lucas followed at first but stopped partway to look back the way they had come. There was some movement, he thought, back in the bushes, but he shrugged it off as being nothing but wind. He was happy he did look back, however, as there were several other paths leading into the woods around the perimeter, and had he gone much farther, he might have lost track of the one they came out of. As Emily and Owen closed the distance to the booth, Lucas hurried back and hastily assembled a small pile of branches and rocks at the mouth of their path. Once he was satisfied it was high enough, he turned to catch up.

Emily was practically running the whole time, and Owen did his best to keep up. He wasn't in bad shape, but he'd dropped Phys Ed as soon as he could, while Emily was on the track team at school. This sprint was nothing to her, and now that she was so close to something that might have answers, she was barely aware of Owen's panting.

"Slow down!" he gasped.

She turned and grinned at him. "Come on, slacker," she said. "I'll race you!" With that, she threw her hair back and giggled. Owen smiled and chased after her as best he could, thinking back to Orion and he's endless pursuit. The one good thing about this whole 'adventure' they were on is that he was getting to know Emily better. She was strong, smart, and capable. Tough, too.

Better be careful, he thought pleasantly. Or she'll crush me.

She raced ahead of him at this point, but he let her go, preferring to watch and smile and daydream rather than run. A quick look over his shoulder showed that Lucas was in no hurry either, and for that, Owen was relieved. He was grateful for the brief alone time with Emily but even more so for the pile of sticks Lucas had assembled. Owen hadn't realized how many paths there were and silently cursed at himself for being too eager. He promised himself he'd be smarter about that kind of thing in the future, assuming he had one.

As he got closer to the booth, his heart sank more and more. It was in the flat stone space similar to the one in the real Toronto and covered in the same sleek black and glass covering, but it was dull, faded, the glass cracked or broken, and plants crowded the base of it. The lights of the sign up above were still on but unchanging and seemed to continue the ripple effect he'd noticed earlier from the treetops. He didn't have to go any closer to know it was a dead end, but Emily was up ahead, so he continued on.

When he caught sight of her, she was half inside the booth, her legs flailing out of the window she was squirming through. For a moment he was worried she would cut herself on broken glass, but he saw that the window was open and intact, so at least she was safe from that. *She doesn't need protecting*, he reminded himself. He was about to call out to her when she started screaming.

As soon as it started, he was running toward her. "Emily!" he shouted. "I'm coming!" Behind him, Lucas was running as well, much faster, as Emily's shriek had reached his ears as well.

As he reached the windows, Owen tried to look in to see what she was screaming about. He looked for blood. He stumbled up the block of windows, but the glare prevented him from seeing clearly inside. All he could make out was a lot of movement and objects being thrown. By the time he reached the window she had climbed in, Lucas had caught up to him. Owen was attempting to boost himself up into the opening when he found himself mid-air and hurtling toward the inside. Lucas, impatient, had thrown him in and was now climbing up to get in himself.

Owen braced himself to fight some horrible creature, to fight the battle the Slate told him was coming, but the room was empty save for Emily herself, still screaming and throwing things, but at nothing in particular. He didn't know what to do or what was wrong. Lucas dropped to the floor behind him and seemed ready to fight the world, but he too was stumped when he saw her raging at nothing.

Eventually, the screaming stopped and the anger subsided. Emily fell to her knees at this point and was sobbing quietly. Owen carefully got up and walked over to her. He put one hand on her shoulder and gently kneeled down beside her.

"There's nothing here," she sobbed. "What are we going to do?" She reached over and clung to him and buried her face in his shirt. He sat there a while, holding her like that, not saying a word.

This was something he understood all too well: grief. She had not lost someone close to her, not that he was aware of, but was lost herself. She was as brave and as confident for as long as she could be, and now that her hope had been dashed, the walls of bravery had come crumbling down. He knew he should be just as devastated, but the tears would not come for him. He had long since cried himself out after his mother had died. There were days when he felt good, strong even, and then all of a sudden the grief would wash over him and he'd feel the grief all over again, crying so hard that he didn't make a sound. When he was feeling like that, it was best to just feel it. After he cried, he would often feel like a weight had been lifted off him, and he could breathe again. Gradually, he cried less often and less fiercely. The grief was still there (it always would be), but it was muted and dim. Bearable.

The best thing he could do for her was just to be here and to hold her in this dead place. The desks were overturned, broken glass was everywhere, and there was no paper or information source to be found. There were bits of garbage and lots of broken furniture — some of it looked like it had been burned — but no answers.

Lucas was rummaging around the place, doing his best to ignore what was happening between Owen and Emily. He'd pick up items and then toss them aside when he saw they were worthless. As Emily's sobs stopped, she mutely watched him as he looked around, a faint hope in her eyes that he would see what she did not. In the end, the boy gave up and sat down, still averting his eyes.

After a while, she pushed herself away from Owen and wiped at the corners of her eyes. "Thank you," she whispered.

"It's all right," Owen said reassuringly. "It's going to be all right. You just needed to let it out."

She let out a small laugh at that. "I guess so," she said. "Sorry it was all over your shirt." Owen looked down and saw that it was stained wet in places from her tears. Any other time or place, and he'd have been thrilled to hold her tight, but this wasn't how he wanted it to happen, nor did he read anything into it. She was sad and needed to cry. He knew what that felt like and wished he had someone like that when he was suffering. His father had tried to help but had his own grief to work through.

They sat for a while in silence.

"So, the booth is a bust," said Owen finally. Lucas nodded.

"What was your first clue?" asked Emily as she wiped her face. "My screaming or the burned furniture?" She laughed lightly, one of the chuckles a small sob, the grief having mostly passed. The old Emily was back: focused and determined.

"A little from column 'A,' a little from column 'B,'" said Owen, grinning. Lucas just rolled his eyes and kicked away a broken piece of chair by his feet.

Emily got up and strolled around the space as best she could. "You would have thought there would be something here," she complained. "It's not like I wanted to control the universe or anything. I just wanted to know where we are."

The chime sound again. This time, however, in the confines of the booth they could all hear it clearly. "Did you hear that?" Owen asked.

Emily nodded as she looked around for the source. "I've heard it before, though it was much fainter. I don't know what it is. I figured it was just ambient noise."

Owen started to get excited. "What did you do to make it go off? I was sitting still. Lucas, were you doing anything?" Lucas shook his head to show that he hadn't. "Emily, retrace your steps."

"Okay," she said, thinking. "I was sitting, got up, looked at burned piles of junk, and said I don't want to control the universe."

"And that you wanted to know where you are," Owen finished. They listened, but there was no sound.

"Don't we all?" she asked. "Hello?" she called. "Chimes again, please. Make sense this time. I need some help, here!"

The chimes sounded.

The three leapt to their feet excitedly. They were close to a solution, they could feel it. "Do it again!" Owen said. "Make the chimes sound! Help us!"

Silence.

Owen gestured to Lucas. "Say something!"

"Something," muttered Lucas. "Help?" he asked quietly. You could tell that was a word not normally in his vocabulary. He had a slightly disgusted look on his face as he said it.

"Strike two," said Owen. "It only seems to like you, Em."

"Help, please?" Emily said loudly and clearly. The chimes sounded.

"Keep asking," Owen said. "Lucas, move around, see if you can figure out where it's coming from."

Emily was all excitement and started to ask for help over and over again. Sometimes it was loud, others quiet, but the chimes followed loud and clear each time. Owen started searching farther out, but the closer he got to Emily, the clearer it became. Finally, he was on his knees in front of her. As the chimes sounded, a tiny pinprick of white light flashed on the side of her now-silver and blue hornbook with the sleek glass touchscreen. "Em," he said. "It's you. You're chiming!"

"You're charming, too," she said, smiling at him.

"Thanks," he said, blushing. "Seriously, though, it's your book. Every time you ask for help, it's making that noise."

Emily picked the book up from her side and looked at it. It was the size of a small tablet, rimmed with silver and an intricate black lace design, and had a blank screen. "Help?" she asked again, and a faint blue light flashed in the corner, and a chime sounded. She tapped the screen, and it suddenly came to life.

THE INDEX v.2.3

Please make your selection:

Map

Locator

Bestiary

Glossary of Terms

Translator

Help

Owen felt like an idiot at that moment. They had been so focused on using his Battledoor that they had completely ignored the tools that Bea and Emily also carried on their waists. The Bookkeeper had said this was an Index from the start! If they were in a book world, then an Index was just the thing they needed to navigate it! Owen was happy to see all of the options it presented, but he was also extremely annoyed. They had been wandering around clueless, and if they had just stopped for a minute to properly look, they could have likely saved themselves a ton of grief.

"Do you feel as stupid as I do right now?" Emily asked him.

"Yeah," he admitted. "But that's over with. Let's see where we are." He reached over and tapped the "map" icon, but nothing happened. Emily tapped it next, and instantly the screen changed to show a detailed overhead map of their current location.

"Looks like I have the magic touch," she said.

"Guess so," he said. "Maybe that's why when Lucas and I asked, nothing happened. It's tied in to you, so unless you ask or work it, the thing is worthless."

"Then it's a good thing I have it," she said with a smile. "You can't get rid of me now."

"I never would," he said. Annoyed, Lucas snapped his fingers to get their attention and then twirled his fingers in a gesture that said *let's get on with it.*

Emily bent over the map to study it more closely. The borders of the map were long and circular, so it was currently limited to the twisted Yonge and Dundas Square or whatever it was. The booth they were in was near the centre and was labelled on the map. There was a small flashing green dot on the booth that they decided was the location of the Index, similar to how a GPS tracker might work. On the rest of the map, open green spaces were marked, paths were labelled, and a few other notations were there, but none of it seemed to be helpful as they denoted either statues or points of interest. They could see no other buildings in the area that were labelled and no clear entrance or exit. It was "path" this and "grotto" that, through and through.

"At least we know where we are," Emily said. "Be nice to know where we were."

The Index chimed, and a green line traced itself back the way they had come through all the paths and back along the wall to the starting point. "Nice!" Owen said. He pointed to where the green line turned at a ninety-degree angle along the wall. "That must be where we left Bea and James."

The logic of it made sense to her, but she wanted to see what else this thing could do. "Show me where James and Bea are," she asked. A faint chime, and two blue dots appeared where Owen had indicated. One of them moved off slightly and into the woods, away from the other.

"Wonder who that is," Owen asked.

"Please label friends," she asked.

Obediently, the Index chimed, and Bea's name floated above the dot moving into the woods. The dot labelled James stayed still.

"Apparently it takes a liberal definition of the word 'friend,'" said Owen. "No offense," he hastily offered in Lucas's direction. Lucas merely grunted.

"Look, it has you two as well," she said. Sure enough, "Owen" and "Lucas" appeared next to the green dot as two new blue dots. "This is so cool!"

Lucas suddenly shoved a meaty finger onto the screen and tapped at it. Between the two groups of friends, not far from Bea, a third blue dot appeared with a question mark over it.

Emily squinted at it. "Who is the mystery dot?" she asked. The chime sounded twice, but the question mark didn't change.

"What does that mean?" Owen asked.

"I don't know," said Emily in a worried voice. "But it's blue, so we have to hope it's friendly." Suddenly, she had a chilling thought. If this could show the location of friends, it could also show other things.

Taking a deep, shaky breath, she asked the Index: "Please show enemies."

The chime sounded once again, and a red dot appeared at the edge. Then the Index chimed again as another appeared. Then another. And another, and another, and another. Some began to appear on top of their position as well. Within seconds, the entire outside edge pulsed red with more dots appearing on them, near them, and a smattering in the woods. The final red dot appeared right next to Bea.

Fear gripped at Emily's chest. "Oh no," she said. "We have to get out of here right *now*."

CHAPTER 12

"They've been gone a long time, don't you think?" asked Bea. Still no answer from James. She shuffled uneasily and stared out at the stone path in front of them. Emily and the others had been gone for quite some time, and she was beginning to feel anxious about their return. She looked over to James for some indication that he'd heard her, but there was nothing forthcoming. She had almost immediately regretted staying behind with him. She wanted to call out after Emily, to apologize, to offer to go with her or, failing that, to try to make it up to her, but she was just so *tired,* and the words couldn't form in her mouth. Instead, she watched her best friend disappear from view down the path, and shortly after that the muffled sounds of the conversation ahead faded away as well. The silence had settled in since then and had not been broken, save for a few weak efforts from her to engage James in conversation. The boy simply sat there and didn't say a word. By now, she almost wished he'd call her "Pig-face" again, just so she wouldn't feel so lonely.

He wouldn't even give her that much attention. He'd been loud, brash, and downright rude when the others were here, but it was like she didn't even deserve his rudeness now that they were gone. The message seemed clear: you aren't important enough or interesting enough to even acknowledge. It hurt, but it was an old hurt. Unless Emily was around, no one ever paid attention to her, unless it was to mock her or push her out of the way. She was an obstacle, not a human being. In her mind, James Vanier was even less of a human being than she was, based on how he treated people, especially Owen. She hated having to stick her nose in to help out that kid because, after all, no one ever did it for her. Two wrongs didn't make a right, however, so she stood by Emily all the same. She wasn't happy about it, but at least she could say she tried, which was more than most of the people at Morton Academy could say.

"You could at least answer me," she said, casting an annoyed glance at the boy. He finally turned and looked at her and offered a terse salute. She gave him the dirtiest look she could manage and gave him the middle finger. One kind of salute for another, she figured.

Serves me right, she thought. *The guy is scum, and you're trying to make friends with him.* She looked back to the path once more for what must have been the hundredth time, but there was still no movement. The second she saw Emily, she resolved to run up to her, hug her, and tell her how sorry she was and how happy she was to see her again. It would all be heartfelt and honest, with extra sugar on top to help blot out the guilt she was feeling.

She was glad to have a friend like Emily. Truth be told, she was Bea's only friend. It rankled her a bit to see someone as popular as Emily who achieved attention without doing a thing for it. Emily Lloyd had it all, Bea knew. She had looks, charm, brains, and this way of magnetically attracting everyone's attention in a room. When Emily walked in, there was a slight hush and then soft sighs from all the boys as she walked by. Emily was the kind of girl, at least on the surface, that Bea normally hated: the pretty ones. Bea didn't get sighs, whispers, or starry-eyed looks unless it was sarcastic or she'd said or done something stupid. She knew it wasn't fair to hate pretty girls based solely on their looks. They'd won the genetic lottery and got to walk around as though their mothers were fashion catalogues and their fathers were celebrities. They had better clothing, more attention, and boys gave them everything they wanted and teachers fell for every line they had.

It drove Bea nuts.

Most girls didn't look like that or act like that and got tossed aside as a result. She wanted someone to see her beauty, her goodness, and her worth the way they assumed pretty girls had it without even talking to them. Instead, she got to walk around with her glasses, her acne, her ugly hand-me-down clothes, and her smart mouth. If she couldn't be noticed because of her looks, she'd try to stand out with a healthy dose of attitude. It gave her a reputation all right, but not one that screamed "date me." Instead, she got called "Piggy" by idiots like James, the newly mute boy.

So when she first met Emily in the seventh grade, she wanted to hate her and went out of her way to shoot dirty looks at the girl any time she walked by. Emily always smiled at her, no matter what she did, which only infuriated Bea all the more. Immediately, Emily had been claimed by the cheerleaders, the preppies, the pretties, and all of the other popular groups when she arrived, but she never seemed to be totally with them. If they pointed and laughed at someone, Emily never joined in. If they gossiped, Emily never gave an opinion. Bea noticed this and took it as a sign that maybe Emily was somewhat human, but it wasn't enough to convince her. Emily sat there and listened and belonged, while Bea often sat by herself eating leftovers from two days ago all the while pretending she *liked* being alone. She went so far as to stuff earbuds into her ears and crank music from her iPhone clone to enforce the image. A pleasant side effect was that for at least one hour a day she didn't have to listen to anyone else's opinion about her.

It was blind luck that she even spoke to Emily in the first place. She was shuffling down the hall to get to class as Emily bolted around the corner and smacked right into her, knocking Bea to the ground and putting a crack in her phone's screen that blotted out any chance of seeing the display.

"Oh my god!" exclaimed Emily. "Bea, I am SO sorry!"

Bea was used to getting knocked around, but no one had ever *apologized* to her before. More shocking than that was the fact that Emily Lloyd *knew who she was.* "S'okay," she muttered as she fixed her glasses and began to gather up the pieces of her music player.

"No, it's not," Emily said sincerely. "I was in a rush to get to class. I should have been more careful." She picked up a piece of Bea's broken music player. "Oh, no, I broke your iPhone!"

"Not real," Bea said. "It's a fake."

"Doesn't matter," Emily said. "Mine is too! I have to make it up to you."

"No, you don't. Really, it's fine." *Emily Lloyd has a fake phone? That's hardly perfect.*

"I can't buy you a new one," Emily said sadly. "We just moved here, my mom and I. We don't have a lot of money left over."

"That's okay. I should have been looking too. My bad."

Emily laughed at that. "I hate that expression!"

Bea felt a drop in her stomach. *Here comes the torment,* she thought. *Pretty girl vengeance in three... two... one.*

"I remember the first time I heard it," she continued. "It was an episode of *South Park*. Cartman kept using it, and it just sounded so silly. I started using it at school all the time, and people kept calling me a nerd for loving the show so much. Nearly ruined my life!" She started laughing at that point, and Bea joined in cautiously. The hammer didn't fall. There was no insult, no sign of insincerity. Was it possible? Was Emily Lloyd *nice?* But she was pretty! It didn't make sense.

"I hate that show," Bea ventured. "It's all fart jokes, and they make Canadians look like they're brain-damaged."

"Aren't we a little bit, though? Who chooses to live in a frozen wasteland several months out of the year?"

"I suppose so," Bea said with a smile. "I know I'm a little brain-damaged after you tried to kill me a minute ago."

"I said I was sorry!" laughed Emily. She stood up at that point and helped pull Bea to her feet. "Look, I totally owe you one. Why don't we have lunch together today? My treat?"

Bea looked uncomfortable. Lunch was alone time. People would look at them and wonder if Emily had lost a bet or something. "That's okay," she said. "You don't have to do that. Don't worry about it."

"Not worried," Emily said. "I'm poor, but I can afford cafeteria food. Although it might seem like I'm purposely picking on you if I make you eat it. Some of it looks like cardboard and tastes worse."

They laughed at that, and Bea said yes. To this day, it had been the best decision of her life. She could have said no and continued on being a loner, but being under Emily Lloyd's wing was nothing short of a revelation.

They talked about their favourite bands (Emily loved U2 and called Arcade Fire their spiritual successors, while Bea remained convinced that Justin Bieber deserved every bit of positive attention he got, despite the fact that he sometimes looked like he was going off the rails with all those tattoos), school work, and, of course, boys. Quickly, they were best friends. Any initial scepticism tossed their way gradually faded away, and Bea's presence was accepted wherever Emily was.

Another cool thing about Emily, Bea came to find out, was that she made no distinctions when it came to having friends. For her, either you were a good person or you weren't. Whether you were popular or not, if Emily Lloyd found common ground she made the effort. She was beloved at school, and no one could begrudge her for it.

And now Bea had let her down. Emily was off somewhere with Owen and Lucas, and she had chosen the armpit of the world to hang out with instead. Even now she wanted to run off after her friend but couldn't bring herself to move. The best she could do now was futilely try to engage James in conversation.

Time dragged on, and slowly Bea could feel the pressure building on her bladder, thanks to the four glasses of water she had downed in the tavern. The thirst had been so great and relieving, it had felt so good, but now the damage was done and there wasn't a toilet in sight. Bea was a city girl through and through, scorning the idea of camping in general. Her idea of roughing it was whatever the walking distance was between stores or hangout spots.

She pushed the feeling down over and over again, promising that she wouldn't leave this spot until Emily came back. Once Emily was back and the apologies were made, she'd pull her friend off into the bush a little bit so she could pee and have someone watch her back while her pants were around her ankles. The need was borderline desperate now, but there was no way in hell she was going to ask James Vanier to go to the bathroom with her. If they ever got out of this place, he'd never let her live it down, and she'd come too far socially to be thrown back into the dark ages. She didn't think she'd be able to handle that.

As though they were sharing the same brain, James loudly yawned and stretched before getting up and brushing off the seat of his pants. "Well," he said lazily, stifling a second yawn. "Gotta drain the snake. Be right back." He winked at her, probably trying to make her feel uncomfortable. Instead, she felt incredibly jealous that it was just so easy for him to go to the bathroom. Normally she loved boys. Right now she hated them and their stupid ability to pee standing up. Life was *not* fair.

The injustice of it all came crashing down on her all at once. James the bully, Owen making googly eyes at Emily while dropping corny-as-crap lines everywhere (*seriously, did he think that was going to work?*), everyone ignoring her, and now boys peeing while she was practically drowning, she had to go so badly. It became too much when she heard the faint splashing sounds coming from the bushes James had just wandered into.

"I'm going too!" she yelled. "Don't follow me!"

James laughed from the trees. "I'll try to restrain myself."

"Just try to be a decent human being and stay away, okay?"

"Whatever," he called.

"Promise me."

"No."

"Why not?"

"Because I don't want to. And I'm not a decent human being. That's no fun."

"Just do it!"

James wandered back into view and made a big deal about pulling up his zipper. "Still here? Quit yapping and go do it." He plopped himself back down and almost immediately reverted back to his catatonic state.

Rather than continue the argument, Bea got up in a huff and walked away from James. She thought she heard him laughing, but when she snapped back around, there was no expression on his face, and he was staring up into the trees.

Boys, she thought scathingly. She pushed her way through some of the thick undergrowth and walked into the woods. She glanced back every so often until she was sure that James couldn't see her and wasn't following.

Finally, she found a large tree surrounded by a growth of beautiful purple and white flowers that looked like it came out of a painting. She walked around behind the tree, careful not to disturb the flowers, and found a bare patch that would do. The height of the flowers was the perfect concealment, though she felt badly that she was about to defile such a beautiful place. The need was too great, though, and she got down to business.

Once she started, the relief was like nothing she'd ever felt before. She felt lighter and almost dizzy with happiness. Once she was done, she pulled up her pants and went back around the tree so she could sit in silence with Mr. Grumpy-PsychoPants some more. Maybe that should be his Twitter handle.

She stopped short, and her breath caught in her chest. Hovering just inches above one of the flowers ahead of her was what must be a fairy. She held her breath until her lungs felt fit to burst, desperately not wanting to move or startle the creature.

Its beauty was incredible. It was a perfect representation of a small human being, flawless in every way. There was not a mark or crease on the cream-coloured skin, and its eyes were large, oval, and a deep black. It had two pointed ears with little tufts sticking out at the very tips. It was not wearing clothing, but the body of the thing had a deeper, darker colour that gave the illusion. All of this Bea noticed at a casual glance before her full attention was given to the wings. They were gold-tipped and veined with silver. They lit up and light flowed through them, pulsing more brightly when the creature found something it liked in one of the flowers. Bea couldn't take her eyes off of it. She wanted nothing more than to run to it and squeeze it and take it home. It wasn't much larger than a teddy bear, so she *could* do it. Now that she had the thought, she needed to take action. She was dimly aware that this was probably a bad idea but pushed it away as she hopped and ploughed through the flowers to get to the fairy, throwing all of her earlier caution to the wind the way a raccoon raids trashcans in the city.

When the fairy saw her it let out a loud, piercing shriek, which stilled everything in the woods except for Bea. She made it a few more feet before the fairy spread its wings wide, and a brilliant flash erupted from them like a thousand cameras going off at the same time, the result of which finally made Bea stop in her tracks. The girl stared at the fairy adoringly, mouth open in a useless grin, eyes wide and loving.

The fairy let use a few more pulses, each weaker than the last, until it was sure that Bea wasn't moving. It hovered a moment or two and then slowly made its way toward Bea.

It's so beautiful, Bea thought. *So wonderful.*

The fairy floated closer, one head cocked to the side as it evaluated the girl.

Yes, come to me. I'll take you home.

A few feet closer, and Bea could see that the smooth skin was actually scaled and rough. *It doesn't matter. So beautiful. I have zits. I can relate.*

Closer still, and the dark skin on the body was actually a mat of barbed thorns.

Please be mine.

A few feet away, and the creature eyes could be seen to have deep red pits in the middle that glowed the colour of blood. Its teeth were razor-sharp, and a milky-white substance flowed out of the corners of its eyes and out of its ears that produced the smooth skin look from afar.

I love you.

It reached out and spread its hand toward her face, the webbing in between each finger as fine as a spiderweb, while its fingers were each as sharp as a knife. It was less than an inch from her face when it let out another shriek and bared its long, sharp teeth.

A sharp crack sounded from above, startling the fairy back a few feet. A large shape crashed to the ground in between Bea and the fairy, scattering flower pollen and leaves all over the place. The fairy shrieked again and let loose a barrage of light pulses that had no effect on the stranger as it rose up and struck out at the creature. The mass swung a weapon at it in wide arcs, narrowly missing each time as the fairy hissed and flashed pulses madly. Finally, the mass lucked out and connected with the creature, creating a twang sound as it knocked the fairy down and sent it crashing onto the ground, where it buzzed and flitted about dazedly.

"Are you okay?" came a voice from somewhere far off. It sounded far off. The mass was waving at her. *How friendly!* Bea thought. *And mysterious! He sounds British. Is it my Neville Longbottom finally come to rescue me and take me away? I'm ready to go!* "Hello?" came the voice again. The fairy tried to fly up again, but was knocked down once more by the mass. "Stupid things," it muttered.

"I love you," Bea said. *Did I say that out loud? I don't care. I do. I love you. Marry me.*

"What?" asked the mass. It moved closer and stood right in front of her, waving its arms again. "Snap out of it." It snapped fingers at her ears and gently shook her shoulders. Bea didn't care. She was content. It was nice here. Nice and safe.

Finally, the mass slapped her hard across the face.

"Oww!" Bea yelled. "What the hell?"

Her vision snapped into focus on a man. At least she thought it was. Huge, thick, steampunk-style goggles obscured most of his dirty face and his eyes. He had incredibly shaggy brown hair, a large brown coat, a torn rucksack, and was holding a badminton racket, which he promptly used again to swat the fairy.

Finally seeing that she was paying attention, he walked up to her and peeled the goggles off his face. *His eyes are GORGEOUS,* she thought. She melted into a puddle at the sight of them. He looked at her, deeply serious and concerned. "Come with me if you want to live," he said.

She giggled. "Okay, Arnold."

"Arnold?"

"Yeah, you know. Arnold Schwarzenegger. *The Terminator?* 'Come with me if you want to live.' His catchphrase." She reached out and caressed his face. "I want to live with you. You can protect me from the fairies." She was breathless. He was so *cute.*

"I don't know who that is, but we need to go. If there's one, there's a lot more around here. It isn't safe."

"Arnold from the movies."

"Okay, fine," he paused. "What's a movie?"

"Film. Movie. DVD. Blu-ray. Netflix. YouTube. Pirate Bay."

"Are you having a seizure?"

"No. He's a movie star."

Sensing he wasn't getting anywhere, the man pushed on. "Okay, tell me later. I think it best we move along, however. This is not the sort of place one lingers."

He is so polite! What a beautiful accent. I love a man with an accent. "I'll follow you anywhere," she said in a husky voice. "Take me to your home. I'll be your queen."

"That's nice," he said ignoring her. "Come on then, your highness."

She reached out and took her arm and held herself close to his chest.

"Call me Bea," she said. "Short for Beatrice. Short for *'I'm yours.'*"

"That does not make any sort of sense whatsoever," he said. "There's no rhyme pattern or similarity. It's just bonkers really..." He cut himself off and refocused. "Right. Back to it. Nice to meet you, Bea. My name is Edgar. Edgar Culshaw. Can we go now?"

"Bea Culshaw. I like that."

"Wonderful. We need to get out of here, Bea."

"And go where?" James Vanier stood on a fallen log ten feet away, arms folded across his chest. He had a large stick in one hand and a tight grip on it.

"Is she a friend of yours?" asked Edgar. "Are there more of you? No matter, help me with her. We have to get out of here before the fairy folk become a problem."

"Fairies?" asked James. "You think I'm scared of Tinkerbell?"

"Who is Tinkerbell? Where are you people even from?" Edgar looked quite agitated at this point, looking around wildly at flowers and treetops, his badminton racket ready in one hand to strike out. "Here I was, enjoying a peaceful day, and you lot show up and make a mess of everything. First, there were sticks all over the damn paths. Took me ages to clean that up! Now I have you two nutters to coddle!"

"I love cuddling," Bea put in.

"Oh, shut it!" said Edgar. He swung his racket in the air one more time at some unseen enemy.

From his posture, Bea could see that James didn't like her knight with his huge goggles and sports equipment. James even acted like her beloved Edgar was probably not all there. Bea was slightly touched at this.

James took a step toward Edgar and readied himself to swing the branch. "It will only take one good sharp hit to the skull, you know," James mused. "Then we can have brains for lunch."

Before he took his swing, the fairy once again floated up in the air and let off a weak flash. James had to blink the light out of his eyes and shake it off. "What the hell is that thing?" he asked as he shielded his eyes.

Edgar quickly put his goggles back down into place and cursed out loud. Another twang sent the creature tumbling down to rest at James's foot. "Fairy-folk," he said. "Don't look at them. The flashes stun you, and then they skin you alive before they eat you."

James shielded his eyes, except for a tiny slit through which he could see the thing groping about at his feet. He took a step back from it.

"They're harmless if you have goggles, though," Edgar continued as he struggled to keep Bea from trying to kiss him. "The racket stuns them but doesn't really hurt them. They also hate the noise the thing makes."

"Why is she acting all goopy like that?" James asked. "You wearing some kind of body spray or something?"

"Side effect," Edgar answered. "They hypnotize their prey, get them to love and adore them so that they will be happy to serve them in any way, including as a course for a meal. Those who are flashed, but live, become quite passionate for a while." Bea muttered something that made Edgar blush at that point. "The effect is temporary, however. Makes them quite valuable at the market, as you can imagine. If you can subdue a fairy and get it away from the others, they fetch a high price and ensure a warm bed for a month. Often not an empty bed, at that."

"Doesn't look like much," James said, nudging it with his foot. The fairy moaned.

"And alone, it's easy to deal with. As I have said, more are likely nearby, and we must move on before this one alerts its brothers and sisters." As Edgar spoke, James raised his foot high over the creature. "As long as we don't kill them or seriously hurt them, we have nothing to worry about."

"Not with you around," said Bea adoringly.

A sickening crunch came from the underside of James's foot. The fairy lay there crumbled, its wing broken and its eyes wild. "Oops," he said with a grin.

"What have you done?" asked Edgar, eyes wide.

"What?" James asked with a shrug. "It'll wash off. Is there a problem?"

The answer never came as the crumpled creature suddenly began to thrash and shriek. It flopped all over the place, and Edgar dashed madly after it, trying to catch it. The fairy tried to fly away, but its mangled wing kept it close to the ground. Edgar finally managed to whack it over the head with his racket once more, which stunned the creature into submission. From his rucksack, Edgar pulled out a dark bag and stuffed the fairy inside it, hoping the dark would calm it. He then gingerly laid the bag on the ground and backed away slowly. In time, the thing would recover and fly off, but for now, Edgar wanted it to nap its temper tantrum away. Once he was done, there was silence for a stretch until Edgar breathed a sigh of relief.

"What are you freaking out for?" James asked. "It's just a stupid fairy."

In the distance, there was another loud shriek. Then another. Then dozens, and soon more than either of them could guess. "You bloody fool," Edgar said. "You've done us in. *Run!*" Without waiting for a response, Edgar ran past James. Once Edgar showed fear, Bea showed twice as much. After all, she dazedly reasoned, if he was scared and he was her knight in shining armour, then she should be terrified.

Bea screamed at nothing in particular and started running after Edgar.

"Don't look at their lights!" he screamed back at her.

Bea dutifully did not look at the lights. In fact, she closed her eyes. That was probably why she ran full-tilt into a tree and knocked herself silly.

She nearly blacked out from the hit. She tried to get up and couldn't. So instead she just lay back down like she was going to have a nap.

"Bugger it all!" cursed Edgar. He pulled himself up short and turned back to get the girl. He lifted her up and unceremoniously slung her over his shoulders, the metal rings of the hornbooks dancing in his face. Had she been less dazed or better capable of rational thought, she would have been thrilled to be carried like this.

James was bewildered by it all. This guy was nuts, and Bea just cold-cocked herself. Between their antics and the shrieking going on all around him, James was clearly unsure what to do next. He looked to his left and right for signs of the fairies but couldn't see a single one.

And then he looked up.

Above them, the lights of Yonge and Dundas Square had stopped pulsing and rippling and were brightening to a shocking level. The signs seemed to crumble away, pixel by pixel, and were streaming down toward them. In horror, James realized that the pixels weren't pixels, but hundreds, if not thousands, of the fairy creatures.

And they looked *pissed.*

CHAPTER 13

B reathless, Owen, Emily, and Lucas did their best to maintain a brisk pace, but the panic was starting to set in. Other than the pile of rocks and branches Lucas had left at the entrance to their path, there was nothing in sight now. They made a right turn, left, continued straight, and were now in danger of becoming hopelessly lost. The thickness of the tree canopies made looking up and getting their bearings difficult, and now that they knew the area was so dangerous, none of them wanted to linger while someone climbed a tree.

Owen was barely paying attention to where he was going. His eyes swept the path back and forth, desperately trying to locate signs of the trail they had left for themselves to follow. It was a perfectly simple plan, and now some oaf or hidden foe appeared to be trying to kill them. "Where are the damn breadcrumbs?" Owen complained. "They were here!" Lucas nodded in confirmation. His scowl was quite terrifying, and Owen had no doubt that if the culprit revealed itself right now, he or she would be pummelled into the ground.

"Moved," Lucas said.

"Yeah, but by who or what?" Owen didn't wait for an answer. He hoped it was the wind, but it was hot and dry down here, and only the leaves at the top of the trees saw much of a breeze. The sticks had been moved. Simple as that. Someone or something was out to get them.

"Keep moving," suggested Emily. They all agreed and kept going down the path as quickly as they could.

Ever since the Index had gone blood red and blotted out the map, they had been running blind. Without looking back, they pushed and pulled each other through the Information Booth window and bolted across the field to Lucas's pile. Without hesitation, they plunged down the path and started to look for their trail, though Owen lamented that in their haste he wasn't as initially observant as he should have been. He remembered the last few twists and turns and followed right away, but soon all the paths looked like the ones before. He and Lucas had been so focused on putting sticks on the ground that they never bothered to look up.

They knew they were in trouble when Owen started to go right down a path and Lucas grabbed his arm, pointing to the left. Both boys were a hundred percent certain they were correct, and it had come down to a coin toss from Emily to resolve the situation. Left it was.

For as long as they could, they ran. Gradually, it slowed to a brisk walk, and now they were stopped, bent over, panting and sweating from the exertion. Luckily, nothing had come out of the woodwork to reveal itself as an "enemy" so far. Best-case scenario had the enemy turning out to be the fairies, and the worst he could imagine was them throwing dust at them to make them sneeze. That's what he told himself in order to feel better, anyway.

"Take a break?" Owen asked. Lucas only nodded and sat himself down heavily. Sweat poured down his forehead.

Emily sat down with her legs crossed underneath her and immediately referred to the Index. Ever since she had asked it to display enemies, the thing had been popping up red circle after red circle, many overlapping each other. It was still doing it now, and no matter what she tried, she couldn't get it to stop. It was a runaway computer program that needed to complete what it was doing before anything else could be done. The only helpful part was that the green dot that showed their position moved with their movements, but the red obscured all the blue showing where their friends were. The path she had highlighted before disappeared when the new command was entered. The Index could be a crucial tool for them, if only she could get it to work properly. "Still nothing," she said. "I can't get it to stop. The good news is that there aren't any red dots showing exactly where we are."

"Keep trying," said Owen rudely.

"Of course I'll keep trying!" she fired back angrily.

Frustration and fatigue was wearing at them all, Owen knew, as he fought back an angry retort. "Sorry, Em," he said. "I know you're doing your best."

She still looked annoyed. "You could try too, you know," she said. "What's the Battledoor showing? You should try talking to it."

They were staying put for the moment, so Owen sat down and pulled out the Battledoor. So far it hadn't done much for him. He'd tried to use it in the situation with the Brewmaster. It kind of worked a little in the market. But really, most of that was just blind luck or timing. Still, Emily was right. It was worth a shot. When he looked at the screen, it was still blank and didn't respond to his touch.

"Battledoor 'on,'" he said. No result. "Display? Function? Commands? Doors!" He was sure the last command would work, but still the screen was blank.

"Try more book-related commands," Emily suggested. More red dots continued to appear on her screen.

"Uh, book?" tried Owen.

"Oh, for god's sake," Emily said exasperated. "Chapter, page, word count, progress, bookmark, table of contents. Anything you can think of when it comes to a book. Something has to work."

One by one he tried the suggestions, and one by one they didn't work. Whatever the Battledoor was, it wasn't cooperative. Once you got to the next part of the supposed story they were in, it would come to life and offer you a choice, but it seemed as though you were on your own once you decided.

He was about to quit when he said "dust jacket." All of a sudden, the thing came to life and Owen got excited. That feeling didn't last long. Simple and blunt, the Battledoor read:

Jacket and synopsis not yet available.
Please complete the story first to ensure accurate results.

He showed Emily the results. "Hmm," she mused. "Not very helpful, is it? At least you got it to do something."

The Battledoor faded once more, and the screen went blank. Owen had to think. There must be some way to get something useful. "It said 'accurate results,' right? Has to be some way to see the story so far," he said to Emily.

The book once again came to life.

THE BATYLDOR
The Adventure of Owen Thomas
Young Owen Thomas wasn't sure what he wanted out of life; in fact he wasn't even sure he wanted to live. Still reeling from the death of his mother, Owen has chosen isolation rather than companionship. All of that began to change the day Emily Lloyd walked into his life.

"What is it saying?" Emily asked. Owen gave a start and bent the book up so she wouldn't see. This stupid thing was going to ruin his chances with her or at the very least embarrass him to death.

"It's just showing a list of what we've done so far," he lied. *It's only a part lie*, he thought. *Enough to keep me from looking like a love-sick puppy.*

Owen read on to see a fairly accurate account of their adventures so far. Surprisingly, the book also knew about everything leading up to them finding it. In a way, this irritated Owen, since it felt like the random chance of it all was more of a predetermined path they were meant to take. "Fate" and "destiny" were words that people like Romeo and Juliet used to justify all of their decisions or outcomes in their lives. They thought they were meant to find each other, and Ms. Gerow loved to talk about how they were meant to die for each other as well. That made him angry. If such a thing were real, if fate ruled their lives, then it meant no decision he ever made was actually worth a damn, because he had no choice. It would mean that his mother was meant to die, that he was meant to suffer, that he was meant to leave his life in Guelph behind forever.

Angry as he was, he couldn't help but look at Emily. *It would also mean I was supposed to meet her.* Tears began to burn at the edges of his eyes, and he forced himself to stare down at the book until he felt under control again.

Path #1 – The Front Door or The Alley
Stepping into the alley was terrifying for Owen. It was a strange place in a familiar setting, as odd as that might be to think about. Once he caught up to his friends...

'*Terrifying*'? *I wasn't terrified!* Now the book was taking artistic liberties. From there, it was a blow-by-blow account of everything else they had gone through. The only interesting part was that the selections he made were greyed out on the screen, and when he tapped the other selection, a warning would pop up:

Path not taken. Story no longer available. You cannot go this way any longer.

Story of my life, he thought. Once you were in, you were in. No going back. *Cause and effect. Action and reaction. Choice and consequence.*

Battle #1 – 'Strange Brew' or 'Straight Through'
This battle was won by luck.

Bite me, Owen thought, though he didn't disagree with the assessment. Much of what they had escape so far had an element of luck with it.

He scrolled down past the entry for the market and paused at the second battle it displayed.

Battle #2 – 'The Fairies' or 'The Furies'
Battle active. Check back later if still alive.

Owen felt sick to his stomach. *No, it isn't,* he worried. *Still alive? What did that mean?* When and where the battle supposedly happened, he wasn't sure. Hopefully they could get out of here before they found out. He dropped the

Battledoor back down to his waist. The thing would tell them where they were going and remind them of where they had been, but unless there was something missing he wasn't seeing, that was about the long and short of it. If it had other secrets, they'd have to wait until later to be uncovered. He envied Emily and her Index (for the brief time it was working, anyway). The Index was something that was useful and would probably guide them out of this mess. All he had done was drop them straight into one problem after another.

"It stopped!" said Emily excitedly. How she could tell, Owen didn't know. The thing was blood-red all over the place. "Clear screen!" she commanded. The Index went completely blank.

"Too far," said Owen.

"Where are we?" asked Emily. The Index chimed, and the overhead map appeared once again. The area was labelled 'The Grotto.' "Show friends."

The Index chimed, but the sound was missed as all three were startled by a high-pitched shrieking somewhere off in the distance. The shrieking was loud, painful, and shocking considering how quiet and serene the place had been a moment ago. "Enemies" shot into Owen's brain, and he looked about, but nothing was out of place. He looked back to Emily, whose face was pale.

"Bea," she whispered.

They were on their feet in an instant. "Show path to friends," she commanded. The shrieking in the distance had sharply cut off. It could be a good thing, but it could be bad. They needed to get back there quickly. The Index dutifully chimed and highlighted a path that went back the way they had just come. Lucas cursed and kicked a rock. This last turn had been his idea.

More shrieks suddenly started, and they all put their hands over their ears. The sound came from all over the place, but mostly it came from above. A quick glance upward showed nothing, but the leaves and branches were shaking with activity. *No wonder we couldn't see them*, thought Owen. "Run!" he mouthed to his companions. He actually yelled, but his voice couldn't be heard above the din.

Together, they raced down the blue line, Owen and Lucas functioning as Emily's guides so she could keep her eye on the Index and call out the turns in the path. The shrieking continued, and Owen could hear fluttering above the treetops and shapes zipping past the rare openings. The sun seemed to have gone crazy as the light above the trees kept flashing like a sort of crazy lightning storm. A million tiny orbs were descending from the heavens above. The sky was falling. Owen hoped it wasn't going to crush them.

Emily shouted out that they were almost there, one turn left, when Owen ran straight into Lucas and fell backward; that was how quickly the kid had stopped in front of him. Owen was about to shout something rude when he looked past Lucas and saw James with his eyes pinched shut, waving his arms around wildly while standing beside a strange man wearing huge black and gold steampunk goggles and whipping around a badminton racket. They had their backs to the wall and were surrounded by a sea of fairies. The whole scene was beyond ridiculous, and Owen fought an insane urge to laugh. The feeling died in his throat when he saw Bea lying in a crumpled heap against a door.

For the moment at least, the fairies hadn't noticed them, they were so focused on tormenting James and the stranger. If it were only James, Owen would be happy to let them get to it, but considering Bea was over there, he knew he had to act.

Fairies frequently buzzed down at the stranger but were rebuked by a loud twang from a badminton racket. Bea was on the ground behind him, and he was fumbling at her belt, trying to pull off one of the hornbooks. Owen couldn't tell if he was trying to help her or steal from her. For all he knew, the stranger had been the one who hurt her. James wasn't a good judge of character at the best of times, so seeing him standing side-by-side with the man didn't do much to vouch for his credibility.

"We need a plan," Owen yelled into Emily's ears. She nodded, her eyes wide with concern for her friend.

Lucas had a plan. It involved roaring and chasing off after the fairies, pinwheeling his arms and knocking them all over the place. Once they saw him, they scattered back and away, shrieking all the more loudly and sending flash after flash against his back. Now that there was an opening, Emily and Owen dashed through it to get to Bea. A few of the fairies dive-bombed at them like birds protecting a nest, but none of them made contact.

Emily got to Bea first and came to a sliding halt by her side. She lifted Bea's face and saw that she was still breathing, though she had a small bump on her head that was already purpling from the bruise. She stroked her hair and kept calling her name, but Bea wasn't responding.

Before Owen could reach the girls, the strange man stepped in front of him and had the racket raised as if to strike him, but instead the man handed it to him. "Swing!" he yelled. "Keep your eyes closed! Don't look at the light! Darkness is your friend!"

Taken aback, Owen couldn't tell if the man was super creepy or helpful in a disturbing way. It didn't much matter given the circumstances, so Owen took the racket and obeyed. He closed his eyes and started swinging. He felt totally ridiculous and almost opened his eyes when he felt the racket connect and give off a twang. He dared not even so much as peek and hoped that if it had been one of his friends he'd just bashed, they'd forgive him.

Edgar had dropped down to Bea's side and pushed Emily aside to get a better grip on the hornbooks at her waist. "Hey!" Emily complained. She pushed him back to try to protect her friend.

"Stop that!" he yelled.

"You stop!" she yelled back.

Groping at the rings, he examined each one for a moment before dropping it back down. Finally, he got excited and saw one he liked best. He grabbed Bea's hand, put it on the ring, and had her pull it off. He stood up, held it above his hand, and yelled "smoke!" before tossing the ring to the ground in front of the fairies. Within seconds, a huge plume of thick white smoke blew out of the ring and into the air, creating a dense fog that threatened to choke all of them. The flashes still came, but far less bright or frequent. The shrieks had quieted down as well.

Owen was unaware of any of this, as his eyes were still closed and he was still thrashing about. He felt a tug on his arm and whacked it as hard as he could.

"Damn you!" the man yelled. "Stop that! You can open your eyes!"

Owen cautiously opened his eyes and saw the stranger gently holding his wrist. "Who are you?" he yelled.

"Time for that later," the stranger replied. "We need an exit!"

Owen grabbed for the Battledoor, and the stranger's eyes went wide. The smoke was too thick and Owen's eyes were watering too much to make anything out.

"Not time for that yet," the stranger said, licking his lips. "Come on!"

Owen followed him back to the wall, where James was huddled into a small ball and Lucas stood over him like a protective watchdog. The stranger moved Emily to the side, much more gently this time, and lifted Bea up into his arms. "Find a door," he said. "Any door. When the smoke clears up, they'll be angrier than ever."

Just any door would *not* do, Owen knew already from his short time in the World. Taking them out of this place and dropping them into winter or fire or a room of angry monkeys or any other hazard would be bad. Finally, he remembered one door that was ideal, if a little boring.

"Nothing!" he yelled out.

"Not much of a suggestion," mused the stranger.

"Nothing is good! Let's go to nothing!"

The stranger was totally baffled by this suggestion, but it seemed to make sense to the others, so he hurried along after them. Wherever "nothing" was, it was beyond the field of smoke, and a stray fairy saw them leave it and called out to its brothers and sisters.

Owen passed one door, then another, then at least ten more before the distinctive heavy oak and stone door marked "Nothing" lay before them. "Hurry! It's here!" Flashes began to appear behind them, and he knew they didn't have much time. He hadn't even seen one up close, but they had unnerved James Vanier, and that was enough for him.

He reached to the door and pulled it open. Without hesitation, James ran inside, followed by Emily and Lucas. The stranger, with the added burden of Bea, huffed by last until Owen got in and slammed the door shut behind them. Many bangs and thumps immediately followed as fairy after fairy flew into the door, causing it to shudder. None of it was more forceful than raindrops on a window, so for the time being they were safe.

Owen tried to turn around but found that he had no room. Everyone was pressed up against one another in the tight space, and no one aside from the stranger seemed pleased about it. The man had a huge grin on his face.

"That was fun," he said, smiling. "I'm Edgar. Pleased to meet you!"

CHAPTER 14

The scent was strong in the air. Two males and a female. Recent. Very recent, in fact, and the sources of the smell could possibly, though unlikely given how quiet it was, be just inside. Basil pawed at the base of the Information Booth below the window Owen, Lucas, and Emily had crawled through earlier and began to growl, hopping up on his short back legs to try to reach up. When that didn't work, he began to bark in frustration. If he could have spoken, he'd have made his intentions as clear as possible. *People were close! People might be right inside! Kill! Bite!* Basil resorted to barks and growls to get the attention of the others.

He was so busy scratching that it caught him unawares when cruel and sharp claws unceremoniously dug into his hindquarters and lifted him into the air. Basil yelped and tried to snap his jaws at the cause of the pain, but he was too long in the body and the claws too far away for his head to reach. Moments later, he was dropped at the top of the windowsill, and he scrambled to find purchase on the shiny surface of the counter. Tail tucked under his legs, he glanced back to see Hatchet come to rest and bend his leathery wings around his chest.

"Bark!" yelled Hatchet tauntingly. "Bark, bark, bark!"

Basil averted his eyes and slunk off to look for a way down so he could investigate the inside of the Information Booth.

"Yes," said Hatchet. "Walk away, dog-thing. Find the human stink and rub your face in it. Master commands it, so we will do it."

The Master did indeed command it, and Basil was ever eager to please. If Master asked him to fetch, he went and got what was asked. If Master asked him to find, he would scent for miles. If Master asked him to bite (his favourite) Basil would bite, chew, and gnaw until told to stop. Basil loved the Master. Basil did not love Hatchet.

The bat-creature clawed at him, scratched, pinched, pushed, and taunted him. If it did not get its way, the bat-creature would screech at him and beat him. Only Master kept him alive, though Master was not above kicking him if he did not perform well.

Determined to do well, Basil sniffed and trotted all around the space. People were gone, but not long ago. They must not be far, and Basil would find them. The Master said to find them. Realizing he had no other way to get out, Basil cast a wary eye toward the bat-creature, preening itself on the window ledge. The bat-creature met his eye, and a toothy grin formed at the edge of its mouth. It gleefully sprang down and skittered toward the dog-thing. Basil growled at it and bore the pain well when Hatchet sunk his claws in, deeper this time, and fairly flung the dog back out through the window. Basil landed hard and scratched the side of his face, letting out an *ark-ark* call of pain. More Groundlings awaited the pair outside and scattered out of the way as the dog-thing limped about to shake off the pain. To a one they tittered, wordlessly, a hundred or more laughs at the expense of the dog-thing.

They all hated him. That was plain enough to see. The Master may have favoured two, but only one was leader of the Groundlings, and that had been a position hard-won. Hatchet had killed more than a dozen other contenders for the leadership position, and his continued ruthlessness meant there were no more challengers. Few were willing to fight in the first place, but none would rise up once Hatchet had shown he was willing to kill his own brood-mate when he tore out its throat. To kill a brood-mate was unthinkable. Hatchet had not only done that but eaten part of the thing as well.

Basil, though a Groundling, was not truly of them. He was one of the few dog-things in the group and the only one the Master had named, a rare gift due to him because of his ability to track, fetch, and understand language. Basil was exceedingly clever for his kind, and so he was prized. Hatchet tolerated no rivals and was allowed to herd his group as viciously as he wanted, but the Master would only let him go so far with the dog-thing.

"One day, the dog-thing will have an accident," Hatchet had said to him once. "One day, only Hatchet will be named and valued." Today, Basil hoped, was not that day. The bat-creature was tolerating Basil's company, but the Master had not said he needed to be nice about it, and Hatchet obeyed what wasn't said as much as what was.

When the Master told them to hunt back at the Spyre, Master had been more excited than either Basil or Hatchet had seen him in years. The Master loved to torture and abuse, but the hunt had waned since the bug-eyed man had denied him of his prize several years ago. The two chief Groundlings had been there, of course, as the Other tossed the book through the door and slammed it shut. The Master had seemed to slow at that point, to diminish somewhat, and sank down into the stone before fading away back to his tower-above-the-dome. But now that had changed. The world had changed, for that matter, and the Master called for the hunt once again.

The Wide-Walker had given the Master hope when he spoke of a new Protagonist and then expressed pleasure soon after as the giant man went to his death. The search could have been long and wide, but quickly enough a clue came about where to start once the lights in the Grotto went all a-flutter and shrieking their angry tune. Hatchet liked to screech as well, but the fairy-sound was too shiny and needed a little more blood to colour it. Once the terrible music began, the Master had pointed to the Grotto and uttered the word "fetch." Obedient without hesitation, the Groundlings moved as one and had flowed down the sides of the Spyre, some clutching brood-mates who could not climb or had no wings, and went off to search. To hunt. How the people below had screamed and fled! Hatchet had no doubt wanted to drop Basil down the length of the Spyre but dared not try with the Master so close at hand.

Now the two circled each other uneasily outside the booth. The shrieking had stopped, but the lights had not returned to their steady places above. Wherever the fairies had gone and whatever had angered them, the fight wasn't over yet. Hatchet wanted to get on with it to begin tearing. Basil wanted to get on with it to keep Hatchet away from him... and to please the Master. Basil was happy if Master was happy.

Basil sniffed the ground furiously and looked to be making little progress in picking up the trail. One Groundling close by got bored waiting and decided to take a nip at Basil's flanks. He got more than he bargained for when the dog-thing turned suddenly and closed his jaws on the thing's throat, killing it instantly. The other Groundlings backed off immediately. Basil might not enjoy very high stature, but he wasn't to be trifled with. The only one who did and got away with it was Hatchet, mostly because the bat-creature could leap away and also because to harm him would be to upset the Master. Besides, the brood-mate killer could fend for himself.

At last, Basil was able to filter the scents out and found a clear trail to follow. He moved ahead cautiously at first, the dead Groundling still in his mouth, and then faster as he grew confident that he was on the right trail.

Hesitating until Hatchet gave the all-clear, the Groundlings waited restlessly. Finally, Basil reached the path and the pile of sticks before turning around and giving a bark to signal the others after he let the body slide out of his mouth. Only then did Hatchet fly forward, the swell of Groundlings at his back.

"Once we are on the path, you are to spread out as wide as you can," Hatchet hissed. "Anything fluttering, scurrying, or baying, feel free to kill it. Anything talking, observe it, subdue it, and call for me. The killing may come later, as the Master will say when the time is right."

The swell nearly caught up, Basil turned at once and headed down the path. The large mass of Groundlings spread out like a dark cloud of dust, tar, and ash as it filtered through the leaves and branches of the wood.

The scent firmly in his snout, Basil never wavered and never slowed. He wanted to please the Master, yes, but he also wanted to stay ahead of the others behind him. Occasionally he would be distracted by trees and scents, but his keen nose told him the trees had been touched or climbed, but the things who did it did not linger.

The scent moved on and thickened, suggesting they had been running. Another scent came through as well then: fear. The one that gave the dog-thing the biggest sense of disquiet was not human at all, but the floaty-birds. The fairies were nearby as well. None of the Groundlings feared the flashes of light; it was merely a nuisance to their kind, but they were not eager to meet their fangs and talons. Fairies cheated, too. They would pick up smaller creatures and carry them to great heights before letting go and dropping them to their deaths. Hatchet had laughed at this once and referred to the practice as "splitting the melons."

Stronger and stronger grew the scent, until it was near overpowering. The trail was nearly obliterated by the hundreds of fairy smells in the air. Slowly, sounds began to mix with smells. The sound of fairy wings produced a large droning noise that the Groundlings disliked intensely, Hatchet in particular, who wasted no time in ordering his pack to attack the things as soon as they were seen. The Groundlings did not have to wait long. The swell came upon the fairies, who were busy buzzing about and throwing themselves one after another at a door in the wall.

The fairies were so intent on the door that they didn't look behind them. Groundling after Groundling burst through the protective cover of the woods and sank tooth and claw into the startled creatures, pulling them down to the ground before tearing flesh and wings from their small frames.

The fairies closer to the wall broke off their useless attack on the door and began to shriek and flash at the intruders. They zipped down at the creatures on the ground or tackled those in-flight. It was an incredible battle of dark versus light. Black shapes tore at the white while the bright shapes permanently shut off the lights of the dark. The wet sounds of "splitting melons" could be heard from time to time. Hatchet yelled with glee as he attacked one foe after the next, never faltering or slowing. Basil barked and snapped his jaws at any that approached, futilely chasing after a few even when they flew into the air.

Though it seemed to last ages, the fighting was over in less than a couple of minutes. The fairies figured out they were outmatched and retreated high above, with several offering shrieks and flashes as they went. Hatchet dropped to the ground and pulled himself, winged hand over winged hand, toward the door they had been attacking. Basil was up against the door now, forepaws clawing at it eagerly.

"Away, mutt," snapped Hatchet and backhanded the dog-thing. Basil tumbled away, whimpering once more, before sitting on his haunches and casting a nervous eye from the bat-creature to the closed door. Hatchet flew up to the door, locked his wings over the knob, and turned it as best he could. Other Groundlings came to his aid to help pry the door open, since it was much too heavy for any one of them to do on their own.

The rest of the Groundlings mixed and surged, a heavy wave ready to crash in on the space. The door opened an inch, then another, then swung the fall way open to reveal the delicious prey inside.

But there was nothing to see. The room, no bigger than a large closet, was empty.

There was no other exit and no way the humans inside could have slipped past during the commotion. Hatchet turned a furious eye toward Basil, who was licking his paws and looking away.

Hatchet shrieked in frustration, with a hundred growling Groundling voices joining in the terrible chorus in support of their leader. Basil cowered and prepared for punishment.

CHAPTER 15

O wen hated Amanda Mitchell. He hated her stupid face, her stupid hair, her stupid lunchbox, and her stupid laugh. Every stomping footstep echoed that sentiment, and the front door shouted it as it was slammed shut behind him.

"Easy there, tiger," said his mother, who had just poked her head out from the kitchen doorway to see what the commotion was all about. "Doors are expensive. Whatever that one did to you, you got it back."

"I hate the stupid door," Owen said stubbornly.

A wry smile poked at the edges of her mouth. He wanted to be angry at her for smiling at him when he was so angry, but he just couldn't. He knew he was being silly and gave up.

"Okay, I *don't* hate the door."

"Progress," she said, chuckling. "A peace treaty has been reached at last! Come, let us dine on peanut butter sandwiches together and toast to the health of the door!"

Angry though he was at Amanda Mitchell, his deep love of peanut butter ruled his heart in a way no girl could hope to match. He followed his mother into the kitchen, half-heartedly stomping for effect.

As she put the finishing touches on his sandwich and cut the crusts, Owen poured a clumsy glass of orange juice each for them. "Want to talk about it?" she asked.

"No."

"Okay."

"I hate Amanda Mitchell."

"That's a strong word."

Owen thought about this for a little as he savoured his first bite, his anger subsiding.

"Is it good?" his mother asked.

Owen nodded. "I gave her a card for Valentine's Day."

"I see. Did she not like it?"

"Well, she said she did. I had hearts on it and drew a picture of a unicorn for her." Owen glanced at his mother and saw the small smile there again. "I hate unicorns," he hastily added. "But she likes them."

"There's that word again," said his mother. "It's not one you should use or feel."

"She lied to me!" protested Owen. "She said she liked my card and that we could play together later, but then she showed everyone the card and said my unicorn looked like a cow and that she would never play with me and that I'm a stupid boy and that she likes other guys like Kyle Shepherd and Maxx Beyer, and I hate her stupid face!"

Through all of it, his mother never said a word but just listened patiently. "That wasn't very nice of her, honey," she said and patted his hand.

Owen began to cry a little, the anger quickly being replaced by hurt. "Why did she have to be so mean?"

"Sweetheart, sometimes people can be mean. They shouldn't be, and sometimes they don't mean to be, but it happens."

"Does it happen to you?"

"Sure, though I try not to let it bother me."

"Do you cry?"

"Not any more, little one. When I was your age, there were several times that I cried over boys who didn't like me or other girls who wouldn't play with me."

Owen didn't believe this. He adored his mother and couldn't imagine anyone not liking her. "That's not true," he said.

"It is," she said. "Not everyone will like you, and it's very hard to please everyone. The best you can do is be a good person, try your best, and make friends with those who appreciate you and want to be around you rather than worry about the ones who aren't interested."

"But I am a good person, and she doesn't like me!"

"She might not," said his mother. "But she might in time. Just be patient, little one. You'll find your true love eventually, most likely when you least expect it."

"Is that how you found Dad?"

"It's how we found each other." His father walked in at that point and saw the tears, the sandwich, and the knowing smile from his wife and decided to pretend he didn't see what was going on. Owen got up, gave his mother a quick hug, and made to leave the room before remembering to grab what was left of his sandwich.

"Mom?" he asked.

"Yes, sweetheart?"

"I don't hate Amanda Mitchell."

"I know."

"But I do hate unicorns."

She laughed at this and gestured at him to run off. "You can't win them all, I suppose!"

As he made his way upstairs, Owen overheard his father ask his mother if there was anything he could do to help. "Young love," said his mother. "He's just eager to be noticed and for the girls in his class to wake up."

"To wake up?" asked his father.

"Yes, wake up!" Why was she repeating herself?

"Wake up!" he heard again.

He felt a gentle nudge at his side. "Owen, wake up!"

Slowly and with great effort, Owen opened his eyes and briefly panicked when he still couldn't see. He wiped the sleep from his eyes and tried to focus once again, but the room was dark and dimly lit. The disorientation was overwhelming, and he felt a surge of panic until a smooth, gentle hand stroked his arm beside him.

It was Emily Lloyd. She was right beside him, and from the position she was in, it looked like she had been asleep as well. She tried to smile, but it was comically distorted as she yawned. "Sorry," she said. "You were talking in your sleep."

"I am?" he stammered. "I mean, I was? Sorry." He flushed a deep shade of red. He was half embarrassed and half thrilled that they had passed out within a few feet of each other.

"Bad dream?" she asked.

"No," he said. "Kind of sad, though. Waking up here is the bad dream. Present company excluded, of course." *Smooth*, he thought as he kicked himself for being so cheesy. Emily was at least smiling.

He wasn't lying about the place being a bad dream, though. It had been a narrow escape from those fairies in the Grotto, though the credit for saving them went to Edgar's knowledge of how to use the Battledoor, not Owen's. *Well, I had to do it, at least,* thought Owen. *But he knew how. I'll have to ask him about that.* At the time, there wasn't a free moment to ask or dwell on it. Once they arrived here in what Edgar called his "Cave Palace," the group sat and relaxed for the first time since their ordeal began. Though they were eager to press on and get going, fatigue won out. Some time during the discussion of all that had happened, Owen fell asleep. Emily must have been close behind him, if she were only waking up now as well.

Being trapped in that closet was not much fun, remembered Owen, though James thought it was hilarious when Edgar had used those words. No one else laughed, because no one else found it funny. James was letting loose his ignorant side. Outside, meanwhile, the fairies continued their relentless assault on the door, but thankfully it had no more impact than hail on a stone cottage.

"Quite exciting, isn't it?" chirped Edgar. He was the only one who seemed to be enjoying himself. It was hard to take him seriously with those giant goggles on his forehead and Bea draped over his shoulder. "New here?" he asked. No one answered as he looked around, and finally he settled on trying his luck with Lucas. "You're a big fellow. Not missed many a meal, have you?" Lucas just glowered at him.

"Sorry, who are you?" asked Owen.

"Edgar!" he said eagerly. "My name is Edgar Culshaw, and I name myself 'Master of the Grotto.'" He said the last part in a mock deep voice. If he expected pleasure or admiration of this title, he was sorely disappointed.

"This Grotto?" asked Emily. Edgar nodded. "The Grotto we're trapped in?" Edgar nodded again.

"Idiot," said James. "If you're the master, how can we be trapped? Shouldn't those fairies listen to you?"

Edgar frowned at the comment, partly because he was called an idiot but mainly because it implied he didn't have a plan. Edgar *always* had a plan. "I *always* have a plan," he repeated out loud.

"Reassuring," muttered James. More fairies thudded against the door.

Nothing happened, and no one spoke for a few minutes. Owen finally cleared his throat in an attempt to get Edgar to reveal his so-called plan. "Sir?"

Edgar turned and stared at him, Bea's hornbook rings clanging softly as he did so. Turning in the confined space wasn't easy, especially with Bea hanging like that, so he wound up bouncing the unconscious girl partly off Emily and James. "Yes?"

"The plan?"

"Right!" he said as though he'd just remembered where he was. "A plan! Good idea!"

Owen nodded and waited.

"What's the plan?" Edgar asked eagerly.

"*I'll kill him!*" James roared as he tried to raise his arms in the tight space. Lucas shifted slightly to somewhat pin the enraged boy against the wall.

The pushing and shoving in the closet had everyone complaining. Emily had her foot stomped on ("Sorry," Lucas muttered), Bea was smacking into people, and James was thrashing about. Emily was asking if there was a way out, and the Index faithfully chimed and suggested opening the door, but no one thought that sounded like a good idea. The fracas did allow Owen a chance to grab the Battledoor and bring it up to look at, but the screen was blank. Edgar's face, however, lit up when he saw it.

"You have it!" he breathed, looking pleased. Immediately after that, his face changed to a mask of agony. "Why do you have it? You shouldn't have it. It's gone. I got rid of it. I saved everything. If it's here, nothing is saved, and I'm in trouble. But that can't be, since I got rid of it. He wanted it, so I stopped him and saved the boy. No, it can't be here. It's not here." At the end of his rant, he relaxed considerably, deciding that the Battledoor wasn't here and he was clearly imagining it.

"You know what this is?" asked Owen as he lifted it higher.

Edgar's eyes focused and unfocused as he glanced at it and then tried to look past it. "Know what *what* is?"

"*This*," Owen insisted and pushed it against the man's face. Normally, Owen wouldn't be quite so direct, but he was stuck in a closet, and whoever this guy was, he hadn't bathed in a while, so the desire to get *out* of the closet was growing steadily.

In his face (one corner was pushing up his nose), Edgar finally had to face facts. "Yes," he said in a weak voice. "I know what that is. But it should be *gone*," he protested.

"Well, it isn't. It's here. With us."

Edgar brightened immediately, forgetting whatever it was that had him upset. "We can use it to get out of here!" he said.

Owen tapped at the screen, but nothing happened. "Can't," he said. "It's not working."

Edgar looked at him as though he were trying to open a door by pushing on it when the label clearly read "pull." "Don't tell me you don't know how to use it," he said scathingly.

Not in the mood, Owen shoved it into the man's hands. "Then I won't tell you. Get us out of here."

Slowly, reverently, Edgar stroked the surface of the Battledoor. "It looks so different," he said. "Stranger than I've ever seen. Much different than when I held it. It changes, you know, to suit the reader. The Protagonist."

That word again. Mangus had used it to describe him when he was in the alley, but Owen dismissed it out of hand. He didn't want to be the one in charge, anyway. A protagonist was the person the story followed, the hero, and meant that everything was riding on that person's shoulders. It had been a heavy burden so far, and if he could pass it on to Edgar, so much the better. "I'm no protagonist," he said quietly.

"No, but you're a pain-in-my-ass-ist," said James. "I don't care which one of you rubs the magic lamp, but use the stupid thing to get us out of here. Crazy-man here smells like a pit stain."

"Nice," said Emily as she shot him a withering look.

For all the arguing, Edgar seemed not to hear. He held the Battledoor like a long lost treasure for a bit longer, and then gently reached out and placed it back in Owen's hands. "It's not mine," he said. "Not my burden. Not my story. Not any more. Mine ended."

"Well, ours haven't," Owen persisted. "How do I use it?"

He hesitated, but the banging on the door was still happening at a consistent rate, and past experience had taught Edgar that the fairy-folk don't give up quickly. "It offers choices," said Edgar, and Owen nodded ruefully. "You understand, I see. I expect you've had to make a couple already."

"Not many, so far."

"There will be more, I fear. A great deal more. Even once you think you're done. There are always more." That was not comforting to hear, but Owen kept quiet and waited. "But you can use it to some degree when it's quiet. You can force a few doorways and a few passages, but the thing needs time to cool off after. It doesn't advance your story any, so don't get your hopes up there, but it can get you out of a tight jam or two."

He reached out for the book. "May I?"

Owen handed it back to him. Edgar lifted the book and rested it against the door. He hadn't noticed it before, or perhaps it hadn't been there before, but there was a small recess in the door itself that the book fit into.

"Place it and speak the words," he mumbled. He held it with one hand and waited for Owen to reach up and hold it in place. Once Edgar let go and Owen held it on its own, the book sank in a bit deeper and the door thrummed.

"What do I say?" Owen asked.

"There are a lot of options," mused Edgar. "I tried a great deal myself. Some worked, others didn't. None led home," he finished unhappily.

"I'll settle for at a way out of here," snapped James.

"My home," said Edgar. "He hasn't found it yet, so it's safe for now. As safe as any place for a Protagonist. For a time, anyway."

"Who is 'He'?" asked Emily. It was the second time Edgar had made a vague reference to some strange man, Owen noticed, and he was as curious as she was. Unhelpfully, the Index did not respond.

Edgar ignored her and focused on Owen. "Yes, it's the best place. Hold it tight, focus on the screen, and say 'Edgar's Cave. I choose this path.'"

Taking a deep breath, Owen did as he was told. The fairies continued to hammer, and their flashes could still be seen through the cracks of the border of the door. Edgar was cheerful again after his brief bout of solemnity and turned the handle. Emily and James both shouted at the same time, convinced that the man was going to send them to their deaths, but the door swung open into a dank, dimly lit cave. A huge boulder hung from the ceiling in the centre with great tree roots holding it in place. A few candles were still smouldering from the rock outcroppings while a great deal of melted wax indicated that he'd been living here for some time. There was a rough-looking mattress and a selection of canned goods strewn about.

At once, Edgar went through the door, Bea flopping gently on his shoulder. The rest stayed in the closet, mouths agape, because every indication had been and still was that there should be fairies where there was now a cave. Still, they had wanted a way out, and there weren't any alternatives. Unlike their previous adventures, there was no second choice.

Except there is, Owen thought. *Making no choice is still making a choice. We can stay and hope they fly away, or I can go with this man who can maybe help me figure out how to use the Battledoor.* Steadying himself, he stepped forward into the cave, taking a moment to pry the book out of the door. As soon as he did, it began to shudder and close. Taking this as a cue to move, Emily, Lucas, and James followed behind. Within seconds of passing through, the door was gone and the smooth wall of a cave replaced it.

They had been down here ever since, though for how long was a bit of a mystery. With no light and his impromptu nap, Owen had no clue if they'd been here for ten minutes or ten hours. The sleep had done him some good, though, as he felt better for having had it. Emily still sat by him, watching him as he shook the last cobwebs from his mind.

"Want to talk about it?" she asked. "Your dream?"

The funny thing was, he kind of did. Normally, Owen refused to talk about his mother because the sharing of it was too raw. It kind of amused him that now that he was in this strange place, he felt like letting someone in. It was just the two of them at the moment, anyway. Owen saw Edgar up ahead, standing by his mattress and gesturing wildly at Lucas and James, both of whom seemed amused and distracted. Bea was either still unconscious or asleep on Edgar's mattress.

"My mom died last year," he said. The words hurt coming out.

"Oh," Emily said, suddenly shy. "I know. I mean, I'd heard. I'm sorry."

"Thanks," said Owen. "I dream about her sometimes. A lot, actually."

"And it makes you sad? Was she very sick? I know that's really personal to ask."

"It's okay. No, she wasn't sick. There was an accident at work. She was fine, then she wasn't. Just like that. My dad said she didn't feel any pain." But Owen had. Even now, he wanted to cry. If he started, he didn't think he could stop, and he didn't want to cry in front of Emily.

"Is that what you were dreaming about?" she asked. "The accident?"

"No," he said. Thinking about it, he smiled. "No, it was a memory. I had a crush on this girl, Amanda Mitchell, and she was a b-word." Emily raised her eyebrow at him, and he chuckled. "Well, okay, she wasn't, but it was the third grade equivalent."

Emily laughed. "Been there," she said. "Though for me it was a jerk of a guy. Hopefully I wasn't the b-word girl back then."

"I don't think that's possible," he said. Blushing, he cleared his throat and continued. "Anyway, my mom made me feel better. My dad, too, later on. She said there was a girl waiting for me and that I'd find her one day. My dad was quite romantic in general and waxed on about how 'true love will find you in the end.' That's also the title of a song."

"Tell me," she said. "What did he say?"

"I asked him when and how that he knew my mom was 'the one.'"

"And?"

"He looked at me and said 'it was this morning.' Before I could ask, he kept going. 'It was yesterday. The day before. Months ago, years ago, the moment you were born, a few moments ago when I saw her in your eyes. You have your mother's eyes.' He told me that he keeps falling in love with her all the time, usually when he least expects it, and that each and every time it takes his breath away and it's the first moment all over again. He said there were so many moments that to just name one would cheapen all the rest. 'That's what true love is,' he told me. 'Not at first sight, but at each new shared moment.'"

Emily had tears in her eyes. "That's beautiful," she said. "Your mom was very lucky."

"We both were," Owen said sadly. Thinking about what he had lost was painful, but he couldn't even begin to imagine how it affected his father to wake up each day and not have your true love beside him. As grateful as he was to have Emily by his side at that moment, Owen wondered if he might not be better off alone to potentially spare himself the kind of pain his father went through each day.

"I like that," she said. "I like the idea that love doesn't just happen across a room, but it builds over time. And through friendship." She reached out and gently took his hand.

Owen looked in her eyes as she said that and felt the unspoken promise just under the words. *This is it*, he thought. *My moment.* He began to lean forward slightly, and she did not move away.

"Hey, butt-stain," came the cold voice of James Vanier, echoing in the dark chamber. "Welcome back. Now that you've had your nappy, can you try not to mess your pants and get us out of here?"

Emily shot him a cold stare and slipped her hand out of Owen's. "You are so obnoxious. We wouldn't even be here if it weren't for you."

James returned her stare with an even harder one. "And you might not be here much longer, if it were up to me."

Before the tension reached the boiling point, Edgar leapt over to join them. He had some netting in his hands and a couple of ugly, wriggling fish caught in it. "Who's hungry?" he asked. "I thought we might even cook them!"

CHAPTER 16

The smell of frying fish was intoxicating and could wake the hunger even in a dead man. The closest thing in Edgar's Cave at that moment was Bea, who was doing her best to fit the bill. The smell won out, and she began to wake.

"Mmmm… whuzzat?" she mumbled as she tried to raise her head. She had a nice, shiny red bump on her forehead that stood out proudly like a trophy on a mantel. She licked her lips and looked around in a daze, her frumpy hair mussed about as though it had earned ten years worth of bed-head all at once. "Breakfast? Mom? Dinner? Izzat cheeseburgers?"

"Get her," came James's snotty voice. "Passed out and nothing wakes her. Not talking, not shaking, not even water in the face."

"That wasn't nice, James," scolded Emily.

"No, but it was funny," snickered James. Lucas joined in but stifled it when he saw the look on Emily's face. "Water didn't do it, but cook some food and… Pig… *she*… wakes right up."

"Food?" repeated Bea dimly.

"Yes!" exclaimed Edgar. "Food is good for you to eat! Even my lovely fried fish. The secret ingredient is…"

"Don't let him tell you the secret ingredient!" shouted Emily, bringing Edgar to a halt. "It smells good. Leave it at that."

"Cheeseburger?" murmured Bea.

"No, fish," said Edgar. "What's a cheeseburger? It sounds delicious!"

Bea sat up and wiped a bit of spittle at the side of her mouth. She was still a little dazed as she looked about the room, but her eyes lit up when she focused on Edgar. "Hey there!" she said in the most seductive voice she could find, which wasn't pleasant given that her mouth felt like it was full of cotton balls. "Cheeseburger. You know. Ground beef flattened into a patty with melted cheese on top."

"Never heard of it. Sounds messy."

"Are you kidding?" asked Bea. "How can you not know what a cheeseburger is? What, have you been living under a rock?"

"Yes!" said Edgar happily and pointed up to the large boulder above them. Bea looked up and stared at it for a moment, before looking around wildly as she tried to figure out where she was.

"Please stop talking about food," groaned James. "I'd kill for a cheeseburger."

"You'd kill for a lot less than that," muttered Owen, though thankfully James didn't hear the comment.

"It certainly *sounds* wonderful!" said Edgar. "Very similar to the Hamburg steak. I've had one a few times. Very popular in Germany. Are you German?"

"No, I'm Canadian," she said. "Where am I?"

Edgar looked puzzled. "You're under my rock. Didn't we just establish that?"

"Why am I under a rock?"

"Because it's where I live."

"But *why?*"

"Because we needed to go somewhere."

Emily coughed. "Give up, Bea. It's no use. You'll just go round in circles with him."

Bea looked delighted at the idea. "I'd go anywhere with him."

Edgar frowned. "Looks like the fairy-flashing has settled in for a mite longer than I suspected. Perhaps I'm just used to them. Might not last much longer, or it could." He shoved his pan from face to face. "Fish?"

Owen reached out for a greasy bit of fish near the edge of the pan and popped it into his mouth. The fish burned a little, but it was totally worth it. This was perhaps the best thing he'd ever tasted. "How much longer will she be like that?" he asked, licking his fingers.

"Oh, a few minutes. Forever. One or the other." Edgar noticed that the other two boys were eyeing the fish and not listening to a word he said. "Of course! It's ready! Let's break our fast together!"

Neither Lucas nor James needed more prodding. They eagerly scooped out the bits of fish closest to them and began to wolf them down. Judging by the happy sounds they were making, the fish was as delicious to them as it had been to Owen. Bea scrambled past Edgar to the pan and began to eat as well. Only Emily didn't join in the frenzy.

"What do you mean, 'forever'?" Emily asked.

Edgar looked back to her, confusion on his face for a minute, then it registered what she was talking about. "In rare cases only," he said in a soothing voice. "But even then it doesn't change anything else about them or hurt them. They're just infatuated. Besides, I'm quite handsome. Perhaps she would have liked me either way."

"But this is awful!" complained Emily.

"I wouldn't trouble yourself about it," he said dismissively. "I have no interest in having a new companion, now or ever. *Adventure* is my bride! *Danger* is my constant companion!"

James laughed. "And rocks are his best friend!"

This stopped Edgar short, and a pained look spread across his face. "No," he said softly. "My best friend is long gone. Happy, I hope. But gone."

Bea looked up at him, a piece of fish slopped against her chin. "Oh no," she said, her mouth partly full. "Wha' happen oo 'im?"

"That did," said Edgar, pointing to Owen's Battledoor. He moved over to the boy and held out his hands for the book. Reluctantly, Owen lifted it and placed it into the man's hands. Unlike the others who had held the book, it thrummed and glowed ever so softly at his touch before going mute again. It reacted to him the way an old friend waves a hand in friendship across a busy street. 'Just passing by, wanted to say hi,' it seemed to say. He looked up and met Owen's eyes. "This was mine, you know. At least, I was the last person to own it. I think. Where did you get it? No matter. No mind. I had it. I owned it. I told the story."

Everyone had quieted down to hear the tale, the only sounds coming from the smacking and chewing of Edgar's fish. Emily moved over to sit in between Bea and Owen, gratefully accepting a helping of the fish that Owen had kept to the side, where it was enviously watched by James and Lucas.

"A story for those in the story?" asked Edgar as he clapped his hands. "Very well! I've told it often enough, and it seems to me that you lot are the ones who most need to hear it. Though there are no cheeseburgers in this story. Do you have one? No matter. As I've told you all, my name is Edgar Culshaw, and I was born into a wealthy English family in Bolton, which isn't terribly far from Manchester. My father was an industrialist and assured me that automation, steam, and factories were going to change the shape of the world. My mother, who did not come from money, had grand aspirations of the kind of social success she had found in the small community. She wanted me happily wed while my father wanted me to follow in his footsteps. To my everlasting shame, or at least to theirs, I wanted neither.

"Wait, what year are you from?" James asked.

"Shhh!" Emily said. "Don't interrupt."

"Yeah, though later maybe we can address that," Owen said. "I'm kinda curious."

"Year?" Edgar asked. "It's this year. Current. Odd thing to ask. Silly, in fact!"

"Please keep going, sweetie," Bea cooed. "Your parents?"

"Yes," Edgar nodded. "Well, the look on their faces as I repeatedly refused their offers was difficult to deal with, I must confess, but I felt my calling lay elsewhere. I had none to confide in but the houseboy, whom I had taken under my wing. He followed me everywhere and listened to my tales and my dreams. If I said I wanted to sail to the colonies, he would have picked up and come with me without hesitation. You know it's funny, but I never thought to ask him what he wanted. One didn't ask servants what they wished for, they were simply to accept what was given or do what was asked. I don't even know if he had parents he lived with, though I surely doubt it. When I first met the lad, he was begging in the streets and stealing from pockets. That's how I met him, you know. I was coming from the theatre and felt a tug on my coat and looked down at a filthy mess of rags and dirt with these large, mesmerizing blue eyes. When he grinned at me, the sides of his eyes crinkled slightly.

"I was about to ask him what his business was when he tugged hard one last time and bolted for it through the streets. The rogue had torn a hole in my new coat and taken my notebook! I had filled its pages with wonders I hoped to see and places I wanted to travel to, and now the wretch had it in his grasp. I gave chase after the lad and finally cornered him in an alley. I told him no harm would come to him if he just returned what he had taken. I got within a few feet of him, and he threw it up into the air, punched me in the stomach, and tried to duck around me.

"Though he had knocked the wind out of me, I stuck out a lazy foot and tripped him up, sending him flat onto the ground. He never yelled, he never even *spoke*, nor complained. He just lay there, looking utterly defeated.

"I headed back to the street, not once wanting to look back, for if I did I might call out to him and insult him or mock him, but I couldn't do it. I was almost around the bend when I did look back, and he was still just lying there, staring at me. It gave me pause. For the first time in a long time, I stopped thinking about *my* book, *my* adventures, *my* plans, and what I wanted for *my* life and wondered what it was this boy was after. Surely not just a notebook, but what that notebook might do for him. Mayhaps he knew someone who would give him some food or a bit of coin.

"I thought of my father in that instance. Though I did not want to follow in his footsteps, I knew he was a great man who was kind and patient. I recalled one instance when we walked down a busy street and shared some food from a vendor selling chestnuts. They were delicious, and I could have easily eaten another bag, and I had a bit of coin in my pocket burning to do just that. When we passed the vendor again later, my father went up to buy another bag, and I asked for the like. As we received our food, we started walking back down the street, and I popped the first warm morsel into my mouth and looked to my father, expecting to see him do the same. Instead, he bent down to a man of the streets who was huddled under a blanket and gave him the whole bag and told him he wished it could be more.

"I felt the fool. I was stuffing my own face while my father gave his away. I never forgot that moment and how proud I was of what he had done. So as I looked back to that boy lying in the alley, I knew I had to go back and do for him what my father had done for that other soul so long ago. I went back, hauled the wretch up, and kept a grip on his collar as we went around the corner into a small shop. The shopkeepers were less than thrilled to have a street urchin in their shop, but the look of my money was enough to get them to hold their tongues. I fed him until he nearly burst and a smile stole across his lips. Afterwards, I bid him farewell and headed home. He followed me the entire way, though at a small distance, and I let him. Once I was home, I put him in the servants' quarters and he remained there until. . ."

Edgar trailed off at that point, and everyone assumed the worst. Considering that he was here inside the story with them, his friend had either been left behind or had come and something had happened to him along the way. Bea reached out a hand and rubbed his arm for support.

James was less tactful. "I call B.S.," he said. "No way. You're talking nonsense. You don't know what a cheeseburger is, you want to travel to the 'colonies' and how 'factories are the future.' You're full of crap. You act like you think it's 1880 or something." Lucas grunted an agreement, and even Emily looked sceptical.

The insult was reflected in the man's face. "You're quite insolent, you know. I am more with the times than that, though as someone who has been there, you ought to show more respect for the efforts of the people who came before you."

Owen leaned forward. "Been there?" he asked. "Edgar, what year is it for you?"

Edgar gave him a look like he had two heads. "The same year it is for all of us. I went into the story three years ago, by my count. The year should be 1895."

There was a sharp intake of breath from all of them. *It isn't possible,* Owen thought. *He can't have been in here for more than a hundred and twenty years. If that holds true, if that much time has passed on the outside world, then is it speeding up for us? Have I been missing for weeks instead of hours? My dad must be freaking out. I have to get out of here. I can't do this to him, not after Mom.*

"What?" asked Edgar, surprised at the silence. "What is it?"

Emily shifted uncomfortably. "Edgar," she began, "I don't know how to tell you this…"

"Tell me what?"

"It's 2018, dummy," said James. He began to laugh. "Either you're crazy or the best-looking old guy ever, but it's 2018. So cut the crap act. Not falling for it."

No one else was laughing, not even Lucas, who looked deep in thought. Tears began to form at the corners of Edgar's eyes. "It's not," he said weakly. "Not possible. The boy? My mother. My father…"

Bea continued to rub his back to try to soothe him. "It's okay, sweetie," she said. "Just keep telling your story." She got only sobs in return, and they all knew not to push it. One by one they moved away to give him time to grieve for the life he had once had. Owen wanted nothing more than to ask when and how the Battledoor came into Edgar's life, but that was to be a story for another time.

OWEN, EMILY, and Bea lounged under one of the gnarled tree roots that had grown into a couch of sorts. Side by side, they fit snugly on the root branch and had been talking over options for the better part of an hour. They knew they couldn't stay here much longer, because they had to find their way back home. The decision made, they fell silent. The only sound now came from the jangle of the green metal-lined hornbooks as Bea tossed them into the air. She seemed especially fond of them now that

Edgar had put one of them to use. Though she hadn't seen it for herself, she clutched the rest of them possessively and elicited a promise from him to show her how they worked as soon as possible.

James and Lucas sat off to the side. They were part of the talks at first, but James's temper had flared more than once, and finally the boy moved off to scowl in the comfort of the darkness. Lucas managed a few more minutes but seemed to sense he didn't quite belong with this group, and he sauntered off to find his friend.

Though none of them said it, they were all waiting for Edgar. Owen in particular wanted a few minutes of the man's time so they could talk about the Battledoor and how to use it. Crazy or not, and who wouldn't be after being forced to live underground for three years, Edgar was their best chance of escape.

Bea lazily tossed a hornbook again, but this time it slipped to her fingers and clattered on the floor.

"Be careful!" shouted Edgar, his voice thunderous after the long silence the group had shared. They hadn't seen him approach in the gloom, but he quickly shuffled into the light and scooped up the fallen ring. He gave it back to Bea as gently as if he were passing a kitten.

"Why does she have to be careful?" asked Owen. "What are they? They were just normal hornbooks before, now they're... different."

"It's this place," said Edgar. "Here, the rules are different. Back in the outside world, books are tomes with words and ideas, but here those words and ideas are made real in the right hands. Or the wrong ones, for that matter."

"What's a hornbook?" asked James. It was the most polite he'd been in a while.

He seemed like he was going to protest, but Edgar nodded resignedly. The shock from knowing he'd missed a century seemed to have poured some sense into him. He was thinking and speaking clearly at the moment, and Owen wanted to get as much out of him as he could.

"Times have changed," Edgar muttered. "A hornbook, in my time... will I ever get used to saying that? It was an instructional tool. They had the alphabet, scripture, or other facts that children needed to study. They were useful items to have. Get you out of a tough situation, so long as you had the right one at hand.

"Here, they're more focused. If you have one here, they develop a specific use, some of them one time only, and all of them precious. You just have to know what it's to be used for, grip it, say the words, then reach in and pull out what you want."

"Like a rabbit out of a magician's hat," said Emily, nodding in understanding. "That's where the smoke came from that you used on the fairies, isn't it? One of the hornbooks?"

"Quite so," said Edgar. "Though sadly, that one is lost to us now. I had to throw it on the ground to get it to work. A great shame. My mother would use the strap on me if she saw me treat a book so disrespectfully."

"Come on," said James. "That's a bit much, isn't it? There was a hornbook about *smoke* in the real world?"

"No, not as such," said Edgar. "As I said, the rules are a bit strange. Each hornbook takes on a particular talent or use here, sometimes unrelated to the real world. Luck of the draw, you might say. It is even likely that these hornbooks have been bent to serve the story of the Protagonist. They might be here to serve your story, Owen. Ooh! Might one of them be the cheeseburger you were talking about?"

Bea lifted the tangle of books at her belt to show Edgar. "I dunno. How can you tell?" she asked.

One by one he inspected them, muttering to himself each time. Finally, he brought one up and traced a finger along a silver line in the middle of the green metal. It was small and faint, and as much as Owen strained, he couldn't make out anything useful.

Edgar reached out for Bea's hand. "May I?" he asked. She blushed furiously and held out her hand delicately, as though they were about to dance. James snorted a laugh in the corner.

Very gently, Edgar used Bea's finger to trace the edge of the hornbook. "You see," he said, "one of the greatest assets of the hornbook is that they require reading. You can't look at one and know what it is. You have to read it. Once you trace your finger or move your hand along it, you can figure it out."

"Maybe throw it in the fire to reveal the secret language of Mordor," Owen said. Everyone looked at him strangely. He guessed that there were no *Lord of the Rings* fans in the group.

"Rope," said Emily, moving on. "It says 'rope'!"

"Quite so," said Edgar with a smile. "Try another."

Eagerly, Bea traced her hands on the other two hornbooks. "This one is 'Light.' That could be useful!"

"It could be," agreed Edgar. "But much like anything here, you should be careful. The hornbooks are literal but not specific. It could be a beam, it could be sunlight, or it could be a light flickering. A trickle of light is one thing. Concentrated sunlight would be blinding. Permanently!"

She traced her finger on the last one. "It's 'food'!" she said excitedly. That made Owen groan. They had a source of food the whole time, meaning that making Harris chase them down had been an unnecessary risk. He felt more foolish now than he did at the start.

"Very good," beamed Edgar. "But remember, it's literal, not specific. It might be fairy food for all we know. Best to leave it be, anyway. We're full of fish!"

"Weren't *we* almost fairy food?" asked James. Edgar raised an eyebrow at him and nodded in agreement, making James recoil in horror once he realized that *any* kind of food might come out. "Oh god!" he said. "Seriously? Yeah, let's pass on the food option. I don't want any of your long pork."

"What's that?" asked Edgar. "Like a cheeseburger?"

"You don't want to know," said Owen. Thankfully, Edgar let it drop.

"Three of you are outfitted for survival, leastways," said Edgar, wiping his hands on his pants. "Though you only have the green hornbooks. It might be that I can help you with that."

"There are other colours?" asked Emily.

Edgar shuffled through a pile of stuff in a corner of the cave. He'd examine an item for a moment then toss it aside. Finally, he pulled out a couple of blue rings and another green, along with a tattered black belt. "Here we are!" he said happily. "Yes, my dear. There are other colours. Blue, for instance, which we have here, are weapons."

James and Lucas perked up at this, much to Owen's dismay. Edgar clearly didn't know who he was dealing with here, as giving weapons to those two was a bad idea on a number of levels. "May I?" Owen asked, hoping to snag the weapons first.

"No!" said Edgar, quite pleased with himself. "You can't! You've got the Battledoor, which is more than enough. It wouldn't tolerate anything else. If you're the Protagonist, you've got the power of choice, which is more than the rest have."

"What about me?" asked Emily. She had shared a knowing look with Owen and knew the danger this presented. "I only have the Index."

"Really?" asked Edgar. He was surprised and worried all at once. They were used to his mood swings, but something about his reaction bothered Owen. Having the Index didn't seem like a positive in Edgar's book. "No, I don't think so. Not quite right."

Finally, the moment Owen dreaded came. "I'll take it," said James. "Not to worry, Owey-boy, I got your back."

This seemed to please Edgar to no end. "Good, good! I see you don't have a belt, but I have one here." He was about to hand it over and paused. "Though I should warn you, I don't like this belt. I got it from a trader, a shifty fellow, and it never quite fit right. Most hang freely, but this one… clings. Belts are meant for support, you see, not to bind you. I felt… dirty."

"Whatever," said James, who grabbed the belt and clipped it on. The tattered black leather smoothed at once and flowed, much like the others had done. It didn't stop there, though, and molded itself to his jeans and up under his shirt. James shuddered when that happened but didn't offer any thoughts or show any interest in exploring it further, so the others let it drop. One by one, Edgar clipped the two blue rings onto his belt.

James traced the lines roughly as though to get it over with. "'Shield,'" he said. "Cool. 'Sword'! Even better." *Now he has two knives*, thought Owen, not knowing the other was safely tucked into Lucas's pocket.

Edgar turned apologetically to Lucas. "I'm sorry, lad, but I am out of tricks." He spread his hands to show they were empty. "But a lad as big and strong as you, I'm sure tricks are the last things you need." He looked around the space to see if there was anything he could offer him. Finally, his eyes lighted on his badminton racket, and he scooped it up. "Here! Take this! This was a handy weapon for me that I pulled out of a blue ring ages ago. Quite useful." He handed it over to Lucas, and it looked even smaller and more pitiful in his hands than it had in Edgar's. Regardless, Edgar looked quite pleased with himself and nodded in approval.

"That's it, then," said Edgar. "You're ready to go!"

"Aren't you coming with us?" asked Owen. It hadn't occurred to him that Edgar might not come, and he was filling with panic.

"My story is done," said Edgar. He seemed to think that was obvious and therefore the end of it.

"But it's not," protested Bea. "You haven't told us how you got here or what happened to your friend!"

"You haven't told me how to use the book," added Owen.

The man hesitated, clearly torn about what to do. "Beatrice, my lady, I am sorry, but the tale will have to wait."

"And me?" asked Owen. "I can't do this without you."

"Of course you can!" said Edgar. "I'm not going. My time is done, and it has already cost me one friend and a hundred years of living. My friends, family, all of them are surely dead by now, and I'm in no rush to join them. I don't belong with you. I don't belong anywhere, really."

Edgar saw the disappointment on Owen's face, and sympathy bloomed on his own. Perhaps he was thinking back to the boy lying in the alley. He had only to take another step and be around the corner back then. One step, and he could have left it all behind. But he didn't. For his sake, for his father's sake, and for the boy's sake, Owen hoped he'd help. He had already fed them at the very least, but knowledge filled the mind the way food filled the belly.

"I won't send you off clueless," he said, settling whatever internal debate he'd been fighting. "Come, Owen, let us go for a walk and learn about choosing your own adventure and making use of the Battledoor."

CHAPTER 17

"You've got to be kidding me," Owen said as he looked dubiously at the small hole in front of him.

"What?" asked Edgar, who was motioning him forward encouragingly. "Not at all, not at all. Go on, then. Squeeze through." He gestured toward the hole with a smile.

Owen wasn't buying it. Edgar had told him they would take a stroll outside and that the only way to get outside was to squeeze through a tangle of roots and rocks before popping out under a giant tree on the other side. "No way," he said. "I'll Winnie-the-Pooh myself. No deal."

"I don't know what that means," said Edgar cheerfully. "Get on with you."

Swallowing nervously, Owen knew he had no choice. The fat fictional bear got himself stuck in a hole like this searching for honey, and the idea of getting trapped underground made Owen sweat and his heart race. Still, Pooh needed his honey, and Owen needed his answers. He got down on his hands and knees then started to push and pull himself through. The rocks and roots scraped and pulled at him but allowed him through. His heart hammered in his chest and sweat poured off his brow, but he made it.

The daylight on the other side was a brilliant thing, and the relief was tremendous. He didn't think even seeing Emily right now would trump his feelings of joy. Edgar slipped out behind him, looking quite pleased. He'd clearly done it many times, as he was totally free of dirt, while Owen looked like he'd been a mudslide victim.

"Right then, let's go for a stroll," Edgar said. He walked off without waiting for an answer. "We won't go far. There's a stone wall and a nice little clearing over here. Sometimes I go here to think."

About what? Owen wondered. *Rocks and stones and crazy thoughts, probably.* He held his tongue. *I just want to know how to use this, get my friends home, see my dad.* He debated within himself for a moment. *On second thought, you can keep James and Lucas.* He immediately felt annoyed with himself for the unworthy thought.

Once they were at the clearing, Edgar spread his arms wide and closed his eyes, letting the smell, the light, and the warmth of the place wash over him. Tired and eager though he was to get on with it, even Owen had to admire how the place seemed like a slice of paradise. Out in the open, he saw the high, domed walls with flickering lights and thousands of doors and felt the fear rise in his chest.

"Edgar!" he said. "We're still in the Grotto!"

"Of course, my lad. This is my home. My story may have ended, but I kept on living. I've stayed in place. I've bookmarked myself, if you can forgive the analogy."

"But why? There must be other places in this world you could have gone. Why stay someplace so dangerous?"

Edgar looked a bit sad, but also resigned. "This is the place of my greatest defeat and my greatest triumph," he said. "I valued friendship over myself. I made a sacrifice that I've never regretted. Also, should anyone ever come looking for me, this is where they would start. I suppose, now, I know that no one is coming."

"Are you talking about your best friend? The boy?"

He nodded. "Indeed. He'd be a very old man now, should he even still be alive. We were being chased by the villain of the piece and his brood. He got away, thankfully. Hopefully he lived a good long life. The villain, however… he's not to be trifled with, especially with that swarm at his heels."

"Who is he?"

"Isn't it obvious?" said Edgar with a wink. "He's the Antagonist."

In a frustrating sort of way, it made perfect sense. Owen had been labelled the Protagonist, which in literature was a fancy way of saying who the reader was in support of, the person the story mostly focuses on. That didn't necessarily mean that the protagonist of a book was a good person, just that the story was told from their perspective. Owen thought of that TV show, *Dexter*, about the guy who works for the police and analyzes blood splatters at crime scenes but in his spare time is a serial killer who hunts down murderers. *Like James*, he thought, before dismissing it. *Hopefully not. I don't want to be in a story that supports a guy like that.* On a show like *Dexter*, even though in real life you'd hope people would be against him, when the story is told from his perspective you find yourself rooting for them, weird as that might sound.

The antagonist of a story was the flip side. It could be a character, a group, an organization, anything at all that worked against the protagonist. Without conflict, there can be no resolution. Without conflict, there's no point to the story and no ending. Without the climax, we can't get to the conclusion. Owen sighed and knew that things were going to get much harder for him before they got easier.

Edgar correctly took Owen's silence for understanding. "Sorry to be the bearer of bad news. No one wants to find out they have an archenemy, especially one they've never met before."

"Why do I have to have an enemy?" asked Owen.

"To fight," said Edgar simply. "To grow. To prove yourself worthy. In a book, to be *entertaining*."

"To get crapped on, you mean."

"Is it really so hard to understand? In the serials I used to read as a boy, the hero of the piece never catches a break. If the hero is happy, then there is nothing to overcome. It's *boring*."

Owen would have loved to be bored right now, but he got it clearly enough. In the comics he read, characters like Spider-Man had been around since the 1960s. They always got beat up, they quit, they fought, they saved the day. If comic characters were ever to come to life, they'd no doubt be ticked off to learn they'd been put through the ringer for the sake of someone's entertainment. When he got back, he'd boycott comics because of their cruelty to their characters. Maybe he'd start an advocacy group. *Think of the suffering of superheroes! Poor Peter Parker! Poor Miles Morales! Poor Bruce Wayne!*

"But this isn't just a story, is it?" Owen asked. "It's my life. It *was* your life. My friends are here, and they didn't ask for any of this either. Not even that idiot James deserves this."

Edgar sat down beside him and put an arm around his shoulders. "My boy, all of life is just a story that gets told the moment we're born to the moment we die. Everything else in between is just leading up to the climax. Even then, the story just rolls on without us. On and on until whatever end comes."

"Death?"

"Perhaps."

"Can we die here?"

"We can die anywhere. No rules about *that.* When I was a lad, I heard about a woman who died falling out of bed one morning. She should have been as safe as pillows, but a two-foot fall was all that was needed."

Grim, thought Owen. "Well, what can I do to put it off as long as possible, then?"

"Ha!" clapped Edgar, rising to his feet. "Now we're talking! Other than a good diet and exercise (not to mention a great degree of luck), here in the World we can *read* ourselves a better way out."

"Does that mean I can avoid this Antagonist? Does he have a name?"

"I don't think so," said Edgar, answering the first question. "I never could, anyway. Always one step behind me. Luck. And those beasts. And yes, he does have a name, though I'm not fond of it. The name isn't important. You'll know him when you'll see him, and I fear you'll see him soon enough. He has a way of finding you. We can deal with all of that later, however. Let's get to it, shall we?"

Owen nodded and got to his feet. Whatever the future held in store for him, he was going to do his best to meet it head-on. It was the sort of thing his mother would have done, and he knew she'd be proud of him right now. "What do I do first?"

"Nothing!" said Edgar.

Frowning and instantly deflated, Owen sat back down. "Insane," he muttered.

Edgar reached out and pulled him back to his feet. "I'm being serious, lad, there's a great deal of nothing to do and nothing to do about it but nothing. The Battledoor is about presenting choices when a decision needs to be made. You could stay in my cave for the rest of your life, and the thing would remain silent because nothing new is going to happen. Once you move out of a safe spot like that, you put yourself on the path of not only your own destiny but anyone else's you cross paths with.

"Look at it this way: you think, you feel, you breathe, but so does everyone else. You only think the world revolves around you because you can't see inside the hearts and minds of anyone else. You make decisions about who to love, where to work, where to travel, and so forth because you want to see them, but you can't control the outcome, only guide it as best you can."

"And that's what the Battledoor does?" asked Owen. "It guides me?"

"No," insisted Edgar. "Backwards. *You* guide *it*."

Looking at the mute tablet in his hands, Owen doubted it. "I can't even get it to turn on."

"Certainly you can, and you will, but only when necessary. Until you've decided to go somewhere or do something and then actually do it, all of your hopes and expectations are merely academic. You can't have experiences without trying. If you go on a trip, you decide where you're going, and once you get there you'll decide what you do.

"The Battledoor has several functions once you're in a story. The main one is that it acts as a physical representation of the choices you need to make to get from the start to the finish. You can go left or you can go right. Once you decide, the book makes it easier for you to get going."

"What if I change my mind?" asked Owen.

"I wondered about that myself," mused Edgar. "It seems that in the real world, you can turn around and go back. Here, however, you can only go forward. You read a book from left to right and turn the page. You can't read a book backward. That would be ridiculous and counter-intuitive."

He's never read manga, thought Owen. He liked the Japanese style of comics well enough, but reading backward took a lot of getting used to. Besides, they still flowed in one direction, even if it was the wrong way. "Okay. The book gives me the choices. I make one then live with the consequences. Got it."

Edgar nodded and continued. "There are two kinds of options the book gives out, in my experience. 'Paths' which direct you left or right (and there's trouble no matter which way I've gone, so don't think you ever get off easy), and then 'Battles,' which, quite literally, involve fighting."

That wasn't something Owen wanted to hear; the experience with the fairies was still fresh in his mind. *Still, it could have been a lot worse.* "One battle it offered me was either 'fairies' or 'furies,'" he said.

Edgar shuddered. "Well, you made the right choice," he said. "Fairies are annoying, but goggles and badminton rackets will do for them. The Furies are a group of very large women with incredible tempers. Greek figures, the Furies. Dated one of them once. Didn't end well. Either way, fighting a battle often leads to a reward to help move the plot along."

Owen laughed. "Are *you* my reward, then?"

Edgar pursed his lips and considered it. "I suppose I am, at that. Hadn't thought of that. Didn't want to think of that. Should stay out of this. Go on, go on, should get going."

Sighing, Owen snapped his fingers. "Go on, then, please."

"Right," said Edgar, coming out his short daze. "The key to using the door is to make the intuitive choice. Go with your gut and don't overthink it. Delaying can be costly. I've heard tales of other Proties who couldn't make up their minds and died for it. Until you, however, I'd never met one, so I couldn't ask to find out for sure."

"If they die, what happens to the book?"

"Don't know," Edgar replied. "Haven't died yet. We must assume it goes back to the real world, though. How else for the likes of us to find it? The point I'm making is that you make the ultimate choice about what happens if you have the Battledoor, and if you work at it you can train your mind and heart to show the clear option."

"How do I do that?" asked Owen.

"Instinct," said Edgar. "Gut feeling. Intuition. And travelling through many more doors to get the rhythm of it. Every now and then, if you're in a pinch and there doesn't seem to be a way out, you can use the book to open a door to a safe point."

"Like we did to get to your cave?" asked Owen.

"Yes," said Edgar. "Exactly. Though it's cheating a little bit. Bending the rules."

"If you can do it, how is it cheating?"

"It's a liberty taken by a higher power than us," said Edgar. "Doors where there ought to be none. Paths that didn't exist a moment before. Kind of like reading ahead or checking out the ending. You spoil the story somewhat and might find yourself in a weaker position for not having earned the knowledge as it was meant to be done."

That much Owen understood. At school, using Google was the main way students sought out information. Much of how Google organizes itself is by what is popular and not necessarily what is accurate. Kids would just go on, copy and paste whatever they saw, not question it, and hand it in. If half of them bothered to read what they were doing, they would know more about the world around them and also would catch some of the facts, or some of the alternative facts, and prevent themselves from looking foolish. In a pinch you did it to stay on top of the work, but making a habit of it would lead to eventual failure. You'd just stay uneducated forever.

"What about the other doors that we saw?" He gestured to the walls around them and the thousands of doors and oddities that lay beyond. These seemed to fall under the category of reading ahead. Unlike the other doors he'd seen so far in his story, they weren't connected to the Battledoor, and nothing was urging them to go through one or more of them. "Are they cheating?"

Edgar took a long look at them all and stared at them wondrously. "They're something different, indeed, and you're wise to ask about them.

Not every door is a path, and not every path is meant to be walked. They're every and any choice that has been made before by a reader, a writer, a creator, a protagonist, or even an antagonist. These doors are ideas made real, and they all come here to live on. I've tried counting and can't do it. I've walked the circumference of this hub of knowledge and never come to the same door twice, even when it should have started over. They move, you see. Every now and then I'll find a familiar door, often when I most need something. It's cheating because it's using the *deus ex machina* of the place."

"What is that?" asked Owen. 'Doing ex macking'?"

"*Deus ex machina*," corrected Edgar. "It's Latin. Translated, it means 'God from the machine' and refers to the control a writer or storyteller has over the world he or she creates. If a writer has painted their characters into a corner, then he or she might introduce a person, an object, or an event that magically gets them out of trouble. It's not always realistic or likely, but it allows the story to move forward. Some call it lazy planning! Others call it imaginative genius. It varies according to skill, of course. That sort of thing is not normally for the likes of us, but the Battledoor allows us to benefit from it in times of great need."

"Is there one here? A door we can use as a shortcut? A secret tool?" asked Owen excitedly, ignoring the confusion on Edgar's face. *If I'm the Protagonist, and this other man is the Antagonist, then that implies someone is pulling the strings the way writers and artists do for the characters in their comics. A higher power. A way out.* "Could we find the Storyteller? Whoever the narrator is, perhaps. A god of sorts."

This idea seemed to stump Edgar, his eyes flickering back and forth as he tried to follow Owen's logic. "I never even considered it," he said to himself. "Makes sense. Of course it makes sense. I've been living in the ground. Someone kept me alive. Telling the story. Bookmarked. Put on hold. Wait list. End of story. He should have killed me. He didn't. They didn't. There and then gone. Me all alone. Waiting." He cast a wary look at Owen. "Waiting for you?"

"I know *I* have been," came a deep, cold voice from the rock outcropping above them. It chilled Owen to the bone until he looked up into the voice's face. One glimpse was all it took, and he was beyond terrified. It was a man, or a shadow of a man. Cloaked in flowing, inky black tar that evaporated into smoke. Smooth grey material pulled tightly over his hands and face. Eyes that shone silver even in the daylight that bent to shadows around his very being. He was every nightmare Owen ever had given form and purpose.

"Ahhh," Vellum said smoothly. *"There you are."*

CHAPTER 18

"What the hell is going on up there?" asked James Vanier irritably. Above them, more booms and crashes could be heard. The noise had started up a few minutes ago. At first it was a low rumble, but the strength and frequency was increasing. Whatever it was, the impacts resulted in scores of dirt and pebbles raining down on them.

Emily Lloyd rocked herself back and forth gently, doing her best to keep Bea calm as a distraction, likely for herself as well so she wouldn't freak out. Edgar and Owen had been gone for a while before the noises came. They had all agreed to wait for them down here, though the decision wasn't sitting well with any of them now that the ceiling was shaking.

"This is freaking stupid!" shouted James as he tilted one of Edgar's tables over and scattered the contents to the ground. It was stupid and pointless and destructive. He felt better already.

"We need to go," he insisted. Almost since the moment Edgar and Owen left, James had been arguing for the need to get going. Emily had tersely suggested he head out on his own to see how far he could get without them, which had shut him up for a little while. Now the boy was pacing back and forth like a caged animal. His raging had scared Bea, who was now shivering and doing her best to hold back tears.

James looked from one to another to see who was with him. Emily and Bea looked away, though Lucas met his gaze. James walked over to the big boy and clapped a hand on his shoulder. "Yo," he said with a smile that never reached his eyes. "You still got my knife?"

At this, Lucas was at a loss for words. The knife was still in his pants pocket, but he made no move to retrieve it. James did a swift burst of mental arithmetic to see if it was worth trying to force the issue. He felt at the hornbooks at his waist and wondered if he could pull out the sword and put it to use.

His hands trembled as he stroked the surface. He was feeling dangerous. The haze of anger that seemed to rule him most of his life was almost upon him. If he pulled the sword now, he didn't know if he would sheath it back in the hornbook or in someone's belly. For the moment, his anger warred with his fear of what he would become if he gave in.

Emily broke him out of his reverie. "We'll go, okay?" she said, getting James's attention. "But we'll do it the smart way."

"Smart, stupid, whatever," James said. "I want *out.*" He let his hand slip from Lucas's shoulder and moved over to the girls. The knife and the sword both, for now at least, were forgotten.

Above them there was another clash of thunder. Dirt and pellets rained in on them, but unlike before, the flow didn't seem to be stopping.

"That can't be good," moaned Bea. "We're going to be buried alive!"

Scrabbling and scratching began to echo off the chambers. The dirt and dust fell a bit more freely.

"What is that?" Emily breathed. "That noise?"

James had been about to say that it was Bea's whining, but then he heard it as well. Behind the scratching came the sounds of growling. It was like the dirt itself was crying out to them.

Lucas stood up and moved over to the wall nearest to him. He reached out and put his palm against it for only a moment before he recoiled.

"What?" James asked. "Talk, dummy!"

Instead, Lucas leaned against the wall and pressed his ear up against it.

Dirt exploded out all around Lucas's head and sent the big kid flying backwards. Emily and Bea both screamed as James did his best to shield his eyes. The room was full of dust and dirt, making it nearly impossible to see. As James looked around, he saw Lucas on his hands and knees a few feet from him while the girls were huddled together and doing their best to get to the exit. Looking back to his friend to give him a hand, James saw that beyond Lucas it was just darkness.

And then the darkness *moved*.

All at once it surged forward, and the darkness split into what looked like a hundred places to show hungry teeth and a mixture of red and yellow eyes. One of them lunged for James's throat, and he barely had time to duck out of the way before the creature's jaws snapped shut.

"Holy shit!" James shouted.

Another creature pounced in his direction but was then swatted out of the air through the timely intervention of Lucas and his newly-bestowed badminton racket.

"Run!" Lucas yelled as he swatted at another one of the creatures.

James didn't need to be told twice. He turned and ran after the girls. He didn't even stop to look back at Lucas. The big kid was supposedly his friend, but no friend was worth dying for. James hated himself for the selfish thought for only the shortest of moments. Try as he might, he just wasn't the sentimental type.

He got to the small opening in record time, only to find that Emily was desperately trying to push Bea through it. The bigger girl was terrified and squealing but not moving.

"Bea, you have to *move!*" Emily pleaded.

James wasn't in the mood for patience. He never was. He grabbed Emily and shoved her off to the side.

"Hey!" she shouted in protest.

James ignored her. He got up right behind Bea, placed his hands on her bum, and shoved as hard as he could.

Bea yelped, of course, but it was enough discomfort that she pulled and wiggled herself forward. The dirt was coming down heavily now, and James estimated they had only a couple of minutes before the whole place caved in. A quick glance behind showed Lucas was somehow keeping at bay a dozen or more of the creatures, many of whom were appearing from freshly made holes or cracks in the ceiling. *Forget minutes*, James thought. *Seconds. Only seconds.*

With a last shove, Bea was through. James wasn't chivalrous, so he followed right behind. If Emily was smart, she'd follow. If Lucas was lucky, he'd live long enough to make it right after them.

Sure enough, only a moment or two after James popped out of the hole, Emily appeared behind him. There was no immediate threat or danger, so he reached out and grabbed her by the shoulders and pulled her free. As soon as she could, she slapped his hands away and stared daggers at him before moving off to comfort a wailing Bea.

There was no sign of Lucas.

The thunder shattered what otherwise would have been a perfectly normal and peaceful day. The ground shook, and James nearly lost his footing. He looked to the hole and beyond it the entire area, including a massive tree that formed the majority of Edgar's ceiling, all lifted up and off the ground before dropping again and sinking into the earth below. Edgar's home was no more. It had all collapsed.

That was it, then. Lucas was dead.

And for a moment, for the first time in a long time, James Vanier felt something. He wanted to scream out in frustration. Maybe even cry. The emotion was so strong, so sudden, and so strange that he didn't know what to do with himself. It had been ages since he'd allowed himself to feel anything. Now that it was here, it was going to consume him.

"Give me a hand here," coughed Lucas from below. The mouth of the hole they had escaped from was still intact, and sure enough, the dirty and bloodied hands of Lucas Walton began to emerge. "I'm stuck."

James laughed at this. It was a laughter filled with relief and perhaps a tint of joy, but of course Emily and Bea took this for cruelty and mockery.

"You disgust me," Emily said. "Get out of the way, you bastard!"

She shoved him hard and began to pull on Lucas to try to get him free. A moment later, Bea joined them to help, though she stayed as far from James as she could and cast a wary eye at him.

Fine, he thought, the fury rising. *I'm terrible. I'm evil. I am exactly what you and everyone else thinks I am. I'm worse than that. If you knew what I was thinking, you'd be running away, screaming. If that's who I am, then that's who I am.*

He walked over to the group, not caring what anyone thought, and pulled on his only friend in the world to get him free. His anger gave him extra strength to make it work. Perhaps a small amount of that came from the shame of having abandoned him only a couple of minutes before.

Lucas coughed and sputtered once he was fully out and held up a hand to show that he was okay and didn't need any more help.

"Now what?" Bea asked.

"We find Owen," Emily said. More thunder in the distance. "As quickly as possible. I don't see any more of those things that got us, but that sound can't be good. He needs our help." This last sentence was directed at James. Maybe she figured they owed him for the Brewmaster thing before. James didn't owe anyone except for maybe Lucas. Even then there were limits. When Lucas nodded his agreement, though, James didn't offer any protest.

Standing up, Emily lifted the Index and called up the map function. It showed the layout of Edgar's cave willingly enough, or what used to be the cave, but the number of offshoots and tunnels and paths related to the area was confusing and hard to interpret without context. They hadn't entered the way they'd exited after all. She had no idea where they were. Emily instructed it to show Edgar and Owen's path, causing all the other options to dim with one light up in a thin blue line.

James was now standing over her shoulder. Emily found his presence repulsive, but he was calm now so she tolerated it. For the time being, they needed each other. "What's outside of this place?" he asked.

Emily repeated the question to the Index, and the familiar map of the Grotto appeared. "We never left," she said in quiet surprise. "We're still in the Grotto. We've barely gone anywhere!"

"Great," muttered Bea, looking up for signs of danger. "Does that mean more fairies? What about my sweet Edgar? He might get eaten!"

"Still talking about food, huh?" sneered James.

"Enough, all right?" Emily snapped at him. Emily used the friend finder function, and two blue dots appeared on the Grotto level of the map. The two dots circled around each other constantly, though she didn't know what to make of it.

"Enemies," suggested Lucas.

She knew it was a good idea, but it had nearly frozen the Index before. "I'll look, but we need to find the right path to take first," she said.

Howls and screams split the air and echoed all around them. The creatures that had attacked them underground had either found their way to the surface, or else others like them were approaching. They didn't have much time.

The Index highlighted the path they needed. Before they had time to do anything other than look down it, arcs of lightning slashed down in the distance. They struck the ground almost exactly where the Index was telling them to go.

James set off immediately. He walked as quickly as he could. He felt drawn toward the chaos. Part of him hoped that it would tear him apart. Maybe then he'd feel free.

"Stop," Emily called after him. James looked over his shoulder at her and tapped an irritated toe. "Show enemies."

As before, the Index began to fill with red dots, so fully that Emily looked like she was going to be sick to her stomach. The outside ring of the Grotto was still red, and a tight blot was concentrated around the Edgar and Owen dots. An ominous black dot stood out amongst the red, though Emily couldn't guess what it signified and only offered that she thought it probably wasn't good.

Then a few red dots at the edge of the Grotto disappeared. She was sure she imagined it at first, but then a few more winked out. Faster and faster they disappeared, and Emily wondered if the Index was glitching. The red dots that represented the fairies were disappearing. Grey-black dots appeared and flickered in their places. It was Bea who named it for what it was. "They're dying," she said.

Determined to make sure nothing happened to Owen, Emily dropped the Index. "We're going," she said. "*Now.*"

If only people had that kind of loyalty for me, James thought bitterly.

The beautiful day in the Grotto was quickly turning to grey and grime. It wasn't a sunset. It felt like the time had come to witness what looked a bit like the end of the world.

Thunder shook again, and far above them the glass in the dome shattered. Doors slipped free of their frames and felt to the ground, many shattering or splintering against the rocks. As they ran down the path, glass and heavy rain fell from the sky. Wordlessly, because words were useless in the tumult, they ran toward Edgar and Owen.

Shapes appeared all around them. They were black and dangerous. Many appeared on the trail to chase after them. A few leapt out to attack and were battered away by Lucas. Others slipped under their feet and nearly tripped them up. James kicked at any that got too close. Emily caught him smiling once, and he did his best to hide it.

Some of the creatures they passed were already busy. The fairies that had been so scary before now looked pitiful and sad as they futilely flashed their lights at the creatures that were on top of them. Several were missing wings. Even more disappeared down the hungry throats of their attackers. James felt no pity for any of them.

"My god," Emily whispered. As she ran, she grabbed a splintered piece of door to use as a weapon. Bea did likewise, though Lucas held on tight to the badminton racket. James, for his part, found the ugliest, sharpest piece of glass he could. He tore a small piece of his shirt off and wrapped it up to make a handle.

Ahead, three of the creatures blocked their path, and the four kids stopped short.

"We need a plan," Emily said.

Lucas charged forward and slammed into one of the creatures.

"Or we could do that," Emily said.

"Or we could do this," James snarled. He ran forward and stabbed one of the creatures in the eye with his shard of glass. The creature shrieked and thrashed as James twisted the shard. The creature stopped the second he pulled the blade out.

The remaining creature turned and tried to flee, but James slammed it down with the bottom of his fist. The creature crumpled to the ground. Before it could get up, James slammed his foot down on it and broke the thing's back. Then he slammed the shard into its neck where it stuck. Try as he might, he couldn't get it free.

He stood up and looked at the others. All of them, even Lucas, stared at him in terrified awe. It made him feel powerful. It made him feel awful.

More creatures appeared behind Emily and Bea. Lucas tried to shout out a warning, but one jumped onto Emily and knocked her to the ground. It got on top of her and tried to bite her, but Bea grabbed it just in time. She almost had it off of Emily when another creature pushed her off. Lucas quickly ran over to help Bea.

Emily's attacker resumed its assault. She was reaching out desperately to grab her door splinter, but it was just out of reach. She almost had it when James appeared, picked it up, and slammed it into the creature's side. It shrieked and hissed at him before running off into the woods.

Emily moaned and tried to get up. James was about to help her but noticed he still had the splinter in his hand.

It would be so easy, he thought. *I could tell them I tried to help her. That I tried to help the person who constantly mocked me. Who insulted me. Who took sides with Oweyboy. They would suspect, but they wouldn't know for sure.*

Emily looked up at him, and her eyes told him that she knew what he was thinking.

He dropped the splinter and helped her to her feet. Dimly, he was aware that Lucas and Bea were watching. Lucas had his hand in his pocket and slowly pulled it out. James knew what he had just been holding. He didn't begrudge his friend for it.

"Let's go," he said.

Before they could, more and more of the creatures surrounded them. The rain fell heavily on them now, and the darkness was broken only by the flash of lightning. This was where they would die.

The creatures advanced slowly. Then they stopped. To a one, they turned their heads and looked down the path for only a moment before they began to run down it. They ignored the group as they went by, and their numbers increased so much that they stopped looking like individuals and instead became one giant mass that swelled up like a wave.

They were heading right for Owen and Edgar.

CHAPTER 19

E dgar had wasted little time in getting Owen to move. They started running blindly through the woods and took twists and turns at random to try to throw off their pursuer. Owen hadn't had time to ask Edgar who the man was or what he had wanted. Without speaking, Edgar had reacted on instinct. Truthfully, it was frightening to have the normally talkative man go dead silent as he had.

Creatures howled and yipped in the distance. Rain had started to fall, causing the ground to become slick. Edgar's face told Owen all he needed to know: there would be no escape.

The earlier confidence Owen had gotten from surviving things like the Brewmaster showdown, Harris and the people at the tavern, or even the fairies had vanished when the man had shown up on that cliff. Just looking at him had made Owen's skin crawl. He wanted to scream, but no voice came out, only a hoarse whisper. He tried to find his voice to yell at the thing on the cliff, to scare it back, to move it away, but nothing would come. He probably would have fainted if not for Edgar standing beside him and helping to prop him up. Each glance he stole was more terrible than the last, and the rotting stench covering the man was starting to reach them. Owen desperately wanted to get away, but every path that led into the woods darkened and was filling with black, hungry shapes that barked, shrieked, and growled.

The man on the cliff spoke to them, Owen remembered dully. Then he had spread his arms, and the black cloak he had been wearing spread out impossibly wide and high, like a black angel of death, and blotted out the sun. The clouds had rolled in. Thunder and lightning shattered the peace and tranquillity of the Grotto. Then the rain had come. All in mere moments.

And then they ran.

All along the path, they were hounded by the creatures. None of them attacked, but they all clicked jaws, bared teeth, and yelped with excitement. The man in the black cloak floated after them, propped up by the darkness, and he laughed. Owen looked back and wished he hadn't.

"I have been searching for you," he said, his voice clear as a bell despite the chaos of the weather. "For both of you, in all honesty, though Edgar is an unexpected treat. Not much of a chase this time, however. For that, I am thankful. Your deaths will be quicker for the convenience."

He heard the man, but something about him had a numbing effect that he felt in his jaw and down to his neck. He wanted to be brave, and he wanted to be witty, but it was hard to think at the moment. He concentrated on putting one foot in front of another. Edgar had a hold of him and didn't let go for an instant.

"Keep moving," was all Edgar said.

Owen ran and slipped in the mud. He didn't fall, but it generated titters of laughter from the dark masses in the woods.

"I have waited as well," the dark man continued. "For my time to shine as the darkest star in the brightest day." He turned his attention to Edgar and floated beside him. Edgar pulled down his goggles and ran harder. "You kept it from me last time. You... hurt me. You sent it away and changed the balance. I needed to keep to the Black Spyre and hug the shadows for comfort. And comfort me they did." He spread his arms and more darkness poured out and clung to the rocks and trees like a fast-approaching night. There was a slight hiss, like a hot surface finding fresh rain falling onto it, but instead of a humid steam, a thick, dark fog rose. The heat caused some of the trees to burst open. More thunder and lightning. "But as you can see, I bring the shadows with me now. You won once, but chance and history won't repeat itself."

"I'll do it again, monster," said Edgar bravely. He at least was able to face the man, though it clearly pained him to do so. The dark man slammed down in front of them and brought them to a halt.

The man chuckled, and hungry animal throats hoarsely echoed him. "No, you won't," he said. "Your time is done. You are no longer the one I'm after, though your death will bring me some joy at least. Long overdue." His cold eyes locked on Owen, and the boy felt he had no choice but to look at him. He fought it as best he could, but in the end he got a long look at the enemy.

The man stood six feet tall and was cloaked in darkness that constantly flowed over his body and cascaded in on itself. To Owen it looked like flowing oil, and he shuddered to think of what the substance might feel like. The gooey stuff was a trench coat, a cloak, and smoke all at once. There was a taut grey substance on top of the oil slick that was pulled over parts of his body and pinned there by silver ringlets. It covered his hands up to his forearms, held tightly in four places beneath the elbow. It also covered his heart and was pinned there within a large silver ring, three grey straps jutting out from it with one below his left arm and two over his shoulders.

The face was the most terrible of all, and Owen looked away once more. The grey substance was tight and perfect as it smoothed out his features. There were two ringlets on his high forehead, two behind where his ears ought to have been, two at the sides of his neck, and one under his chin. The look was so flawless, it might as well have been porcelain. The only thing that betrayed the perfection was the creeping horror Owen felt at the idea of what might be under that mask.

Owen had seen the enemy now and wanted no part of it.

"You know who I am, of course?" asked the man.

Numbly, Owen nodded. "The Antagonist."

The man roared in anger, the act pulling the taut mask even tighter. The Groundlings shrank back from the noise and cringed in terror. Many of them had been creeping out of the edge of the woods. They slunk back in terror. Edgar, too, flinched and looked away.

"Should have warned you," he said quietly. "He hates being called that."

Impossibly, the man seemed to flow from where he stood as he moved toward them. It looked like no more effort than someone out for a Sunday stroll in a park. The cloak gripped the surface of the ground beneath him and the trees around them before it and slid back into place, like a man climbing hand-over-hand down a ladder. Owen would have run if the option were there, but there was no place to go. The small black creatures were blocking every path. Summoning courage he didn't know he had, he stood his ground.

He still screamed when the man touched him. Roughly, Owen felt his face and chin held between cold, dead fingers that were impossibly smooth. As brave as he had been a minute ago, it still took all of his willpower to open his eyes and face the man.

"MY. NAME. IS. *VELLUM!*" he shouted. Owen's eyes watered, and his ears felt like they wanted to bleed. Vellum's breath was hot and dry on his face. Around them, the woods darkened further, and rain began to fall in earnest. The lightning strikes landed all around them, one of them splitting a tree in half. It burned slowly. The smoking ruins rose higher into the air. "And *I* am the Protagonist."

"Stupid name," Owen said. He didn't know who looked more surprised that he said it, himself or Vellum. The man dropped his chin, looked into his eyes, and a sprig of confusion showed and the man recoiled.

"*You...*" Vellum said uncertainly. "You are..." Distracted and without finishing the thought, he flowed higher up into the air. No one seemed to know what to say or how to react to this. Even the Groundlings were strangely quiet. Edgar was almost catatonic. *I did something*, Owen thought. *Something unsettled him. Cause and effect. Try, try again.*

"So you're named after cow skin, and you want everyone to know it. Pleased to meet you, Cow Skin." He hoped and prayed that the remark wouldn't get him and Edgar killed. He grinned at Edgar, but it faded when he saw that Edgar was looking at him as if he were insane. When the crazy guy thought *you* were nuts, maybe you should check yourself. Still, it was the only strategy he had. *If I can throw him off long enough, maybe we can make a break for it.*

It didn't work. There was no change, and Vellum still said nothing, just looked lost in thought. It was Edgar who spoke first. "Vellum isn't just dried *animal* skin used for paper, Owen. There were other kinds used as well. Entire books have been bound in it."

"What kind of skin?" asked Owen. He didn't want the answer.

"Human, of course," said Vellum, who had his full attention back on the pair. "My name reflects my gift. My face reflects the lengths I will go to in order to ensure I have control over anything and everything. Like the Golden Slate itself, the Battledoor."

Unconsciously, Owen's hand dropped to his waist and gripped the side of the book. "Sorry," he said. "Not done with it yet."

"You're done with everything," Vellum said simply. "Including your life. I'll have the book regardless. I want it, so I'll take it."

"It won't work for you," said Edgar. "Let it go."

Vellum only laughed. He spread his arms, and his cloak of darkness went wide. "You know nothing," he said. "There is more than one story. There is more than one perspective. There is more than one *book*." On the man's right hip Owen thought he saw a similar slate, though it was as black and evil-looking as Vellum. Three black hoops dangled from the man's left hip.

"No," said Edgar in a hushed voice. "*No.*"

"A yang for every yin. A con for every pro. Balance, fool, in all things."

"What is it?" asked Owen. "What's going on?"

"He has one," said Edgar. "I'm such a fool. How else could he have found me so easily and so quickly so many times?"

Owen grabbed Edgar and shook him. "No riddles. What does he have?"

"A Battledoor," he said, meeting his eyes. "Or at least the equivalent of one. He *is* the Antagonist, after all."

At this, Vellum roared again and flicked his wrist, bringing up one of the black hoops to bear and lifting it high over his head. The darkness that had been trickling out of him seemed to be coming from that hoop, and when he held it up, it began to pour out in earnest. The fairies, those that had survived and since returned to their roosts on the walls of the Grotto dome, saw the encroaching darkness, started to shriek, and flew free from the walls closest to the gloom. Their flashes, too far to do any harm to those on the ground, looked like lightning in a storm. As the darkness reached them and touched them, one by one the lights went out and came crashing to the ground. Thunder boomed and echoed in the dome. Lightning strikes split the darkness, several of which smashed and shattered the doors and the glass walls and ceilings of the Grotto itself. It rained beautiful shards of sparkling death. Owen thought of Emily then. He hoped she was safe.

Several creatures snapped and barked. "Keep your Groundlings away, Vellum," Edgar snarled. "Or I'll give them a solid thrashing!"

Vellum laughed. It was deep and guttural. There was no mirth.

The Groundlings, acting on some unheard command, then advanced on the pair while knocking each other over in their eagerness to get to them. Edgar scrambled around and found a large stick and began to swing it in wild arcs to try to keep them back. Owen, meanwhile, found a selection of rocks and tossed them at the creatures. If he hit anything, it was lost in the blackness of their bodies.

For the moment, at least, Vellum's wrath was concentrated on the sky and the dome itself, though Owen knew that wouldn't last for long. Once he looked back down to them, it would only be a matter of seconds.

Too quickly, Owen was running out of rocks, and it was harder to keep his footing with the pounding rain. A Groundling inched closer, flashing its teeth at the boy as it leapt for his throat. Just before it could sink its teeth in, a jagged shard of glass tumbled from the sky and pinned it to the ground, sending great gouts of brackish-blood onto Owen's shirt.

This got the attention of the other Groundlings, who shied back and turned their attention to the sky. Edgar was busy swinging away, but Owen risked a glance upward himself. Whatever Vellum was doing, it was ripping the place apart. The high ceiling was cracked and broken. More doors that had been mounted for countless ages were falling free from their frames and smashing into kindling on the ground below.

"Edgar!" screamed Owen. "He's going to bring the whole place down on us!"

A sickening crunch was heard as Edgar connected his stick with the head of a Groundling that had been dribbling a bright green substance from its mouth. His goggles had partly fallen down his face so that only one eye was covered. When he saw what Vellum was doing to the doors and the beautiful Grotto itself, he looked like he could cry. "Oh, no," he said mournfully. "He can't do this! These have stood for as long as man has put pen to paper. He's ruining all of creation and creativity!"

"We'll have to deal with that later," Owen shouted at him. "Let's focus on *not dying!*"

Edgar nodded and swung at a few more creatures, but in the end it wasn't going to be enough. They had seconds, at best, before they were overwhelmed. Only Edgar's stick was having any effect, and with their backs to the stone wall and Vellum perched above them, the end was coming soon. Vellum pulled a black hornbook from his side and held it above his head. More black foulness poured out of it toward them. It was beyond terrifying.

Books should have happy endings, Owen thought sadly. *It can't end like this. There should be more to it than this.*

A sharp crack sounded the end of their resistance. Edgar looked down to his stick, where it had split in two, leaving only a few inches left in his hand. He threw the shard at the Groundlings and cursed in frustration. One, a dog-like creature, caught it in his mouth and wagged his tail with pleasure. The next object tossed to the thing might very well be an arm or a leg.

Slowly, Owen and Edgar backed up to the wall and watched helplessly as the swarm encroached on them, glass and rain falling and reflecting what little light there was left in the world.

Just a little brightness more would be wonderful, thought Owen. *Just a small glow. Warmth and comfort before the end.*

Mom, help me.

In answer to his prayers, the reflected light grew stronger, ever so slightly, bringing a sad smile to his face. The Groundlings stopped in a ring around the pair, and in the centre they began to merge and blend together.

More came from the paths to join their brood. Together as one, they swelled up like a wave about to crash down on them. As one, they roared and began to topple forward. Owen closed his eyes and awaited his fate.

THEY WERE panting from the exertion of running through the woods. The weather and rain made the exertion all that much more painful. Bea, who wasn't considered athletic on her best day, was huffing and puffing so hard it looked like she might pass out. Emily reached out a hand to steady her.

That was Emily's role in life, it seemed. She was always the force that steadied things and provided balance. Whenever her parents fought, which was often, Emily would play peacekeeper as they used her to speak to one another. She would defend one parent and then have to defend the other. It made her loved by her parents, of course, but she resented being used as a pawn. No matter where she went, she always was trying to defuse the situation.

When will someone notice my *pain?* she thought sadly.

Even here, in this strange place, Emily found herself taking up the mantle of the defender and protector. At first it had been for Owen. He was sweet and kind and clearly in pain. He could stand up for himself but never seemed to know how to keep himself from going too far. Now it was for Bea. She was an amazing person and a good friend who was mistreated by far too many people, including herself. Emily had sought her out as a friend because she looked like she needed one. Being Bea's friend was an act of pity. It turned out, though, that after a couple of years together and Bea never leaving her side and being loyal to a fault, she had finally found the support she had been missing from her parents. Bea wasn't someone who needed a pity friend. Emily herself was the pity friend.

Well, maybe they pitied each other. Then, once they garnered enough strength from one another, they pitied anyone who tried to get in their way. It felt fantastic.

Yes, she was a peacekeeper. But Bea had taught her that strength through adversity and resilience sometimes means standing up to conflict. Not to fight, necessarily, but to take a stand. She liked that. It was so similar to what she had already been doing for her parents for years.

Looking ahead to James and Lucas, she tried to find the same hidden qualities that she and Bea had pulled out of one another. She could see when Lucas was trying to be good and move past the image people had of him. When she looked at James, she desperately wanted to find the good, but all there seemed to be was more darkness. Even then, the darker he got, the more desperately she looked to see where bits of light might be creeping out.

What happened to you? she wondered, not for the first time.

In between supporting Bea and checking ahead to see Lucas and James, Emily spared glances for the Index. The path was still clearly laid out before them, though the debris from the damage to the Grotto was making it slow going. One glance too many wound up knocking her off her feet. She cursed and thought of all the ads warning against texting and driving. She should have been more careful.

Lucas was in the lead, and he caused them all to crash to the ground when he suddenly stopped short at the edge of the clearing. James cursed loudly, and Bea made a slight whimpering sound as she wiped the mud from her eyes. Bea's hands dropped to her side and curled around the edge of one of her hornbooks.

It was Emily who got to her feet first to get a look at what had stopped Lucas.

Ahead, Owen and Edgar were pinned against the wall with a whole host of black creatures snarling and snapping at them. Edgar waved a stick at them, which promptly snapped in half. Floating in the air above them on what looked like a black watery cloud was the most grotesque man she had ever seen in her life. He held a black disk over his head with all kinds of foulness dripping out of it.

She called out to Owen and started to run toward him, but Lucas grabbed her and tackled her to the ground first, driving mud up into her nose and eyes. She struggled to get away from him to help Owen, knowing that it would mean her death as well. *I won't let him die alone*, she thought.

"No," he said simply. Going there was suicide.

But Owen was going to die if she didn't go. She saw it clearly and went limp. Helplessness descended upon her. The creatures rose up like a huge wall and tottered back and forth.

As they began to fall on their prey, a bright shaft of white light cut right through the centre of the Groundling horde, burning any caught in the glare and sending the rest scurrying away. Several of the creatures yelped in agony as fire scorched their fur and skin and they rolled in the mud to put it out. More burst into flames and squealed. Some were incinerated on contact and didn't have time to scream.

Emily looked back to see Bea, of all people, holding her hornbook out in front of her, directing the beam that shot out of it like a searchlight. There was a maniacal grin on the girl's face.

"Get away from *my man*, you bastards!" she shouted.

I'M NOT dead, was Owen's first thought.

Or maybe I died really quickly.

But maybe not.

The rain was still falling, and his heart was still pounding, so Owen chanced to open his eyes just in time to shut them again. The light he prayed for was there with a vengeance. The Groundlings were scattering as the torrent of light swept back and forth all around him. He squinted through it to see Bea running toward them, screaming and shouting insults the whole time. Behind her came Emily and her Index, and, to his shock, Lucas and James.

The Groundlings were terrified of Bea and did everything they could to get away from her, but in her wake the other three were easier targets. They lunged and snapped at Emily, Lucas, and James, some drawing small cuts as they ran through the Groundling ranks. Lucas managed to catch up with Emily and was swatting Groundling after Groundling away with the badminton racket while James was ineffectually trying to use his new hornbook to pull out a sword. He finally gave up and just started punching and kicking anything that came near him.

Slowly but surely, the group was approaching the trapped pair. Owen strained to hear as Emily was shouting something at him, but he still couldn't hear above the din of the collapsing Grotto. She was pointing and gesturing wildly, but he was distracted by the voice of Vellum.

The man spoke, and his friends, now a few feet away, stopped running as they all stared at him in horror. Owen had only been around the man a few minutes longer and could barely make himself look at him. He could imagine what the others were thinking and feeling all too well.

Vellum began to move toward his friends. Without thinking, Owen dashed forward and slammed bodily into him. The grime and grease of Vellum tried to stick to Owen, but it wouldn't take hold.

"Away from me!" he yelled. He backhanded Owen and sent him flying several feet.

Unsteady but very much alive, Owen pushed himself to his feet. He reached down to grip the Battledoor in his hand. A quick look showed nothing on the screen, but the Golden Slate glowed from an inner light. Warmth spread throughout his body as Owen noticed the damp and cold slip away from his body.

"No," Vellum said. "NO! It's MINE!"

He moved forward and reached out for Owen while allowing his cloak to extend the reach. The glow of the Battledoor expanded to encompass Owen all around. Instead of smothering him, the black filth burned away to nothing.

Vellum poured on more and more of the darkness. His rage was out of control.

Strong at first, Owen began to buckle under the assault. His eyes remained determined, but the fatigue was starting to seep into his bones.

"You have no place here," Owen said. "I'm the Protagonist. You can't beat me."

He put all of his will into what he was saying. The book glowed in assent but was quickly reaching its limit. There was still so much Owen didn't know about the Battledoor, and it looked like that limitation might get them killed yet.

I won't give up, he thought.

"You will yield," Vellum said as if reading his thoughts. "Stop this foolishness. Death is here for you to embrace as you would an old friend."

"Embrace this, turd burglar," James replied. Vellum spun around to face him, and his eyes went wide with shock and confusion and a look of recognition. Owen supposed the man knew doom when he saw it. James had grabbed Bea's hornbook, still blasting light, and was about to direct it at Vellum.

An instant before it connected, Vellum's mouth dropped open in shock and surprise at the audacity of it all. *And maybe fear*, thought Owen. *Fear and confusion*. The light swept over to Vellum's position but hit nothing as the man was suddenly gone in a puff of smoke sucked away into a vacuum. Owen had blinked and the man had vanished.

"Did I get him?" asked James excitedly.

James screamed suddenly and rocked forward, clutching frantically at his back. His shirt was torn into rags, and red was blooming all over it. Vellum's form solidified behind him, and he laughed coldly as James's warm blood dripped from his fingertips.

As he fell, James dropped the light hoop, and a Groundling made a grab for it with its teeth, burning the thing's face and scattering its companions back as he dropped it in pain. Luckily, the path of the beam swept over Vellum's position and seemed to blast him into nothingness once more.

"The book!" Emily shouted. "Owen, use the Battledoor!"

It won't work, he thought wildly. *Where can we go?* He lifted the book and saw two choices:

CHOOSE YOUR PATH:
'Ashes to Ashes' or 'Dust to Dust'

He did as Edgar had told him and went with his gut. He barely read the options before selecting "Dust to Dust." He looked around for the door, but none presented itself. The conflict had pushed them to the edge of the Grotto, where there were nothing but hundreds of smashed doors, rocks, and wrecked trees. Ahead of them the Groundlings were mustering themselves for a final assault. Vellum, for the moment, was nowhere to be seen.

His friends were around him, though. Alive, but wet, bloodied, and bruised.

Have faith, he told himself. *Make your fate. Let's do a little magic here.*

He lifted the Battledoor up high and then brought it down in a wide arc as hard as he possibly could and smashed it into the ground. There was a thunderous crack below them, which split the ground in two and dropped them between, the rock itself having become a door. The Groundlings scurried back from the edge and watched Owen and his friends tumble into black nothingness. Before they could get the courage to follow, the rock swung back up and crashed together, scattering debris and Groundling alike.

A silence settled onto the Grotto. The ground had stopped shaking, the fairies had stopped dying, and the glass had stopped falling. A ray of light broke through the clouds, but neither Owen nor the rest of his group were there to get a chance to enjoy it.

The blackness pulled itself together, and Vellum rose slowly out of it. The Battledoor was gone once again from his clutches. Pawing at his own slate, Vellum couldn't help but smile.

He wasn't done yet.

ACT III
DOWN THE RABBIT HOLE

CHAPTER 20

The fall came so suddenly that none of them really had time to register what was happening, let alone scream. As they fell deeper into the black abyss, Owen watched above them to see the gloomy daylight of the Grotto quickly recede before being cut off completely as the ground swallowed itself back up above them. After it all closed off, they continued to fall in total darkness.

Somewhere in the blackness, Bea finally gave up the brave act and screamed. They all screamed at that point. Owen's eyes were wide as he tried to look at anything, his pupils dilated to their extreme, but still nothing came into focus. Edgar was trying to shout out helpful pieces of advice, but "tuck and roll" and "try not to hit anything" were awfully vague, not to mention useless in the dark.

Though they couldn't have been falling for long, it felt like an eternity in the dark. Seconds passed, though it felt like minutes. Finally, Owen's butt hit something that made a metallic thump. He yelped out in pain and surprise as he bounced off it and kept falling. Soon after, he hit it again and again, until it became a steady, smooth surface. Finally, he was sliding down into the dark instead of falling. Similar thumps and bumps in the darkness told him the same thing was happening to his companions.

A little light crept back in at this point from dim and indistinct sources, enough that Owen could see they were travelling down a large metal chute. They were sliding quickly thanks to the momentum of their fall. Soon the smooth ride began to jerk them back and forth as the chute introduced twists and turns. The light only allowed quick glimpses of several other entries and exits to the chute that passed by too quickly to try to grab on to and use. A wad of laundry connected with him as he looked back, then more clothing spilled in from the sides and below him. None of it smelled good. Where was it coming from? Why would all of this be here? The realization dawned on him. He was in a giant laundry chute! From the amount of time they had been in it, though, it was a chute the size of the CN Tower.

Finally, he saw Emily a few feet back and to his left, as she was trying to free herself from a tablecloth. He yelled for her and reached out a hand. She did likewise, but just before their fingers met, she disappeared down another path. He looked around for help, but he was sliding too fast. One after another, they slipped from each other's view down the passages. First it was Emily, then Lucas, then James's unconscious and bloody body, then Bea, and finally Edgar, goggles askance on his shaggy head, who let out a big whoop of surprise as he dropped straight down out of sight. They were gone, one by one, and now he was all alone. He could still hear them yelling and shouting for one another, so at least they weren't too far away, and none, except for James, seemed hurt.

It wasn't long until Owen heard Edgar's voice from somewhere below him, shouting something urgently. "Ung n groul," it sounded like, and he was shouting it over and over again. Owen strained to listen or to slow himself so he could better hear. He was focusing so intently that it was quite a shock when he suddenly popped out of the chute into a room filled with blinding light, and he crashed into a pile of laundry the size of a small house. He tumbled down the side of it before skidding to a halt face-first at Edgar's feet.

"Why didn't you listen to me?" Edgar shouted angrily down at Owen, who was blinking away the light. "Tuck and roll! *Tuck and roll!*"

Owen tried to look up but couldn't see. He pulled at his head and face to free himself from some article of clothing and was slightly disgusted to see that it was an overly large pair of women's underwear. There were little hearts all over it. He yelped and threw them away. He blinked some more to find that the room wasn't so bright as he had thought as his eyes adjusted to his new surroundings.

Everyone aside from himself and Edgar was there as well, sprawled out in a similar fashion as they disentangled themselves. Emily's ride had stopped up higher on the pile, and she was trying to make her way down as gracefully as possible when one was in a giant pile of dirty linen. Lucas was off to the side, using a bed sheet to gingerly slide James down the last few feet. The boy was awake and moaning softly. Bea, who had been on her butt a few seconds ago, hurried over to stand beside Edgar, her hair all messed up and her glasses askew. She was sweating, which made her acne glisten. She was looking at him lovingly.

"I tucked and rolled!" she said while clinging to his arms. "Did you see me? It was the best thing anyone has ever said."

"Agreed," said Edgar, who was trying to pry her off his arms.

The fall had not been very gentle, and as Owen got up he felt bruises and bumps in places he didn't even know existed. He ignored Bea and Edgar and instead turned his attention back to Emily, reaching out to support and help her make it down the last couple of feet. "Where are we?" he asked.

"How would I know?" she said. "You've been here longer than I have." He rolled his eyes before pointing at the Index, causing her to blush. "Oh, right," she said. She pulled it up and turned away to cover her embarrassment before she began trying to figure it out.

"Help," said Lucas. The word sounded pained and foreign coming from him. Owen didn't think the guy had ever asked anyone for help in his life. It just wasn't in his nature. As Emily worked, Owen, Edgar, and Bea made their way over to him and saw that he wasn't asking for himself, but for James.

He didn't look good at all. His shirt was torn and useless, and Edgar wasted no time stripping it off him. Though Owen despised him, he had to admit that James was in pretty good shape, save for the long, ugly gash down his back. Flecks of Vellum's grey hand were apparent, as was a dark black fluid mixed in with the blood. It took everything he had not to throw up at the sight of it.

"Oh my god," said Bea in a hushed voice. "I can't look!" She began to gag and ran back over to Emily's side. Owen couldn't blame her. Heck, he wanted to join her, but James needed help now.

He would totally hate this, thought Owen. *Waking up and seeing that it was me helping him. He'd probably threaten to kill me for saving him.* It was kind of a perverse pleasure, really, to annoy his foe by helping him.

Gently — very gently — they pulled the shirt off of his back. The slash from Vellum had made a mess, but thankfully it had not gone terribly deep. If they could properly clean it and keep it that way, then with the help of some strong antibiotics, it should be fine. No matter what they did, it was going to leave a scar, but that was a small price to pay for living. Infection was the primary concern, however. If Vellum's touch made the problem worse, those little red lines would start to appear, and the skin would darken and putrefy. Owen had never had the pleasure of sniffing dead flesh, except from whatever it was that Vellum reeked of, and didn't want to start again any time soon. They needed to clear all of the gunk away and hope for the best. To Owen's eyes, it already looked bad. *It's too fast for it to have gone so bad.*

Edgar was optimistic, as usual. "At least we landed in a pile of rags!" he said cheerfully. "*High-quality* rags! I wish I had my rucksack. I'd take several of these home. Very useful!" He tore a few strips off a pink bed sheet and passed them over to Lucas and Owen. Lucas raised an eyebrow at the colour.

"It doesn't matter," said Owen in response. "They'll all be red soon enough." Sombrely, Lucas nodded and began to wrap up his friend. When they were done, Edgar eased him into a t-shirt he had found. It wasn't pink but rather a deep blue, something Owen thought would hide bloodstains nicely enough if the wound were to soak through.

"He should be fine," said Edgar, though he looked worried.

"Should be?" asked Owen.

"The cut is bandaged, but we need to get him some medicine to make sure."

"How soon?"

"Now would be good, but we have none. We have time, I think. It may not even be needed, but better safe than sorry."

Emily approached them at this point. "Is he okay?" she asked. Owen knew Emily had about as much love for James as she did for the plague, but it was a testament to her character that she cared for another person in pain. Besides, neither of them could ignore the fact that James had fought beside them rather than against them. They owed him some kindness now, at the very least.

"Better than okay," said Edgar, trying to put on a brave face. "The best ever! No one has ever been healthier. Or he might die. But he's probably fine. Or he will be soon enough."

"Oh, Edgar, you were amazing!" cooed Bea, batting her eyelashes at him. With James covered up, she had slipped back over to stare doe-eyed at Edgar.

Edgar flushed at the compliment and said nothing.

"How much longer is that going to last?" Emily asked as she looked at her friend. "The fairy dust stuff."

"Ideally, not much longer," Edgar said. "It's rather awkward, isn't it? Never heard of it taking so long. Not that I mind. Attention is nice. I *have* been looking after myself, you know. Not many compliments in the cave. Once, I imagined I had one from a turtle. Nice fellow. Named him after a High Renaissance architect and painter. Raphael was his name!"

Owen was about to comment on that but let it go. It was just easier that way.

"Can I meet him? I'd love to meet your friends," Bea said.

Owen knew they needed to get on with it, so he pressed Emily for information and overrode the conversation. "Well?" he asked. "What does the Index say?"

Emily picked it up and showed the group. "We're in a laundry room."

"Master of the obvious," mumbled James. His eyes were half open, and when he spoke Lucas hugged him tightly, causing him to groan. "My back, idiot!" he shouted in pain. Lucas eased up immediately and stepped back with a wide grin. It was infectious, and James returned the smile easily enough. "Nice to know you care."

"You were injured," reported Edgar.

"Like I said," James replied. "Master of the obvious. Keep going. Where are we?"

"Basement level of a building," said Emily. "It's not showing me a name, but the place is pretty big." She tapped at the screen, and it showed what looked like a series of pipes. "It looks like the Battledoor opened us up at the top of this place into the space between the walls they built for ventilation. We fell down and were lucky enough to slip into a series of tunnels and chutes they made, obviously, for laundry. Otherwise, we'd probably be dead."

"Unlikely," chimed in Edgar. "The Battledoor is random, sometimes, yes, but it doesn't usually take you from one dangerous situation and then place you in front of a train."

"Tell that to the cliff Bea met earlier," Emily said.

Edgar looked interested. "That would be exciting! But no, wherever Vellum is, we have time. How much time, I don't know. But some. Maybe seconds. Or hours. Time is relative."

"I'll take however much I can get," said Owen. "But no chute can possibly be as long or as complicated as that was in a building. Doesn't make sense."

"Well, perhaps it wasn't a straight trip, strictly speaking," Edgar said.

"What do you mean?"

"There are places in between the pages. Spaces you don't notice but are still there. The Margins."

"Well, it was convenient," Owen said.

"Yes!" Edgar agreed. "Though usually it means death."

Okay, then. "Please get us upstairs, Em."

Carrying James between them, Owen and Lucas brought up the rear of the group as Edgar took point with Bea and Emily trailing between. They agreed that Emily needed to be protected so she could consult the Index, and the three boys were going to be slow, no matter what, so it was best if they formed a kind of rear shield. If something came at them from behind, the temptation was going to be to drop James and run for it, but Owen knew Lucas would stand his ground, and for better or worse Owen decided he'd stay with them. Emily and her Index were going to be the key part of avoiding trouble and getting out of here quickly. They really would have been in trouble without her, since the building they were in now was a maze of doors, hallways, and stairwells to Owen's eyes. They saw no one else in their travels that would account for all the dirty laundry they had seen, nor even the beds and bathrooms that might use it.

The World was a strange place. It was full of buildings, but no substance. *Kind of like a movie set where they build the front of the buildings but there's nothing inside… or the opposite, where there are views of buildings or cityscapes out a window, but it's just a picture.* Owen had seen the people of the World with his own eyes, so he knew people were here, but where they were was a mystery not likely to change any time soon. Either the group was lucky or they were being avoided. Watched, maybe. Owen didn't care as long as they were left alone and allowed safe passage.

"Main floor," said Emily once they climbed yet another stairwell. Bea gave a wheezy thumbs-up in her direction. Owen didn't know why she was so tired, since he and Lucas were the two carrying another person. James shuffled and dragged, but he still needed help to support his own weight. "The main entrance should be through those double doors up ahead. Looks pretty large and open, though the floor map seems all messed up."

"Messed up how?" asked Bea as small beads of sweat slipped down her forehead.

Emily held up the Index and showed them. It was a normal building at the moment, but past the doors it became a series of sharp angles jutting up and out, like the building had thrown up or time had been frozen as it exploded. On paper, it was an ugly mess.

"I know what this place is," Owen said eagerly. He was sure he was right about its Toronto-based equivalent in any case. Why wouldn't he? He passed it every day on his way to school. Quickly, they passed through the double-doors, and everyone else but Edgar clued in.

The old building gave way almost immediately, and ahead it was smooth stone, polished marble, and points of glass and metal that expanded outward from the building. The open area was full of light and quite impressive in terms of scale and grandeur. Above them was a balcony with a glass rail that Owen himself had once stood at to look down at the people coming in, the bones of dinosaurs resting at his back and the sounds of simultaneously delighted and terrified children that ran around them. They were in a famous landmark that thousands visited each year. They were in a museum.

Though why a museum would have bed sheets is a bit beyond me, thought Owen.

"It's so *pretty*," breathed Bea.

"Indeed," Edgar agreed. "Quite impressive."

"I always thought it was a bit of a travesty," Owen admitted. "The poor ROM. What did they do to you, girl?"

Edgar was transfixed as he looked about the place. "It's wonderful," he said. "How could you not like this place? It's industrialization given form!" He paused and looked thoughtful. "What's a ROM?"

"It stands for the 'Royal Ontario Museum,'" said Emily. "It was built in 1912 here in Toronto and was a beautiful old building. The city wanted to help increase tourism and make it stand out more, so they modified the outside of it a few years ago in an attempt to make it look like a crystal bursting out of the building."

"Modified! Ha! Ruined it, you mean," grumbled Owen.

"How is this ruined?" asked Edgar. "It looks spectacular!"

Don't even get me started on why they changed the name of the Skydome, thought Owen. *The Blue Jays play in the* Skydome, *not the stupid Rogers Centre. Names, like buildings, should be shown more respect.*

"Well, I like it," said Emily. "I think it adds class and sophistication."

Case in point, thought Owen. *Best not to argue about it, though.*

"I like it, too," said Edgar.

"I like it if you like it, Edgar," said Bea.

Lucas declined to comment, and James was busy gritting his teeth from the pain in his back. Owen figured that was the end of the conversation and ushered the group toward the door and whatever awaited them next.

"Leaving so soon?" a voice drifted down from the balcony behind them. Bea shrieked and dropped into the fetal position, while Lucas and Owen both dropped James at the same time as they spun around ready to fight. James cried out in pain as he dropped to his knees, but he shakily pushed himself up and turned, one hand gripped tightly on his hornbook. They all feared the worst and were ready to fight back.

Luckily, it wasn't Vellum, the Groundlings, or anyone else Owen had ever seen before. It was a tall man in a dusty brown overcoat, tweed jacket underneath, wire-rim sunglasses, and a muss of black hair. He lounged against the glass railing and lazily waved at them like a man without a care in the world.

"DJ!" called Edgar happily as he recognized the man. "Where have you been, you crazy bugger?"

"Hello, Ed," the man replied. "You know me. I've been here and there, covering as much ground as I can." Edgar thought this was a very witty comment, and he laughed loudly. The rest of them were confused but happy that this man didn't appear to want to cause them harm.

"I've been looking for you for ages," Edgar said. "I check the booth daily, but the place is a mess. You couldn't leave a bloody note?"

"Sorry, my man. Not my style. It was time to wander, so I wandered. I don't often get free time." He took off his sunglasses and looked at them. There were no eyes to speak of that Owen could see. They were all white, with small traces of black that flitted across them, too quickly to make out the shapes and symbols. It was incredibly strange and hypnotic, but Owen did his best not to stare. "I'm still retired, but now I'm back on the clock out of curiosity more than obligation. Got a story to cover, after all! This him?" he asked, indicating Owen.

"It is indeed," confirmed Edgar, who proudly put his arm around Owen. "The latest and greatest Protagonist!"

"I'm..." began Owen, but he was sharply cut off.

"Owen Thomas. Walmer Road. Originally from Guelph. Mother died in an accident last year. Relocated. Not having the easiest go of it. Loving father. Unrequited love" (he cast a nod in Emily's direction) "and the fate of many hanging on your ability to use the Battledoor to conquer the villain and escape the book." He slipped his glasses back on and looked at each person in turn. "Emily. Bea. James. Lucas," he said. "Welcome to the World. Have a statement you'd like to give?"

The others just stared stupidly.

"Hrm," mused the man. "I'll quote you warmly."

"Who *are* you?" asked Emily.

Instead of answering, he exploded in a fluff of dust that seemed to be sucked down to the main level and swirl in front of them before solidifying again in human form. "I'm DJ," he said. "Short for Dust Jacket." The move had been all flair, but the effect was impressive enough. Bea actually clapped.

James snorted at the name. "What happens if you get wet? Are you 'Mud Rag,' then?"

Edgar kicked him gently. "Show some respect!" he said. "This is the Dust Jacket. The beginning and end of a good book. He teases the story to be told, like a reporter does with a good headline. He's what pulls the casual readers in the outside world into the stories told between the covers. He gives the image, the impression, the hype of it all!" From his enthusiasm, Owen thought he sounded like a preacher trying to convert the masses.

DJ swept his arm back in a grand gesture and bowed before them. "All true, I must confess, though my services and uses have been limited since you threw the book out of the World, Edgar."

"I had to!" insisted Edgar. "It was the only way!"

"No, it wasn't," said DJ. "It was *a* way, and you took it. I call it selfish."

"I was not selfish. I saved the boy!"

"And nearly doomed the rest of us." The man sighed and peered over his glasses at Edgar, the black bits in his eyes swirling around. "Edgar, this World is about balance, you know that as well as I do. When you tossed the book without properly resolving your story, you gave Vellum the edge and tilted the balance. You left off on a cliffhanger and nearly pulled all of us in here off the edge with you. But you don't see it even now, do you? Haven't you noticed how poor everyone is in the market? Vellum taxes them and sits on the profits. They pay them too, unless they want Groundlings to destroy their work and kill their families. Most have fled to the outlands and to the prairies lest they get trampled on by Vellum. They barely have enough coin to get the latest batch from that crazy giant. Meanwhile, for fun, he watches from the Black Spyre and takes those who might rise against him and tosses them over the side. Here, the Antagonist rules. You've been hiding under your rock and swinging your sporting equipment content to let everything play out without you. I'm surprised you're even here with them."

Edgar shuffled his feet under the verbal assault and said nothing. Owen was thinking about their conversation a short time ago, when Edgar had said pretty much this exact thing. He was going to send them on their way and go back home. *No need to rub salt in the wound*, thought Owen. *It's not my place to judge him or to call him out.* "We would be dead without him," said Owen. Edgar looked at him and smiled in gratitude.

"That may be," said DJ. He strolled around the open space, taking it all in. He tsked as he saw all the glass and metal. "I hate what you've done with the place."

"Who? Me?" asked Owen. "What are you talking about?"

"This is my home," said DJ in a disappointed tone. "Or at least it was. I'm here, retired and resting, and all of a sudden the walls are bending and sticking out. My privacy is gone, and now anyone strolling down the street can peek in and see what I'm up to. I used to like to dance naked in here. Though the help like the change, probably for the same reason."

"Awkward," James said.

"Totes, man," Bea agreed. James didn't look pleased for the assist.

"I didn't do anything to this place," protested Owen. "I picked up a book and walked through a door. I didn't touch this building." He was angry with the man for trying to make him feel guilty, but more so for trying to give him credit for the modern-day architectural disaster that the ROM, in his opinion, had become.

"Sure you did," said DJ. "The moment you entered the World, this building changed. The story bends around the Protagonist and is told from his or her point of view. The outside reader sees the World how you see the World. They rely on your perspective and opinion to form their own mental images. If you see your home, they see your home. Or at least your version of it. So you popped in, and my house popped out... and at rather a sharp angle, too. What's the matter with you, anyway? Can't think in straight lines?"

"Listen, there is a museum in Toronto and the city..."

DJ waved the explanation away. "I know all about it. I know your story. It's my gift. I know what you know, and I give the long and short of it to others. I'm a reporter of sorts. In a newspaper, you get a story that tells the highlights of what happens without getting into the nitty-gritty. I'm the highlights, so to speak. I avoid the rest. TL;DR, if you catch my drift."

Edgar looked confused, so Bea clarified. "It means 'too long, didn't read,'" she said. "Like in email. Twitter. Instagram. Or Facebook." Edgar looked even more confused. "Don't worry, I'll explain it all later."

"Wonderful. We're stuck in here with the guy in charge of the blooper reel. You can't trust the media to tell a true story, even when they're trying to," said James pessimistically.

DJ peered over the top of his glasses at James, the black shapes flitting impossibly fast over his white eyes. He shifted form back to dust and floated over to where James was seated on the floor. Only his head reverted back as he examined the boy. "Ah, I see it now," he said, sighing. He shook his head sadly. "I see it all." He pushed his glasses back up his nose and shifted back over to Owen, where he became fully solid again. "Can't help it. Shame, though."

"If you can see it all, you can get us out of here," said Owen. "You can tell us how we can get home."

"Could, that's true," said DJ. "I am lucky enough to see how the story begins and ends, as long as you do it correctly, anyway." That last comment was directed at Edgar, who bit his tongue and looked away. "But I won't say."

"Why not?" asked Emily. "If you can help us, why wouldn't you?"

"Not my place," said DJ. "Not my function, either."

"That's not strictly true, though," put in Edgar. "You ran the Information Booth for years! Everyone came to you for answers."

DJ nodded. "For queries, for quests, for ideas about things, sure. But this is different."

"How is it different?" asked James. "What the hell is your problem?"

"It's different because *I don't want to*," said DJ with a chuckle. "Not worth it to me."

"Please," begged Bea. "We just want to go home."

"Not my problem."

"How can we make it your problem, then?" Emily asked.

DJ smiled at this and crossed his arms. "You can't. I hold the cards here. You don't. My job is to remain impartial. To tell the story."

"Is that it, then?" asked Owen hopefully. "Are you telling us that *you're* the Storyteller?"

DJ shook his head. "Ah, well, no. I'm *a* storyteller, not *the* Storyteller. Big distinction. I report, but the Storyteller writes. Even I'm just fiction to the Storyteller."

"Can you tell us how to find him, then? The Storyteller?" asked Owen.

"How do you even know if it's a 'him' or a 'her' you're looking for?" DJ asked mysteriously. "One should never assume. You know the old saying about what happens if you do? That's a good puzzle. Always liked that one. I can't help it if I love puzzles. They're my thing, you know." He rolled up his sleeves and cracked his knuckles before speaking in a loud, booming voice. "'Answer truthfully (yes or no) to the following question: Will the next word you say be 'no'?'" He cackled in delight.

Owen thought about it, but the question itself was a trap. If he said no, then technically he was lying. If he said yes, then it was truthful but inaccurate. The whole thing made his head hurt. "Whatever," said Owen, knowing there was no good way to answer. "Do you know where the Storyteller is? If you won't show us the exit, can you at least point us in the right direction? Then you can still be impartial. You aren't taking sides, you're pointing out a path. The Battledoor led me here to you. I *picked* you." He was thinking of the two choices. "Dust to dust" had been the instinctual choice. It had felt right then and felt right now, even with the added aggravation.

DJ just laughed at him and began to walk away. "If you don't get what I am, you don't get an answer. I thought you were smart. That's what I put on the sleeve with all the other good stuff, anyway."

Something about what he said got Owen's brain working. *What is he?* thought Owen. A dust jacket. *They all wrap around books, tease and hint, but don't outright reveal the plot. They also have pictures on the cover, maybe the author on the back, and...*

"Your price," Owen said, completing the thought out loud. "The barcode. You can't read a book without paying for it first."

The Dust Jacket stopped and sighed. "Yes," he said. "There's always a price. I can hint, I can tease, but if you want more, you must pay to get at what lies between my coverage. There are rules." He looked at the boy appraisingly. "Are you willing to pay?"

"Yes," said Owen without hesitation.

"Careful, now," warned DJ. "What if I said 'your mission is not to accept the mission.' Would you accept? There are riddles and impossible questions, any of which could be your undoing. It won't do anyone any good if you don't know what you're getting into. I'll tell you what you want to know, but first you must battle for it. If you win, I'll tell you what you want to know and set you on the path to success. If you don't, well... the story will end for one of you quite abruptly."

Death, thought Owen. *He means to kill one of us if I'm wrong.* "Why would you do that?" asked Owen. "We're nothing to you! Besides, killing us isn't very impartial of you!"

"What?" squeaked Bea. "I don't want to die!"

"Hush," said Edgar as he put an arm around the girl. "Let this play out."

"There are rules," shrugged DJ. "The rules say I'm the reporter, but if you push for information, then in the World I can also act as an antagonist of sorts. If you challenge me, I have to make it hard. I have to make it count. I can't just roll over. I'm an obstacle you must get past, and then I can give you a bit of information." He waited a few moments for the details to sink in. "That's my price. You win, or one of you dies."

Action and reaction. Cause and effect.

Emily was at Owen's side and placed her hand in his. "I believe in you," she said. "You can do it. I'm right here beside you."

Edgar walked up to him and nodded. "Me too. I agree. Faith and all that." He looked to Bea and Lucas, both of whom nodded. Finally, he looked to James.

"Go ahead, Owey-boy. Roll the dice. If you screw it up and my name comes up, I'll just make sure to take your sorry ass with me," James said. It was about as encouraging as he could hope for.

He turned to face the Dust Jacket. "I'm in."

The Battledoor chimed.

CHOOSE YOUR BATTLE:
'Riddle Me This' or 'Brain Candy'

"Wonderful," muttered Owen. "Aren't these just different wordings for the same thing?"

"Ah, if only that was the question itself," said DJ. "You'd have won or at least placed in the top five."

"Instinct," said Edgar. "Choose by instinct. Guess through logic. That's all most puzzles of this sort really amount to."

The Dust Jacket moved in front of Owen and covered the slate with his hand, forcing the boy to look him in his sunglasses-covered eyes. "I'll give you this much before you choose. Not every battle you'll fight will be with your hands. In your case, I've given you a battle of wits. Both are puzzles, brain-teasers, with problems to solve. Give the right answers, and I'll speak."

Owen took a deep breath and prepared to make his choice. This battle was on.

CHAPTER 21

H is hand hovering between the two options, Owen Thomas knew the options were more for show than anything. One meant the other and vice versa. But still, there it was, loud, black, and threatening as ever on his Battledoor:

CHOOSE YOUR BATTLE:
'Riddle Me This' or 'Brain Candy'

It's all redundant, thought Owen. *One or the other. The question is likely to be the same.* He tapped 'Riddle Me This,' simply because it reminded him of a *Batman* villain and watched as the question formed.

'Would you rather a lion attack you or a tiger?'

For a moment he was stumped, but he took his time and carefully read it over and over again to see if he could find a way to solve it. At a glance, the question seemed to be asking if he'd rather face a lion or a tiger, neither of which he'd likely survive. The wording, however, was cleverly arranged. If you read it correctly, it asked if you wanted the lion to attack you personally, or if you'd rather have the lion attack a tiger. Confident, Owen presented his solution.

"I'd rather it attack the tiger, thank you," said Owen.

The Dust Jacket laughed and clapped. "Very good!"

The others cheered behind him. Emily and Bea hugged each other while Lucas breathed a sigh of relief.

The celebration was cut short.

"Next!" Dust Jacket called out.

The Battledoor chimed, and another question appeared on the screen.

'What's black and white and red all over?'

"Hey!" protested Owen angrily. "I answered the question! What gives? Why is there another one?" The others murmured their dissatisfaction as well. For a moment, they all had thought they were in the clear, only to have their hopes dashed by this laughing dust cloud.

Smiling, the Dust Jacket shrugged. "I never said it was only *one* question. Where's the fun in that? I don't get to participate in the events I cover very often. I need to make it interesting for myself. Oh, don't look so hurt. I never lied, you see. I said it would involve *riddles*. Plural. Learn to read between the lines. That's free advice, by the way. No charge. Just for you." He winked at them.

Frustrated, Owen turned his attention back to the screen. He was angry at the feeling that the Dust Jacket was toying with him, but at least this puzzle wasn't any harder than the first. Everyone Owen knew could get this one. It had been a revelation in the sixth grade when it passed around the group like wildfire.

"A newspaper," said Owen matter-of-factly. If you substituted "red" for "read," the answer made sense. "It's in black and white and then read."

Dust Jacket frowned. "Aw, sorry, kid," he said. "The correct answer is a panda in a strawberry pie-eating contest. Don't you know most modern newspapers are in colour? And people think *I'm* behind the times. Oh well, thanks for the playing, though." He looked greedily from one person to the next. "Now, which one of you will die?"

"That's not fair!" protested Emily. "His answer makes sense! Yours is just stupid. There are lots of different answers to that riddle! You could have said a zebra being eaten by a lion, for Pete's sake!"

"Emily, my dear, are you volunteering?" asked the Dust Jacket as he pointed his finger at her. Dust dripped from the tip of it and swirled about in the air toward her. Emily backed up instinctively. "Dust in the throat and eyes is painful. It's a lot like drowning on dry land. Quite unpleasant, I should imagine. You know, dust is made up of skin particles floating through the air. You'll choke to death on skin and your own arrogance. You wouldn't be the first. Wait till you hear about what's going to go down in Saskatchewan."

"No, wait!" shouted Owen. "Me. If you need to punish someone, punish *me*. Leave her alone."

This made the Dust Jacket pause. He looked at Owen appraisingly and slowly lowered his hand. "I'm feeling generous. Perhaps the last question was too vague and allowed for multiple choice. That's kind of a theme in the World, you know. Lots of different outcomes based on any one action. It can be quite fun, though more often than not it can be quite deadly. However, out of respect for Edgar and our shared, bizarre history, I suppose I'll allow one last question. Though this time, if you're wrong, I get to end *all* of your lives. Agreed?"

"Fine," said Owen without hesitation. James was the only one who protested, but Bea gave him a vicious kick and he quieted down. Owen raised the Battledoor and read the final question out loud:

When asked, I bring you fresh insight,
and through the darkness we find new light.
In the empty silence I speak loudly,
and it is through your eyes that you'll hear profoundly.
I bend, though if you are careful I will not break,
and together new knowledge we'll awake.

"I know what it is!" said Emily excitedly, but before she could continue, a wave of dust flooded into her face, causing her to cough and choke.

"No cheating," said the Dust Jacket simply.

Luckily, Owen didn't need any help this time, either. The image of the old man in the store that started off this whole adventure came flooding into his mind. The towers of volumes, the ideas in between, and the suggestion that it was magic, not words, that crowded the many pages.

"A book," he said reverently. "The answer is a book."

"Well done," said the Dust Jacket, his demeanour instantly changing to quite calm and happy, with none of the menacing tones he had shown moments before. "To be honest, I wasn't sure you'd get it, even though it wasn't very hard. Maybe you stand a chance after all. Maybe not."

"The deal?" asked Owen.

"No need to worry. I honour my agreements." His voice showed a mixture of disappointment and optimism. Owen hoped that the disappointment was because his riddles had been dispatched quickly, but Edgar seemed to like the man and trust him. Owen figured that was the optimism. Rules have to be obeyed, the man had said. Maybe he bent them by making his questions as easy as he possibly could. "You wish to know how to find the Storyteller?"

"Yes," said Owen.

"A door, a lock and key, a handle, and the fate that the hinges help all to swing freely upon." DJ twitched slightly at this and looked like giving the information was paining him.

Suddenly weary and tired of riddles, Owen sighed and dropped his head. "I can't take this much more," he said. "Can't you just tell me flat-out?"

"I'm the Dust Jacket," he said simply. "I hint. I tease. I suggest. I don't tell. That's what the Storyteller does. That's what you get to experience."

"Yes, yes," said Edgar. "Very deep and mysterious. All of that. DJ, can you be a little less vague, however? Old times' sake?"

DJ shrugged and shifted back and forth from his dust form as though he were thinking it over in rapid-fire progression. He shifted up to the balcony, over to the front door, and then back in front of them. "It hurts," he said once he became solid again. "It's against the rules." He shifted some more.

"Break the damn rules," said James, grimacing from the effort of sitting down. His pain was obvious, but he was bearing it all surprisingly well. DJ looked at him for a while before shifting over to him again.

Once he was solid, the Dust Jacket looked at James and nodded. "I suppose a *little* rebellion won't hurt," he said as he appraised James. "You didn't ask for this, so I'm offering it freely. You'll need more strength to continue, and sadly this story needs you still, though I fear I'm not doing you the kindness you may think I am. You aren't wholly what I expected. You may not thank me later." He reached into his jacket and pulled out a long flask filled with a grey-white fluid. "Take this," he said, offering it to James.

"What the hell is it?" asked James.

"For the pain and to clean the wound. It won't cure what has been done to you, but it will help."

"I'm not drinking this," said James. He uncorked it, sniffed it, and gagged at the smell. He tried to push it back into the Dust Jacket's hands, but the man had shifted away back to the centre of the room.

"I'd do it," said Edgar seriously. "DJ is as well known for his medical knowledge as his blasted riddles. Many would come to see him daily for his potions and remedies."

"What does it do?" asked Owen.

"It helps," said DJ nonchalantly.

"That the best you can do?" asked James irritably. "'It helps'?"

"Yes," he said simply. "I hint. I tease. I suggest."

"I get bored, I ignore, I do what I want," snapped back the boy, but he drank anyway. Relief flooded his face almost instantly, and the tension flowed out of his body. The deed done, the Dust Jacket began to shift and blow away slightly.

"Thank you," said Owen. A gift was a gift, but it wasn't the price they agreed upon. They needed answers. "And for us?" he pressed. "Our deal? Can you help us? Explain what you mean about doors, locks, keys, and everything else?"

"I know what I agreed to pay, but I wasn't expecting this much discomfort," said DJ as he winced and clutched at his chest. The hand shifted away and only returned once he lowered his arm. "I can't stay solid for long. Every time I speak, I slide apart again. The Storyteller knows what I'm doing, I fear. I told you, it's not allowed."

"Try," said Emily. "Please. What do we need to do?"

"Split apart," he said hoarsely before shifting again. This time part of his upper body drifted down to his feet. Through concentration, it came back together. Owen thought for a moment that the man was referring to what was happening to his own body, but DJ repeated the idea. "Split up. Your group. Your *paths.*" The shifting started again in a flurry of movement. Each time he gained solid form, he looked more wasted and haggard. The effort of giving up this information was tearing him apart.

"How?" asked Owen. "Where are we going?"

"Three paths, three objectives," said DJ tiredly. "If you want to get to the Storyteller, you have to find the right door to take. One exists, but it can't just be opened. You must undertake incredibly dangerous quests to get the parts you need to make it work. Get the parts, open the door. The Storyteller is behind the door, waiting by the hearth. All will be explained. The story will end. Be careful of this kind of ending. Unfinished narratives can plague you more than your imagination."

"Like we care if it gets us home," Bea said sullenly.

"How can we find the paths?" asked Emily. "Which one is closest? We'll leave right away to go and get the pieces."

"Not that easy," said DJ. The shifting was looking more dramatic now than ever. He looked like he was going to be sick. Owen had paid for the information, but the cost was too high if it was hurting the man this much. "You have to split up. Two of you must go to the End of the Line; there you'll find the lock and key. Two halves of a whole that work together despite their differences. Two of you must travel to the Block, a prison cloaked in darkness and guarded by the Stone Warden. There you'll get a handle on things, something you both need anyway. Ha! Forgive me my puns. The last two must brave the Underground Maze to find your true selves. Find the centre, find the hinges that swing open the door and show the way, both out of the maze and through to the Storyteller."

"That's it? Is that all we need?" Truthfully, it sounded like a lot to Owen. He wasn't ready to split up the group or send them into harm's way.

"Not quite," gasped DJ. "You have one already. The Battledoor must be set in the door. The Golden Slate of good from the Protagonist. But everything in balance. You need the other one as well. I'm sure you can take a hint."

"Vellum," said Owen flatly.

Boom.

As if on cue, the sounds heralding the approach of the man began to sound. There wasn't much time. Everyone tensed up and looked around, but the sound was distant and faint. There was time yet.

"Yes," DJ said, reading their expressions correctly. "He is coming."

Owen sighed. The last thing he wanted was to see that monster again. Deep down, part of him knew it was inevitable. If the World was like any other story, you needed a climax in order to see the end of the book. Face your fears, confront the villain, save the day. He looked at Emily. Get the girl? It was wishful thinking, but perhaps his story would have a happy ending. It would be hard-won, however. They'd won one battle, kind of, by escaping him in the Grotto. *It was a victory, but not the final or ultimate one. It always comes down to a final battle. But if we're lucky, that battle is a good time away yet. Our story isn't done. Why am I afraid that this is just the beginning?* Beating Vellum wouldn't be enough. There was also the Black Slate that rested at the man's hip. "I need to take his slate as well."

"Ha!" James said. "Just grab it. Dine and dash."

"Yes, I'm sure it's as easy as all that. Just point and yell 'look over there, a sasquatch!' and he'll totally fall for it," Bea said sarcastically.

The red haze flared up in James's eyes for a moment. "What did you say?"

Boom. A little louder this time.

DJ cleared his throat. "My time is growing short. Violating the rules is one thing. The Mechanical Man will not be pleased, but it's not so great a thing to him. Not yet, anyway. Keeping *the other* at bay is another." He looked to Owen, urgency taking over his features. "Can you guess where the door is, Owen Thomas? Edgar, how about you?"

"Oh no," said Edgar, the colour draining from his face. "It's up there, isn't it?"

DJ nodded and gasped for breath. "The Black Spyre. At the top. A long way up to the door of no return."

The Black Spyre, thought Owen. If the World was a modified, twisted version of home, then that meant the highest point in the city was the CN Tower. He had to climb it to the top to find the door. It would take forever to climb but wouldn't take long to get down it if he failed. He shuddered at the thought. He did not love heights.

Boom.

Emily broke into the conversation at that point. "How can we do all of that?" she protested. "Get all of those things? Vellum is chasing us with those Groundlings of his. There isn't that much time, and there's only one Battledoor. Owen has the book, and he can't be in several places at once."

"Didn't you study English, girl?" asked DJ. "Can you think of no stories that exist with more than one hero? There are books with multiple protagonists. Stories can follow more than one. Think of *Teenage Mutant Ninja Turtles*. Think of *X-Men*."

"Yeah, but isn't *X-Men* always about Wolverine? That guy is everywhere," said James.

"What are you talking about? Will someone please make sense? How could a turtle possibly have the manual dexterity to be a ninja?" Edgar asked.

"Later, sweetie," Bea said. "As much time as you want."

"You are greater than just one person," said DJ as he looked each of the group in the eyes. "You each must take on part of the story now. Split the book and hand out the pieces. You can do that. It's still yours, but you can share. Like a lending library of sorts." He looked at Owen, though the man had almost completely lost shape, and dust was blowing around the room.

"Three pieces. Three paths. Three groups of Protagonists to combat the one Antagonist. Once you've collected your pieces, head for a reunion at

Union Station. All paths lead there, eventually. If you make it." He coughed and retched violently.

"Choose your battles wisely."

Then he was gone.

BOOM.

The noise was significantly louder than it had been before. A small amount of dust trickled down from the ceiling. It wouldn't be long now.

Owen held the Battledoor in his hand and looked at the group. He had mixed feelings. On one hand, it felt wonderful to even consider sharing the burden of the book, but the thought of putting others in danger put butterflies in his stomach. It wasn't a decision he could make on his own. If it came down to it, he was prepared to do it all. His friends and companions had earned the right to decide for themselves.

"Thoughts?" he asked.

"It's insane," said Edgar. "But I'm in."

"I thought you wanted to stay behind," said Owen. "Give up the chase."

"So did I," agreed Edgar. "But DJ doesn't lie. If I'm partly to blame for the problems in the World, I would do well to try to fix them rather than hide from them. I thought I was saving the boy, not dooming a world. I miss my rock. I miss the fish. I miss my Grotto. But I suppose I can't hide any more. I'll take part of the book again, though it was something I thought I was long done with."

A loud click accompanied this, and a fine thin line appeared on the Battledoor. Owen was able to slide a third of the book apart and watched as the border flowed around the new smaller book. The screen was intact, and writing formed on it:

CHOOSE YOUR PATH:
'The Block'

Behind him, a door appeared with writing to match the slate. Edgar turned around to face it and put his hand on the doorknob, sighing as he did so. "See you soon," he said.

"I'm coming with you!" shouted Bea, who rushed over to his side.

"Ah, little busy-Bea. I'm glad for the company," he said and looked back to Emily, whose mouth was half open in protest. "Don't worry, I'll keep her safe." Emily closed her mouth, nodded, and said nothing. He turned the handle, opened the door, and they stepped through, closing it behind them as they went.

BOOM.

Emily stepped up then, wiping a tear from her eye. "Give me one," she said decisively. "I'll take the maze. I have the Index, so it makes sense." A loud click followed her declaration, and the book slid apart again. Owen actually tried to keep it together, but the book had a mind of its own. Owen hesitated and didn't want to pass the book over to her. He wanted to keep her with him to keep her safe. But he knew that would mean leaving James and Lucas on their own, and this was too important to trust that the pair would follow through and not leave them.

"Em…" he began. "No."

"I'll be okay," she said quietly, then leaned forward and kissed him on the cheek. "That's for now. We'll see where later takes us." She hesitated and looked at the ceiling. Cracks were beginning to form. "Just be careful, okay? Hurry up and get out of here before he gets here. Maybe we'll get lucky, and the doors will disappear behind us." She tossed a nervous glance over to Bea and Edgar's door. It hadn't moved or changed.

Owen smiled sadly at her and wanted to hold her and kiss her, but she was already heading toward the second door that appeared. Lucas was already there ahead of her, and she smiled at him. "Going to keep me company?" she asked. They looked at the piece of Battledoor together.

CHOOSE YOUR PATH:
'The Underground Maze'

Emily tapped it and looked up at her companion. Lucas nodded and opened the door, though he hesitated and looked back at James, who was now standing under his own power. Whatever the Dust Jacket had given him, it seemed to be working quickly. James waved his friend off casually, like he was going to see him again in a few minutes. They shared one last long look, and within seconds Emily and Lucas were gone and James and Owen were alone.

BOOM. BOOM. BOOM.

Dust and plaster fell from the ceiling. Scratching and clawing could be heard. Vellum would be here in seconds, yet still Owen hesitated. James seemed to sense Owen's discomfort and how the pairings had wound up, but logically Owen knew it was what made the most sense. Emily and Bea would be well looked after, even if Edgar was a bit crazy and Lucas was little more than a thug.

"Not how I would have wanted it either, Owey-boy," James said. "But Lucas has a soft spot for your girl. Hopefully she'll have a soft spot for him later on, if you know what I mean."

Owen did and wanted to punch James in the face, but the villain was behind them, the quest was ahead, and starting out with a fight seemed a waste of energy. *I'm on a path with my enemy. We're yin and yang. I wouldn't wish him on anyone else, so now I have to roll the dice and see what happens next.* Instead, Owen looked to the Battledoor and the final choice:

CHOOSE YOUR PATH:
'End of the Line'

"Screw it," James said as they looked at the third and final door that appeared before them. The whole building began to make a sound like an eggshell cracking. "Who wants to live forever?" He grabbed the handle and roughly thrust open the door, and the two of them took a long moment to stare through to the uncertain path ahead of them.

And then they stepped through.

End of Book One

A SNEAK PEEK AT *BATTLEDOORS:*
THE BLACK SPYRE

The wind rushed in through the open double doorways and brought with it a foul smell and a deeply negative energy. The black cape fluttered in the breeze while the creatures all around him skittered about uselessly. It was all useless. It was all out of control.

It was all happening again.

Defeat in the Grotto years ago had left a bitter taste in Vellum's mouth. He had been within a few feet of the Battledoor, Edgar Culshaw, and the ultimate victory that he now feared would never come. He had amassed the Groundlings from the Margins of this World and the many beyond that he sometimes visited and together they had surged forward, ready to claim their prize.

And then the bastard threw the book through the door.

Now it was all happening again. So similar and yet differently this time. Almost like it happened from a different perspective, really. He knew it would happen again unless he was able to change the outcome, but knowing what needed to be done and actually bringing it to fruition were two different things. All of it formed a jumble in his mind. He was so many people in so many places in so many times… keeping track was difficult to impossible. Travelling the dark places did that to your mind. It took you where you wanted to go through all the places lesser men would fear to tread.

Beyond all of this, Vellum was tired. *I have waited a long time. Patiently. Watched from the top of the tower, waited for the return. I thought it would be different. It was supposed to be different.* A hundred other thoughts, fears, and doubts crept into his mind and for each one he pushed down and away another dozen took its place. It spread throughout his body like a virus.

Victory had seemed so certain when he chanced across the pair in the Grotto earlier. The Groundlings had pushed some of the group out of the ground, the fairies were ripped and shredded, and the two he was after were cornered with nowhere to go. He had beat them. Punished them. Tormented them.

Lost them.

Culshaw, whom he knew very well, and Vellum's new Antagonist... the boy named Owen who had dared name himself the Protagonist despite the proclamations in every corner of the World that this place belonged to Vellum and Vellum alone. It had enraged Vellum to hear that bit of blasphemy on the boy's lips as he well knew that in *this* story it was he himself that was the only Protagonist worth following. If any reader was in support of a character in this story that he had been spinning without contest for years now, then they surely must want him to win. Why wouldn't they? Vellum wanted to win, to rule, to be in control. Isn't that what all beings want, ultimately, from their rulers? To be able to give up control to others who will make them feel safe and secure? It was madness to deny him. Any in the World who did were the Antagonists to his vision and he would suffer no rivals or impediments.

For a while, at least, he had none. It was as smooth a transition of power as one could hope for. In the beginning, he had been prepared for more of a fight than he got. Vellum had expected many different primary Antagonists to stumble in and out of the World after Culshaw tossed the book, or even for the people to attempt more of an uprising, but none had appeared until this boy. As long as the trains ran on time, no one cared much who was blowing the whistle.

Yet there was something about this boy. Owen. Looking him in his eyes stirred something deep within Vellum. Then the boy's companions appeared and strengthened his feelings of dread and uncertainty. There was something there. Something new. Something old. Something dangerous.

It would not do.

Beside him, Basil whined and began to tentatively lick his arm. Vellum's only acknowledgement of the dog-thing was to bat him out of the way.

Basil tumbled down a few rocks, yelping all the way, until he skidded to a stop in front of Hatchet and the other Groundlings, all of whom laughed and sneered at the dog's misfortune.

The noise caused Vellum to stir finally. He had been motionless in the Grotto since he reappeared out of the slick substance on the ground. He surveyed the chaos and carnage of his attack all about him. It was cold comfort as none of it save for one small pool of blood belonged to his opponents. He rose from the shredded doors, shards of glass, and ground-up earth to survey his followers. To a one they awaited, rapt with attention, for the Master's word.

He despised them all. They were cowardly, snivelling, obsequious creatures, single-minded in their desire to kill, hunt, and maim. They were useless and numerous, better to have as part of his flock than as an obstacle in his way. He had won them over in the Margins years ago with his displays of cruelty and utter lack of remorse. Those were qualities to be admired. As far as he knew, he was the only being they feared, a fact that he exploited time and again so long as it got him what he wanted.

And Vellum always got what he wanted in the end.

But will it always be that way? He knew what was likely to happen, but fought against it in what was left of his shredded heart. He had expected some resistance, some defiance in the eyes as he pulled the life out of his victims, but when the others had appeared, one shining that accursed light... They had not only resisted, but found new strength. They had also escaped.

Hatchet half-limped, half-flew forward. "Master," he hissed carefully. "We have been waiting for you. The boy and the rest of our food slipped into the earth itself. They are crushed. They are dead. We are denied our feast, but at least they are denied their lives."

Vellum's eyes flared and Hatchet shrank back a few feet. "No," he said quietly. "They are not dead. They are escaped once again. It always comes down to you and your followers. You are too slow, too stupid, too weak."

Hatchet bared his teeth and growled, but at least he was smart enough not to attack. His anger he was brave enough to show. "We are not weak!"

he shrieked proudly. "We hunger for blood!" He swept his wing back to his companions. "The light burned us. Many of us were killed but we do not fear. We do not hide. We are the shadows and we will consume the light!" Behind him, the Groundlings cheered as one, but the sound was horrible, even to Vellum's ears.

"No," insisted Vellum. "You are weak and hide behind your numbers. You have failed me. And not for the first time."

Basil barked at this, picked up an object in front of him, and trotted up beside Hatchet. He dropped it out of his mouth, and even in the dim light Vellum could see the bloody and torn clothing. The dog-thing was a good tracker and a better killer, but torn clothing was not torn flesh. Hatchet relieved his frustration by batting and buffeting Basil until the dog slunk back into the ranks. Vellum watched it all but cared not a bit.

It is true, they have failed me, thought Vellum. *But when the light was bright, I pulled myself back. I'm not even sure it would have burned me, but all I knew was that I couldn't let it touch me. That was all they needed, though, to get away. I am partly responsible. I stopped pulling down the Grotto and they sank into the earth… but there are only so many places to go. Culshaw will guide them. But where will he take them? What will he do next? Who could guide him?*

The answer came to him quickly. "We're leaving," he said.

Hatchet bobbed his head up and down in agreement. "Yes," he said. "To the Spyre?"

"Eventually," mused Vellum. "No, we're going for a history lesson. We're going to the Dust Jacket."

AUTHOR'S NOTE

The first draft of *Battledoors* was completed on November 2, 2011 and was written as the first gift of many for my son, Owen, who was born not long after. Nothing brings your life into focus like the impending arrival of a child. I realized that this little boy might eventually want something to hold that was uniquely me, the way I sometimes find myself looking at objects that belong to my parents that somehow sum up our relationship. What I quickly found was that everything in our house was just stuff... none of it held any deeper meaning or true significance other than it was something that I liked. Writing a book, however, with the main character named after my son, and set in the city where we live, was a way I could make something truly special for him. And now he gets to share his book with readers like you. You can't beat that.

There's a photo on my desk of Owen as a little boy of about a year and half, sitting on my shoulders as we both stare off into an exhibit at the zoo. Just two dreamers seeing the world through different eyes at the same time. All I could think of in that moment was "I'm the one who gets to show him these things. I can't believe how lucky I am." And so now, I'll get to show him this book. Two sets of eyes sharing the same dream. This book is for you, son. I hope I made you proud. Being your father changed my life for the better in more ways than I can count. I love you more than you'll ever know.

This book would not exist without the tireless support of my loving wife, Catherine, my wonderful daughter Nora (who has her own book, *Paramnesia*, which was her own "welcome to the world" gift), my dog Toby, and the continued enthusiasm and support of my mother, Edith, and my father, Graydon.

My family of supporters who love and believe in me include but are not limited to my brother Graydon and his wife, Tammy, my in-laws, Peter and Rhonda, my brother-in-law David and his wife, Libby, my Uncle Brian and his wife, Barb, and my good friends Jeremy, Josh, Jamie, Paul K., Vicky, Nicole, Mark, Taina, Eric, Meredith, Sydney, Kyle, Via, Amanda, Dave, Lois, Wendy, Ellie, Patti, Aaron, Christa, Chris, Tom, Paul H., Jack, Jalen, Reno, Ali, Robin, the D.A. Novel Club, the staff and students at the school where I teach, and so very many others who all inspire me every day to be the very best man I can be.

I also want to thank the incredible team at Blue Moon Publishers, including Heidi, Talia, and my unbelievable editor, Allister, who told them to take a chance on this unknown writer. Luckily, they listened.

Lastly, I need to thank Scott Carter, the DJ to my Edgar, who acted as my guide and sounding board. He believed in me before I believed in myself, and that made all the difference.

That is where my adventure started. You, hopefully, are where it continues.

Adventure awaits beyond the next doorway.

ABOUT BRIAN WILKINSON

B rian Wilkinson was born in Guelph, Ontario. He completed a Bachelor of Arts degree in English Literature at the University of Guelph in 2000, received a diploma in Journalism from Humber College in 2004, and finally graduated with a Bachelor of Education degree from the University of Toronto in 2007. He has been a high school teacher and librarian since 2007, where he has mostly taught English and now works to pass on a deep love of stories as a head librarian.

He has worked in various capacities for the *Toronto Sun*, *Eye Weekly*, the *Toronto Star*, *Kidscreen Magazine*, and the online comic news site *Comixfan. net*. His love of comics led to a writing job at Marvel Comics, where he co-wrote *X-Men: The 198 Files*.

He currently lives in Toronto, Ontario, with his wife Catherine, their son, Owen, their daughter, Nora, and their very loud dog, Toby.

Find Brian on Social Media:
Official Website: bewilkinson.wordpress.com
Twitter: @The7thParallel
Instagram: bewilkinson77

BOOK CLUB GUIDE

1. Imagine that you found the Battledoor instead of Owen. Would you have made the same choices or would you have gone a different route? Discuss what you adventures you think may have happened on some of those other paths.

2. How did the Bookkeeper come into possession of the Battledoor? What possible reasons could he have for giving the object to Owen? If he knew it was dangerous, why would he knowingly pass it on to someone so young?

3. James is a bully with severe anger issues. What kind of life or circumstances do you think he might have experienced that would have led to him acting this way? Would any possible scenario he might have had then justify his actions or attitude?

4. Lucas seems more calm and measured than his hot-headed friend. Why would he remain loyal and by James's side knowing how dangerous he could be?

5. What do you think of the friendship between Emily and Bea? What do each of them bring to the table in their relationship that makes their bond so strong?

6. Throughout the book, Owen deals with the tragic loss of his mother. Often he thinks back to times he shared with her, and he even opens up about her loss a little bit to Emily. How may have this event shaped Owen's life and personality?

7. Edgar has been on his own in the World for three years. Take the time to discuss and imagine what life must have been like for him and how it may have influenced his personality.

8. Many of the elements of the World revolve around literary conventions, terms, and ideas. What were some of the elements that you noticed, and what might be some you'd like to see explored further in the future?

9. How does the setting of the book (a warped version of Toronto) influence or impact your reading of the story? If you have been to Toronto, do you imagine these places more clearly? If you haven't been to Toronto, how might the story impact the way you choose to visit and view the city?

10. The story ends on a bit of a cliffhanger. Discuss your theories about what you think might happen next.

WRITE FOR US

We love discovering new voices and welcome submissions. Please read the following carefully before preparing your work for submission to us. Our publishing house does accept unsolicited manuscripts but we want to receive a proposal first, and if interested we will solicit the manuscript.

We are looking for solid writing—present an idea with originality and we will be very interested in reading your work.

As you can appreciate, we give each proposal careful consideration so it can take up to six weeks for us to respond, depending on the amount of proposals we have received. If it takes longer to hear back, your proposal could still be under consideration and may simply have been given to a second editor for their opinion. We can't publish all books sent to us but each book is given consideration based on its individual merits along with a set of criteria we use when considering proposals for publication.

THANK YOU FOR READING
BATTLEDOORS: THE GOLDEN SLATE

If you enjoyed *Battledoors: The Golden Slate*, check out these exciting young adult titles from Blue Moon Publishers!

The Immortal Writers Series by Jill Bowers
Immortal Writers
Immortal Creators
Immortal Suspects

The Hit the Ground Running Series by Mark Burley
Hit the Ground Running
Flow Like Water

The Nefertari Hughes Mystery Series by Bethany Myers
Asp of Ascension
Diadem of Death
Medallion of Murder
Relic of Revenge

The Deadish Chronicles by Brian Wilkinson
Paramnesia
Hypomnesia
Hypermnesia

Fall In One Day by Craig Terlson

NemeSIS by Susan Marshall

And don't miss the next book in the Battledoors series: *Battledoors: The Black Spyre*.

BlueM⊃on
PUBLISHERS